"YOU REALLY LOATHE FRAUDS, DON'T YOU?"

asked Catlin, lacing his fingers through Lindsay's in a single smooth motion, bringing their palms together, holding them that way.

The texture of Catlin's touch caused sensations that spread through Lindsay as surely as the wine she had just sipped. She looked up, wondering if he could feel her surprised response in the pulse beating just beneath the skin of her inner wrist.

"Yes," she said simply.

"Why?"

There was a silence for a long moment while Lindsay absorbed the question, and the fact that the question had even been asked. Her response to fraud was something that she had always taken for granted about herself. She hated lies of all kinds.

"Doesn't everyone?" she asked.

Catlin's answer was a smile that made Lindsay wonder what he had been doing for the lifetime before he had come to her and asked about Qin bronzes.

"Not everyone, Lindsay. Not even most people. It's truth they fight, not lies."

Available from Elizabeth Lowell

TELL ME NO LIES

An international crisis was about to explode, and expert art appraiser Lindsay Danner was caught squarely in the middle. Only renegade ex-agent Jacob Catlin could save her—but what price would she have to pay for her salvation . . . ?

TOO HOT TO HANDLE

She'd been warned Ethan Reever had the devil's own temper, but she was desperate for this job. She could handle it. And one look at Tory had Ethan heating up—but not with anger. Tory Wells was simply too hot to handle.

SWEET WIND, WILD WIND

Years ago, Lara Chandler had fled the Rocking B Ranch in humiliation, her innocent dreams of love crushed. Now she'd returned to face the man responsible for her heartbreak—Carson Blackridge . . . a man who'd do anything to get Lara back.

ELIZABETH LOWELL

TELL ME NO LIES

Silhouette Books®

Published by Silhouette Books New York

America's Publisher of Contemporary Romance

SILHOUETTE BOOKS
300 E. 42nd St., New York, N.Y. 10017

TELL ME NO LIES

ISBN: 0-373-48250-7

Published Worldwide 1986

Published Silhouette Books 1992

Printed in the U.S.A.

1

CATLIN BARELY CONTROLLED a sound of disbelief. Adrenaline poured through him, ripping away the comforts of the present, revealing the bones of the past when a woman had taught him the true meaning of betrayal. The lesson would have cost his life had it not been for the speed of another man. The woman had died. The other man had died. The man known then as Jacques-Pierre Rousseau had lived.

He looked at the ancient Chinese coin lying in his palm. The metal had been cut deliberately in half, sundering the vague, graceful lines of a swallow in flight, leaving a bird with one wing. Inside the cut, the copper's untarnished core shone like a pale wound. The coin was both familiar and subtly alien. He was used to seeing the other half of the swallow, the half that he carried as a good luck charm, the half that had come into his hands a world and a lifetime ago.

Long ago, far away, in another country.

Catlin's eyes shifted from the coin to the slight, erect figure of Chen Yi.

"An interesting keepsake," said Catlin neutrally. "A shame about the mutilation. Han coins like this are rare."

"A man of your connections could join both halves," pointed out Yi in a soft voice.

"Oh? Did you bring the other half with you?" asked Catlin, but the verbal fencing had already lost its urgency. He had the other half in his pocket. All that remained was to be sure that Yi's possession of the coin wasn't an accident or a trick to win Catlin's confidence.

Yi waited, his face as impassive as Catlin's.

"How did you get this?" asked Catlin.

"From a man who was also named Chen."

"There are literally millions of Chens in China."

"Yes."

Yi took a hard pull on the evil-smelling Chinese cigarette he held. The act was a sign of addiction, not nervousness. Yi was not a nervous man.

The distinctive odor of Yi's cigarette, the odd cadence of Yi's English, and the ancient Chinese coin all combined to give Catlin a feeling of dreamlike unreality. He wasn't fool enough to give in to the feeling. The adrenaline expanding through his body in a chemical shock wave told him that the night and the moment were all too real, potentially deadly.

"Which Chen gave this to you?" asked Catlin, flipping the mutilated coin absently into the air, catching it, flipping it again. His voice was like his body, totally controlled, poised for whatever might come next. Including death.

"It came with word of my—" Yi stopped speaking abruptly as he searched his memory for the exact equivalent of a Chinese word. It did not come to him. "What is the English word for my father's brother's nephew's nephew's son?" asked Yi.

"Shirttail cousin," Catlin offered sardonically.

"Ah!"

The sound was not the soft near-sigh used by Americans. It was a blunt verbal punctuation mark signifying that a point had been made. That, and the ever-burning unfiltered cigarette, branded Yi as a modern mainland Chinese more surely than his folded eyelids or the subtle golden cast of his skin.

"The cut coin came to me with the notice of the death of my shirttail cousin, Chen Tiang-Shi," said Yi.

The name caused a chain reaction of memories in Catlin's mind. For an instant he lived again in Southeast Asia, felt again the delicacy of Mei's hands searching over his hot flesh, smelled again the heady scent of her aroused body, knew again the moment of blank shock when at the instant of his own release she raised a gun barrel toward his head. He knew then that he was dead, that the woman who was climaxing beneath him at that moment would kill him in the next, that he had been betrayed in ways that he could not begin to name or number.

Then the shots, the convulsive leap of flesh, more shots, the red ruins of a woman he had loved lying across him. And Chen Tiang-Shi slumped at the foot of the pallet, apologizing even as he died cursing his treacherous cousin Geneviève Mei Chen Deneuve.

Later the mutilated coin had come to Catlin, bearing only the message that one day the other half would also come to him, and with it a small request that he could ignore or honor as he chose.

Catlin's eyes focused on the silent figure waiting for his decision. "If it is in my power, it is yours," said Catlin simply. "And the English word to describe Chen Tiang-Shi is *man*. His life gave honor to his family and to his ancestors."

Yi bowed slightly, making light stir within his fine, nearly white hair. "As I was told," he murmured, "no matter what name you wear, you are a man of great face."

Grimly Catlin waited for the flattery to end so that he could find out what kind of bargain he had made for the redemption of his younger, more foolish soul.

"You no longer work in Indochina," said Yi.

It was a statement, not a question, but Catlin answered. "I no longer work in Indochina."

"You no longer work for your government."

This time Catlin hesitated, counting all the gradations of lie up to the final truth. "I don't work against my government, either."

"Ah." Yi noted the caveat, absorbed it and continued. "You owe no loyalty to family, community or tradition."

"Not in the Chinese sense," agreed Catlin.

"You walk in no man's shadow."

"Not if I can help it," Catlin said dryly. "I love the sun."

Yi looked at him with black, shrewd eyes set wide in a face the color and texture of parchment. Yi was clean shaven; the People's Republic of China had little use for the thin beards that had been the Chinese style since Confucius. Yi's nails, though long for Western tastes, were not so lengthy as to draw immediate attention. Although his hair had little black left in it, and his voice was breathy from a lifetime of cigarettes, his eyes as they probed Catlin were those of a young man—clear, quick, intense.

Catlin underwent the scrutiny with patience, sensing that Yi was trying to understand him by describing him. To a Chinese, Catlin's lack of blood and community ties was unthinkable, abhorrent.

"You worship neither the Christian God, the Muslim Prophet, the Buddha, the silent Tao, the once-voluble Mao nor your own ancestors," continued Yi. "Yet you are a man of great face. A man of honor."

Catlin made a gesture with one hand that could have signified agreement, disagreement or anything between.

"I am grateful to Chen Tiang-Shi," murmured Yi, "that you survived a woman's treachery to enlighten this poor intellect on the true nature of the impossible."

Impassively Yi continued studying the much larger, much more powerful man whose name had once been whispered in tones of fear and admiration throughout Indochina. Yi nodded abruptly, having reached a decision. He lit a crumpled cigarette from the ragged stub of the previous one and began to talk about events more tangible than honor, enlightenment and the nature of impossibility.

"You are familiar with the archaeological explorations at Xi'an?" asked Yi.

Again, it was more statement than question, but again, Catlin answered.

"I no longer collect Warring States bronzes," Catlin said deliberately, "but yes, I know about Xi'an and the Emperor's Army. It is arguably the greatest archaeological find in the history of man."

Yi looked for an ashtray, found none and tossed the thinly smoking butt into the fireplace.

"If you did collect such bronzes," asked Yi, "what would you pay for a charioteer, chariot and horses inlaid in gold and silver, half life-size, from Emperor Qin's own grave?"

Catlin didn't bother to conceal the swift intake of his breath, for he knew that his interest would already have been revealed by the equally swift dilation of his pupils. He hadn't had to live undercover in several years. He had gotten out of the habit of making his body live the same lies as his mind.

And the offer itself was breathtaking. It was like asking an avid Egyptologist if he would like to own King Tut's solid gold coffin.

"If I were still collecting, I would pay whatever I had to for such a bronze," Catlin said quietly.

"Five hundred thousand American dollars?" pressed Yi.

"Easily."

"One million American dollars?"

"If I had it. And if I were sure that the bronze was neither fraudulent nor available in quantity." Catlin smiled rather grimly, thinking of the Chinese government's stand on the exportation of antiquities. "Given the PRC's position on the illegal export of cultural treasures, I don't think that Emperor Qin's bronzes will be a drug on the art market anytime soon. Unless there has been a change of policy?"

Yi's dark glance didn't waver. "There has been no change."

"Then this discussion is, as we say, academic."

The cigarette glowed urgently between Yi's narrow lips.

Catlin waited, sensing that the Chinese had approached a point of no return.

"It should be," Yi said curtly. "It is not."

"And I'm not a collector of Chinese bronzes." Catlin's voice was smooth and hard, leaving no doubt that he meant each word.

Yi's hand moved in a sharp gesture, trailing smoke. "This is known. But you once were. If you were again to become a collector, would you be approached by people selling Qin bronzes?"

"Under the name of Catlin? I doubt it. It would take time to establish myself as a collector of that magnitude."

"If the name were Jacques-Pierre Rousseau?" Yi asked, his normal staccato delivery making the question sound even more blunt.

"Didn't you hear? The poor fellow died. Somebody chucked a grenade into his hotel room a few years back. Must have been a hell of a mess."

Yi looked into eyes that were the pale, clear amber of a winter sky just after sunset. But there were no stars to illuminate the depths of Catlin's eyes, only the certainty of night to come. Dragon's eyes, alive with predatory intelligence.

"There were people who doubted that a man of Rousseau's abilities would so easily die," said Yi, pulling sharply on his cigarette. "There were rumors."

"There always are." Catlin hesitated, then shrugged. The man who had brought him the other half of the Han swallow deserved the truth. "Rousseau could be more trouble to you alive than he is dead," Catlin said bluntly. "He wasn't exactly a friend of the People's Republic of China."

Yi thought about that possibility for several silent minutes. "When the nest is overturned," he murmured, "all eggs are broken."

Catlin smiled thinly. "The nice thing about Chinese sayings is that they can mean everything. And nothing. Whose nest? Whose eggs? And who's turning things upside down?"

With an abrupt motion Yi threw his spent cigarette into the fireplace. "Is it necessary for the tool to know the mind of the artisan?"

Catlin weighed the half coin in his hand. An image came to him: China's beautiful Li river at twilight, when the fishermen lit lanterns on their narrow rafts and poled out onto the river. At their feet were cormorants that had been hand-raised from birth to answer to their master's distinctively pitched cry. When the rafts were joined in a circle, fish rose to the fascinating shimmer of lantern light against the dark surface of the water. Then the cormorants were released into the river to dive and fish. A string tied around each bird's throat prevented it from swallowing the fish it caught. The cormorant returned to its master's raft, surrendered the fish, then swam back down into the black water to hunt again. When the master's basket was full, the strings were removed from the birds and they fished for themselves.

"Tell me, Chen Yi. When the fisherman of Li take their cormorants out onto the dark river, do they tie the throat string so tightly that the birds strangle?"

Yi's response was seen only in the slight hesitation before he flicked open a lighter whose design hadn't changed since the Chinese first learned how to copy Zippos. "The string should be tight enough that the bird cannot swallow the fish it catches," said Yi, drawing sharply on the fresh cigarette. "Any tighter and the bird is useless." The lighter snapped shut with a metallic click. "Any looser and the bird eats his master's meal."

"I'm more intelligent than a cormorant."

"And therefore far more dangerous."

"How badly do you want to catch fish?"

Yi replaced the lighter in the pocket of his very Western suit coat. He looked again at the half coin resting on Catlin's hard palm and remembered just a few of the things he had heard about the man called Rousseau.

Trustworthy. Intelligent. Quick. A man of great face. Deadly.

"Perhaps if you told me what fish you wanted to eat," offered Catlin, "I could suggest ways of catching and cooking it."

Yi looked around the room as though orienting himself. He knew that the apartment belonged to the Pacific Rim Foundation and was used when its employees came to give expert testimony before Senate committees or more private advice to the powerful men who worked in Washington, D.C. Yi also knew that Catlin *was* the Pacific Rim Foundation. Despite Catlin's experiences in Asia, or perhaps because of them, the foundation had gained a reputation for being neither advocate nor enemy of Asian aspirations.

There was nothing Chinese in the room, neither modern nor ancient, to hint that Catlin had spent a decade and a half of his life immersed in a foreign culture. Yet even so, Yi sensed something in the room that made him comfortable. In the design and placement of the furniture there was an austerity and discipline that recalled the great Chinese calligraphers. In the richness of fabric and rug there was the same celebration of the senses that characterized imperial silks.

It was apparent that Catlin was a man of taste and intelligence. And power. Deadly power. But then, that was why Yi had sought him out. Yi needed a man both intelligent and deadly.

Unfortunately, it was rather like fishing with a dragon instead of a cormorant.

Yi pulled at his cigarette, swallowed the smoke and said, "There is a woman."

Catlin smiled sardonically, remembering his own past. "There usually is."

Without smiling, Yi looked amused. "She is American, raised in China. Her parents were Christian missionaries in the Shaanxi province until 1959." He noted Catlin's surprised expression and nodded. "Yes, even after we became the People's Republic. Her father was Canadian and her mother was American, although few people knew about her mother. It was too dangerous. Americans were not—" He hesitated, searching for a word that would not be insulting. "Applauded."

The thin curve of Catlin's smile told Yi that Catlin was well aware of just how dangerous it was to have been an American in China during the first years of the People's Republic.

Yi smiled widely, quickly, a sign of embarrassment rather than amusement. With a curt "Ah!" he dismissed the years when to be an American in China was to be under a death sentence. "New governments are like children. They must learn," continued Yi. "The People's Republic has learned the value of harmony between distant republics. That is why I am here. The harmony is endangered."

Ghostly fingernails traced Catlin's spine and stirred the tiny hairs along the back of his neck. As both part owner and full-time employee of the Pacific Rim Foundation, his job was to project, predict and advise the foundation's powerful clients on

he subject of relations with Asia in general and China in par-
icular. Yet he had heard no rumors, no hints, nothing to in-
licate that the delicate mutual courtship of the U.S. and the
?RC was faltering.

Yi studied Catlin through a curl of blue-gray smoke. Noth-
ng showed on Catlin's face or in the set of his body. There was
no physiological clue as to whether one of America's foremost
and least-known experts on Asian affairs was surprised by the
blunt statement that there could be a rupture in the tenuous
fabric of diplomacy that had been woven so carefully between
he two countries.

"Where does the woman fit in?" Catlin asked quietly.

"She is the key in the lock."

"Does she know it?"

"No."

Catlin waited. Only silence came to him, and then more si-
ence. Chen Yi was reluctant to part with more information
han he had to. Catlin understood the Chinese's discomfort; it
vas the nature of secrecy to perpetuate itself.

"Keep talking." Catlin smiled grimly. "The string isn't long
enough for fishing yet."

"Will it ever be, Rousseau?" Yi's laughter was a short, harsh
ound. In the apartment's restrained light, Catlin's eyes were
he color of hammered gold. They offered no comfort, simply
understanding.

"My name is Catlin."

"Your name is dragon," muttered Yi, puffing savagely at the
ast burning length of his cigarette before flinging it into the
hearth.

"But I'm your dragon," retorted Catlin, flipping the half
coin high into the air, watching the flicker of untarnished metal
n the wound. "Or as we say in America—I may be a son of a
bitch, but I'm your son of a bitch. For now." He caught the
ancient bronze coin easily, looked at it and decided that it was
ime to rattle Yi's cage just a bit in the hope that unexpected
nformation would fall out. "Will you have some tea, Chen Yi,

Comrade Minister of Archaeology, Province of Shaanxi, People's Republic of China?''

If Catlin hadn't been looking for the betraying flicker of Yi's eyelids, he would have missed it.

"How long have you known?" asked Yi.

"Since you asked about Qin bronzes. There are millions of Chens in China, thousands with the name of Chen Yi; but only one of them controls access to the richest archaeological find in human history." Catlin caught the half circle for the last time and slipped it into his pocket with the other half coin he had carried for many years. "Tea?" he asked politely.

Yi hesitated, showing his surprise, silently telling Catlin how disturbed the Chinese was.

"Thank you," said Yi.

"Chinese or English?"

"Do you have lemon peel?"

"Yes."

"English, please. It has been many years . . ."

Catlin gestured toward a chair that was near the fireplace, which Chen Yi had preempted as an ashtray. In a few minutes Catlin returned with an elegant scarlet-and-gold porcelain teapot and matching cups on a lacquer tray. When Catlin lifted the pot to pour fragrant, steaming tea, a dragon was revealed—sinuous, malevolent, powerful. Savage intelligence gleamed from the dragon's hammered gold eyes.

Yi dropped two sugar cubes and a twist of lemon into his tea. He showed no surprise when Catlin did the same. Using lemon peel rather than juice was customary in the part of Indochina where Catlin had once worked. It was the Asian way of coming to terms with the brutally strong tea that the English preferred. Although Catlin didn't brew his tea until it was the color and consistency of tar, the acquired taste for lemon's piquancy remained.

"Your English is very good," Catlin said matter-of-factly. Despite the odd tonality and staccato delivery that were quintessentially Chinese, Yi's words were easily understood. Nor did he employ the euphemisms, honorifics and circumlocutions that many Chinese used when speaking a second language. There was an unusual flavor to Yi's speech, though. He had an elusive accent and a turn of phrase that was more British or Canadian than American. And yet there was definitely an American flavor to Yi's English, too. Perhaps he had had teachers from more than one country. "Did you attend school in Vancouver before the revolution?"

"Your Chinese is very good, I am told," retorted Yi. "Did you attend school in Beijing?"

"No." Catlin smiled slightly at Yi's riposte. "Not even when it was still called Peking."

"Did you kill many Chinese?" asked Yi without warning. It was an interrogator's trick—the unexpected, deadly question dropped in the midst of neutral chatter.

"Did you spend much time torturing English-speaking prisoners in North Korea?" countered Catlin, his tone uninflected.

Yi and Catlin exchanged impassive stares while tea steamed upward between them like dragon's breath.

"An unhappy past," said Yi finally, touching the fragile rim of the teacup with sensitive fingertips. "It is our duty to see that our governments do not repeat past errors of fear and greed."

"Are we on the verge of doing that?" asked Catlin. "Repeating past errors?"

There was a metallic click, the hiss of flame, then another click as Yi closed the lighter. "Yes."

Catlin was silent for a long time, weighing the urgency that must be driving the outwardly calm Chinese official sitting across from him and sipping tea. Yi's bluntness was unusual in the extreme. The Chinese people had lived under gradations of tyranny and despotism for thousands of years. Such governments taught people a hundred ways to say yes and none to say no. Indirection and lying were the very arts of survival, as though the people themselves had to live undercover in their own land. The modern age had been no kinder to the Chinese. First the West humiliated them, then followed the horrors of civil war and a political fervor indistinguishable from religious ecstasy.

Unfortunately, ecstasy made lousy economics. Twenty million Chinese starved while Mao found his feet as a leader. When his feet began slipping again, millions more Chinese were uprooted, displaced and disgraced in the Cultural Revolution. Ecstasy continued to make lousy economics. When the fervor burned to ash, the survivors blinked and looked around. The specter of fiscal ruin blinked and looked back. Deng Xiaoping stepped into leadership, bringing with him very delicate murmurings of rewards based on work rather than need.

Capitalism, in a word.

The word was never used except by enemies of Deng Xiaoping. The flirtation with capitalist heresy continued, encouraged by the sudden spurt in output from farm plots "owned" by peasant families. The courtship broadened as American and Canadian business advisers were invited to the People's Republic to teach the fine art of making money while paying lip service to the spinning ghost of Mao. With each new factory, with each new commune in which peasants earned profits as well as food for their cooking pots, the relationship between the U.S. and the People's Republic deepened into one that had the potential for becoming a fine and enduring marriage of mutual interests: China's entry into the twentieth century's technological sweepstakes; and the West's entry into a market that comprised one-quarter of the population of earth.

There was no public announcement of connubial bliss between America and China, simply a gradual withdrawal of running-dogs-of-capitalism rhetoric. Chinese Communists sat down to dinner with Western capitalists, and all participants used long spoons, for wise men knew there was no other way to sup with the Devil from a communal pot. It was an interesting meal all around, one that gave promise of fattening the participants.

"Who's pissing in the soup?" asked Catlin.

Yi looked utterly blank. "Please?" he asked, jarred from his nearly perfect command of English.

"An idiom," said Catlin with a hard smile. "It means to ruin things for everyone, including yourself."

"Ah! So! Pissing in the soup." Yi grinned. "Very good. Thank you. That I will remember."

Catlin had no doubt Yi would remember. At an age when most Americans were embracing the precarious salvation of Social Security, Yi was still expanding his own grasp of the increasingly complex world around him.

"I do not know who is pissing in the soup. Ah! I do know that piss is present in my bowl. The smell is very bright."

"Strong," Catlin said automatically.

"Strong. Ah." Yi murmured an apology. "It has been many years since I speak English with an American. Very difficult."

"You speak better English than nine-tenths of the natives do," said Catlin quietly, "but if it tires you, we could try Mandarin, French or Cantonese instead."

"Or Vietnamese?" asked Yi, his voice bland and his eyes impenetrable.

"Or Vietnamese," agreed Catlin, not bothering to conceal his background for the simple reason that if Yi knew he was Rousseau, Yi knew that Catlin spoke Vietnamese as well as the other languages. It had been his gift for languages that had gotten him into covert operations in the first place. Not for the first time in his life, Catlin was grateful that his mother was French, rather than, say, Russian. Siberia was not a place that intrigued him. He would take Saigon's steamy heat any day.

Catlin took a sip of his tea, giving Yi a chance to gather his thoughts. It was the type of politeness that Chinese expected and rarely received from people raised in Western cultures. Yi noted the gesture and felt himself warming slightly toward the man who had once been China's foe, and might become so again if the Four Modernizations of Deng Xiaoping were undermined by enemies within and without the country.

Yi discarded a glowing stub of tobacco, lit a new cigarette and began to speak in staccato phrases about modern treachery and ancient Chinese bronzes. It was clear that he was once more in control of himself and the English language.

"Did you know that there is buried at Xi'an a bronze army that surpasses in artistry the famous terra cotta army of Emperor Qin Shih-huang-di?" asked Yi.

"I've heard a few rumors." What Catlin didn't say was that even though Rousseau's "death" had forced him to stop collecting bronzes, he still collected information from many of the old sources. "I didn't know that you had started excavations."

"We have not. We sank trial shafts to discover the extent and content of the find, then sealed the shafts."

"Why?"

"We should not gulp knowledge like starving dogs at their first meal," said Yi.

Catlin smiled cynically. "And then there's the fact that when the public tires of one archaeological circus, there will be a new one to take its place," Catlin said. "Handled correctly, the finds at Xi'an will be a balm to China's wounded pride for decades to come. All the world will look at the People's Republic in continually renewed wonder at Qin's accomplishments. China will be seen as the center of the civilized universe." Catlin took a sip of tea and continued, "By the time you've milked the finds at Xi'an, the People's Republic might have managed to pull its science and technology into the twentieth century. With that achieved, you can forget the humiliations of the nineteenth century and take your place as first among equals in the councils of the powerful. Once again, you will have great face in the world."

Yi swallowed smoke and said nothing for a moment. "You should have been born Chinese. Ah! Without doubt, you would have been one of our great Legalists."

Catlin laughed softly at the double-edged compliment. When it came to pragmatism, the Chinese Legalists could have given lessons to Genghis Khan and Machiavelli combined. In silence Catlin waited for Yi to continue, sensing that whatever was said next would cost Yi some of his precious store of face.

"It has come to me that some of Qin's bronze army have found their way from darkness to light," said Yi. "American light. Have you heard this?"

"No, but it wouldn't surprise me. If the bronzes have half the quality of the terra cotta, collectors would quite literally kill for them."

"The bronzes are—" Yi's voice dropped. "There are no words," he said softly. "No words." He drew in smoke sharply. "Xi'an is the soul of China. I believe someone is selling it to America." Yi looked narrowly at the big black-haired man sitting so easily across the hearth from him, like a dragon at rest, confident of his own power. But there was no peace in those amber eyes, only intelligence. "Can you imagine what would happen if Deng's enemies could point to a looted Xi'an and say, 'See what capitalism does? It blackens the face of China! They treat us as lackeys and dogs. We have no face!'"

Catlin set down his cup very carefully. He could imagine all too easily how an illicit traffic in Qin bronzes could be used in the lethal internal propaganda battles that characterized political disputes in the People's Republic of China. Deng's careful, discreet, determined courtship of a non-Communist economy would be the first casualty. Deng himself would be the second. America's hope of peaceful relations with China would be the third. It was extremely doubtful that the next Chinese leader would be open to anything but hostility with the West.

"You said that you *thought* Qin bronzes were being smuggled out. Aren't you certain?" asked Catlin.

The cigarette burned brightly, then dulled. Yi brushed a fallen ash onto the floor. "No. Grave robbers could be at work even as we speak and we would not know until the time came to excavate and we discovered that thieves had preceded us. Mount Li is huge. It is impossible to guard everywhere against tunnels dug in the night and concealed in the day. Ah!" Yi sucked in smoke with a harsh sound. "I have seen no evidence of stolen bronzes. I have heard only rumors."

Catlin was quiet for a long time. Then he took a final sip of tea, swirled the residue in a dark spiral and set the cup aside.

"There are several possibilities," said Catlin, his words clipped. "One: Qin bronzes are being stolen and sold in America. Two: Qin forgeries are being sold in America. Three: rumors are being sold in China. If number one is correct, then obviously someone in the Chinese government is involved. Someone very high up in the bureaucracy of Xi'an. You, perhaps. If not you, then someone you trust. The betrayal wouldn't stop there, either. It would go all the way to Beijing. Theft of a chariot, charioteer and horses simply would not be possible without the complicity of powerful people within China's government."

Yi waited, watching Catlin through an expanding spiral of smoke.

"If forgeries are being sold," continued Catlin, "government officials may or may not be involved. It wouldn't matter. Face is not lost over the sale of forgeries." He paused, smiling thinly. "Except by the buyers, of course. But that isn't the PRC's problem, is it?"

Yi's cigarette glowed and dulled again, quickly, like a heartbeat.

"Number three is more tricky," said Catlin neutrally. "Rumors can undermine governments faster than any truth, no matter how damning. It's the old saw about not being able to disprove a negative. You can't prove that bronzes have *not* been stolen and sold. As you said, Mount Li is huge."

Yi nodded curtly.

"So the odds are against you two to one," Catlin pointed out calmly. "If there are real Qin bronzes being sold in the U.S., the prodevelopment forces in China lose to the Maoists, and so do you. If there are rumors of such sales, you still lose, because you can't prove that the rumors aren't true." Catlin shrugged. "Unless you can find Qin bronzes in America and prove that they're forgeries, you're shit out of luck, my friend. The Maoists will hang your ass so high you'll think you're Peking duck."

2

LINDSAY DANNER sat in her office, seeing nothing of the exquisite Oriental teak desk with its Chinese lacquer pen boxes and an appointment calendar graced by elegant calligraphy. Lindsay's eyes were fixed on her hands, but it was the past that she was seeing, voices and scenes that would never come again, times and people gone as surely as yesterday's sunlight.

Yet the nightmare would not go into the past where it belonged. The nightmare not only endured, it grew stronger, feeding on the irrational sadness that had all but overwhelmed Lindsay at her mother's recent death. There was no need for such grief. Her mother had died quickly, painlessly, cherished by the people she had loved more than she had loved anything except God.

Nor was there need for the nightmare that came more and more frequently, claiming the dark hours after midnight, making Lindsay twist and turn helplessly while a faceless Chinese man pursued her through a world that was black and silver and red, blood red, her hands warm and sticky and she was screaming, screaming.

No! Lindsay told herself harshly, clenching a gold pen in her fist. *I'm not a child anymore. If I wake up screaming, no one will come and comfort me and tell me that it's all right and that—what? What did I want my mother to tell me? What was the question I never found the courage to ask and ask and ask until it was answered?*

In the next instant Lindsay shivered, feeling as though the nightmare were turning over inside her, sliding up from the black well of the past. *Whatever the question was, it doesn't matter anymore. It's too late. Somehow I always thought that the next time I saw mother I would have the courage to ask. But she's dead now. There's no one left who even knows what it was like in China then. It's as though it never happened.*

But it did happen. Ask the nightmares.

"Miss Lindsay Danner?"

The voice was unusual in that, though polite, it held an underlying command. Lindsay's head jerked up. A man stood in the doorway of her office. Automatically she summed him up: medium height, blue eyes, pale skin, a few years older than her own thirty years. He was dressed in the manner of Washington, D.C., professionals, with conservative clothing conservatively cut. In a city where politics and rumor ruled supreme, most professionals left stylish dressing to their less vulnerable counterparts in Manhattan or L.A.

"May I help you?" asked Lindsay, her voice neutral, controlled, belonging to the curator of Ancient Chinese Bronzes for the Museum of the Asias rather than to a vaguely frightened, grieving daughter. Discreetly Lindsay checked her calendar. For the past three days she had been in Vancouver, British Columbia, appraising a minor collection of early Chou bronzes. No names had been penciled onto her appointment calendar during her absence.

"Steve White assured me that you would be able to solve a little problem we have," said the man.

Lindsay registered the first-name familiarity of her visitor with Mr. L. Stephen White, director of the Museum of the Asias—and not incidentally, a man of considerable inherited wealth and arrogance.

"I'll be glad to help Mr. White in any way I can," Lindsay said dryly. "He is, after all, my boss. Please sit down Mr.—"

The man closed the door behind him and walked over to the massively elegant teak desk that dominated the room.

Lindsay noted the firmly closed door with a sharpening of curiosity. After a childhood in politically torn China, and an adulthood that had included going down dark streets to appraise objets d'art of dubious provenance, Lindsay recognized a naked bid for secrecy when she saw it.

She would have been worried about the possibility of robbery if it weren't for the fact that all the museum's items were meticulously photographed and cataloged, making their resale through normal channels both unlikely and unprofitable. Nor could the contents of the museum be looted and melted down as had too many of Mexico's and South America's pre-Columbian artifacts, a looting that had begun with the Conquistadores and continued unabated to modern times. Much to modern grave robbers' disappointment, ancient Chinese artisans had used little gold and silver in their creations.

That didn't mean Lindsay couldn't recognize gold when it was dangled under her nose. The shield her visitor held out to her was of the expensive, gold-plated, blue-enameled variety that only the FBI carried. Lindsay looked from the gleaming metal to the polite, professionally assured face watching her from across her desk.

"Special Agent Terry O'Donnel," said the man. Then, in case Lindsay hadn't noticed, he added, "Federal Bureau of Investigation."

The smooth, top-quality leather folder closed over the shield as it was returned to the agent's dark blue suit coat pocket.

"Sit down," offered Lindsay, hoping her sudden curiosity wasn't too obvious. "Will you be here long enough for coffee?"

"We were hoping," said the agent, "that you would come with me to the Hoover Building." He smiled suddenly, turning on the Irish charm. "The coffee there isn't great, but it's free."

"Is Mr. White part of the 'we' you mentioned?" asked Lindsay.

"Indirectly."

Lindsay gave the agent a measuring look. Some people hated modern art or rock music or nuclear power plants. She hated evasions, euphemisms and prevarications. Lies. In a profession where many of the artifacts had been looted in one way or another, at one time or another, Lindsay's absolute refusal to deal on the lucrative, pervasive "double market" was rare.

"How indirectly?" she asked bluntly.

Terry O'Donnel reassessed the slender, bronze-haired woman in a single glance. He decided that the elegant lines of Lindsay's face and the generous curves of her mouth concealed an unusual intelligence and will. If he doubted it, all he had to do was look into the cool, assessing clarity of her very dark blue eyes. Abruptly he decided to change his approach.

"I have a feeling that if I gave you the usual your-government-needs-you speech," said the agent, "it wouldn't work."

"It might. The truth would work even better."

O'Donnel's mouth turned up in a wry smile. "In this case, it's the truth, the whole truth, and nothing but the truth, so help me God. Your government needs you. And," he added swiftly, seeing a question taking shape on Lindsay's lips, "it's something I would rather not discuss here. If it helps you to make up your mind, your boss is with my boss right now. Want to call him?"

"Why didn't he simply call me?"

O'Donnel shrugged. "Guess he was too busy."

"Too busy to pick up the phone, so he sends an FBI agent to fetch me," muttered Lindsay. "That sounds like L. Stephen." She pulled her purse out of a drawer, locked her desk and stood up. "Your cab or mine?"

"Mine. It doesn't have a meter in it." He smiled again, deciding that Lindsay standing up was even better to look at than Lindsay sitting down. The sensual promise of her mouth was repeated in the curving line of breasts and waist and hips. "Having a car is one of the few perks of a civil servant."

"Is the car air conditioned?" she asked hopefully.

He gave her a pitying look. "You've never worked for the government, have you?"

"The government isn't terrifically interested in ancient Chinese bronzes," Lindsay pointed out, locking her office door after the agent had stepped through.

"It is now," O'Donnel muttered too softly for Lindsay to hear.

Lindsay walked next to O'Donnel through the museum's long, narrow hall. Beneath their feet was a rich Chinese silk carpet designed in the dragon motif that had begun in the Shang dynasty more than three thousand years ago and had continued into the modern age of the People's Republic of China. The passage of time, political dynasties and artistic styles had changed the appearance of the dragon, but not its ubiquitous presence. In some unknown, untouchable way, the dragon was China's soul, unchanging.

"Sherry," said Lindsay, pausing by an open office door and leaning inside, "I'll be out for a while. Could you pick up my phone?"

"Sure thing." Sherry looked at the man waiting next to Lindsay in the hall, wondering if he were a buyer, a seller or a knight in shining armor come to take Sherry away from the boredom and near-poverty of being a museum secretary. When the man looked away from her without so much as a hint of a sexual come-on, Sherry sighed and turned her attention back to Lindsay. "Will you be out long?"

Lindsay didn't know, but from the way O'Donnel shifted impatiently behind her, she assumed that his tolerance for chitchat had just run out. "I'll give you a call," promised Lindsay.

The instant the museum's mahogany door swung open, the outside air draped around Lindsay like wet fur. Immediately the teal-blue silk of her dress molded itself to her body. Even so, the cloth itself felt cool against her suddenly flushed skin. The weaving of silk had been invented and brought to perfection in the south of China, where the climate was even hotter and more humid than Washington's infamous summers.

As always, the rush of torrid, steamy air made memories stir deep within Lindsay... a child waking in Hong Kong's smothering darkness and screaming, screaming. The nightmare was old, as were the memories of her mother saying *Nothing is wrong, Lindsay. Go back to sleep. Forget what happened. Forget. Forget.*

Grimly Lindsay turned her mind away from the past with all its irretrievable questions and regrets. And pleasures, too. Despite the nightmare, despite whatever she had finally forgotten, there was much that she loved of the past, and the past was China. She had missed it bitterly when she had been sent to the United States as a teenager. Although she had finally come to love her aunt, the summers spent in Hong Kong with her mother were rich with memories of laughter and voices and the seething humanity that was the Orient.

"This way," said O'Donnel, touching Lindsay's arm, startling her out of her thoughts.

In defiance of local parking regulations, O'Donnel's car was waiting at the curb. The car was American-made, neutral in color and had no visible auxiliary lights or siren. Even so, there was no ticket decorating the windshield. D.C. cops quickly learned how to read government license plates. Some cars would never be ticketed and towed away, even if they were parked right in the lap of the Lincoln Memorial.

As soon as O'Donnel pulled out in traffic for the short drive to the Hoover Building, Lindsay started asking the question that had been tickling her tongue since she had first seen the rich, gold-plated shield.

"Who lost some ancient Chinese bronzes?"

Now that he had Lindsay safely in tow, O'Donnel didn't need to rely on charm, Irish or otherwise. "I'm not free to say any more than I already have, Miss Danner."

"Mr. O'Donnel."

He turned and looked at her quickly, surprised by the self-possession he heard beneath her soft tone. "Yes?"

"If Mr. White isn't on the other end of this drive, you might as well take me back to the museum right now. I won't work with people who lie to me, no matter how pretty their badges are."

O'Donnel's mouth moved in an unwilling smile. "He's there, Miss Danner."

Nothing more was said during the short drive, nor as O'Donnel led Lindsay through the blank-walled, air-conditioned corridors of the Hoover Building. He handed a laminated plastic visitor's badge to Lindsay, which she clipped onto the wrap-front of her dress. O'Donnel clipped his own ID card to his coat pocket and said nothing of interest until he closed an office door behind her.

"Here she is, Steve. You didn't tell me she was a tiger."

"Sharpened her pretty little claws on you, did she?" asked L. Stephen White. "Do you good, boy." Without looking up from the photographs he had been sifting through, White said, "Naughty baby, Lindsay. And from such well-behaved missionary stock, too."

Five months of proximity had accustomed Lindsay to her employer's manner, but she hadn't learned to enjoy it. She doubted that she would ever learn to enjoy being treated like a backward third-grader by the distinguished L. Stephen White. She knew that there was nothing personal in his treatment. He acted toward everyone like that, man and woman alike. It was the result of being raised by parents with more money and less compassion than Fort Knox.

"Was there something you wanted?" asked Lindsay.

White glanced up, looked her over from softly curling chin-length hair to high-heeled sandals, and murmured, "Yes, baby, there most definitely is."

"Then it better be in my job description," shot back Lindsay, impatient with her employer's relentless supply of sexual innuendos.

O'Donnel snickered. "Go get 'em, tiger. If you need any help filing a harassment case, I'll be glad to lend a hand."

"Down, boy," said White, standing and stretching. "Lindsay and I get along just fine, don't we, baby?"

"Especially when I'm not three days behind in my work because of an unscheduled trip to Canada," Lindsay agreed tartly.

"You're cranky. You had lunch yet?" asked White.

"Yes."

"Must be your period, then," he said, yawning.

Lindsay turned and started back toward the hall door.

"They'll arrest you," taunted White.

Lindsay ignored him and opened the door.

"Ah, hell, Lindsay. You know I'm just kidding. Sit down and drink some coffee."

Lindsay looked over her shoulder at her boss. He was tall, dark, very wealthy, twice-divorced and considered handsome by women who lacked the desire or brains to look beyond his surface. His father and grandfather had been avid collectors of Oriental objets d'art. White was an avid collector of weekend affairs. There were days when Lindsay seriously considered becoming one of his two-day stands simply to end the relentless pressure. She had no doubt that once he had bedded her, he would lose interest in her. Again, it was nothing personal. It was simply the way L. Stephen White was with women. Like many collectors, whatever he hadn't yet acquired had far more allure than all the pieces that had been bagged, tagged and filed under Yesterday.

"Cream or sugar?" O'Donnel asked quietly.

Lindsay's indigo eyes measured him and saw only a desire to defuse the situation. "Yes, please," she said. "Both."

"Coming up." O'Donnel vanished into an adjoining room.

"How was Canada?" asked White. "See anything good?"

Lindsay thought she heard more than the usual amount of interest in the latter question. "Beautiful. No."

"In that order?"

Lindsay nodded.

"Hell," sighed White. "My father's all over me like a rash about the hole we have in our Warring States and early Han bronze collections."

"Then why did you send me to look at an early Chou collection?" she asked.

"Not close, huh?"

"You missed it by several centuries," said Lindsay dryly. She was accustomed to the fact that the director of the Museum of the Asias was militantly *un*interested in ancient Chinese bronzes. That was why she had been hired—to placate the grandfather to whom Chinese bronzes represented all that was sublime in art. It was unusual, however, for White to miss the mark so widely.

"Nothing else, uh, turned up?" he asked.

This time Lindsay was certain she heard more than casual curiosity. "No. Were you expecting something?"

O'Donnel came back through the connecting door, carrying two mugs of coffee. Lindsay murmured her thanks and looked at the mug curiously. It was thick, cream-colored and emblazoned with the FBI seal in gold and deep blue. She looked up as another man came into the room, a man who needed neither badge nor seal to mark him. From the short steel-gray hair to the wing-tipped shoes, the man fairly shouted FBI.

"That was quick, Brad. Did you get him?" asked White, looking up from his coffee. Despite the first-name familiarity, there was respect in White's voice as he spoke to the older man.

The man shook his head. "Still busy. I'll give it a few more minutes and then send a car for him."

"Bradford Stone, Lindsay Danner," said O'Donnel, completing the introductions with admirable economy.

Suddenly White's familiarity with O'Donnel and his boss made sense to Lindsay.

"Mr. Stone," said Lindsay, holding out her hand. "Jason White has mentioned you many times."

"Still telling Korean war stories, I'll bet," Stone said, smiling and shaking her hand firmly.

"More than one Oriental art collection began then," said Lindsay. "The spoils of war."

Stone smiled enigmatically and changed the subject. "Have Terry and Steve told you why you're here?"

"No."

"Please sit down, Miss Danner," Stone said politely. "Or is it Ms.?"

"Whichever you prefer."

"Well, then, Miss Danner, I understand you're an expert on old Chinese bronzes."

"Er, yes," murmured Lindsay. She sipped the potent coffee. Like the rest of the FBI setting, it was masculine and utterly lacking in finesse.

"I also understand that you have an uncanny talent for telling forgeries from the real McCoy."

Lindsay blinked and wondered if now was the time for modesty. "Any expert—" she began carefully.

"Don't get coy on me, Lindsay," interrupted White, cutting across her cautious words. "You know damn well that's why I hired you. You kept old Jason from making a fool of himself over that half-baked bronze pot."

"Actually," Lindsay said, smiling slightly, "that 'pot' was a *kuei* and it was quite thoroughly 'baked'. One of the best frauds I've ever seen."

"But still a fraud," said Stone, watching her closely.

"Yes."

"How long did it take you to find out?"

"Oh, I knew the second I looked at it," said Lindsay. "It took me several days to prove it, though. Jason didn't want to take no for his answer. He loved that *kuei*."

"But you knew," said Stone. "Instantly."

Lindsay wondered at the satisfaction in Stone's voice, but refused to evade or ignore the implicit question. "Yes."

"How?"

Lindsay looked at the three men who were watching her intently and wondered how she could explain the inexplicable. Besides violence and fear, one of her most vivid childhood memories was of standing in front of a Hong Kong shop window and knowing that something was wrong with one of the old bronze *ti* vessels on display. She had stood and stared until her mother had taken her by the hand and led her back to their quarters behind the shabby Christian church. She had been eleven years old, exposed since babyhood to the bits and pieces of the ritual grave furnishings that her father and uncle had collected around Xi'an. Though the intent of the ritual vessels was unabashedly pagan, both of the Danner men had been fascinated by the art itself. And so had Lindsay.

"I grew up with Chinese art," said Lindsay finally.

"So did the Chinese," Stone responded. "Can they tell fraud at a glance?"

Another memory surfaced, that of the owner's amazement when she had marched into his shop and asked him what was wrong with the *ti*. Only years later did she realize that the vessel had been a clumsy fraud, the first of many that she would see. But there were other frauds, far more subtle and expert. Those, too, she came to recognize for what they were. Lies.

"Some people are born with the ability to discriminate perfectly among musical notes," Lindsay said finally. "Others are born with the ability to create extraordinary paintings or poems that ravish the soul." She shrugged. "My ability is much more mundane. All art experts have it to some extent. They will run tests as confirmation, but they depend on their instincts and experience to form their opinions."

Stone looked at Lindsay for a long moment, as though judging her, using his own instinct for lawlessness and fraud. "Whatever is said here will go no farther than this room. Agreed?"

Lindsay hesitated. "So long as I don't have to actually lie about it. Frankly, I'm a terrible liar."

"If anybody asks you questions, refer them to me."

"All right."

Stone looked away from Lindsay. "Thanks for your help, Steve. I'll call Terry if I need either of you."

O'Donnel took White's arm and headed for the hallway. "C'mon Steve. One of our agents just busted a porn ring. He's got a file full of evidence that's guaranteed to make you go blind."

The door shut firmly behind the two men.

"The FBI finds itself in the position of needing some immediate, reliable and very discreet advice on ancient Chinese bronzes," Stone said bluntly. "Normally our own resources are enough to cover anything that comes up from counterfeit Paul Revere silver to fake Old Masters. In this case, though—" He made an impatient gesture. "Our labs won't have access to the bronzes. If there are bronzes."

Lindsay took an unobtrusive sip of coffee. She knew that Stone was irritated at having to reveal anything to an outsider. That simply wasn't Bureau policy. Even so, his elliptical approach to the subject told her that whatever was at stake was very important.

"Yet," continued Stone, "with or without recourse to our labs, it is absolutely imperative that we know whether or not the bronzes are fraudulent."

Lindsay wanted to shout *What bronzes?* but instead took another sip of the lethal coffee. Though she was a naturally spontaneous person, being a buyer, seller and appraiser of art had taught her the value of a poker face and silence.

"No comment?" prodded Stone.

"I'm sorry. Is one required?" Lindsay asked politely.

Stone made a sound that could have been a muffled laugh or a grunt. "You don't give away much, do you?"

"Neither do you, sir." She smiled. "We'd be a lethal bridge team."

Unwillingly Stone smiled in return. He fiddled with a pen, brushed it aside and said, "There are some bronzes down the hall. I want your opinion of them."

"Certainly." Lindsay set aside her coffee and stood with barely concealed eagerness.

The phone rang.

Stone picked it up, listened for a moment. "He what? Who the hell does he think he is?" Pause. "They're *here*? Judas H. Priest!"

The receiver slammed back into the cradle.

"Sit down, please, Miss Danner," said Stone in a tight voice. "Someone will bring you more coffee. There's been a slight problem with the, er, exhibit."

Stone was out the door and down the hall before Lindsay could say a word. Not that Stone would have listened if she had managed to say anything. He was focused on the problem waiting for him down the hall. He had been against this assignment from the first moment he had heard of it. Nothing had happened since to change his mind.

Without bothering to conceal his irritation, Stone yanked open a door, stepped through and forcefully pulled the door shut behind him. "All right, Terry. What in hell is going on."

It was a demand, not a question. Before O'Donnel could respond, an interior door opened. An old Chinese man entered, accompanied by a large, solidly built male Caucasian who moved like a commando.

"Mr. Stone," said O'Donnel quickly, "this is Mr. Chen Yi and his, er—"

"Fishing buddy," supplied Catlin. He looked at the older FBI agent. He had worked with men like Stone before, respected their strengths and knew their weaknesses. Part warrior, part bureaucrat, part prima donna, part team player. Shrewd, hard and more than a little vain. A good soldier and a lousy guerrilla.

Chen Yi held out his hand in the accepted Western manner, clasped Stone's hand briefly and said, "It is an honor."

Stone's pale blue eyes fastened on Yi's impassive face as they shook hands. "The honor is mine," said Stone. Then he added bluntly, "The State Department told me to expect several Chinese. Nothing was said about an American."

"A small misunderstanding," murmured Yi. "My comrades were delayed in Los Angeles by illness. Something in the water, I fear."

Catlin wondered whether the "something in the water" had been added by Chen Yi rather than the Greater Los Angeles Metropolitan Water District. It was what Catlin would have done if he had reason to distrust his comrades—or they had reason to distrust him.

"I came ahead alone to prepare the way," continued Yi, his voice breathy and yet staccato, giving a sense of pressure or urgency to everything he said. "Mr. Catlin was gracious enough to agree to advise me on the intricacies of your American customs and government."

"Mr. Catlin," inserted O'Donnel in a neutral tone, "is the Pacific Rim Foundation's leading Asian expert."

Catlin held out a hand that had a thin white knife scar across the back. Stone took the hand with the firm grip of a man who has to do a lot of politicking to maintain his power.

"We weren't expecting you," Stone said.

"It came as a surprise to me, too," said Catlin.

"Mr. Yi—" began Stone.

"Chen," interrupted Catlin quietly. "Mr. Chen. Native Chinese reverse the order of their names, family name first and personal name last."

Stone nodded abruptly. "Pardon me, Mr. Chen." He glanced at O'Donnel. "Why don't you take Mr. Catlin down to the coffee room while Mr. Chen and I talk."

Yi's hand moved in a silent gesture of protest. "Pardon *me*, Mr. Stone, but Catlin is necessary. He is also very discreet."

The words were polite, but no one in the room doubted that Yi meant to have his way. Any discussions would be held in Catlin's presence—or they wouldn't be held at all.

"Where are the bloody diplomats when you need them?" muttered Stone under his breath. He took a deep breath. "Mr. Chen, the director himself impressed upon me how necessary it was that we do everything within our power to help you."

Yi bowed slightly, accepting the implications of Stone's words with a uniquely Chinese combination of modesty and arrogance.

"I have no wish to offend you," Stone continued carefully, remembering the extreme clarity and bluntness of his orders: *Do whatever you have to, but make goddamn sure Chen Yi doesn't go home unhappy.* "But the fact is that your presence presents me with some, er, difficulties."

"That is why Catlin is here," agreed Yi calmly. "He is one who removes obstacles from my roads."

Stone said nothing, but color heightened beneath his skin. "If you will excuse me for a moment," he said tightly, turning away.

Catlin decided it was time to dynamite some of the obstacles out of the roadway. "Certainly, Mr. Stone. But when you've finished talking to your boss, and he's talked to his, and so on up to the Oval Office, the answer will come back down the line that Chen Yi has the keys to the city. Believe it. He could commit sodomy on the White House lawn and receive only congratulations on his form and prowess."

Stone grimaced. O'Donnel smothered a smile. Neither one argued the point.

"Politics," said Stone in disgust, turning back to face Catlin.

"Precisely." Catlin smiled crookedly. "Think of it as budget time, Mr. Stone, and Chen Yi is the Appropriations Committee."

Stone looked from the frail, politically powerful Chinese to Catlin. "May I be very blunt?" asked Stone.

Catlin looked at Yi. Yi nodded slightly.

Catlin turned back to Stone. "Yi understands enough of our customs not to be insulted by things that an American of equal rank wouldn't be insulted by. So when it's just us chickens pecking away at each other, we'll observe American customs and you can be as blunt as you like. But outside here, you treat Yi like the Second Coming of Christ. Nothing personal. Just a question of face."

A quick look told Stone that the Very Important Chinese was amused rather than insulted by Catlin's boiled-down version of diplomatic protocol.

"Is that acceptable to you, Mr. Chen?" asked Stone with the caution of a man who had survived changes in political administrations and the more vicious fraternal infighting that bedeviled any large bureaucracy such as the FBI.

"Yes, Mr. Stone," said Yi, lighting a cigarette. "As Catlin kindly explained it to me, he may be a son of a bitch, but he is *my* son of a bitch." Yi swallowed smoke, gave Stone a cool look and asked, "Have you chosen an appraiser from the list I gave you?"

"Three of them were out of the country. One just got back."

"What of the five who were here?" asked Yi. "Have you interviewed them?"

Stone shrugged. "Since we're being blunt, I'll tell you that I wouldn't trust most of them as far as I could throw them uphill. Including the women."

"Buyers, sellers, smugglers or thieves?" Catlin asked casually.

"Where the hell did Chen find you?" retorted Stone.

"Same place you're going to—under Catlin, Jacob MacArthur, in your computer files." Catlin looked at O'Donnel. "Normal spelling on all three names. Go ahead. We won't miss you."

O'Donnel looked at Stone. Stone jerked his head toward the door. "We'll be down the hall," said Stone. Then he added too softly for anyone else to hear, "Sic her on the bronzes."

"It's been a pleasure meeting you, Mr. Chen, Catlin," said O'Donnel politely before he turned and left the room, shutting the door behind him.

Stone turned to Yi. "Would you like to watch the sixth expert appraise the bronzes we rounded up?"

Chen Yi nodded. "I would like to see them myself."

With a wolfish smile, Stone gestured toward the door. "Are you familiar with two-way mirrors, Mr. Chen?"

"Yes."

"The room we'll use is soundproofed. You'll have a clear view of the bronzes."

"And the appraiser? Who is he?" asked Yi.

"She. Lindsay Danner."

With a quick breath Yi took the last of his cigarette down to a burning stub, which he threw into a sand-filled ashtray. "Ah!"

Only Catlin noticed the slight jerk of Yi's hand when he heard Lindsay Danner's name.

3

CATLIN TOOK IN THE ROOM with a single, sweeping glance. The area was small, soundproofed, well ventilated and dimly lighted. There were chairs scattered about, facing the large pane of glass that dominated one wall. Through the subtle distortion of the special glass, another room was visible. That room was empty but for seventeen bronzes waiting in a row on a long conference table. The table was wide and placed so that whoever looked at the bronzes would face the hidden room. The lighting in the room was so bright as to be just short of pain.

In all, the setup was about as subtle as a sonic boom. Only a total innocent would be unaware of the possibility of watchers hidden on the other side of the mirror.

"Sit down," said Stone, gesturing toward the chairs. "Don't worry about talking. You could set off a bomb in here and nobody would hear it on the other side."

Chen Yi went directly to the window and peered through. "Those bronzes," he said. "Where did you get them?"

"Museum basements from here to Manhattan. You told me that we couldn't use any of the more famous pieces."

"Good." Yi's lighter snapped open and he drew in sharply on the cigarette. The flame surged.

"I wouldn't do that too close to the window when someone's on the other side," said Catlin, remembering a time long ago when the flare of a match coming through a whorehouse "mirror" had given him an inadvertent warning of danger. "A direct, nearby light source bleeds right through."

Stone gave Catlin a measuring glance as Yi snapped shut the lighter and stepped away from the glass.

"You seem to know a lot about two-way mirrors," Stone said. "You spend much time in police stations on the wrong side of the glass?"

"Not if I can help it," said Catlin as he went closer to the window and looked at Chinese bronzes for the first time in years.

"And if you can't help it?" shot back Stone.

"You're the investigator. Read my file," Catlin suggested softly.

The door in the other room opened. O'Donnel ushered in a woman. Hidden microphones picked up each sound, giving the three watchers the eerie sensation that they were immaterial, invisible spirits hovering over the bronzes, seeing but not being seen, hearing but not being heard. Stone was accustomed to the feeling. So was Catlin. Yi was not, and proved it by the sharp intake of his breath when O'Donnel seemed to speak right to him through the glass.

"Mr. Stone had to take a phone call, but he wanted you to get right to the appraisal."

"What does Mr. Stone expect?" asked Lindsay, walking toward the bronzes.

Catlin's amber eyes narrowed as he took in the self-assured elegance of Lindsay's clothes and carriage. Under the bright fluorescent lights her smooth, chin-length hair gleamed like a freshly minted bronze coin. The color was rich, textured, alive with shades that went from pale flax to a deep chestnut gold. The effect was like her voice, shades of silky richness.

"Expect?" asked the agent.

Lindsay looked away from the bronzes and back over her shoulder at O'Donnel. The motion outlined her breasts in silk that was the same clear indigo as her eyes.

"Does he want me to assign an age to the bronzes? A price? What does he expect?" Lindsay's voice was supple, slightly husky, intriguing.

Catlin shot a sideways glance at Yi. "Is she the one?" asked Catlin in Mandarin.

"Yes," answered Yi in the same language.

"He wants to know if the pieces are forged or not," said O'Donnel beyond the mirror. "We're not buying, so the price doesn't matter."

Lindsay moved to the table and bent over the first bronze. Her hair drifted forward gracefully, a motion echoed by the silk dress. A triangle of fine-grained skin was revealed when the wrap front of the dress fell slightly away from her body as she bent to study the bronze. The men in the room were treated to a view of smoothly swelling breasts that were barely concealed by dark blue silk.

"Daughter of a missionary," murmured Catlin in Mandarin. "By the spirits of my ancestors, if the daughter of my minister had looked like that, I would have gone to church seven days a week and twice on Sundays."

Yi smiled. "The mother was pleasing" he said, also in Mandarin.

"Is the daughter a broken pot?" Catlin asked, his delivery as staccato as Yi's.

Yi shook his head as his soft voice filled the room with the clipped, sliding tones of Mandarin, "After the mother, there is no other woman. Her hair was a golden river. Her voice dreamed in shades of silver. To be near her was to know the serenity of the lotus blooming beneath the summer moon."

Catlin's eyes narrowed as he looked at the Chinese who stood and stared through a two-way mirror into the hidden past. Living in Asia had taught Catlin that Chinese men were not noted for their tender view of women, despite a persistent strain of eros and romance in Chinese poetry. Yet in Yi's voice there was both remembered desire and something else, something deeper and more enduring. If translated into ideographs, Yi's description would have been ambiguous, capable of referring to both the spirit and the flesh. But then, the hallmark of the written Chinese language was that most ideographs had more than one meaning. China's multileveled, evocative, imprecise ideographs were a joy to poets and a curse to scientists.

The sound of Lindsay's words drew Catlin's attention back to the present and the woman who stood on the other side of the mirror.

"Number one is a rather ordinary *i ch'i* of the *ting* type. Or *ding*, if you follow the recent spelling and pronunciation guide approved by the People's Republic."

"Whoa," said O'Donnel. "Run that by me again, in English."

"Taking notes?" asked Lindsay, smiling.

"Nope. You're being immortalized on tape. Didn't Mr. Stone tell you?"

Lindsay shook her head, making light run like threads of molten gold through her hair. "The first bronze is a ritual vessel, a three-legged caldron used for serving meat and cereals. Late Shang period."

"Genuine?"

"Yes. There's no particular artistry in it, however. It's simply a bronze vessel made for the grave of a man of middling importance who died three thousand years ago. Excellent patina, if you care."

O'Donnel shrugged. "Not me. My boss might. I don't know."

"Most collectors care more about patina than about the intrinsic artistry of the vessel itself," explained Lindsay. She smiled slightly as she bent over another bronze, remembering collectors she had known. They were a diverse and unpredictable breed, as even the most casual visitor to any museum could see.

Lindsay used both hands as she turned the second bronze toward the light. Though the piece was less than a foot high, the craftsmen hadn't stinted on the bronze. "And if the collector is Chinese," she continued, turning another aspect of the bronze toward the light, "he will probably care more for the quality of the inscriptions than anything else about the piece."

With an expression of distaste, Lindsay returned the bronze to the table. "This is a *kuang*, a vessel for wine or water. It aspires to be Shang. It isn't. It's probably a Sung forgery. The

Chinese have been faking early Shang bronzes for at least seven hundred years.''

"Really? Why?'' asked the agent, looking at the bronze and finding nothing worth counterfeiting. To his taste it was squat, overwrought and ugly.

"Fashion.'' Lindsay's smile turned down at the corners. "And survival. In Sung times there was a very powerful magistrate who would excuse all manner of antisocial behavior in exchange for ancient bronzes that carried inscriptions. Wise crooks cast their apologies in advance. With appropriate inscriptions, of course.''

O'Donnel's smile was wide and understanding, if not wholly approving. "But how did you know this one was fake? Wasn't the surface dirty enough?''

Lindsay's laugh was soft, rippling, as sensuous as silk sliding over skin. Catlin sensed Yi's indrawn breath as the Chinese leaned toward the glass like a man seeing a dream condense just beyond his reach.

"Mr. O'Donnel,'' she murmured, trying not to smile, "that isn't dirt, that's patina, the pride and glory of mature bronze. And no, there's nothing wrong with it. After the first five hundred years, it's almost impossible to date a bronze on the basis of its patina alone.''

She turned toward the third bronze.

"Then how did you know that this was a fake?'' persisted O'Donnel.

Lindsay glanced up from the table. "The inscriptions.''

"Oh.''

With a cynical smile of male understanding, Catlin saw O'Donnel admiring Lindsay's legs as she bent over the table again. Catlin himself was watching each of her movements, listening to each nuance of tone and word choice, trying to find the person beneath the smile and the indigo silk. Two things had come through very clearly to Catlin so far: Lindsay handled the bronzes with love; and she disliked the fraudulent Shang bronze with a feeling that went deeper than an art buyer's desire to avoid being cheated.

O'Donnel came closer and bent to peer at the rejected bronze. Catlin noted the brush of bodies and the fact that Lindsay took a small step aside that ended the physical contact without making an issue out of it. O'Donnel noticed, too. Without looking up from the bronze he was studying, he eased away, no longer crowding Lindsay.

"What inscriptions?" asked O'Donnel after a minute, baffled by the mazelike patterns that covered the *kuang*.

"On the body," Lindsay said absently, "beneath the handle."

She picked up the third bronze and turned it slowly in her hands. The piece looked rather like an artichoke sitting in a bowl, with triangular leaves overlapping in an elegant pattern. Holes were cut in the bronze to allow incense to escape. Unlike the other bronzes, the patina on this one was an even cinnamon color that showed off the gold-inlaid hunting scenes to spectacular advantage.

O'Donnel picked up the rejected *kuang*, grunted at its weight and peered at the faint line of ideographs. "What's wrong with the inscription?"

With great care, Lindsay set down the hill-censer she was holding. Catlin saw the slow caress of her fingertips up the bronze's curved side as she withdrew her touch and gave her attention to O'Donnel.

"The inscription shouldn't even be there," said Lindsay. "Of all the scientifically excavated Shang sites, not one of them has yielded an early bronze with an inscription. Even a simple tribal mark is rare."

O'Donnel squinted at the damning ideographs and set the *kuang* back on the table with an audible thump. "What about the third one?"

"Genuine," Lindsay said quietly, her voice husky. She touched the bronze again, savoring it with her fingertips as well as her eyes and mind. "Exquisite. Han dynasty."

Catlin sensed Stone's sudden attention and guessed that Lindsay's estimate of the bronze disagreed with that of the other experts the FBI had brought in. Yi, too, seemed surprised. As was Catlin himself. The patina on the piece was simply too even, too perfect. Suddenly he wished that he were in the room himself, able to question Lindsay personally, and to hear her husky answers.

"But it's smooth, not rough like most of the other bronzes," protested O'Donnel. "And it's a different color."

"Patina forms quickly in water or wet ground, very slowly in air. That hill-censer was a prized family possession passed down from hand to hand through the centuries, and used only for the most important rituals. It was never a funeral offering buried with its owner."

Lindsay smoothed her palm over the incense burner that had been cast to resemble hills rising to a central peak. "And the gold," she added, tracing a hunting scene with a delicate fingertip, "never corrodes. This is an extraordinary piece. Where did you get it?"

"Then the other one must be real, too," said O'Donnel, ignoring her question as he pointed toward a *kuang* that was twice the size of the one she had rejected and much better preserved. The patina was an even dark brown.

"That's a fifty-footer," said Lindsay, glancing up from the beautifully wrought hill-censer toward the *kuang*.

"What's that?"

"A fraud you can spot at fifty feet," Lindsay said dryly. "It's trying to be Shang, but the designs are Chou. The patina is a standard vinegar spray job. The proportions of the animal are wrong. Totally inept all the way around."

Behind the mirror Catlin laughed softly. Like Lindsay, he had nothing but contempt for an amateurish job of deception. Unlike her, he had a professional's admiration for a fraud that passed unnoticed. After all, his life had depended on the success of being a living fraud—a covert agent living in enemy territory.

As Lindsay proceeded down the line of bronzes, Catlin divided his attention between the two sides of the deceptive mirror. Stone, in particular, interested Catlin. Whatever Stone's area of expertise in the FBI, it obviously wasn't in art fraud, illicit traffic in antiquities or anything having to do with dubious artifacts of any kind. Beyond scoring Lindsay on a piece of paper, Stone spent his time watching Yi and Catlin rather than the bronzes.

Catlin had a suspicion that amounted to a certainty that Stone was a member of the FBI's elite Foreign Counterintelligence Division. The certainty increased as Catlin listened in amused understanding while Stone tried to get more information from Yi than Stone had gotten from his superiors.

"I hope your comrades will be well soon," said Stone.

Yi acknowledged the conversational gambit with a nod of his head, but his black eyes never wavered from the glass.

"Do you know when they'll join you?"

"No."

Stone watched Yi for a moment, then flicked a glance at the next room, where Lindsay's quiet comments made a counterpart to his own, more pointed, questions.

"Are those bronzes anything like what you're looking for?" asked Stone.

"No."

"Do we have any deadline for finding your missing bronzes?"

"No."

"Where do you want to begin? West Coast? East?"

"We have begun," Yi said simply, watching as Lindsay bent over another bronze.

"Do you want to wait while we go through the whole list of experts?" continued Stone. "Two of them are still out of the country."

"That is up to you."

"It's your expert we're picking," Stone said.

"Is it? Your government insisted on giving me an expert to help in my search." Yi tossed his cigarette into a nearby ashtray. The butt rolled once, then lay and smoldered like a banked fire. Pungent smoke curled up, disturbed by random currents of air in the room. "I submitted a list of four Americans who are qualified to tell Chou from Qin under the most stringent circumstances. Your government submitted a list of twelve. We agreed to interview eight. You have interviewed six.''

The lighter snapped open as Yi turned away from the mirror, shielding the flame with his body and cupped hands. He inhaled, snapped the lighter shut and focused his black eyes on Stone.

"Shall we compromise?" continued Yi in a clipped voice. "*Our* expert. As soon as we choose him."

Silently Catlin admired Chen Yi, the consummate actor. Catlin knew what Stone did not: Yi would maneuver until the FBI chose Lindsay Danner. Catlin didn't know how the trick would be accomplished, but he was sure that it would be.

"Some experts," Stone said sarcastically. "More than half of them are under suspicion as either crooks or con artists. Wouldn't trust them to tell me if a nickel was wood or metal."

"Caveat emptor," said Catlin, "is the motto of the art trade."

Yi looked sideways at the man he had gently blackmailed into helping him.

"It's Latin. It means let the buyer beware," said Catlin, translating without being asked.

"Ah!" Yi laughed abruptly. "Not every wise man was born in China."

Stone took a deep breath and went back to chipping away at Yi's imperturbable exterior. "The director wasn't entirely clear as to what you expected from me."

Yi puffed on his cigarette, shielding the glowing tip from the glass with his hand, and ignored the conversational gambit.

"How many men will you need?" persisted Stone.

"I requested none."

Catlin smiled slightly. Yi was having an FBI escort shoved down his throat in exactly the same way that Yi was being shoved down Stone's throat. There were polite protestations of brotherhood and helpfulness from everyone involved—and no trust at all. He doubted that Yi and the FBI would get around to dining with each other. No one on earth made spoons long enough for either side to sup comfortably from a communal pot.

"Do you have a plan?" asked Stone, lighting a cigarette of his own with curt motions that said a great deal about exasperation and self-control.

Yi made ambivalent gestures with his hand, leaving a trail of smoke like a dissolving ideograph hanging in the room.

"Well?" pressed Stone.

"I am quite well, thank you," Yi said, deliberately misunderstanding. "And you?"

Catlin spoke swiftly in Mandarin, for he sensed that Stone's patience was right up against its limit. Making an enemy of the FBI at this point in the game wouldn't help Yi at all.

"In the circuses of China, do they have signs warning people not to tease the tigers?" asked Catlin.

Yi bared his teeth in something that only a diplomat would have called a smile. "The tiger is caged."

"At the moment, yes. But there will come a time when the tiger is taken from the cage to perform for its keepers. What then, Chen Yi?"

There was silence, then a reluctant "Ah!" Yi turned to Stone and said in English, "The course we take depends on the expert who is chosen."

Silently Catlin wondered what Yi had in mind for the woman on the other side of the deceptive glass.

Stone looked from Yi to Catlin and back again. The FBI agent's eyes were like clear crystal against the heightened color of anger showing on his skin. There was a long moment in which there was no sound but that of a bronze wine vessel being shifted from one place on the table to another. Finally Stone nodded abruptly and turned back to the two-way mirror.

In silence the three of them watched while Lindsay worked her way down the line of bronzes. O'Donnel followed, asking questions about the various pieces. She worked quickly, confidently, until she came to the final piece. It was a wide, shallow bowl resting on a broad, low foot. Though hardly delicate, the bowl nonetheless gave a feeling of balanced tension rather than earthbound heaviness.

Lindsay picked up the bronze and turned it slowly in her hands.

"Something wrong?" O'Donnel asked casually, leaning his hip against the long conference table.

"A *p'an* like this has never been found earlier than the Chou dynasty. Yet the execution of this vessel is definitely Shang, not Chou. Monumental yet simple. The designs are less complex, less flamboyant than Chou. The piece as a whole is less... leaden...than most early Chou." Lindsay put down the bowl, stepped back several paces and simply looked at it.

"Another fraud?" asked O'Donnell after a long silence.

Slowly, Lindsay shook her head. "No, just a type of *p'an* I've never seen before, a link between the art of two long-ago dynasties." She smiled softly to herself, remembering her excitement when she had found a genuine bronze that was neither in the Huai style nor yet Han, but rather an elegant combination of the two artistic traditions. "After all," she said quietly, approaching the bowl again, "the break between dynasties is never as clean and quick as the dates in history books make it seem."

"But if you've never seen a bowl like this one before, how do you know it's not a fraud?"

For a time O'Donnel thought that Lindsay wouldn't answer, that she had attention only for the unusual bronze bowl. Finally she turned to him.

"Beyond a professional's trained instinct, you mean?" she asked, her voice light, her dark blue eyes serious.

O'Donnel grinned, understanding instantly what Lindsay was saying. He, too, used instinct in his work. Every good cop did, reflexively dividing the people he met into categories of honest and crooked and in between. "Yeah, that's what I mean."

Lindsay gestured again toward the *kuang* that was a seven-hundred-year-old forgery. "The Chinese of the Sung dynasty valued inscriptions. The Shang did not. Therefore, when Sung forgers went to work, they made pieces that appealed to the fashions of Sung times. They added inscriptions.''

"So it boils down to inscriptions again," said O'Donnel, gesturing toward the bowl.

Lindsay smiled ruefully. "I wish it were that simple. Art inevitably reflects the tastes of the artist's time. Even forged art. Have you ever seen a comparison of Old Masters forged through the ages?''

O'Donnel's blue eyes narrowed intently, but he said nothing, knowing that the question was rhetorical. She no more expected him to be an expert on Old Masters than he expected her to be expert in FBI procedures. He, at least, was correct in his expectations. Before coming to the counterintelligence division, O'Donnel had worked art fraud. He knew a great deal about Old Masters.

"In the times when epic art was in fashion," continued Lindsay, "forgers subtly altered the feel of the Old Masters they imitated until the proportions were more epic, and therefore more pleasing to potential customers. Today, the forgers tend to simplify some of the old paintings that are, to our present tastes, overwrought. If baroque comes back in vogue, the Old Masters will be recast yet again in subtly baroque form and sold to collectors who can't believe that new Old Masters don't turn up in grandma's attic every day.''

"I didn't think forgers were that smart," said O'Donnel. "Changing old paintings to please modern tastes. Very clever.''

"It's not cleverness," Lindsay said. "It's simply that no matter how hard you try, you can't escape the subtle, pervasive influence of the culture and time you were born into. Forgers paint a subtly modernized version of an Old Master not because they sense that it will be easier to sell, but because they can't help it.''

With a graceful motion Lindsay turned back to the table. "That's how I knew that bronzes number twelve and fifteen were frauds. The forgers used the correct designs for the times they were imitating, but they used the symbols themselves incorrectly. For their decorations, Shang bronzes have symbols that make very clear statements about the relationship of man and the universe according to Shang precepts. Sung forgeries of Shang ritual vessels copied aspects of the Shang design quite accurately, but they garbled the underlying philosophical statements every time.'' She shrugged. ''Not surprising. The forgers usually were illiterate peasants. To them, the symbols were simply flourishes to catch the eye, decorations empty of meaning.''

O'Donnel looked at the bronzes as though memorizing them before he turned back to Lindsay. ''Want to go over them again?''

She shook her head. ''I would like to study the last one more closely, though. Could you lend it to the Museum of the Asias? Or at least allow us to photograph it for our own education, perhaps even do an article on it? Ideally, we would like to purchase the bowl, of course. And the hill-censer, too,'' she added, gesturing toward the incense burner inlaid in gold. ''If the owner wants to sell, my museum wants to be among the bidders.''

O'Donnel smiled and held his hands out, palm up. ''I'll pass it along, but it's really not my department. For all I know, the boss cooked up these bronzes at the local foundry.''

There was a distinctly cynical edge to Lindsay's answering smile. She knew that while O'Donnel probably wasn't lying outright, he wasn't telling much of the truth, either. He certainly wasn't telling her what she wanted to know—who owned the bronzes she had just looked at.

''I'd appreciate whatever you could do,'' she said. ''I'm sure L. Stephen White will be more than willing to make the request a formal one.''

''Never hurts,'' said O'Donnel, widening his smile. ''More coffee? Or would you prefer to go back to the museum?''

Lindsay hesitated, then shrugged. ''The museum, please, if Mr. Stone has no more need for me.''

''If he does, you'll be the first to know,'' O'Donnel assured her.

He led her out the door without even looking over his shoulder at the audience he knew watched behind the mirror.

"Hell of a performance," Catlin said.

"Miss Danner?" asked Stone. He shrugged. "The others have a better score than hers on the bronzes."

"I meant O'Donnel. He didn't look at the mirror once. And he acted like he'd never seen a piece of art in his life."

There was a long pause before Stone asked, "Just what makes you think he has?"

"Instinct," Catlin said laconically.

Yi gave Catlin a swift look that Stone couldn't see. Catlin was certain that Yi was thinking about tigers and teasing. But Catlin knew Stone's type of tiger very well. There was a vital difference between teasing and shouldering for position in the coming battle. Catlin had no doubt that a battle was coming. Stone would get one look at Catlin's file and everything loose would hit the fan. Yi would have to fight hard to keep his undomesticated dragon.

Not that Catlin blamed Stone for the coming battle. In Stone's position, Catlin would have done the same. The last thing a company man wanted was a renegade spook poking his nose into an FBI counterintelligence pie.

"Let's decide on an expert," said Stone, drawing a paper from his pocket. "Then we can get together on a plan."

The paper contained a list of the seventeen bronzes down one side. The sheet had been divided into seven columns. In the first was the information that had come with the bronzes from their various museums. Each of the other six columns contained the name of one of the experts who had been tested. The arrangement made it very easy to score each expert against the rest.

Stone took out his pen, finished filling in Lindsay's column and handed the sheet over to Yi. He studied the paper with every evidence of acute interest, holding it so that Catlin could read, as well.

There was agreement on most artifacts. It was easy enough to justify dismissing the "expert" who had overlooked bogus inscriptions. Four other experts had agreed all the way down the line with the museums' assessments. Two of them were people whose names had been added to Yi's original list by the FBI. The other two had had their names crossed out by Stone.

"Why do you dismiss these?" asked Yi. "They performed as well as the people you selected."

"Their backgrounds don't inspire confidence," Stone said flatly.

"Ah!"

Calmly Yi drew out a pen and inked through the names of the two people put forward by the FBI. Stone's mouth flattened into a line, but he said nothing. He knew a quid pro quo when one was politely shoved down his throat.

Yi shrugged. "That leaves us with Miss Danner, I believe."

"But she missed two of the bronzes," protested Stone. "The two people you crossed out—"

"Overlooked what Miss Danner's more sensitive eye discerned," Yi interrupted, impervious to Stone's objections. "The *p'an* is indeed Shang. I saw photographs of its twin not two months ago. It was found at a newly excavated Shang site. Very worthy. Very rich."

Yi's cigarette glowed once, then made a flat arc from his fingers to the ashtray.

Expressionlessly Catlin watched the final moves of the mental chess game the two men had been playing since the instant they had been introduced. At this point, Stone was checked. There was no way he could argue that Yi was wrong on the basis of archaeological evidence only Yi had access to. Even as Catlin understood the gambit, he admired Yi's shrewdness. Lie, truth, or half-truth, only Yi knew, for only Yi held the proof.

"What about that incense burner?" challenged Stone. "Every one of the other experts declared it a fake."

"The Beijing Museum has some very ancient bronzes whose patinas are of similar color and perfection," Yi said, watching Stone with shrewd black eyes.

Checkmate.

Stone no more had access to Beijing's museum than he did to recent archaeological excavations in China. He could either call Yi a liar or he could accept Lindsay Danner as the FBI's chosen expert on ancient Chinese bronzes.

Stone started to speak, stopped, stubbed out his cigarette and turned smoothly to face Yi again. "Would you buy the incense burner?" asked Stone.

"Is it for sale?"

There was no hesitation. "Yes."

"Ah!" Yi turned to Catlin. "That will be your first acquisition. See that Miss Danner handles it for you. It will be an excellent return to the market for an absent collector."

"None better," Catlin said dryly. He didn't know whether the incense burner was a fake or whether the bowl was a genuine late Shang rather than an early Chou fraud. In terms of what he would have to do to earn back half of the mutilated coin, it didn't matter. Yi had won. Stone had lost.

It was time for the dragon to go fishing.

"Will you inform Miss Danner of her new client," said Yi, gesturing toward Catlin with a fragile, long-nailed hand, "or should I?"

"Client?" asked Stone.

"Yes. According to the information you have supplied to me," Yi said, "Miss Danner's activities are not limited to the Museum of the Asias. She also serves independent collectors, as does every other expert on that list."

Stone nodded.

Yi smiled coolly. "Mr. Catlin is a collector of fine Chinese bronzes. His special interest is in third century B.C. bronzes. Especially the Qin dynasty period."

Instantly Stone understood. "You want us to set up a sting."

"Please?"

"That's where the cops pretend to be crooks," explained Catlin. "They get close to the crooks like a bee on a flower. They buy stolen merchandise, talk crooked, walk crooked, eat crooked and wait until they have enough evidence to hang the real crooks. Then the cops sink in the stinger and fly away to the next rotten flower."

"Ah!" The technique was not an unfamiliar one to a man who had survived China's bitter fratricidal strife. Yi was a man with many public faces and no private ones. "A sting. Another idiom to remember. Very useful. Thank you."

Stone shifted impatiently. "It shouldn't take long to set up a team. I'll give you a call tomorrow and—"

"Excuse me," interrupted Yi. "You will do nothing. The team is Catlin and Miss Danner. Your job is to protect them at the moment of the sting. Nothing more."

"And the dragon's job?" Catlin asked in Mandarin, cutting off Stone's explosion.

Stone held his temper and waited, remembering that the last time Catlin had started talking Mandarin, Yi had given in. Yi met Catlin's eyes unflinchingly. Catlin had the gut feeling that whatever was said next would be the simple truth.

But when it came, it still surprised him.

"You are to protect Miss Danner," answered Yi.

"Who do I protect her from?" Catlin shot back in Mandarin. "Buyers? Sellers? Policemen? Thieves?"

"Everyone."

"Including you?"

Yi smiled sadly. "I above all, dragon. Ah! I above all."

4

CATLIN WALKED along the Capitol Mall, weaving in and out of tourists. The massive, elegant needle of Washington Monument rose out of the green ahead of him. Catlin didn't look at the sun-struck whiteness of the obelisk, nor at the mixture of races and nationalities seething slowly among America's monuments to itself. He had already discovered the only thing of importance—the number of the men who were tailing him.

There were four. They were quick, professional and operated like a close-order drill team. It had become an open tail, the kind designed to let the mark know that someone was keeping him on a very short leash. Open or closed, it didn't matter to Catlin. He had sensed the presence of a follower two blocks before the other three team members had fallen in to place. It wasn't that the first man had been careless, but rather that Catlin had lived too long in enemy territory ever to forget his vulnerable back.

Without seeming to, Catlin picked up the pace. His stride was long, powerful, difficult for a less fit man to equal. Because his life had depended on reflexes or strength too often in the past, Catlin had honed himself into an efficient fighting machine. Although he no longer lived in enemy territory, the habits he had learned there were too deeply ingrained to be discarded. Today he was as hard and potentially as dangerous as he had been long ago and half a world away.

The men behind him were fit enough for most purposes, but they hadn't been through the kind of wars Catlin had. Within a mile they were sweating heavily in Washington's smothering humidity. Within two miles they were dragging. By the time Catlin took pity on them and turned back to his apartment, a new team had been called in. Catlin watched the handoff, gave everyone involved high marks for professionalism, and vanished into his apartment for a shower. He had learned all he needed to know.

The FBI computer had finally caught up with Catlin, Jacob MacArthur. The shit had well and truly hit the fan.

Catlin assumed that Lindsay Danner had an honor guard, too. The thought made him smile as he lathered himself beneath the pulsing needles of water that all but filled the steamy shower enclosure. At least the men following Lindsay would have something good to look at. Her walk was clean, resilient, subtly provocative, the kind of movement that made a man want to pull her close around him while he found other ways for that sleek body to move.

Idly Catlin wondered if Lindsay would bring half the skill and intensity to bed that she had shown with the bronzes. She had touched that incense burner with an unconscious sensuality that had intrigued him at the time. But when O'Donnel had tested by crowding her gently, she had eased away. No fuss, no sidelong glances, no protests of dismay or disinterest. Just the discreet withdrawal of a woman who didn't rub up against men on a casual basis.

That, too, intrigued Catlin. Beneath her social polish and gentle smile, Lindsay Danner was a rather private person. That could be a real problem. For the charade he had in mind, he would have much preferred a woman who had the casual sexuality of a singles bar on Saturday night. Lindsay didn't come across like that, either on the surface or at the level of reflex, as O'Donnel had discovered. Which meant that Yi's shanghaied dragon was going to get a workout trying to stay close enough to Lindsay to keep her from getting killed.

Who do I protect her from?

I above all, Dragon. I above all.

With a muttered curse Catlin shut off the water and reached for an oversize towel. Beyond that cryptic statement, Yi had refused to say anything about himself in relation to Lindsay Danner. Nor would he say anything more about Lindsay herself, no matter how Catlin had pressed. He had been forced to seek information in other ways. Sooner or later, Lindsay's file would arrive at his apartment. He hoped that it was sooner rather than later. He didn't doubt that her file would arrive, though. He knew too many powerful people in Washington and Langley for such a simple request to be disregarded.

A buzzer rang just as Catlin was buttoning up the conservative white shirt that he trotted out of his wardrobe for Washington visits. With quick movements of his hands he tucked in his shirt, fastened his slacks and pulled a gun from the holster lying on top of the bed.

The sound of knuckles meeting wood substituted for the sound of the doorbell.

Catlin crossed the living room silently and stood to one side of the door. He didn't put his eye to the little spy hole installed by building security. That would have been like standing in the center of a target and begging someone to shoot.

"Who is it?" asked Catlin.

"Bradford Stone, FBI."

"Who else?"

"No one."

Catlin opened the door. "Come in, Stone. You're late."

Stone walked through. With a glance he took in the apartment and the barefoot man standing in front of him with a 9 mm pistol in his hand. "Late? Did we have an appointment?"

"Yeah," Catlin said dryly. "The second my file hit your desk." He gestured toward a chair with his free hand. "Sit down," he called over his shoulder as he went back to the bedroom. "I'll be right with you."

A few minutes later Catlin came back wearing moccasins, a belt and a 9 mm holstered in the small of his back. "Coffee or something stronger?"

"Coffee."

"An official visit, then."

Stone smiled unwillingly. "Have any beer?"

"Coming up."

Catlin pulled two beers out of the refrigerator, opened the long-necked bottles and returned to the living room. "To teamwork," he said ironically, saluting Stone with the beer.

Stone took a long drink and then asked, "Where were you between 1975 and 1982?"

"Around."

"Around where?"

"India. I spent a lot of time in various ashrams. Meditating."

"Bullshit," snapped Stone, slamming his beer bottle onto the coffee table. "You were in covert operations after Saigon fell."

"Really?" Catlin paused to enjoy the intimate bite of the beer as it curled across his tongue and caressed the back of his mouth. "That's going to surprise the hell out of the good guru Rajeenanda—not to mention the CIA and the IRS."

"Look, I was hoping we could work together on this," said Stone, turning away, reaching for his beer again.

"There's not a doubt in my mind that we will."

Stone's head snapped around. There was no mockery in Catlin's expression or voice.

"But we're faced with the problem of the lesbian lovers," continued Catlin. "Who does what and with which and to whom?"

There was a short bark of laughter, followed by a silence as Stone drank from the icy bottle of beer once more. "You know, Catlin," Stone said as he lowered the beer, "under other circumstances I think I could enjoy working with you."

"I doubt it. I don't take orders worth a damn. You're used to giving them."

"What about Yi?" Stone asked smoothly. "He gives you orders."

"Does he?"

"How did you hook up with him?"

"I didn't."

Stone made an angry gesture. "Is this what you call cooperation?"

"You read my file. You should have a rather exact appreciation of just how cooperative I am."

Catlin waited while Stone decided whether a show of anger would be useful. The FBI agent went up in Catlin's estimation when he decided to abandon physical intimidation and go straight for blackmail.

"You know," Stone said quietly, "if someone tipped a senator from Massachusetts or a *Washington Post* reporter that the CIA was conducting operations on home ground, you could be in a world of hurt."

"I could. If I were with the CIA."

"You are. And I'm going to dig until I prove it." Stone paused, drank and added, "Unless I get some cooperation from you."

Catlin smiled faintly. "You can dig until hell freezes solid. I don't belong to anyone anymore. Ask around. They'll tell you the same thing you're going to learn the hard way. I'm as free as any man ever born."

Stone had heard enough truth to recognize it in Catlin's voice. Stone had also heard enough lies never to give up short of absolute certainty. He would keep digging, but he would no longer expect to hit gold. He lit a cigarette, examined his remaining options and sighed.

"Do you trust Yi?" asked Stone.

"I don't have to. I know what he wants. That beats the hell out of trust."

"What does he want?"

"From you? I imagine he'll be happy if you stop crowding him."

Stone grunted. "What does he want from you?"

"A stalking horse that will let him get close to the bronzes without being spotted as a representative of the PRC," Catlin said in the matter-of-fact tone of someone stating an obvious fact.

It was a reasonable lie and might even be part of the truth. In any case, there was no point in telling Stone that Yi wanted a full-time bodyguard for Lindsay Danner, the woman he had manipulated the FBI into using. Then Stone would want to know why Lindsay was in danger. It was a question that had occurred to Catlin at least once a minute since he had seen Yi's sad smile.

I above all, dragon. I above all.

None of the possible answers that had occurred to Catlin had been comforting.

"Why did he choose you?" asked Stone.

"I've done some consulting for mainland Chinese businessmen. He could have heard of me through them."

That, at least, was true. It just didn't happen to be a truth that applied to the specific question Stone had asked.

For a moment Stone stared into Catlin's nearly yellow eyes and wondered if the man owed allegiance to anyone or anything. Even himself. People who lived in deep cover for much of their lives ... changed. That was why the FBI had resisted having undercover agents at all until a few years back, when circumstances had forced the Bureau into it. Stone wasn't comfortable with the type of man who could vanish without a ripple into another, usually crooked, culture. To survive with his true identity intact, such a man would have to be very strong.

Or very weak. A moral chameleon able to fade into anyone's background, no matter how degraded or vicious.

Stone shifted uneasily and looked away from Catlin's eyes, wondering which category he fell into. Then Stone shrugged and accepted what he could not change: he had been ordered to work in close, to get all the counterintelligence information he could from both Catlin and Chen Yi. The true state of Catlin's morality didn't have a damn thing to do with Stone's job.

"What if I told you that Chen is a spy?" asked Stone.

Catlin smiled. "Are you telling me that he is?"

"We have to assume it."

"So?"

Stone's color heightened. "You don't mind working for a spy?"

"Do you?" Catlin asked smoothly.

Red washed Stone's cheekbones. "I didn't volunteer," he snarled.

"Neither did I." Catlin set his empty beer bottle down on the table with a distinct snap. "Look, Stone. I'll save you the trouble of hinting around that if I don't play your game, the U.S. government will shut down the Pacific Rim Foundation. It won't happen."

Stone didn't argue. It was the first ploy he had tried with his boss. It had been shot down without a prayer. The Pacific Rim Foundation was one very sacred cow, in and out of the intelligence community.

"You're a smart man," continued Catlin, settling back into his chair, watching the older man with eyes that gave away nothing. "You've figured out by now that you're not going to intimidate, blackmail or insult me into going along with your program, whatever your program might be."

"Would flattery have worked?" Stone asked curiously.

Catlin laughed, enjoying the agent's determination. "We'll never know, will we?" Then all humor faded from Catlin's face. "But we do know this: Yi is an important man in China. America very badly wants China opened to trade. If the question of the Qin bronzes isn't cleared up, U.S.-Chinese relations are in the toilet. And so are you."

"Maybe. And maybe the bronzes never were missing." Stone leaned forward. His light blue eyes were intent and his voice was hard. "Maybe this is all just an elaborate lie so that the Chinese can get a guided tour of the internal security apparatus of the CIA overseas and the FBI's counterintelligence operation in America."

Catlin nodded. That kind of intelligence gambit was the first thing that had occurred to him when he had heard Chen Yi's stated reason for being in the U.S. There was no way to prove or disprove Chen's honesty. There was simply trust. And lack of it.

"Christ," Stone continued in a disgusted voice. "I'm being ordered—goddam *ordered*—to tell Chen anything that our informants in and out of the Asian communities turn up. The same goes for overseas operations, from what the guys at Langley said when we screwed pieces of your file out of them. They're as pissed as we are."

Catlin nodded again, understanding the dilemma of Stone and Stone's counterpart in the CIA. If the Chinese wanted to know how deeply American intelligence had penetrated Asian communities at home and abroad, it would be a simple matter to leak "confidential" information about Qin bronzes in China and see where and how quickly the information surfaced elsewhere. Like dye markers tracing otherwise invisible river currents, the leaked rumors of Qin bronzes would outline the American intelligence network as informants and agents brought the information to the CIA or to the FBI—and thence directly to Chen Yi himself.

"A Chinese sting," said Catlin flatly.

"Yes." Stone's light blue eyes pinned Catlin. "Does that change your mind about cooperating with us?"

"I am cooperating."

"Yeah?" challenged Stone. "How?"

"I agreed to work for Chen Yi."

"You mean you were ordered to work for Chen?" asked Stone.

"Another beer?" Catlin asked, coming to his feet in a single smooth movement.

"No." Stone stood up quickly, knowing that his last question, like nearly all the others he had asked, wasn't going to be answered. He looked up at the man across the table from him. "I hope I get a chance to bust your ass, Catlin," said Stone matter-of-factly.

"You've read my file. You've read Yi's." Catlin glanced at his watch. "Pick your devil, Stone. I've got a date."

Suddenly Catlin looked up from his watch. The bleakness in those amber eyes made Stone remember all the years missing from Catlin's file.

"I'll tell you this," Catlin added softly. "If someone helps me, I never forget it."

He didn't need to add that if someone hurt him, he never forgot that, either.

There was a moment of electric stillness. Slowly Stone nodded. He headed for the door, not waiting for Catlin to show him out.

"Tell your boys to be more discreet," Catlin called after him, "or I'll take them out at night and lose them. There's no point in scaring the Danner woman before she's agreed to help us. If she agrees."

"She will," Stone said grimly.

Catlin raised one black eyebrow. "Flattery, blackmail, intimidation or bribery?"

"Would you believe patriotism?" Stone asked, his tone sarcastic.

"Would you?" Catlin asked curiously.

Without a word Stone shut the apartment door behind him.

Catlin finished dressing, shrugged into the specially tailored suit coat that fell without a wrinkle over gun and holster, and left the apartment. He was followed by two men who were discreet and a third who was very nearly invisible. Curious about the third man, Catlin maneuvered until he was close enough to identify him. O'Donnel.

Only one of the men followed him into the Museum of the Asias. It wasn't O'Donnel. Catlin stood in the door of the secretary-receptionist's office. The sign on the desk said Sherry. Her face said available. She looked at him the way a cat looks at fresh cream. Catlin smiled and silently wished that Lindsay reacted to men in the same way. It would have made things so much cleaner, less complicated.

Safer.

"Jacob Catlin," he said. "I have an appointment with Lindsay Danner."

When Lindsay heard Sherry's light laughter and the click of her high heels as she crossed the margin between two hall rugs, Lindsay knew that her afterhours appointment was a man who fell into that broad category called "interesting." Other men, and all women, who checked in at Sherry's office on their way to finding Lindsay were given verbal directions rather than a smiling close-up of Sherry's personal charms.

"Lindsay, this is Mr. Jacob Catlin," said Sherry, stepping over the threshold.

Lindsay smiled professionally at the man who was being led into her office by Sherry's crimson-tipped fingers, which were buried in the sleeve of a custom-made silk suit coat that L. Stephen himself might have envied.

"A pleasure to meet you, Mr. Catlin," Lindsay said, rising and extending her hand. The name was familiar, but she couldn't quite place it. She decided that Catlin must be one of the many collectors she had heard of but never met.

"Just Catlin, Miss Danner," he said, smiling and holding out his hand in return. "My father was Jake, I refused to answer to Jacob or Junior, so that left Catlin."

Her smile changed, becoming more personal, less professional. "I wish I'd been that stubborn. I hated my name," she confessed. "I've learned to live with it, though. Please call me Lindsay."

The handshake surprised Lindsay. Catlin's hand was hard, with a distinct ridge of callus along the outer edge of the palm. He was powerful underneath the tailored silk. Even as she registered the unusual strength of him, she realized that he had eyes that were the exact golden brown of an amber and bronze pendant she had just purchased for the museum.

"You don't like the name Lindsay?" he asked. "Why? It's like you, restrained and elegant." His glance moved around the office. "No bronzes?" he asked, giving her no chance to either react to or retreat from his personal comment.

Lindsay blinked and caught herself just before she looked around the office, too. "Er, no. Mr. White wasn't very specific as to which period of Chinese bronzes interested you."

She retrieved her hand from her visitor's hard yet gentle grasp. He didn't try to hold the contact, but he let go of her hand in such a way that his fingertips caressed her from her palm all the way to her bronze-tinted nails. She gave him a swift, sideways glance, but he was absorbed in his study of the office, apparently unaware of the almost intimate way he had touched her. The paradox of the man intrigued her, particularly the civilized exterior on what she suspected was a very uncivilized interior. The best of the bronzes she dealt with were like that—three dimensional embodiments of human paradox.

"I collect Warring States and Qin dynasty bronzes, or Huai style, if you prefer that description," he said, acknowledging with a smile the fact that every expert seemed to divide Chinese bronzes differently. "Third century B.C. bronzes, particularly those of Qin's time, are my passion, but—" he shrugged "—of course they're very rare. I've collected some early Han, as well, but it has to be spectacular to interest me."

Instantly Lindsay thought of the hill-censer. O'Donnel had called an hour before to tell her that the bowl and incense burner were both for sale. Mr. White had approved the purchase of the bowl, but had refused to even consider the hill-censer. Nor would he give any reason, although he had assured her that he had no personal doubt as to the piece's authenticity.

"Mr. White didn't mention what price range you were looking in."

Catlin turned toward Lindsay. "There's no limit on a piece that I like."

She listened to the faint roughness underlying the deep male voice. Like his callused palm, his strength and his nearly gold eyes, Catlin's voice was unusual. Combined with the thick, sleek pelt of black hair, and the mustache that contrasted with the white curve of his occasional smile, Mr. Jacob Catlin was a definite change from the slim-hipped, vaguely male curators and white-haired collectors who were the museum's usual clients. No wonder Sherry had walked him down the hall, doubtless watching hungrily the whole way.

"Have you known Mr. White long?" asked Lindsay.

"Senior, junior or very junior?" Before she could answer, Catlin continued, "I haven't been collecting for a while. I was told that you would be an excellent adviser on any acquisition

I make. I'll pay the usual fee, of course, plus a bonus for any Qin bronzes you find for me.''

Lindsay's previous question was forgotten in her sudden curiosity about the man who had stopped collecting and wanted to begin again. Like everything else about Catlin, that was unusual. Collectors were noted for their obsessiveness. A collector didn't simply abandon collecting unless his heart stopped or he ran out of money.

"You realize," Lindsay said carefully, "that the museum gets first refusal on everything I find, whether in or out of business hours."

Catlin nodded, wondering if it were true. There was a built-in conflict of interest between Lindsay's work as a private consultant to collectors and her job at the museum. It would take an unusual degree of scrupulousness to avoid the temptation of pleasing one of her private—and fee-paying—clients at the cost of her employer's interest. On the other hand, the combination of museum work and self-employment as an expert was common. It often benefited the museums, which as a result had a direct pipeline to serious collectors and thus knew instantly when a private collection was up for sale. The cream could be skimmed long before the collection as a whole went to auction. There were other, more subtle benefits, too, involving tax write-offs and untaxable trades for existing, surplus museum stock.

Catlin was sure that Lindsay would be glad to point out all the benefits to him.

"You're in luck," said Lindsay, smiling at Catlin. "Follow me to the workroom. My boss has just turned down an absolutely exquisite bronze hill-censer."

"Why?" Catlin asked as he fell into step alongside her.

"You'll have to ask him," said Lindsay, unable to conceal her irritation. "I still don't believe it."

Catlin smiled slightly. He believed it. He had been there when Yi gave the order.

Lindsay watched Catlin's small, hard smile and decided that wherever White senior or junior or "very junior" had met

Catlin, it hadn't been on the lawn bowling circuit. Yet despite his dissimilarity to most of the men she was accustomed to meeting in Washington, Catlin was oddly familiar to Lindsay. She hadn't really realized it until she saw his cool, private smile. He reminded her of the men who years ago had slipped into her uncle's house while she lay awake, men who spoke in low voices of things she was too young to understand, men who moved like beautiful, hungry tigers through the darkness. Like Catlin, beside her. Lean and powerful beneath a deceptively silky hide.

She wondered if, like the long-ago men, Catlin would bring terror and death in his wake.

Even as her skin tightened and moved, sending a tiny ripple over her arms, Lindsay put aside the unwelcome thought. There were parts of her childhood she had forgotten how to remember. There were other parts that she remembered only in dreams and woke up screaming and wondering why.

Lindsay took a slow, careful breath and tried to control her unruly thoughts. Shaanxi had been a long time ago. Surely it should stop haunting her. Surely she could look at a strong, self-confident man without waiting to hear gunfire and screams.

Surely that wasn't blood running between her fingers.

"Lindsay?"

The quiet, deep voice lured her out of the past's paralyzing fears. She realized that she was standing in front of the stairway, her hand gripping the railing as though she were afraid of falling.

"Is something wrong?" asked Catlin.

He steadied Lindsay with his left hand even as he reflexively unbuttoned his suit coat with the right, making it possible to reach his gun quickly. He didn't know what was wrong, but he had seen raw fear too many times to mistake it in her eyes now.

"I—" Lindsay cleared her throat, loosening muscles constricted by a need to scream. "I'm sorry. I was thinking of something else." She let out her breath and forced herself to ignore the irrational fear sweeping over her, as though nightmares pursued her even when she was awake. "Watch your footing," she said briskly, starting down the stairs. "This house is almost a century old. When we took it over, nothing but rats had lived in it for years. We've done a lot of repair work since then, of course, but we've tried to keep the Victorian features intact. That means steep, narrow steps to the basement."

Catlin followed very closely, ready to reach for Lindsay if she stumbled. She didn't. She recovered her composure with a quickness that made him wonder if he had imagined the instant when fear had tightened her features into a mask. Then he saw the fine trembling of her hand as it slid down the oak rail. Adrenaline still coursed through her, primal response to terror. He wondered what had triggered it. The shadows pooled at the bottom of the stair? The musty scent rising out of the basement? A word? A sound?

Lindsay's fingers fumbled, then found the wall switch. Very bright, un-Victorian work lights glared down. Throughout the basement, long tables were covered with artifacts in various stages of being unpacked, cataloged and, if necessary, repaired or restored. The unusual Shang bowl shared one end of a table with the Han incense burner. A discarded packing carton and scattered Styrofoam chips gave silent testimony to Lindsay's eagerness as she had unpacked the bronzes.

"Both of these bronzes are very unusual," said Lindsay, touching the bowl possessively as she turned to face Catlin. "They—"

Her voice died. Catlin's face was hard, intent, and in the relentless light his eyes glittered like yellow crystal. The back of his right hand was resting lightly just behind his hip. He was examining every part of the basement as though he expected something to explode out of the black shadows beneath the tables. His stance radiated danger as surely as the metal-topped table reflected light.

"Yes?" he asked encouragingly, turning to face her fully. "They . . . ?"

Lindsay took a grip on her overactive imagination. There was nothing dangerous about Catlin except his effect on her mind.

Or perhaps it was simply the humid air and heat that were playing tricks with her memories, calling up Hong Kong and with it a host of older, more frightening memories. Or near-memories. She would never know, now. The last person who could have told her was dead. She would never know why in her nightmare last night she had run with her hands covered by blood.

"These—" Lindsay's hands clenched as she reassured herself that they were clean, dry, not bloody at all. "These two bronzes are nearly unique among their own kind," she said, her voice husky. "The bowl is a Shang precursor to the more familiar Chou *p'an*."

Even as Lindsay spoke, she realized that Catlin was like the bowl, an enigma, showing the stamp of no single time or culture.

And like the bowl, he was genuine.

The realization calmed her at the same irrational level where fear had bloomed. She let out a slow, silent breath. Whatever danger there was in this man, he wasn't dangerous to her. Only lies and deceit were.

Catlin walked over to the table. The silence of his stride struck Lindsay. Not once since she had met him had she heard the sound of his shoes against the floor. Yet he was hardly a dainty man. She was five feet six inches in her high heels, and he still had at least six inches on her.

"May I?" asked Catlin, his hands poised over the bowl.

"Of course," answered Lindsay, curious to see how he would handle the bronze. She had discovered that it was possible to tell a lot about a man from the way he handled objects.

Catlin's hands were both careful and confident as he picked up the bowl. He turned and tilted it slowly, letting the basement's unforgiving illumination pick out every potential flaw. His eye followed the discrete line of each design. There was no overlap of decoration from foot to bowl or from interior to exterior. The symbols were appropriate to the time and to their placement on the *p'an* itself.

There was no inscription.

"Amazing," said Catlin, meaning it.

"Genuine, too," Lindsay said dryly.

He nodded, his eyes intent upon the bronze resting coolly, heavily, in his hands.

"There's no doubt of that," Catlin said, his mind utterly involved with the smooth, green-gray bronze. "Only on forgeries do the designs overlap the functions. Shang artists saw life as an assembly of individual pieces. One animal symbol for the foot. One for the outer bowl, and so on. The symbols themselves are quite openly savage," he continued, looking into the bowl as though it were a crystal ball. "The Shang world was one of terrifying demons and human sacrifices to appease the unknown. Shang art reflects that, as does the art of the Maya and the Inca. Quite similar, as a matter of fact."

Then Catlin heard the echo of his own musings and remembered that he was talking to an expert in the field. With a soft laugh he shook his head ruefully. "Sorry. It's been a long time since I held a Shang bronze in my hands. It went to my head."

Lindsay smiled at Catlin with genuine pleasure. It was rare for her to meet someone who shared her complex appreciation of ancient bronzes. And she had no doubt that Catlin did. It was there in his voice when he spoke and in his hands as he held the bowl. He loved ancient bronzes, not because they were rare or valuable or fashionable, but because they whispered to him across an immense bridge of time, telling of people who had lived and laughed, wept and died. And if the people had been lucky, very lucky, they had a genius among them who could preserve their fears and dreams in art, passing on to the future the very soul of the past.

"Don't apologize," she said, her voice husky. "It's a pleasure to meet someone who appreciates art for more than its investment value."

For a moment Catlin didn't know whether Lindsay's perceptivity or her honesty was more startling. Then he decided it didn't matter. Both were as unusual and evocative as the bronze in his hands. He looked into Lindsay's indigo eyes and heard Yi's words again: *To be near her was to know the serenity of the lotus blooming beneath the summer moon.*

Grimly Catlin wondered if he were going to redeem the mistakes of his past only at the cost of Lindsay Danner's future.

5

LINDSAY STOOD in front of the mirror, brushing her smooth cap of hair into place, wondering if Catlin had meant what he had said about her when they first met. *Elegant and restrained.* His casual compliment had wedged in her thoughts where the more pointed compliments of other men had not. Perhaps it was just that he had responded to the bronzes as she herself did, but she had the feeling that Catlin had been honest in his words. Nor had he tried to follow up the compliment immediately with a pass, subtle or otherwise.

That, too, was unusual. Washington, D.C., was a city where political power was king and sex was queen. If Hollywood was a magnet for girls of flamboyant looks and lackluster minds, Washington was a magnet for girls of high polish, both mind and body. The competition for dates with politicians and power brokers was unrelenting. Nearly all the bright, eager secretaries and shopgirls who poured into the city from the South and Midwest soon learned to settle for lovers instead of fiancés and serial relationships instead of lifetime commitments.

If the girls were lucky, they eventually found a rising young lawyer and settled into motherhood in suburban Virginia or in Georgetown. If they were unlucky, they grew too old for the mating-go-round and were forced to retreat to their less sexually competitive hometowns. Once home, they also settled into motherhood, raising another generation of the nubile and the ambitious who would in their own turn be drawn by power's cruel magnet to Washington, D.C.

Lindsay had never really fitted into the D.C. cycle. She had come late, at twenty-nine. By then she had already discovered the limitations of marriage and the self-recriminations of divorce. She also had discovered that those same limitations and self-recriminations applied to an extended affair as well as to marriage. At thirty, she had finally accepted the fact that the concept of fidelity simply was foreign to men, and to many women as well. Her aunt had been the first to point that out to her, but Lindsay had had a hard time believing. The example of her parents' marriage had remained, silently proclaiming that anything was possible, even enduring love.

Possible, yes. Probable? Well, not really.

Ultimately, Lindsay had decided that lasting love wasn't necessary for emotional survival. There were other beautiful, enduring things to be enjoyed, things that didn't require the passionate commitment of two people in order to work. For some people that life focus was politics, especially in Washington. For others it was gambling or sex, religion or law, dog breeding or duplicate bridge. For Lindsay, it was art.

She glanced at her watch, wondering if she would have time to dip into one of the auction catalogs piled on the table. Although she rarely found any ancient bronzes of museum quality in the big public auction houses, the catalogs provided good indicators of the changing fashions in public taste that inevitably had an impact on museum acquisition and display. No matter how excellent a museum's collection of Aztec war axes, if Polynesian feather capes were in vogue, then the museum had better have something bright and colorful and plucked from birds to attract the public.

Trends often went the other way, too, from museum to general public. After the King Tut exhibit, every curio importer on two continents had dusted off scarabs and sold them all, no matter how ugly or obviously fraudulent. The museums that lacked the prestige to attract the traveling Tut exhibit had been forced to rummage in their basements amid turn-of-the-century boxes and dig out overlooked and often mundane Egyptian artifacts. These had been cobbled together into displays whose only redeeming grace had been that they had brought money into often starved museum accounts.

At the moment, all things Chinese were in vogue, a reflection of the increasing trade ties between the two nations. In less

han a decade Lindsay had seen the value of even the most ordinary Chinese objets d'art double, triple, quadruple and then
simply soar. A decent bronze that would have brought several
thousand dollars at auction ten years ago would now sell for ten
times that much. There simply were not enough artifacts to
supply the needs of American decorators, much less enough art
or the discriminating collector.

Which was why the catalog held so little lure for Lindsay at
the moment. She knew she would see item after item that was
artifact, not art. Even worse, some of the items would be arti-
fice—three-dimensional lies created to fill the gap between demand and supply. She frowned at the slick catalog, but in the
end she picked it up. Perhaps a truly rare, truly superb objet
d'art had eluded collectors and museums alike and had found
its way into this catalog. Like love, such a thing was possible,
if not particularly probable.

In any case, looking at the catalog would prevent her mind
from spiraling uneasily down and down into the past, where
unanswered questions waited, questions whose very existence
she had ignored for years. That wasn't possible any longer.
Somehow the death of her mother had released the chains
holding down the past. Now the nightmare came to Lindsay
nearly every night, and she awoke shaking, remembering the
sound of screams and the color of blood.

But now it was too late to ask her mother why the dream
came, why it would not go away, why Lindsay had the cold
feeling that she had forgotten something crucial. Something
cruel.

"Stop it," she told herself sharply, suppressing a shudder.
'Most of what's bothering you is just a lack of sleep. Fright-
ned people sleep badly, which is something you learned a long
time ago."

With a grimace, Lindsay opened the catalog. Chimes
sounded a moment later. She tucked the catalog under her arm
and went to the front door of her apartment.

"Who is it?"

"Catlin."

The voice identified Catlin to Lindsay even more than the name. Reflexively she peeked through the spy hole. As though expecting it, he was thoughtfully standing far enough back from the door to be fully encompassed by the tiny lens.

With the catalog held precariously under one arm, Lindsay began opening the various locks that were de rigeur for modern city living. Even if she had been living in a cornfield, she would have locked her house in exactly the same way. The uncertainty and fear of her childhood had taught her that locks could be a definite aid to peaceful sleep. Lately, though, locks hadn't been enough. She was thinking of getting a dog or a cat, something that would be warm and real in the small hours of the morning when nightmares pursued her.

As Lindsay opened the door, the catalog slithered out from under her arm. Catlin's hand shot out with startling speed, grabbing the catalog before it fell farther than her hip.

"Window-shopping?" he asked, glancing at the cover.

For an instant Lindsay was too unnerved by both Catlin's speed and the hard warmth of the back of his hand moving over her hip to answer. She said the first thing that came to her mind. "Actually, it's more like hunting snipe. Come in."

Catlin caught her eyes and smiled suddenly. "Snipe?" he asked, glancing again at the catalog as he walked into the living room.

"Right," she said, closing the door and automatically throwing the dead bolt. "Lots of false trails, giggles from the tall grass—and no snipe."

Catlin's laughter was as warm and unexpected as the touch of his hand had been. After a moment Lindsay laughed with him.

"What kind of snipe did you have in mind?" he asked.

"How about a perfectly preserved bronze charioteer inlaid in gold and silver, half life-size, taken from Emperor Qin's very own tomb?" Lindsay asked whimsically, putting her own private fantasy into words.

Though Catlin still smiled, a subtle change came over him. "That," he said distinctly, "would be one hell of a snipe."

She looked at him suddenly, reminded of the moment in the basement when he had looked like a man anticipating danger. The rational part of her mind said that she should be afraid of this man. The irrational part of her—the part that she depended on for her visceral judgments of bronzes—told her that she was safer with Catlin than she had ever been in her life with anyone. As soon as that realization came to her, she relaxed, accepted Catlin without further questioning, just as she accepted her gift for discerning genuine from fraud among ancient Chinese bronzes.

"Yes, a charioteer would be a hell of a snipe," she agreed. Her smile turned down slightly at one corner. "But don't hold your breath, Catlin. The Chinese discovered the Emperor Qin's bronzes in 1980—and then they covered them right back up!" She shook her head slowly. "Ever since I heard the first rumor, I've dreamed of seeing just one of Qin's bronze charioteers. Just one."

Catlin heard the longing in Lindsay's voice, saw it in the indigo depths of her eyes and in the soft curve of her mouth. "Have you?" he asked quietly.

"No. I've been to Xi'an three times. Each time I've wangled the VIP tour of Mount Li and the digs."

"And?"

"Terra cotta," she said. Then she heard her own words and laughed very softly. "Don't misunderstand me. To stand among Emperor Qin's resurrected army, to see rank upon file of soldiers erect in the trenches, faces as individual as yours or mine, men rising from the earth and marching down through time . . ." Her voice died, then resumed quietly. "To see that is to see a great people's soul given form and substance and texture. It's beautiful. It's terrifying." She hesitated, trying to explain the eerie magnificence that was Xi'an. "It is art," she said simply.

"And this?" asked Catlin, raising the fat catalog.

"Commerce," she said. "And maybe, just possibly, some true art."

"The auction house would be offended."

"I doubt it. They're better than most at finding quality artifacts and weeding out frauds, and they know it."

"But no Qin dynasty bronzes?" asked Catlin casually, riffling through the pages with a blunt thumb.

"No."

"How about rumors of Emperor Qin's bronzes?"

Lindsay shrugged. "Occasionally."

"Lately?"

She looked up from the pages flying by beneath Catlin's thumb and found him watching her. She felt as though she had stepped into a searchlight. His eyes were clear, intent and missed nothing.

"No more than usual—why?" she asked.

"What's usual?" countered Catlin.

"Ever since the first of the emperor's mortuary bronzes were found, every Tom, Dick and Hop Sing has one for sale," Lindsay said dryly.

"Bought any?" asked Catlin, idly fanning through the catalog again.

"No, but I've appraised a few for clients who had bought them elsewhere."

"And?"

"The worst of the bronzes had hardly cooled from the casting process."

"What about the rest?"

"One Sung forgery. Several genuine Han bronzes. One bronze from the Warring States period."

Catlin closed the catalog with a snap. The small sound startled Lindsay, who had been watching Catlin as intently as he had been watching her.

"Fascinating. I collect rumors as well as bronzes," said Catlin. "They, too, tell about the soul of man." He smiled. "Why don't we swap rumors over squid with ginger, Sichuan rabbit and shrimp with garlic?"

"Throw in pot stickers and you've got a deal," Lindsay said, suddenly realizing just how hungry she was.

"You're on."

Mentally Lindsay crossed her fingers, knowing that for every excellent Washington restaurant, there were three that were at best adequate. When the taxi deposited Catlin and Lindsay in front of the steps leading down into the Sichuan Garden, she mentally crossed another set of fingers. She had heard of the restaurant, but had never eaten there.

"Relax," said Catlin, smiling. "This place is owned, run and staffed by the People's Republic of China. You won't find a menu like this anywhere outside China and probably not inside, either. The Sichuan Garden is the PRC's showplace of Chinese cuisine."

The first thing Lindsay noticed as the door closed behind her was that in the restaurant's low light, Catlin's eyes became the clear, luminous brown of fine cognac. Then she noticed the enormous vases and intricately painted temple dragons that were on display. A Tang horse pranced in place, as vibrant today as it had been a thousand years ago.

"Some of the artifacts are genuine antiques," said Catlin, as he seated her. "Others are antique or modern copies. All of them are beautifully crafted."

"It's rare to find such valuable things on open display," Lindsay said. "I know a museum that would kill for the vase by the entrance."

"Displaying the art without barriers or guards is a subtle and very powerful display of face," said Catlin, picking up his chopsticks.

Lindsay glanced at him with increasing interest, realizing that he was right—and that he must know a great deal about the nuances of Chinese culture. When the meal was served, she realized that he must be as familiar with the everyday aspect of Chinese life as he was with the cultural. He used chopsticks as easily as she did.

"Were you born in China?" asked Lindsay, looking up from her plate, a tidbit of rabbit poised in her chopsticks.

"No. Why?"

"You use chopsticks like a native."

Catlin looked down at the chopsticks as though just realizing that he wasn't using a knife and a fork. He looked back at her. "So do you."

"I was born in Shaanxi province."

"Really?" Catlin asked, his voice encouraging. He wanted her to talk about herself rather than ask questions about his own past. Her file had shown up at his apartment, along with Yi's file, but there had only been time enough to skim the pages before he had to pick Lindsay up for dinner. Besides, he would find out a great deal about her inherent truthfulness if he could compare what she said with the information in her file. "I thought Americans were thrown out of China by then." He smiled suddenly, looking at her with open male appreciation. She was wearing a tourmaline green sheath that owed far more to Paris than to the Orient. "And don't try telling me you were born before 1949. I wouldn't believe it."

"You're right. I wasn't," said Lindsay. She paused to savor a bite of her very spicy shrimp dish before she continued. "Dad was Canadian. Mom was American, but they kept that a secret as long as they could. When I was eighteen I had to declare citizenship in one country or the other. I was living in San Francisco by that time, so I chose to become American."

"Was your father in the import-export business?"

"My parents were missionaries."

Catlin's black eyebrow arched. "Tough job under any circumstances," he said. "In the early stages of the People's Republic it must have been hell."

Lindsay's chopsticks hesitated for an instant over the shrimp as memories sleeted through her, screams and shots, blood turning black in the moonlight. And something worse. Something she remembered only in nightmares, forgetting again the instant she awoke. "Yes," she said huskily, "sometimes it was just that. Hell."

"You must have been glad to leave," Catlin said, seeing again the shadow of fear tighten Lindsay's face, hearing fear in the thinning of her voice.

Again, Lindsay hesitated. "It was home, and childhood, and now all I have left are memories. Some of them are very good. Oil lamps and candle flames, so graceful, so warm. The scent of ginger and garlic sizzling in hot oil on a frosty night. The women in the kitchen laughing and talking and chopping vegetables with miraculous skill. The pungent smell of cigarettes and the click-click of stones as the men played mah-jongg."

Lindsay looked beyond Catlin, seeing not the gleaming restaurant but the seething past. "We all lived together, our houses leaning against one another. The church was little more than a handmade altar hung with scarlet, the Chinese color of joy and good wishes. We sang hymns in half scales." She smiled. "I didn't realize what 'Onward Christian Soldiers' really sounded like until I got to San Francisco. Do you know," she said, focusing on Catlin instead of the past, "that hymns sung by Americans using the European scale sounded alien to me?"

Catlin nodded, understanding exactly what Lindsay meant. When he finally had returned to America, it had been years since he had used English to do anything but break coded communiqués. His native language had sounded foreign to him.

Suddenly Lindsay realized that she had been monopolizing the conversation. That was unlike her. She had learned that few people could relate to the experiences she had had as a child, much less understand them. Usually it was she who listened, other people who talked, and her memories slept. Catlin was different. He was a good listener. His quiet questions, his genuine interest in her answers, and the feeling of safety she had with him peeled the years away, leaving only memories silently welling up like blood from an open wound.

"How did you learn to use chopsticks?" asked Lindsay.

"Hunger is the best teacher," Catlin said wryly. "Sticky rice helps. In no time you're eating like a native." He glanced around the restaurant. "Well, almost. True natives hold the bowl under their chin and shovel as fast as they talk. If we did that, the Anglos around here would think we were barbarians."

"They certainly would," agreed Lindsay, laughing. "A polite Western child says grace and bends at the waist to bring the mouth closer to the food. A polite Oriental child says grace, brings bowl to mouth and lets the devil take the hindmost."

Catlin's smile flashed. "Did your parents have a large congregation?"

"Hardly. Christianity wasn't very popular at the time. You know how it is—when things go wrong in China, foreign devils are blamed." She glanced at her plate heaped with food and the full rice bowl beside it, remembering all the times she had gone hungry. "Lots went wrong in China after the turn of the century. The half-century mark was no treat, either."

"I'm surprised your parents stayed, particularly with children."

"Child," she corrected. "I was the only one. That caused great despair to the congregation," she added, smiling. "Large families in general and sons in particular are a source of great face in China. To follow a man who had only one child— and that one a girl—required courage of a sort that most Americans just don't understand."

"Similar to the kind of courage it took to accept the teachings of a man who had only one name and no children at all: Jesus."

Lindsay's eyes widened in surprise. She had met no one outside China who understood the Chinese people's immense need to place themselves in history through their ancestors and their own offspring. A man with no family name and no children had no face. To emulate such a man was not only ridiculous, it was offensive to one's own ancestors.

"The fact that Christ was a bachelor living away from home didn't help the Christian cause in China," Lindsay agreed wryly. "The Chinese men who were responsive to religion often chose Islam. They could more easily admire a man who had a wife, concubines and many sons."

"How long were you in China?" Catlin asked as he deftly lifted a shrimp to his mouth. The texture and flavor were both superb. With a silent, ironic laugh, he realized that the Chinese food he was eating tonight in Washington was far better than most of the food he had eaten during all his years in Asia.

"My parents were forced to close their mission when I was seven," said Lindsay. Her voice changed, thin again, remembering fear.

"Out with the foreign devils?" guessed Catlin.

She nodded, but said nothing, not wanting to pursue the subject. Since her mother's death, the recurring nightmare of China was too close, too frightening. Lindsay wanted to remember as little as possible about that time of violence and fear. She was alive, safe, a woman in America rather than a child in Shaanxi province, China.

"We went to Hong Kong," Lindsay said quickly. "Dad divided his time between there and Taipei while mother ran a small mission among the poor. Later I was sent to live with my father's sister in San Francisco."

"How old were you?"

"Twelve."

"It must have been difficult to leave your parents and the only world you had ever known."

"Yes," said Lindsay. She searched her rice bowl as though she expected to find a diamond hidden among the glistening white grains. "It wasn't the first time, though. Hong Kong was also a foreign land to me. The climate was different. The people looked different. Cantonese rather than Mandarin was the common dialect."

"Did you learn to speak Cantonese?"

Lindsay shrugged. "A little. Dad's congregation was mostly displaced northerners, both in Hong Kong and Taipei, so I had little use for Cantonese. The school I went to was English."

Catlin hesitated, wondering how to ask the next question without revealing what he already knew. "I guess your parents wanted you to get a better education than was available in Hong Kong," he murmured, "so they sent you to America."

"My father died. My mother stayed with the congregation in Hong Kong. I went to San Francisco."

The words didn't tell Catlin as much as the tension of Lindsay's fingers holding the chopsticks; she would talk no more on the subject of Hong Kong and her father's death and her relocation in America. Despite the fact that she hadn't told Catlin as much as he had seen in her file, he didn't think that Lindsay was being dishonest. He, too, had a deep reluctance to talk about aspects of the past that had nothing to do with government secrets. Some parts of the past were simply too painful to remember.

"How did you end up in China?" asked Lindsay abruptly, her tone determined. She was through talking about herself and the past. She had done far too much of it tonight. Dreaming about the past was bad enough. Talking about it was impossible.

"Airplane," Catlin said laconically, not bothering to correct her assumption that China rather than another part of Asia had been his destination. "You were right about the Chenin Blanc," he continued, pouring more of the wine into her glass. "It's quite good with the rabbit. I'll have to remember that. It's hell finding Western wines to go with Oriental foods. The dry whites can't compete with Sichuan seasonings, the reds overwhelm the subtle flavors of the nonspicy dishes, and the Reislings are sometimes just too sweet for anything but fortune cookies."

Lindsay laughed.

"Have you tried one of the Merlots coming out of California?" he asked, smiling in return. "Lighter than Cabernet, more interesting than Beaujolais." He signaled a waiter. "Let's experiment."

Lindsay was so grateful to have the conversation shifted away from her past that she didn't notice Catlin had avoided answering any personal questions about his own past. Eagerly she entered into a discussion of the possibilities of various wines when drunk with various international cuisines. By the time the discussion shifted to Chinese bronzes, Lindsay was relaxed again, enjoying the company of the man with amber eyes and a very quick mind.

"White told me that you had never made a mistake when it came to sniffing out fraudulent bronzes," Catlin said, not specifying which of the three White males had praised Lindsay.

"He exaggerates," she said, smiling. "I've made mistakes. Without the help of a highly sophisticated laboratory, it's very hard to spot a modern copy of an ancient bronze. Bronze art isn't like painting. If the craftsman is exquisitely precise—literally an artist at his work—a bronze copy can have almost the same vitality as the original."

"But it won't be exactly the same?"

Lindsay hesitated. "I've never seen a copy that had the same sheer *presence* as an original. Or if I did," she added honestly, "I didn't recognize it as a copy. Fortunately, most forgers have neither the patience, the tools, the knowledge nor the talent to do a really top-notch job of copying. Also, when outright fraud is the object, the tendency is to copy the larger, more expensive pieces. Those are also the most famous bronzes. Any knowledgeable collector being offered a bargain bronze will check it very carefully against existing catalogs, or pay someone like me to vet the purchase for him."

"And the unknowledgeable collectors?" asked Catlin.

"Have no business buying any kind of art." Lindsay hesitated and frowned slightly. "That's harsh, but it's true. The idea that great art can be found at bargain prices is just plain naive, and any art dealer who tells you otherwise doesn't have your best interests at heart. If the piece he's pushing were such a fantastic bargain, the dealer would buy it himself and resell at a profit. After all, that's the way legitimate dealers make a living. And the dealer who protests that he'd buy the piece himself, but his inventory is full or you're such a swell friend that he wants to let you in on a good thing . . . well, when you hear those words, grab your wallet and run like hell. The dealer has seen you coming, and you have sucker written all over you."

In the silence Lindsay heard her own words echo. She smiled in self-mockery. "You pushed the wrong button, I'm afraid. I have very little patience with art scams or the people who make them possible. And that includes greedy buyers as well as greedy sellers.''

"You can't con an honest man?" suggested Catlin, smiling.

"Exactly."

Catlin nodded, but he wasn't wholly satisfied with Lindsay's explanation of her strong feelings on the subject. He doubted that the question of fraud and deception was that simple for Lindsay. Something other than the expert's contempt for the inexpert was driving her. She wasn't that kind of intellectual snob. If she were, she would have condescended to O'Donnel even while she answered his ingenuous questions about the seventeen bronzes. But she hadn't condescended. She had answered carefully, trying to share her love of the bronzes as well as her knowledge of them. It had been the same when Catlin had thought aloud about the Shang bowl, telling Lindsay things about art and culture that she already knew. She hadn't been haughty or protective of her superior knowledge; she had smiled and told him what a pleasure it was to meet someone who shared her passion for old Chinese bronzes.

"You really loathe frauds, don't you?" asked Catlin, lacing his fingers through Lindsay's in a single smooth motion, bringing their palms together, holding them that way.

The texture of Catlin's touch caused sensations that spread through Lindsay as surely as the wine she had just sipped. His hand was large, smooth between the long fingers and hard along the edge of the palm. Warm. She looked up, wondering if he could feel her surprised response in the pulse beating just beneath the skin of her inner wrist.

"Yes," she said simply.

"Why?"

There was silence for a long moment while Lindsay absorbed the question, and the fact that the question had even been asked. Her response to fraud was something that she had always taken for granted about herself. She hated lies of all kinds.

"Doesn't everyone?" she asked.

Catlin's answer was a smile that made Lindsay wonder what he had been doing for the lifetime before he had come to her and asked about Qin bronzes.

"Not everyone, Lindsay. Not even most people. It's truth they fight, not lies."

A lighter flared at the next table. The unmistakable odor of a Chinese cigarette drifted over to Lindsay. The candle in the red bowl near her hand flickered suddenly, making scarlet light ripple like flames over the cloth, turning it into the landscape of her nightmare, smoke and fire. Her hand tightened within Catlin's until her skin was pale where it pressed next to his. Remembered screams writhed silently in her mind, memories of futile pleas, the overpowering smell of incense and blood that would not stop spurting, blood all over her hands and a voice rasping *Betrayed!*

Or was that nightmare, not memory? Did someone cry betrayal in her dreams?

Lindsay's bleak eyes met Catlin's over the wavering candlelight. "It's been a long time since I smelled incense," she said in a flat voice. "I've never really liked it. I need fresh air."

Catlin didn't point out that it was a Chinese cigarette rather than incense burning in the restaurant. He had seen fear in Lindsay's eyes, heard it in the tightness of her voice, felt it in her hand laced through his. He signaled to the waiter, paid the bill and took Lindsay outside. Washington's summer night flowed over them in a dark, moist embrace. Low clouds diffused the city's lights, making the sky appear to slowly seethe.

As Lindsay and Catlin walked, he took her hand again, anchoring her to his warmth and strength. She accepted the gesture as it was meant, comfort rather than seduction. She didn't say anything until they had walked down Nineteenth Street to Pennsylvania Avenue and turned left past the Executive Office Building to the tree-studded open space called the Elipse. The smell of grass and the tang of salt air from the Tidal Basin blended with the urban odors of asphalt, concrete and car exhaust. Lindsay breathed deeply, feeling like a fool for letting childhood memories and a lingering nightmare upset her so much. She faced Catlin but made no effort to remove her hand from his.

"I'm sorry," she said quietly. "My uncle was murdered when I was seven. I believe I was with him. At least I have memories of blood. Sometimes. At night, late—" Her voice broke. She made a curt gesture with her free hand. "Memories or nightmare, it—"

Catlin pulled Lindsay into his arms, muffling her fragmented words against his chest. He held her while she trembled, her skin cool to his touch. He didn't have to hear the rest of her story in order to understand. He still remembered the first time he had seen violent death, the shocking profusion of blood, the slaughterhouse smell, the terrible stillness of cooling flesh. He had been twenty, and he had vomited until he was too weak to stand.

How much worse it must have been for a child of seven. The fact that Lindsay didn't remember it only underlined the intensity of the horror. She had simply blotted it from her mind. Or tried to. Memories could turn into dreams, and dreams into nightmares.

Slowly Catlin rocked Lindsay against his body, smoothing her hair with one hand, murmuring words that had no meaning beyond reassuring her that someone was there with her. As he brushed his lips over her hair he wondered how many times she had gotten the night shakes and fought them alone. Like him. Now the shakes came to him only rarely, in dreams, when he was young again and a woman whispered love against his mouth while she raised a gun to his face. Mei, who had loved treachery and lies more than she had loved any man—and she had loved him better than her other men. Mei, who had killed and never dreamed. The perfect conspirator, the ideal assassin.

You've picked the wrong player, Yi, Catlin raged silently. *Lindsay's not the kind of woman who can survive your power games. The best way I can earn back the other half of that coin is to grab her and run like hell for cover.*

But there was no cover.

Catlin didn't need to turn his head to see another couple standing close together beneath a tree. It wasn't love or even lust on the couple's mind. Catlin had noticed their presence when they left the restaurant with their meal half-eaten. The pair had stayed behind Catlin and Lindsay every step of the way since. So had two other men, seen only as shadows crossing parallel intersections, their steps hobbled to match Lindsay's high-heeled stride.

Lindsay stirred against Catlin's chest. The trembling had gone, leaving only the awareness that she was standing in a stranger's arms, absorbing the comfort he gave without question—but Catlin didn't feel like a stranger. There was no awkwardness, no uncertainty in his touch. He held her as though he had known her for a very long time. She had held him in the same way.

"Better?" he asked, his voice soft and deep.

She nodded and took another slow breath. "It hasn't been that bad for a long time. I'll be all right now. It—passes," she said. Then she heard her own words echo and felt embarrassment sweep up in a hot tide. Very softly she added, "I'm not really crazy. Sometimes the nightmare just—"

"Yes. I know."

There was such certainty in Catlin's voice that Lindsay looked up, meeting his eyes. "How?"

"I've been there, Lindsay. And then, like you, I finally came home." He brushed his mouth over hers, taking the question that had formed on her lips. "That's what I'm going to do with you tonight. Take you home. I'll feed you a brandy and we'll play mah-jongg until dawn. If you fall asleep between turns and the nightmare comes again, I'll be there."

Lindsay let out her breath in a rush of sound, feeling a vast relief at not having to go back and face the nightmare alone. "You don't have to do that," she said. "I'm used to—"

"I know," he said, interrupting her with another brush of his lips over hers. "Did you ever think that maybe I dream, too?"

Her eyes widened in surprise, their deep blue color turned to black by fear and the night. "What do you dream about, Catlin?" she whispered.

He gathered her hands from his shirtfront, kissed both palms and hoped that she would never know.

6

"YOU'RE ONE HELL of a fast worker," O'Donnel said, looking up as Catlin came into the office. "One date and bang! Home with the lady you go, never to leave until dawn. And here she wouldn't even play footsie with me."

"Where's Chen Yi?" asked Catlin.

O'Donnel opened his mouth to pursue the subject of fast work, took a look at Catlin's narrowed eyes and decided that the other man wasn't going to kiss and tell. "In with Stone."

"Who's the referee?"

O'Donnel rocked back in his office chair and gave Catlin a long look. "You volunteering?"

"I'm insisting."

Although Catlin smiled, nothing about his expression was genial. Without another word O'Donnel came to his feet and led Catlin to Stone's office. The room was redolent of Yi's strong cigarettes. Catlin glanced quickly around the office, noting both the executive furniture and the obligatory framed photos on the wall showing Stone shaking hands with three presidents, a brace of senators and the man who had once counted for more than any mere politician—J. Edgar Hoover.

"I understand from the surveillance report that you and Miss Danner got along like a house on fire," said Stone, his tone revealing both approval of Catlin's prowess and disapproval of Lindsay's easiness.

"Do you have a room where Yi and I could talk privately?"

"No."

Catlin turned to Yi and began talking in Mandarin. Stone took it for a few moments, then swore and got to his feet.

"You can have this one," Stone said, stalking out the door and shutting it hard behind him.

"Are we truly alone?" asked Yi, looking around the office.

"Probably," Catlin responded in English. "After Watergate, only a fool would bug his own office."

"Ah!" Yi waited, watching the man opposite him with opaque black eyes.

"Let her off the hook," Catlin said without preamble. "She doesn't have what it takes for this kind of work."

"She has precisely what is needed."

"Crap!" retorted Catlin. "She's so damned naive she didn't even know a two-way mirror when she saw it."

Yi nodded. "That is why I have you, dragon. You see through walls for her."

Catlin made an impatient sound. "It won't work, Yi. She's not hard enough. She still gets the shakes over a murder that happened nearly a quarter century ago. She has a fetish about honesty. In short, she's just not a player. Try to make her into one and she'll blow up in your hands."

"She has a gift for the genuine," agreed Yi, inhaling quickly. "Her mother had that gift, too, only with her it was for people, not art."

"Had?" asked Catlin, remembering that Lindsay's file had listed her mother as still living.

"She died two months ago."

"Christ. No wonder Lindsay has the shakes. She's reliving the past while she tries to cope with losing it."

"Please?" asked Yi.

Catlin's hand moved in a savage gesture. "Lindsay is an only child. Both her parents are dead. No one alive remembers her childhood. No one. The child that was Lindsay died with her mother."

Yi's eyes widened as he absorbed the ramifications of Catlin's harsh words. "You speak as one who knows."

Catlin shrugged. "We all face it sooner or later, unless we die out of turn."

"Not in China," Yi said softly. "Very few of us know that kind of isolation. Our families are large, our communities are small, and we share our lives many times, with many people."

He looked down at his own hands, thinned by age, and thought of his family stretching back through history, a net of blood relationships woven across the face of Asia and time itself. "It must be terrible to be so alone," he said after a long pause. "I grieve for the daughter." He glanced up, meeting Catlin's eyes unflinchingly. "I would free her if I could, but I cannot. She is needed."

"Why?" demanded Catlin. "There's a world full of experts out there."

"The bowl," murmured Yi, "and the hill-censer. As I have said to you before, she has a gift for the genuine. This is known about her in China, as well as in America. Even as a child she had that gift. Whatever she says about bronzes will be believed. It would not be so with other experts. Whether they said forgery or fine art, there would be doubt, for the experts were not born of China. They did not grow on millet and rice, hunger and politics, fear and danger. Other bronze experts may have knowledge or greed, but no gift." Yi's cigarette flared fiercely. When he spoke again his tone was staccato, harsh, allowing no argument. "Lindsay Danner is necessary to me. To China."

Catlin thought of the woman he had laughed and talked with until dawn so that no dark dreams could ripple through her mind, making her twist and turn as though trying to evade a hunter. He knew that she could not stay awake every night, and he knew that the nightmare was patient.

"Yi—" began Catlin.

There was a knock, then the door opened immediately. "Finished?" O'Donnel asked, looking from Yi to Catlin.

"Yes," said Yi.

"No," said Catlin.

"Well, put a cork in it for now," advised O'Donnel. "She's here," he added, looking at Yi.

"Ah!"

Catlin snarled an obscenity, knowing that he had lost. He turned toward Yi with a speed that made O'Donnel flinch in surprise. When Catlin spoke, it was in Mandarin. The words were clipped, as harsh as the sound of stone grating over stone.

"If she is hurt, most honorable Chen Yi, you will wish that you had not gone fishing with a dragon."

Yi traded stares with Catlin for a long moment, then bowed slightly, accepting Catlin's promise. O'Donnel hesitated, sensing the tension in the room but not knowing its cause.

"Ready now?" O'Donnel asked dryly, poised in the doorway.

Yi tossed his half-smoked cigarette into an ashtray and stepped toward the door. Catlin followed. Neither man said a word as O'Donnel led them down the hall and into the same "Conference" room where Lindsay had looked over the seventeen ancient bronzes. The long table had been replaced by comfortable chairs circling a smaller table. The careful intimacy of the arrangement brought a cynical smile to Catlin's lips, but he said nothing. He simply turned around, went back down the hall a few steps and opened the door that led to the concealed room.

"I'll watch from here," said Catlin. "If she sees me before she says yes, she might say no."

O'Donnel's eyebrows climbed. "And here we thought you were our secret weapon."

"I'm nobody's secret weapon," Catlin said flatly.

Yi watched Catlin leave, but said nothing. After a short look around the room, Yi took a chair near an ashtray, lit another cigarette and waited for Lindsay Danner to arrive. The wait wasn't long. A door opened and a voice floated down the hall into the room. Yi closed his eyes for a moment, listening, remembering what life had been like many, many years ago.

"Mr. White didn't tell me what you wanted," Lindsay said, looking over her shoulder as Stone held open the door for her. "Is it about the bronzes I saw yesterday?"

"Indirectly."

Lindsay walked into the room, smelled the unmistakable pungency of a Chinese cigarette and closed her eyes for an instant, fighting memories. When she opened her eyes again, she saw an elderly Chinese man sitting in an oversized chair, watching her. Though his clothes were Western, she had no doubt that he had come from half a world away. He stood, bowed slightly when Stone introduced them and sat again.

"Have a seat, Lindsay," O'Donnel said, gesturing to the chair next to Yi. "Coffee?"

"Yes, please. Extra cream, too," she added, remembering the last cup of coffee she had drunk in the Hoover Building.

"Mr. Chen?"

"Thank you, yes," said Yi. "No cream. Much sugar. Is there lemon peel?" he added rather wistfully.

"I'll see if I can scare some up," promised O'Donnel.

Stone waited until the door closed before he took a chair opposite Lindsay. "Thank you for coming here again. Before I go any further, I want to stress that though Steve doesn't know the precise details of what we have in mind, we have his fullest cooperation in this, er, endeavor."

"Yes, I gathered that," said Lindsay, her voice neutral. What she didn't say was that J. Stephen had called the cab for her, loaded her in and given directions to the driver before she could either agree or object.

"A rather unusual job has come up," Stone said, eyeing the cool, poised woman who had gone out once with a stranger and then taken him home until dawn. "A job that can only be done by you."

Lindsay fixed Stone with dark blue eyes and murmured encouragingly. Her curiosity was fully aroused. "More bronzes?" she asked.

"Yes."

"Mmm. Treasure hunt time," said Lindsay, smiling widely, letting her excitement show. "You're on! Lead me to them, Mr. Stone."

"Actually," Stone said, grinning in response, "we were hoping that you would lead *us*."

"I don't understand," she said, looking at the three men. Then a possibility occurred to her. The smile vanished as her expression became remote, cold. "Neither I nor any of my private clients deal in suspect bronzes," she said in a clipped voice.

Yi measured the emotion coiled just beneath the silvery voice and remembered Catlin's warning: *She has a fetish about honesty.* Yi had wondered at the time if that were the legacy of a missionary upbringing. He still wondered, but he no longer doubted that whatever the source, Lindsay was committed to honesty in the same way that other people were committed to God or Marx or Mao. Lindsay's commitment to the truth came as no real surprise. That, in addition to her gift for discovering fraudulent bronzes, had been what made her uniquely suited for dealing with Emperor Qin's bronzes. Her reputation for honesty was known and accepted on both sides of the Pacific.

Sadly Yi acknowledged to himself that the daughter was like the mother in more than voice. Both women would face down a hungry tiger over a matter of principle. Unfortunately, while necessary and even admirable, Lindsay's honesty would make things much more difficult, infinitely more dangerous.

Yi's cigarette glowed sharply, twice.

"No one meant to imply any dishonesty on your part," Stone said calmly. "Frankly, we've researched you rather thoroughly. You have an enviable reputation. That, in addition to your expertise, is your major attraction for us."

Lindsay weighed the words, nodded and settled back into her chair. "All right, Mr. Stone. What do you want me to do?"

"Brad," he corrected, smiling. "May I call you Lindsay?"

"Of course."

"Thank you. It will make working together easier."

Yi gave Stone an opaque black glance, silently reminding the FBI agent that whatever happened, it would be Catlin and not Stone who worked with Lindsay.

"Mr. Chen," continued Stone, "is from the People's Republic of China. He has come to us with a difficult problem. He believes that someone is stealing ancient bronzes from Xi'an and selling them in America."

"Xi'an?" Lindsay asked, giving the name the quick tonal shifts that revealed her intimate knowledge of Mandarin. "From Mount Li?"

Yi nodded.

"Emperor Qin's tomb?" persisted Lindsay, unable to believe what she was hearing. Adrenaline spread through her in a wave of excitement. "My God," she breathed. "Are you saying that some of Qin's funeral bronzes are here in the United States right now?"

"If not now, then soon," said Yi.

"Where? When? Who's bringing them in?" demanded Lindsay, questions tumbling out one after the other in her eagerness.

Stone laughed curtly. "That's why we need you. We don't know."

"But—" began Lindsay. She shook her head when words simply didn't come. "If you don't know, how would I?" she asked finally.

"You haven't heard any rumors?" asked Stone.

She made an exasperated sound, remembering a similar conversation with Catlin. "Mr. Stone—Brad," she corrected hastily, before he could. "I've heard nothing *but* rumors since 1980, when word of the bronze find at Xi'an was released by the Chinese government." She turned suddenly to Yi, remembering his name in another context. "You're the Minister of Archaeology in Shaanxi province, aren't you?"

Yi nodded.

Lindsay's breath came out in a rush. "It's an honor to meet you, sir," she murmured, bowing her head briefly, gracefully, in the manner of a Chinese woman greeting an elder, powerful male.

For the first time, Yi smiled. The expression transformed his face, making him appear to be a kindly grandfather rather than an aloof, perhaps even cruel, patriarch. "The pleasure is mine, daughter," he said. "Ah!"

Stone shifted in his seat, impatient to get back to the rumors Lindsay had mentioned. Yi threw the agent a black glance, nodded curtly and tossed his cigarette into the ashtray to smolder sullenly.

"About those rumors," Stone prompted.

Lindsay looked away from Yi. "Nothing came of them. Each time I tracked down the rumors, the bronzes were either forgeries or genuine Han or sometimes even Shang. But never Qin."

"Any new rumors?"

She laughed, but there was little humor in the sound. "All the time. Every collector and curator is obsessed with the idea of owning something from Emperor Qin's grave. As long as there is a demand like that, someone will find a way to meet it. Or," she added dryly, "to appear to meet it."

"None of the bronzes were from Xi'an?" pressed Stone.

"I can't speak for all of them. The ones I saw definitely were not."

Stone grunted. "But you haven't seen all of them?"

"Hardly," she said, her voice cool. "I don't do business in that market."

"What market?" asked Stone.

"Some people call it the shadow market or the gray market. Most people call it the double market."

"What do you call it?"

"Thieves' market," she said, her contempt clear in the line of her mouth.

"But some of your clients do business there," suggested Stone.

"Not through me."

"How can you be sure?" Stone asked, drawing out a cigarette and lighting it. "Are you positive that each and every piece that goes through your hands never has been bought or sold or traded on the double market?"

Lindsay opened her mouth for a hot reply, then closed it again. After a moment she sighed. "No," she said quietly. "I can't be positive. But I try very hard to spot dubious goods."

"What sort of thing do you look for?" asked Stone, blowing out a stream of mild tobacco smoke.

"Frauds," she said simply. "If the piece is genuine, I look at the person bringing it to me. If their reputation is—" she paused.

"No better than it has to be?" Stone suggested ironically.

Lindsay nodded. "If the dealer's reputation is dubious, I have to assume that the provenance of the bronze is equally doubtful. So I check very carefully. But even so—" she hesitated again.

"Even so?" prodded Stone.

"Say a piece is stolen from its legitimate owner or looted from an archaeological site," said Lindsay, her indigo eyes focused inward, seeing something that made her mouth turn down. "A few dealers will buy artifacts that don't come with documentation. The first thing such a dealer does is forge a document to make it appear that a legitimate sale took place. Then he sells or trades the artifact to a slightly more scrupulous dealer and documents that transaction with another bill of sale."

Lindsay looked from Stone to Yi, wondering if she were telling them things they already knew. Both men looked back at her with complete attention. She took a deep breath and continued. "The artifact is sold or traded for a third time, and a third piece of documentation is added. Now remember, except for the first bill of sale, all the paper is legitimate. Nor are repeated sales suspicious in themselves. Dealers trade more often with each other than with anyone else. It's a way of broadening and upgrading inventory without spending a lot of cash."

Stone nodded. His narrowed eyes watched her intently, silently encouraging her to keep on talking.

"By the fourth sale, even the most scrupulous dealer will accept the provenance of the artifact in question as legitimate. In fact," admitted Lindsay, "it's rare that more than two pieces of documentation will ever be asked for. There simply isn't time, especially if the artifact is of only modest value."

"And the dealers who aren't careful of documentation?" asked Stone. "What about them?"

"They exist," Lindsay said flatly. "Every profession has its rogues. Even the FBI."

"Who are your rogues?"

"Do you want a list?" she asked, half curious, half angry.

"No. I want an introduction."

Lindsay blinked. "You want what?"

"We want you to take us to the dealers who might have knowledge of stolen Qin bronzes," Stone said bluntly.

Slowly, Lindsay shook her head. "They won't see me," she said. "And if they did, they wouldn't say Bo-Peep about stolen art."

"Why?"

Her mouth turned down wryly at the corner. "I've made no secret of my opinion of such dealers. In fact, I've done a series of articles on the subject for a collectors' magazine. My contempt for thieves and double-dealers is well known. It has been years since I was approached by someone who had a bronze of doubtful provenance to sell."

Stone threw a look at Yi. "Well?"

Yi grunted. "It is her reputation that makes her necessary to my comrades."

Bronze hair gleamed as Lindsay turned her head suddenly. "What do you mean?"

"It is known that you cannot be bribed," said Yi, drawing sharply on his cigarette. "It is also known that you can determine rapidly whether or not a bronze is genuine. You are precisely what my comrades need to find the emperor's bronzes."

"Mr. Chen, I would gladly help you if I could, but stolen bronzes won't be brought to me because of that very reputation," Lindsay said.

"Sure they will," said Catlin from the doorway. "You wouldn't be the first good girl gone wrong in the name of love."

The voice was unmistakable. Lindsay whirled and looked over her shoulder at the dark, powerful man lounging so casually against the doorframe. Catlin's words didn't register on her, but the impact of his sudden presence did. She had laughed and talked with him, and had even fallen asleep watching him take his turn at mah-jongg. When the click of the tiles had awakened her, she had been tempted to ask him to come to bed with her, to hold her so that if she woke up with her skin cold and a scream frozen in her throat, warmth would be right there, next to her.

But she hadn't. She knew that if he had come to her bed last night, it wouldn't have been simply to sleep. She didn't want the complication of a lightning love affair in her life right now. It was difficult enough coping with the tide of memories that kept rising powerfully within her, all the questions about the past that she had never asked her mother, questions whose answers would never come now, for the past was beyond her reach.

She only wished that nightmare was, too.

"Catlin?" Lindsay asked. It was the only word she could say in her surprise. "What are you doing here?"

He looked into her indigo eyes and swore silently, even as he ruefully acknowledged that she had a way of cutting through the fat to the bone beneath with just a few words. Honesty—a sword with two edges and no sheath at all.

"I'm recruiting you for a job that might well destroy you," he said bluntly.

"Dragon—" began Yi in Mandarin, his tone a sharp warning. Then he remembered that Lindsay, too, spoke Mandarin. With a harsh sound he fell silent, but his eyes spoke blackly of betrayal.

"You see," continued Catlin, his tone as hard and unflinching as his eyes, "these men have read your file backward, forward, upside down and inside out, but they're still blind to your overriding reality. Honesty. So I've been sitting on the other side of that mirror and listening to them tiptoe around what is really a very straightforward proposition."

Reflexively Lindsay turned to look at the deceptive mirror. As the implication of Catlin's words sank through her confusion, color stained her cheekbones. She turned back toward him sharply, an angry question on her lips. The question died as she realized that at some very deep level Catlin was far more angry than she was.

"What proposition?" Lindsay asked carefully.

"Find Emperor Qin's missing bronzes, and in doing so prevent relations between America and the PRC from slipping back to the Bamboo Curtain days."

"But—"

"I know," Catlin interrupted curtly. "You can't help, because you have a reputation for honest dealing, and the people who will be handling these bronzes wouldn't qualify as honest even in Hong Kong." He smiled, but it wasn't comforting. "So we're going to have to take that beautiful reputation of yours and smear it from D.C. to Xi'an."

Lindsay flinched subtly. "No one would believe it."

Catlin's smile became even less reassuring. "Sweet innocence," he said, shaking his head. "It's a miracle you survived this long without a keeper." The smile vanished, leaving only the cold near-yellow of his eyes. "People can't wait to stand around and sing a chorus of 'Oh How the Mighty Are Fallen,'" he said sardonically.

Lindsay's breath came in sharply, but she didn't argue what she knew to be the truth. "I have no objection to helping," she said, turning to face Chen Yi. "China has given much to me. It would be an honor to give back something in return, however small. But I don't see how I can."

"Become a crook," Catlin suggested coolly.

"No one would believe it," she retorted, turning to face Catlin again. "Why would I suddenly turn dishonest? Money? I'm not in debt because I don't live beyond my means. I've turned down bribes for years. I love bronzes, but I'm not obsessed by them, so I can't be bribed by even a spectacular piece of goods."

"No?" he asked softly. "How about me?"

For the first time the implication of Catlin's earlier words burst inside Lindsay: . . . *good girl gone wrong in the name of love.*

Catlin saw knowledge go through Lindsay in a wash of color beneath her clear skin.

"They'll never believe I'm dishonest," she said tightly.

"Will they believe you're in love?" asked Catlin. "Will they believe you're so much in love that nothing else matters to you? It happens to women, I'm told," he added coolly.

"Does it happen to men?" she challenged.

"Sometimes. With the right woman." Catlin's voice changed, softer now and even less comforting, sparing her nothing of the truth. "But love doesn't enter into the reality of what we'll be doing. For the first time in your life, Lindsay Danner, you're going to have to live a lie. You're going to have to watch people smile slyly and nudge each other as you walk past. People you wouldn't have wiped your shoes on will suddenly consider themselves your moral superiors—"

"Catlin—" interrupted Stone roughly.

"Shut up." Catlin's words were calm, neutral, and all the more effective for it.

Lindsay sat without moving, watching Catlin with eyes that were almost black.

"But that won't be the hard part," Catlin continued relentlessly, "because you don't give a damn about the opinion of thieves and fools. It's the people you respect who will tear the guts out of you. You have to deceive those people, too. All of them. All the way to the wall. No hedging, no flinching, no secret winks, no hand signals. And no exceptions. Not one. You'll know you've succeeded when the people you admire turn away when you approach, and maggots invite you to dinner."

For a moment it was utterly quiet. Nothing moved but the smoke curling up from the cigarette held between Chen Yi's fingers.

"That's when you'll be useful to us," Catlin said. "When you can eat with maggots and not gag."

There was no color left beneath Lindsay's skin now, but she said nothing, did nothing, simply watched Catlin as though she had never seen a man like him before. Which was the exact truth.

"That isn't the worst of it," continued Catlin. "You'll get to the point where carrion tastes like tenderloin, and maggots turn out to be pretty human, after all. And one day you'll look in the mirror and see a maggot looking back at you."

Catlin smiled. Lindsay looked away.

"Maybe you'll be lucky," Catlin said. "Maybe we'll find the bronzes before you lose your illusions about yourself. Even if we do, the worst is still to come."

Lindsay looked back in startled disbelief, only to find herself caught and held in Catlin's cruel, compassionate glance. Her protests died in her throat.

"The worst part is that when the whole mess is wrapped up, when Chen Yi goes back to China a hero or a dog, when Stone goes on with his career intact or in pieces, that's when you'll be patted on the head and turned back out into your own world. Only it won't be your world anymore. A good reputation is like virginity. You lose it only once."

"Hold it," Stone said grimly. "We'll certainly tell Lindsay's boss that—"

"What about the rest of the world?" Catlin retorted. "Are you going to take out ads in the trade magazines saying that Lindsay Danner isn't really a crook, that she helped her government pull some very, very delicate chestnuts out of a nasty international fire? Are you going to tell everyone to stop sneering and go down on their knees to thank God that one of His children was brave and foolish enough to risk everything she had of value in the hope of helping out two governments that don't give a damn about one Lindsay Danner?"

"We'll do everything we can," Stone said firmly.

Catlin's laughter coiled through the room, a sound darker than smoke, colder. "Sure you will, Stone. And when word comes down that all you can do with the Emperor Qin affair is hit it with a Top-Secret stamp and bury it in the files, what then? Who's going to help Lindsay put her life back together then? You? Yi? Her boss?"

"We'll do everything we can," repeated Stone.

Catlin smiled.

Lindsay closed her eyes, but still she saw the cold yellow fire burning in Catlin's glance. Silently she asked herself how she had ever found his presence comforting.

"There it is, Lindsay," said Catlin, "the unvarnished truth that you prize so highly. Open your eyes and look at it. Take a good look. Win, lose or draw, there's no going back from this moment. Learn to live a lie or walk out of here and never look back. Make your choice." He waited until her eyes were open again before he added softly. "Make a choice you can live with, because once you make it, no one can live with it for you."

Lindsay held Catlin's eyes for a long moment before she looked at Yi, then at Stone. "Is there really a possibility that relations between the U.S. and China could be destroyed over the Qin bronzes?"

"Not a possibility," Stone amended, his expression grim. "A certainty."

She looked at Yi, who said quietly, "There is no doubt. The time when America was the enemy is still bright in many Chinese minds. Nor is there another person with your unique qualifications who can help us in our difficulty," added Yi.

Without realizing it, Lindsay turned toward the man who waited so quietly in the doorway, dominating the room with his silence.

"Catlin?" she whispered.

He saw, and knew why she turned toward him, trusting him. He had told her the whole truth when the other men had told less than half. This moment was the reason why he had not seduced her last night when he could have, when he had wanted sensual oblivion as much as she had, and had known that he would find it in her, and she in him.

"In that much, you can trust them," said Catlin. "For America it is economics, pure and simple. For China, it is a question of face among nations."

Lindsay let out her breath in a long sigh, doubting no longer. The concept of face might seem elusive or ludicrous to most Americans, but she was not most Americans. She had lived in China, where face was as real as life and death. More real, for face transcended both, passed down through the generations from hand to hand as surely as ritual bronzes.

"Then the only real question to be answered is whether I could live with myself if I said no," Lindsay whispered.

Catlin waited, showing nothing of his thoughts.

"There is no choice," she said quietly. "I'll do whatever I can, whatever the cost."

Only Catlin saw the fine trembling of Lindsay's hands in her lap as both Stone and Yi congratulated her on her choice. Without a word, Catlin watched the betraying quiver, knowing exactly how a judas goat felt. It was a feeling out of the past, a feeling he had sworn he would never know again.

He had been wrong.

7

"SHE WAS RAISED to love and serve China.
Even so, that was a terrible chance you
took," Yi said, staring at Catlin through a veil of smoke.

Catlin stood at his apartment window, watching as the street
below turned ruddy with the light of the dying sun. It was too
soon for the street lamps to be on, but a few taxis prowled
white-eyed through the streets, trying to attract fares.

"No worse than the chance you took," Catlin said.

"Explain."

"She's an innocent," he said flatly. "She was made to be
protected, not to be put in the line of fire."

"We are all born innocent. And we all go into the fire."

Catlin turned with a feline motion that was very quick, very
controlled. Predatory. "Have you never met a genuinely good
person?" he asked softly.

"Yes. One." Yi made a sharp motion, sending his spent cigarette into the fireplace. "Do not mistake goodness for weakness. A fatal mistake, dragon. A very American mistake."

"Do not mistake innocence for stupidity," retorted Catlin.
"A fatal mistake, Yi. A very Chinese mistake."

Yi stood with his hand in the pocket of his suit coat, waiting
for Catlin to continue.

"If you had told Lindsay only half the truth—that China
needed her—she would have volunteered without hesitation."
Catlin's voice was flat, calm, even though anger seethed just
beneath his careful surface. "But then she would have come
apart the first time an old friend drew back from her in distaste. That would have been the moment when she realized
what living undercover really meant. Then she would have
known that you had lied to her by not telling her the whole
truth. She would have begun to question everything you had

ever said to her, *including the worth of the ultimate goal.* And then, my friendly enemy, it would all go from sugar to shit in a hurry. Lindsay won't sell her soul for people who lie to her. She's innocent, not stupid.''

Yi's lighter flame hissed in the silence before the top shut with a metallic snap. He inhaled sharply and stared at his too-intelligent dragon, remembering the moment when Lindsay had turned to Catlin as the only source of truth in a room full of near-truths and outright lies.

"Ah!"

The guttural sound was followed by a very thin smile as Yi returned the lighter to his pocket.

"So. Now it is you whom she trusts?" asked Yi, but it was not really a question. It was a statement of discovery.

"Yes."

Yi laughed and laughed.

"What next, dragon?" he asked finally, smiling as he pulled on his cigarette.

Catlin turned back to the window because he didn't trust himself to look at Yi any longer. "When are your comrades due?"

"That is not known."

Catlin's mouth flattened into a line. "Do you trust them, Yi? More important, do they trust you?"

Nothing answered Catlin but silence. He turned around. "Do they know about half of a Han coin?" he asked. "Do they know that you chose Lindsay long before you arrived in America to watch a farce through a two-way mirror? Are your comrades part of your plan, whatever that plan might be?"

"They chose you to advise us in this matter," Yi said.

"The way the FBI 'chose' to use Lindsay?" retorted Catlin caustically. "Do your comrades know about my past?"

Smoke curled silently from Yi's lips. "We have not discussed it. It does not matter. A sword is a sword, no matter the hand it was made for."

"But a cormorant comes only to one master's call."

"What a pity that you are not a cormorant." Yi made an abrupt gesture. "What is it you wish to know from me?"

"Did you choose the people who came with you to the United States?"

"No."

"Then they are your enemies," Catlin said flatly.

For a long time there was only silence and smoke dissipating in random currents. Catlin thought that Yi wasn't going to answer. Finally his voice came, as soft and astringent as the smoke curling up to the ceiling.

"A wise man assumes that everyone is his enemy."

Catlin made a disgusted sound and looked back toward the red light flooding the street below. The wind blew, making twilight shadows twist while branches shifted and shivered as though trying to escape the descending night.

"How are you going to manage it?" Catlin asked after a long silence. "Are you going to travel with Lindsay and me? Are you going to pretend that you don't know us? Are your comrades in on the sting?"

"I will travel in many of the same places that you do, but not as the Minister of Archaeology. I will be a resident of Taiwan, a buyer of old bronzes. That will give me an acceptable reason to openly approach Miss Danner on occasion, through you."

"If your comrades are working for the thieves, your cover was blown before you ever left China."

"Yet for them to act upon that knowledge would be to proclaim that I am in the company of betrayers. That would not be wise. As for the rest, I have strongly advised Mr. Stone not to tell my comrades anything about interviewing Miss Danner. They will assume that you are merely being attentive to her in order to use her for their purposes."

"True enough," said Catlin. His eyes were hooded, his blunt cheekbones thrown in relief by the angle of the sunset light. "But will your comrades believe it?"

"Mr. Stone will tell them that he has spoken with several experts, told them of the missing bronzes and will await their information. When word of bronzes comes from those dealers, it will go to you, as well. Mr. Stone will say nothing about you, because he is not supposed to know that you are working directly for me. My comrades will accept that, because it has always been their intention to purchase you as their own expert and source of information in America."

"If your comrades are helping the crooks, won't they try to prevent me from getting information that might get back to you?"

"That is one possibility. If, indeed, one of my comrades is guilty of treachery."

Catlin grunted. "Then Lindsay is in immediate danger."

"Perhaps. Perhaps not."

"Why not?"

"Who," Yi asked softly, "will authenticate the bronzes if not Miss Danner?"

"The dealer making the purchase," retorted Catlin.

"But if the person is not a dealer, or is not trusted to be unbiased in his appraisal? What then, dragon? Who will my comrades trust not to cheat them? Who will the buyer trust not to cheat him in turn?"

There was no answer except the obvious. The thieves would end up wanting Lindsay Danner's opinion for the same reason that Chen Yi and his comrades did—her expertise would not be questioned, even after she had been compromised by taking as her lover a man who had a reputation for buying and selling bronzes of verifiable authenticity and very dubious provenance.

Yi drew hard on his cigarette, matching for an instant the red glow of the setting sun. "Candidly, I do not expect to find the bronzes through the experts and dealers I listed for the FBI," continued Yi. "As you pointed out, the thieves must be well connected to my government. They will know whom the FBI has talked to and whom it has not."

"So that's why you put three of the biggest crooks in the business on the list," Catlin said. "You wanted them out of the game early on. The same for the best-known legitimate experts. You cut the heart out of the competition. A brilliant move, Chen Yi. My compliments.''

"It will limit the thieves' potential outlets," agreed Yi, "and make it even more likely that Miss Danner will be called upon to authenticate the bronzes.''

"Why? Lindsay was on that list. They'll know about her.''

"Two women appeared on that list. If someone wishes to check, one of them was blond, and rather careless of her reputation as a dealer. Mr. O'Donnel brought her to be tested just after Miss Danner left the building. The woman came and went through the public entrances. Miss Danner did not.''

"Nice of your comrades to get sick in L.A.," Catlin said. "Saves Lindsay having to play hide-and-seek with them, too.''

"That was quite fortunate, yes.''

Catlin watched a lone pedestrian walk toward a cab parked by the curb. After a moment the person retreated with angry steps and flagged a passing cab. Catlin smiled wryly. He suspected that if he went down to that cab he would be taken anywhere in town, anytime. There was another watcher parked down the street in an ordinary car. FBI, no doubt. There would be a similar surveillance on Lindsay's home.

Yi's cigarette made a flat arc into the fireplace. He didn't watch the flight. He had eyes only for the man who stood with his back to the room, asking questions whose answers Yi would just as soon not give. But that was the price of fishing with a dragon.

"When will the bronzes arrive in the States?'' asked Catlin. "I do not know.''

Catlin didn't bother to believe or disbelieve Yi's statement. The only truth that mattered was that Catlin wasn't going to know the arrival date of the bronzes right now. Nor did he know how much time he would need with Lindsay, how long it would take to turn her into some semblance of a player.

"How much time does it take to ruin a reputation that took a lifetime to build?'' he wondered aloud, his voice bitter.

"A moment only,'' said Yi. "The right moment.''

"Which you will no doubt provide.''

Yi shrugged. "What is it that you Christians say? God will provide?"

"We're more likely to say 'The Lord giveth and the Lord taketh away, blessed be the name of the Lord,'" Catlin retorted, his voice as hard as the line of his mouth.

"An unusual sentiment," said Yi after a moment.

"It isn't mine," Catlin said, turning around with feral swiftness. "I respond more to the line of reasoning that goes 'An eye for an eye and a tooth for a tooth.'"

Yi smiled. "As I said, you are a Chinese Legalist beneath your Western surface."

"What do you respond to?" asked Catlin.

"History. Family. Face."

Yi turned away from the man silhouetted against the dying sun. Catlin watched as Yi went to the door, opened it and closed it noiselessly behind him. Catlin stood to one side of the window, staring out, waiting for Yi to appear on the street at the front of the building. After a few moments Catlin closed the drapes.

Yi hadn't reappeared.

Catlin showered, shaved and dressed quickly. There was a fund raiser for a senator that night, one of those glittering dinners requiring the attendance of wealthy patrons, collectors, curators and anyone else who wanted to contribute to the campaign chests of the senator whose committee oversaw the disbursement of federal grants to the arts. Originally L. Stephen White had been slated to attend in the name of the Museum of the Asias. White, however, had come down with a touch of flu. Lindsay would be attending in his place, with Catlin as her escort.

How long does it take to ruin a reputation?
Just one moment. The right moment.

Catlin wondered if that moment would come tonight. The thought did nothing to soften the grim line of his mouth as he stepped into the street and walked to the taxi that had been turning away fares for the past two hours. He opened the door himself, slid in and gave directions to Lindsay's home. When the cab arrived, Catlin slid out, closed the door and walked away.

"Hey, what about my fare?" complained the cabby.

"Tell Stone I stiffed you."

There was a shocked silence, then a curse. "How did you make me?"

"You're the first cabbie I've had in years who speaks English."

The driver's rueful laughter followed Catlin up the walkway. He didn't bother to ask the cabbie to hang around until he returned with Lindsay. The taxi would be there when he came back, waiting by the curb like a well-trained hound.

Lindsay opened the door on the first knock. She was wearing a beaded gold silk blouse over a matching full-length skirt that glittered with more of the tiny crystal beads. The slit in the fitted skirt showed her long, elegant legs to advantage. The blouse was loose, but the weight of the beads made the material cling to her breasts, outlining her in shimmering light with each breath she took. From the burnished bronze smoothness of her hair to the elusive, tantalizing fragrance she wore, everything about Lindsay was clean, untouched, radiant.

Abruptly Catlin felt like turning on his heel and walking out, telling anyone who asked why to go to hell, he wasn't going to ruin a woman like Lindsay just to redeem a debt incurred by a younger, much more foolish man.

"It's not too late to back out," Catlin said flatly.

Lindsay's eyes widened in surprise, revealing depths of blue. Slowly she shook her head, causing light to ripple through her hair.

"Listen to me," he said, catching her chin in his hand, holding her very still. "There's no way for words to convey the truth of being undercover. You aren't tough enough."

For an instant the nightmare rose in Lindsay like a dark whirlwind, a twisting spiral of screams and fear and a child running through the night with blood on her hands. Behind the nightmare was the reality of the past, a childhood spent with whispers and gunfire, hunger and the kind of silence that came only to hunted animals.

"I've survived more than most," Lindsay said in a husky voice. When she saw that Catlin was going to argue, she put her fingers over his lips in a gesture that surprised her as much as it did him. She lifted her hand quickly. "I'm going through with it. And," she added, smiling crookedly, "I won't say you didn't warn me if you won't say I told you so."

There was no answering flash of humor in the harsh amber eyes watching her. "You're a fool, Lindsay Danner."

"Then what does that make you?" she retorted.

"A judas goat."

The humor curling her mouth died. "But I know where I'm being led. You told me."

"Did I?"

"Yes. Hell."

"And you didn't believe me."

"Oh, but I did," said Lindsay. "I could see it in your eyes, hear it in your voice."

"Yet you're following me."

She shrugged, making silk and crystal move sensuously. "I'm not the first woman to follow a man into hell. And," she added with quiet determination, "I won't be the first to come out of hell carrying the seeds of spring in my hands."

"Persephone carried winter, too," said Catlin, remembering the old myth.

"Yes. Makes for a more interesting world, doesn't it?"

"Tell me that in a few months," he retorted. He looked at Lindsay's unflinching eyes for a moment longer before he removed his hand, releasing her. "So be it," he said bleakly.

Catlin closed his eyes for a moment. When he opened them again there was no emotion, neither passion nor compassion, anger nor encouragement. There was only predatory intelligence and an equally predatory control.

"Will any of your clients be at the dinner tonight?" asked Catlin.

Like his eyes, his voice was devoid of emotion, almost in-human. Lindsay stared at him, hardly able to believe this was the same man who had knocked on her door just moments ago, taken one approving look at her and tried to talk her out of finding Emperor Qin's bronzes.

"Will they?" rapped Catlin.

"Y-yes," she said, stumbling over the word, off balance. "How do you do that?" she asked before Catlin could ask her another question.

"Do what?"

"Just—vanish. Emotionally."

"It's a trick you learn in hell," he said indifferently. "Which clients?" he asked, pursuing all that mattered now—Qin's bronzes and the other half of a mutilated coin.

"What?"

"Which clients will be there tonight?"

There was neither patience nor impatience in Catlin's con-trolled voice, simply a sense of vast stillness waiting to be filled by answers. Lindsay shook her head in silent disbelief.

"No wonder Chen Yi called you dragon," she whispered.

There was no answer.

"Sharen Kerry," said Lindsay. "Dave Goldstein. Mr. and Mrs. Tom Stoltz."

"In order of their honesty?"

Lindsay hesitated. "I—they're all honest with me."

"Cut the crap, Lindsay," he snapped. "You know what I mean. If you had a bronze of dubious provenance to unload, which one of the three would you go to first?"

Unconsciously Lindsay bit her lip. "Mr. Stoltz. He does a lot of buying from Jackie Merriman. She isn't dishonest," added Lindsay quickly, "just careless. If she likes a piece, she won't ask uncomfortable questions about where it came from, no matter how odd the papers accompanying it might look."

"Next."

"Dave. He's very competitive."

"That leaves Sharen Kerry."

"Forget it. She's teaching art at a private school in the suburbs. She would faint at the suggestion of a dubious bronze."

"And you won't?"

"No. I just won't buy it myself or recommend that a client buy it."

"How does Sharen get the money to collect?"

"Born with a platinum spoon between her perfect teeth," Lindsay said wryly.

"Will any dealers be there tonight?"

"Overwhelmingly."

"Honest? Dishonest?"

"Yes," she said succinctly.

Catlin turned several ideas over in his mind, rejecting them one by one. He knew what he had to do. He just didn't like doing it.

"All right," he said abruptly. "Tonight you're going to give your best imitation of a woman being swept off her dainty little feet by a man. You'll conduct the normal amount of business, but you'll do it with me by your side. You will appear distracted. Not rude, simply absorbed in the man who is your new lover. Can you handle that much acting?"

Lindsay remembered watching Catlin over mah-jongg tiles and thinking that it would be good to lie in bed with him, to have his comfort and warmth and power wrapped around her. "No problem," she said honestly. "You're a very distracting kind of man."

Catlin's first reaction was to wonder if she meant it. His second was to realize that she did. She wasn't an actress. That was the problem. He smiled a bit grimly, surprised in spite of himself that she admitted an attraction to him. Again he regretted that she wasn't a different kind of woman. Having an affair with her would provide a high gloss of realism to her actions, the kind of realism that might just make the difference in an amateur undercover's performance.

Not to mention being a real pleasure for him.

But Catlin knew that Lindsay wasn't the kind of woman to take a lover for a night or a week, to put up with unwanted sex to create a fake atmosphere of intimacy. Her discrimination was written all over her file, all over her body, all over her life, revealing a pride, intelligence and integrity that simply refused to settle for casual screwing.

"And," continued Lindsay, "I believe you're very, very good at this kind of acting. I'll watch you for cues."

Catlin nodded, relaxing just a bit. At least she hadn't flinched at the idea of appearing to have an instant lover. For a woman like her, that was the first hurdle.

"What about other men?" he asked. Her file hadn't said anything about a current lover, but then, her file hadn't noted her mother's recent death, either.

Bronze strands swirled as Lindsay shook her head. "There's no one I owe explanations to, if that's what you mean."

"Good," he said bluntly, "because you wouldn't be allowed to make any that didn't agree with the image of a woman thrown headlong into a flaming affair."

Lindsay's unexpected smile made every one of Catlin's male instincts come to full alert. Then her smile faded, leaving the honesty that was such an intriguing, dangerous aspect of her personality.

"I've never had one of those," she murmured, smiling at Catlin even as her eyes approved of the male planes of his face, lingering on the clean shape of his lips. "You'll have to tell me how to act."

"Do you want one?" he asked bluntly.

"What?"

"A flaming affair."

Lindsay's eyes widened in surprise.

"Then don't tease me," finished Catlin, his voice cold.

She flinched as though she had been slapped. Heightened color appeared above the blouse and swept up to her hairline. There was a long silence, because Catlin waited until the blush faded before he spoke.

"Listen to me, Lindsay. Listen to me as though your sanity depended on it. Because it does."

Beneath the resonance of his voice, she sensed anger and irritation, compassion and control. Control most of all.

"Look at me," Catlin demanded.

Lindsay made a small gesture with her hand, as though she lay restlessly in her bed, warding off attacks born of nightmares. The gesture went through Catlin like a knife, telling him that he had hurt her. He hadn't wanted that, but once she had accepted the job, he had known that hurting her would be inevitable. He could keep her body reasonably safe, but her mind was beyond his ability to protect. She had to do that herself, and he had to tell her how.

"One of the hardest parts of being undercover is keeping the public lies separate from the private truths," Catlin said, watching Lindsay's downturned face with brooding eyes. "You can flirt with me all you like in public—in fact, it's required for the sake of appearances. But you be damn sure that you keep the act separate in your mind from the reality."

"There should be no conflict," Lindsay said, her voice neutral, her face still turned away from Catlin. "I don't flirt in public."

Her body language said that she didn't plan on beginning with him tonight, either. Or any other night in the foreseeable future. As far as she was concerned, he had just hit the bottom of the list of the world's desirable males.

Catlin's hand traced the slanting line of Lindsay's high cheekbone, smoothed over her hair, teased the sensitive curve of her ear. He tested the softness of her lips with the pad of his thumb as he bent down to her.

Then he spoke, and his voice was like a whip. "Quitting?"

Lindsay shivered and jerked away from his sensual touch. "What do you want from me?" she whispered, looking at him with wide, dark eyes.

"An act. That's all. Just an act."

"But—"

"I know. You're a terrible actress. So get out while you can, Lindsay Danner. Get out *now*."

Color rose in her face again, but this time its source was anger rather than embarrassment. "Go to hell, Catlin! I said I would do it and I will!"

He looked at the wash of heat and the intensity of her indigo eyes, the flash of emotion heightening every aspect of her beauty. He could not help wondering what it would be like to call that response out of her with passion rather than fury. The thought brought a hot shaft of desire that he ignored. Mei had taught him the deadly folly of being ruled by his own sexuality. It was a lesson he would never forget.

Catlin glanced down at his watch. They would be more than fashionably late if they didn't leave soon. Yet it was very clear that Lindsay wasn't ready to do a convincing performance of a woman enjoying an evening with her latest lover. Deliberately he reached for her, sliding his hand around to the back of her head, burying his fingers in the silky coolness of her hair. As he had expected, she pulled back.

"Not good enough," he said in a clipped voice. "When I open that door, you're going to have to convince the world we're either already lovers or soon will be. Kiss me, Lindsay. Act like a woman humming with desire."

"The door is not open," she said, biting off each word.

Catlin's hand shot out and opened the door. He stood there, waiting.

Lindsay took a deep breath and stared up at him, her eyes nearly black against her pale skin. Then she smiled, but the curve of her mouth owed much more to anger than to sensual anticipation. She put her arms around Catlin's neck, stretched up on tiptoe and threaded her fingers deeply into his black hair. Her hands tightened, pulling his hair as her teeth closed less than delicately on his earlobe.

"You're a genuine bastard, Catlin," she whispered huskily.

"My parents will be surprised to hear that," he whispered in return, closing his arms around her in a grip that reminded her that two could play the punishment game. He turned his head suddenly, capturing her mouth.

Lindsay stiffened, expecting an angry male invasion. She was wrong. As always, Catlin managed to catch her off balance. He nuzzled her lips softly, gentling her. His hands moved slowly down the length of her back, stroking all the responsive points, caressing her with a sensitivity that she had never known from a man before. Without realizing it, she softened against him, seeking greater contact, not less.

There was a heady flow of warmth over her silk-clad body as he lifted her until her mouth was on a level with his. Her breath sighed out and she turned her head to follow the teasing, tantalizing lips that refused to hold still for the kiss she suddenly wanted. If he had tried to force her mouth to open for him, she could have resisted. But there was no force in his embrace, no punishing aggression, nothing but the skillful teasing of his tongue following the shape of her lips.

"Catlin," she said, torn between anger and sensual response, not knowing what to feel, what to do, how to act, how to—

And then her questions vanished as he moved his head again, taking her mouth with the same delicacy that he had used to seduce her lips. The taste of him swept over her senses, transforming anger into an entirely different response. Her hands loosened their too-tight grip on his hair. She savored the crisp thickness of it between her fingers even as she shivered at the hot touch of his tongue sliding over hers. She forgot her anger, her uneasiness, the front door open for all the world to see. She forgot everything but the heat and strength of the kiss that was consuming her.

It was a long time before Catlin lifted his head. "That should do it," he said very softly, measuring her flushed, slightly swollen lips and dilated eyes. "You look the part now."

Reality returned in a rush, making Lindsay feel as though she had been dropped into icewater. "Why are you doing this to me?" she whispered.

"You're doing it to yourself. You volunteered, remember?" He let her slide down his body until her feet touched the floor again. "No," he said quickly, covering her mouth with his own when she would have said more. "We'll argue about it later," he murmured, nuzzling against her ear like a lover even as his fingers closed just short of pain on her arms. "Don't ever forget the act when the door is open."

Lindsay looked up at the intent, saturnine face and comfortless amber eyes. She shook her head as though disoriented. The soft heat that had been unfolding deep within her body curled back on itself, leaving her empty, shaken. For a moment she closed her eyes, appalled at what a gullible fool she had been to let her own attraction to Catlin convince her that he was attracted to her, too.

Even as the thought came, she realized that there was no time for recriminations, no time for anger, not even time to regain her balance. The door was open, so the show must go on. *I'll get better at this,* she promised herself fiercely, silently. *I have to!*

"How—how do I introduce you to people?" she asked numbly, hating the betraying catch in her voice.

"Catlin, Jacob MacArthur, Genuine Bastard," he suggested coolly, his voice low, reminding her that other people could appear at any moment.

"No disagreement there," Lindsay said in a voice as understated as his, "but what do you do for a living?"

"Didn't Stone brief you?" murmured Catlin against her hair. He took her keys because her hands were shaking too much for her to lock the door easily. He hoped that anyone watching would assume that desire rather than anger was the cause.

"Stone said you'd tell me whatever I needed to know," she muttered, holding out her hand for her keys as Catlin finished locking up. She put them in the tiny crystal-encrusted purse she carried. "I'm supposed to call him tomorrow."

A hard smile tightened the line of Catlin's mouth. He knew that Stone would be eager to talk to Lindsay. The FBI agent would pump her for every bit of information he could, hoping that Catlin had gotten careless and told her more than he had told Stone.

"I'm part owner and one of the resident experts at the Pacific Rim Institute," Catlin said, taking Lindsay's arm. "That's a think tank on Asian affairs," he added, assuming that the name was unfamiliar to her.

There was a shocked silence while Lindsay realized that Catlin's name had seemed familiar to her not because he had collected bronzes in the past, but because he had earned a reputation for the kind of intelligence and insight into Asian affairs that made his advice de rigueur for Washington's legions of foreign affairs specialists.

"That's like saying Lafitte-Rothschild owns a nice little winery," muttered Lindsay, looking at Catlin as though she had never seen him before. She had heard the Pacific Rim Institute mentioned in the same terms of respect as were used for Rand's more highly publicized think tank. "You really do that?" she asked, hardly able to believe that this cold, controlled, physically powerful man was also one of the gray eminences who advised kings, premiers, presidents and lesser politicos on the state of the Asian nations.

Catlin gave her a sideways glance. "I really do. Why?"

"It's so, er, respectable."

For just an instant humor replaced coldness in Catlin's expression. "And I'm not?" he asked, his mouth lifting at one corner in an almost hidden smile.

Lindsay found herself smiling in return. "Are dragons respectable?"

"When it serves their purpose, yes," Catlin assured her smoothly.

"Is this serving your purpose?"

"It must be. I'm here."

"Then—"

Catlin made an impatient gesture, cutting off the questions he knew were coming. He turned and pulled Lindsay into his arms, easily overwhelming the instant of stiffness before she remembered her role. He bent and brushed his lips over hers, but his words were an icy counterpoint to his caressing touch.

"Think before you ask me anything else, Lindsay," he whispered against her lips. "Before this is over, you're going to need someone you feel you can trust. I won't lie to you, but I won't tell you more of the truth than I have to, either. And sometimes I won't answer at all. Do you understand?"

Lindsay stared at the impeccable ruffled shirt and sleek black dinner jacket that were just inches away from her face. "Ask you no questions and you'll tell me no lies, is that what you're saying?"

"Yes."

She hesitated, then looked directly into Catlin's unusual eyes. "Have you had a lot of experience living in hell?"

"Yes."

"Then I couldn't have a better guide, could I?"

"Remember that," Catlin murmured, tightening his arms painfully around Lindsay. "When we're alone, utterly alone, you may question me if you feel you must. But out in public you may not. Ever. If you can't accept that, call Stone right now and tell him to find another sucker. Our lives may depend on people believing that you are so infatuated that you will do anything to please me. Including sell your unblemished soul." Catlin stared down at Lindsay, his expression closed, offering neither comfort nor encouragement. "The act must begin tonight."

"I thought—I thought it had begun *last* night," Lindsay said, her voice catching with the question she would not allow herself to ask.

Catlin said nothing. He knew that she was wondering whether he had stayed with her last night out of compassion and a desire for companionship, or simply as a calculated effort to win her trust. He also knew that she was too proud to ask. He was grateful for that, because he didn't know the answer.

He didn't want to know it, either.

8

LINDSAY WATCHED in amusement as Mr. and Mrs. Stoltz unbent and became Tom and Harriet after a few moments of listening to Catlin's amusing conversation. The pomposity of the afterdinner speaker had helped to melt the social ice. It had been all Lindsay could do not to laugh aloud herself at Catlin's more outrageous asides to the speaker's pious phrases. She wondered if Catlin were as put off by pretensions to cultural superiority as she was, or if he simply had guessed that the Stoltzes disliked being lectured to on the subject of high art by a neon-nosed politico who couldn't tell painting from sculpture without a label.

Even as the question occurred to her, Lindsay shunted it aside. In public she must accept Catlin at his word. If she tried to dissect each action, each glance, each sentiment, she would turn in tighter and tighter mental circles until she was tangled hopelessly in a sticky net of her own weaving. She couldn't promise Catlin that she would become a great actress, but she would guarantee that she would learn the essentials of her role as quickly as possible. She would laugh at his incisive observations and not ask whether he was being witty in order to get closer to Qin's bronzes or because he genuinely was enjoying the evening with her.

Besides, did she really believe there was any doubt as to what motivated Jacob MacArthur Catlin?

"What do you think, Lindsay?"

Belatedly she realized that Mr. Stoltz had asked her a question. She turned away from her brooding study of Catlin's profile and said, "I'm sorry, Tom. I didn't hear what you said."

Mr. Stoltz gave her a knowing smile. "Admiring the scenery, huh?"

"Er, yes," she mumbled, ducking her head to hide her annoyance at his genial leer. With an effort she schooled her features into their familiar expression of professional attentiveness. As she did, she wryly conceded to herself that being an actress might not be too hard after all; a variation of it was required in her daily work.

"Catlin was telling me you found a flawless Han hill-censer for him," continued Mr. Stoltz. "Old, but never buried."

"Yes," said Lindsay, sipping the late harvest Riesling that had been served with the rich cheesecake.

"Treasures like that don't come on the market very often. Wonder why the family gave it up?"

"Maybe they didn't" Catlin said matter-of-factly, turning toward Mr. Stoltz with a slight smile. "Maybe it was lost."

Catlin's expression said that a more appropriate word might be "stolen," and he didn't really give a damn one way or the other.

Lindsay bit back an instinctive defense of her own honesty as she remembered the role she had volunteered to play. On the other hand, she decided that it would seem odd if she changed completely overnight.

"I don't think so, darling," she murmured. "The papers showed that some other museum bought the censer from a refugee family early in 1920."

"And you always believe everything you see in print, hmm?" asked Catlin, running a fingertip indulgently down Lindsay's nose. He shrugged negligently, a motion that drew the fabric of his coat tightly across his wide shoulders. "All that matters is that the piece is genuine, and the museum didn't recognize it. You did." He bent and kissed her slowly on the lips. "Clever little honey cat. How did I get so lucky as to find you?"

A flush stained Lindsay's cheeks. Grimly she hoped that no one would recognize it for what it was—anger at being so obviously patronized. When she trusted herself to look, Catlin was watching her. His eyes did not reflect the smiling indulgence of his mouth. They were like candle flames imprisoned within ice—brilliant, entirely without warmth.

"You must have done something utterly marvelous in another life to deserve me," Lindsay said, her voice husky with the effort of controlling herself.

Catlin's laugh was soft, deep, as unexpected as the sudden flicker of real warmth in his expression. "Do you believe in more than one life?" he asked, watching her with the satisfied smile of a man who is sure of his hold on a woman.

"Having met you, how could I believe anything else?" she retorted throatily, smiling with more teeth than warmth.

Catlin's smile thinned as he realized that Lindsay was deliberately referring to the double life he had once led and that both of them were leading right now.

"You don't have any more Han bronzes up your sleeve, do you?" asked Mr. Stoltz.

Before Lindsay could answer, Catlin's hands moved slowly from Lindsay's shoulders to her fingertips. "Not a one," he said, turning toward the other man. "Sorry."

Mr. Stoltz's laugh was a harsh male bark. Vigorously he shook his half-bald head, lifting wisps of fine white hair. "No you aren't, and in your shoes I wouldn't be, either."

"Don't worry, Tom," said his wife, leaning forward, her sleekly cut gray hair gleaming like pewter in the light. "Catlin assured me that the Han purchase was unusual for him. His true passion is third century B.C. bronzes."

"Especially pieces from the time of Emperor Qin," added Catlin.

"Qin's dynasty lasted only fourteen years," Mrs. Stoltz said, dismissing it with a flawlessly manicured hand.

"Ah, but what years those were," countered Catlin, leaning toward the woman, his eyes intent. "In 221 B.C., one man unified all of China. One man's vision was imprinted on the face of the greatest nation on Earth. Think of it. In all Europe's history, where cultures and races were much less diverse than in China, there never was unity of government. Not even Rome managed it, though Lord knows they spent a lot of men trying. The northern cultures always evaded the Roman Peace. Perhaps all that Rome lacked was what Qin discovered—the many and bloody uses of highly mobile cavalry against heavy war chariots.

"Qin's vision didn't stop with military maneuvers," continued Catlin, picking up Lindsay's hand and absently smoothing the pad of his thumb down the soft inner skin of her wrist as he spoke.

Sensation radiated through Lindsay from the warmth of Catlin's touch. She watched him with an intensity that matched his as he spoke softly of one of the great rulers in human history. Like Catlin's words, the slow stroking of his thumb sent ripples of awareness through her.

"Qin knew that to hold his conquered lands and peoples together, he had to standardize everything from the size of axles on carts to the width of the roads to the law itself," said Catlin. "Qin did just that with a ruthlessness that has since become legend, burying rebellious Confucian scholars alive to make his point.

"Nor was he satisfied with simple tyranny. He knew that food as well as soldiers had to be moved freely from one end of his huge country to the other, so that famine in the north could be balanced by the south's bounty. A network of roads was built, China's greatest river was subjected to man's control, and the Great Wall was completed, ending the barbarian raids and removing the need for warlords with personal armies to protect personal fiefs."

Lindsay watched Catlin openly, making no effort to conceal her interest in both the man and his words. She was accustomed to a certain amount of scholarship in the men she dated, but she wasn't accustomed to a mind that was both educated and highly pragmatic. The combination fascinated her.

"The result of Qin's military and administrative genius was precisely what Qin had in mind—the destruction of feudal China," summarized Catlin. "Qin gave land to the peasants and then he taxed those peasants directly, erecting a framework for imperial control that endured largely unchanged into the twentieth century."

Lindsay watched as Catlin's amber eyes changed subtly, signaling a shift in his attention from his dinner companions to something much farther away in time and place. She felt herself being pulled along with him, for the intelligence and restrained passion in him as he spoke of Qin was as electrifying to her as the thumb delicately caressing the inside of her wrist.

"But Qin's greatest accomplishment," Catlin continued softly, "was his preparation for the comfort of the half of his soul that would remain on earth after his death. A million peasants, as well as the artists and artisans of an entire continent, worked for more than a decade to build the twelve square miles of grave mound that we know as Mount Li. Perhaps seven thousand life-size terra cotta soldiers were made and painted in individual detail, as well as horses and chariots and weapons. Nor did Qin stop there. Another army was cast, this time in bronze. It guarded another entrance to the grave mound. The bronzes were made in the style men came to call Qin—inlaid with gold and silver, using designs as graceful and fluid as the terra cotta soldiers were powerful.

"There must be other treasures at Mount Li, too," said Catlin, "grave furnishings in all that was precious to the Qin culture, metals and jade, ivory and fantastic silks brocaded in silver and gold. Through the centuries men have talked of a bronze map of Qin's China that was as big as a football field. The map had seas and rivers of mercury that coursed over its surface, circulated by pumps. All to amuse the soul of Qin."

Lindsay barely controlled a shiver as Catlin's thumb slid from her wrist to her fingertips, caressing them slowly while he spoke. The passion that had vibrated subtly through his words was more apparent now. His voice deepened suddenly, becoming as supple and smooth as a quicksilver river created by a long-dead emperor for the future entertainment of his own soul.

"I'd trade all the gold and silver, incense and silk, ivory and jade, all of it, for a single bronze chariot and charioteer," said Catlin. "No one anywhere, in any time or culture, attained the artistry and understanding of bronze that was achieved under Qin's reign. In Qin bronzes, there is true greatness."

Catlin turned and fixed Lindsay with his uncanny golden brown eyes. She met the glance without even being aware of it. She was aware of nothing but the emotion coiled in his voice, an emotion very like her own when she thought of man's greatness cast in enduring bronze for all the ages to share. She didn't remember that there were other people at the table, other voices in the room, an act to be conducted on a public stage. Only Catlin existed for her, and his deep voice was describing emotions she had always believed only she herself felt. It was like the moment when she had seen how confidently and yet reverently he had handled the unique Shang bronze. It was like seeing a reflection of her own soul—dizzying, confusing, almost terrifying, for Catlin was very much unlike anyone she had ever known, especially herself.

"I would give anything I own," he said, watching her. "I would give anything you asked, for one of Qin's bronze charioteers."

"If there is one to be found," Lindsay promised, her voice husky with the yearning she sensed in him, a yearning frighteningly like her own, "I'll find it for you, Catlin. It will be yours."

"Sweet Lindsay," he murmured, kissing the palm of her hand. "You are much too good for me."

"Don't tell her that," said Mr. Stoltz, horrified. "She might believe you!"

"It would be only the truth," Catlin murmured. He released Lindsay's hand as he turned back to the other couple. "What about you, Tom? You know of any Xi'an bronzes for sale?"

Lindsay could barely conceal the shock she felt. Catlin's tone was matter-of-fact again, holding none of the complex emotions that had enthralled her and made her forget where she was and who he was. With fingers that wanted to tremble, she reached for her small glass of Reisling. Forcefully she told herself that she had to stop being taken in by Catlin. With him everything was an act, even passion. Especially passion.

Yet even as she told herself that, she didn't believe it. She had known too many collectors, too many artists, too many scholars, to mistake the truth of the emotion in Catlin's voice when he spoke of history and bronze, greatness and man. He might fake an attraction to her for the sake of the job, but he loved ancient Chinese bronzes as passionately as she did.

"Right, Lindsay?" asked Mr. Stoltz.

Frantically Lindsay tried to recall the conversation that had eddied about her while she thought of passion and bronze and Jacob MacArthur Catlin. Nothing came to her but the realization that, despite the certainty that he was as ruthless in his own way as the long-dead Emperor Qin, Catlin was becoming more and more attractive to her with each moment she spent with him.

"Tom claims that all rumors of Qin mortuary bronzes have ended up being scams of one kind or another," said Catlin, smiling at Lindsay like an indulgent lover.

She took a grip on her fraying concentration and smiled blindly at Catlin—blindly because she refused to really meet his eyes. He was much less distracting when she wasn't caught like a foolish, fluttering insect in their cool amber depths.

"Well, yes," admitted Lindsay. "That's true. But—"

Taking her courage in both hands, Lindsay put her fingertips against Catlin's forearm with the casual intimacy of a woman who is accustomed to a certain man. Immediately she realized that the small embellishment on the act hadn't been a good idea. She wasn't accustomed to Catlin, to feeling the heat and power of him radiating through the dress shirt and dinner jacket. It was unnerving. Before she could snatch back her fingers, his hand came down over hers, firmly holding her captive, caressing her soft skin.

"But I'm—I haven't tried all possible sources for bronzes from Xi'an," Lindsay said quickly. She rushed on, wanting to say what was necessary for the act before her distaste became too obvious. "There are other—other dealers. People I don't usually—'' Her words dried up suddenly. She looked at Catlin in helpless, painful apology.

Catlin wanted to come to Lindsay's aid, to finish the sentences that were sticking in her throat, to somehow make it easier for her to open her mouth and compromise a lifetime of work in a few words. Ruthlessly he controlled the impulse to speak for her. Nothing he could say or do would be one-tenth as convincing to the Stoltzes as the flush on Lindsay's cheeks and the strain in her voice as she offered to sell her vaunted principles for a man.

In the end there was nothing Catlin could do but lift Lindsay's fingers from his sleeve and gently kiss her palm, breathing warmth into flesh that was too cool, almost chilled. Even as he caressed her hand, he knew that he should not. It wasn't part of the act.

Why not? he asked himself harshly. *Just because a man is a ruthless bastard when it comes to collecting bronzes doesn't mean that he's a ruthless bastard when it comes to women.*

The answer came even as the question silently formed. The man called Rousseau had not been noted for his compassion— and he had made no distinction between men and women when it came to getting the job done.

People change, he argued silently with himself.

Sure they do, he retorted. *They die.*

There was no answer to that. There never had been.

Lindsay took a deep breath, letting the warmth of Catlin's caress radiate through her. She smiled at him with real gratitude, knowing that he was trying to make it easier for her to go on with the act. His understanding gave her the courage to keep on talking.

"I—I'm sure I'll be able to find someone, somewhere, somehow," Lindsay said, meeting Catlin's eyes. "There are so many dealers, so many rumors. One of them is bound to lead to a bronze for you. I won't overlook any lead, darling. No matter how—unusual."

At the corner of his vision, Catlin saw the speculative look the Stoltzes exchanged. He brushed his lips across Lindsay's palm again, then folded her fingers over as though to hold the warmth of his caress in place.

"We'll both keep our ears open," said Catlin. "One of us will hear something." He glanced up at the Stoltzes. "If you happen to hear anything, I'd appreciate knowing in time to make a bid. I'm a very generous man. Ask Lindsay."

Mr. Stoltz smiled. "Generous enough to sell a Han hill-censer?"

"If your information led to my acquiring a Qin charioteer, yes."

Mr. Stoltz looked both surprised and excited. "I'll keep it in mind."

"Do that," Catlin said. "More wine, darling?" he asked, shifting his attention to Lindsay.

She shook her head.

"Then perhaps the Stoltzes will excuse us." He moved his head enough to divide a smile equally between husband and wife. "Lindsay has promised to introduce me to the rest of her friends."

Lindsay felt the heat of Catlin's big hand through the thin silk of her blouse as he guided her between tables and open spaces toward a group of people across the room. Half humorously, half seriously she decided that in the future she would wear clothes that were thick enough to remove any sense of intimacy from Catlin's casual touches. Medieval armor, perhaps, or its modern equivalent.

"What are you smiling about?" Catlin asked, bending down until his lips brushed the shining thickness of her hair.

"Bulletproof vests," she said softly.

One thick, very black eyebrow arched upward. "What about them?"

"Do they conduct heat well?"

"No."

Lindsay realized that Catlin was serious. "Are they heavy?"

"The new ones aren't. Quite comfortable, all things considered. Why? Thinking of getting one?"

"It occurred to me," she said dryly.

Ignoring the people circulating around them, Catlin stopped and turned Lindsay toward him. He put his hands on either side of her face, holding her gently, irrevocably in place.

"I'll protect you, Lindsay. I swear it," he whispered against her mouth. The words were too soft for anyone to overhear and they were sealed with a slow kiss. When he lifted his head it was to look into eyes as pure and blue as high-mountain twilight. "But if you want body armor," he added, nuzzling her lips, "I'll get it for you. Do you?"

Lindsay shut her eyes, feeling off balance again. Catlin had touched her often enough in the last few hours that she should be getting used to it. She was not. She was becoming more sensitized to his caresses, not less.

"Will it protect me from your touch?" she asked helplessly.

Catlin heard the desire and the truth in Lindsay's question. The honesty of her response to him was more potent than any aphrodisiac. Hunger quickened in him, the hunger he had first felt when he saw the soft outline of her breasts while she bent over a table of bronzes. A hot wave of desire swept through him before it focused low in his body, letting him count every heartbeat in the growing heaviness of his sex. The speed and force of his response caught him unaware. He had few defenses against honesty, because he had known so little of it from women—or men.

"You are too goddamned honest," Catlin said softly, distinctly, wanting to kiss Lindsay again and not trusting himself to stop with just one kiss. "I don't think they make Kevlar chastity belts. Too bad. One of us sure as hell is going to need it before this is over."

"Kevlar?" asked Lindsay, grasping the only safe part of the conversation that he had offered to her.

"That's what body armor is made out of."

"Oh." She laughed a little shakily and then took a deep breath. "I think maybe I'd better have some more wine. Maybe a lot more."

"I think that's a really lousy idea."

He turned her around, put his hand in the small of her back and pushed her toward a group where a redhead in a black sheath and scarlet bugle beads was describing Chinese bronzes with graceful sweeps of her long-nailed hands.

"That's the famous Ms. Merriman, isn't it?" Catlin asked softly.

Lindsay looked away from Catlin's face, saw the blaze of red hair and nails, and agreed. "That's Jackie."

"Anyone with her we should meet?"

"The man on her left, I guess. Mitch Malloy. I wonder who had the bad taste to invite him tonight?"

"What's wrong with him?"

"Nothing, if you like slime mold," Lindsay said in a voice that went no farther than Catlin. "Malloy sells spurious bronzes," she explained. "He sells them very carefully, mind you, and mainly to nouveau riche out-of-towners. But he sells bad bronzes just the same. It's rumored that he sells others that are genuine enough, but not very honestly come by. That's only rumor, though."

"Our kind of guy."

Lindsay's mouth flattened. "If you say so."

"I do. Anyone else?"

"I don't recognize the woman. One of Mitch's, I suppose. The man to Jackie's right is Sam Wang, her latest lover. He's from either San Francisco or Vancouver, depending on which gossip you believe. Some have him born of a French colonel and an ethnic Chinese woman living in Vietnam. Others say he's Taiwanese. Others say his family has been American since the first railroad was built." She shrugged. "You get the idea. Everybody knows something about Sam, but nobody agrees on just what. Except one thing. He gets his hands on some truly stunning bronzes from time to time."

"Dubious provenance?"

Lindsay hesitated. "I don't think so. Sam's family still has ties overseas, and he's well connected to refugee communities all over the West Coast. Family treasures that are being sold to finance resettlement in a new land could easily come to him first. In that he's like Hsiang Wu, an old friend of my family. Wu was a respected man in Shaanxi before the revolution. Newcomers seek him out and old-time residents ask his advice. Naturally, the results show up in Wu's antique shop."

Catlin waited, but Lindsay didn't go on to point out that a man like Sam Wang or Hsiang Wu was in a perfect position to fence stolen bronzes under a cover of eminent respectability. "Is Wu honest?" asked Catlin, keeping his voice low.

"Of course," said Lindsay instantly. She looked at Catlin with wide, shocked eyes. "Wu was my mentor. He taught me a great deal about how to tell genuine from fraudulent. He would allow no dubious merchandise in his shop. I know, Catlin. I was in and out of his shop every day until I moved to Washington. I still see him whenever I visit my aunt."

"And Sam Wang? What's his reputation?"

Lindsay shrugged. "If you collected bronze seriously at one time, you know what the art business is like. Everybody is slandered, most of the time without much cause. Sam comes in for his share of it, but nobody has caught him in anything dishonest or even truly dubious."

"That's hopeful."

"It is? Why? Aren't we looking for thieves?" asked Lindsay, her voice very low.

"I doubt that the Chinese thieves, whoever they are, would trust their treasures to an idiot with a bad reputation," murmured Catlin, brushing his lips over Lindsay's hair as though he were whispering endearments to her.

"But an honest person wouldn't handle stolen goods," objected Lindsay.

"Who said they were stolen?" he whispered.

Lindsay looked at Catlin for a long moment. "Are you saying they aren't?" she whispered.

"Let's get me introduced around," he said, his voice normal again.

Lindsay started to press Catlin, to ask again if the Qin mortuary bronzes were indeed stolen goods. Then she remembered

Catlin's warning about questions and lies. Apparently this was one of the times when he simply wasn't going to answer.

Without a word Lindsay allowed Catlin to guide her toward the group he had selected. As she had half expected, Jackie wasn't overjoyed to see her. Jackie was one of those women who preferred to be the undivided center of whatever male attention was available. Then she glanced over Lindsay's shoulder to the tall man standing behind her. If there was one thing Jackie appreciated more than an outstanding bronze, it was an outstanding man.

"Lindsay," said Jackie, smiling widely, "how marvelous to see you here tonight. I heard Steve was sick. Nothing serious, I hope?"

Lindsay murmured something appropriate and smiled professionally as the introductions went around. Catlin's smile matched hers in sincerity and social polish. She was relieved to see that he made no overt response to the frankly sexual signals Jackie was sending out. Pretending to be Catlin's lover was difficult enough for Lindsay. Pretending to be one of a slumber party would be beyond her acting abilities. It also would be so far out of her known character as to be unbelievable, no matter how intense her supposed infatuation.

"And this is Sam Wang," Jackie concluded, resting her fingertips on the back of Catlin's forearm as she urged him closer to her side. She looked up at him out of large gray eyes. "You're new to the art scene, aren't you?" she murmured.

"Not really," said Catlin. He switched his attention to Sam Wang. The Eurasian's calm expression was at odds with the bleak calculation of his eyes. Catlin had met a lot of people like that. He smiled, feeling better about the prospect of the night not being a total loss in terms of coming closer to Qin's charioteer. "I've been looking forward to meeting you, Mr. Wang. Lindsay told me that you come up with some astonishing bronzes from time to time."

Wang gave Lindsay an enigmatic look. "Did she?"

"Do you?" Catlin asked, smiling.

Wang made a dismissive gesture with his hand. "What is astonishing?"

"One of Emperor Qin's bronze charioteers," Catlin said succinctly.

There was a hissing sound in the instant before Wang controlled his surprise. "Astonishing indeed," he said quietly. "As well as very, very valuable. You have such a bronze?"

"I want such a bronze."

Wang's eyes crinkled slightly. His laugh was soft, surprisingly low. "So do I, Mr. Catlin. So do I!"

"For yourself or for sale?"

There was a moment of silence, then Wang sighed. "For sale, I'm afraid. That's too much capital for me to tie up in a single piece of art."

"Not for me," Catlin said distinctly. He looked from Wang to Malloy to Jackie. "I'll pay a generous finder's fee."

"What about Lindsay?" asked Jackie, looking at the other woman with barely restrained curiosity.

"Lindsay will authenticate the bronze," Catlin said flatly, "no matter who I buy it from." He turned and drew Lindsay to his side, running his fingertips from her cheekbone to the pulse beating just beneath the soft skin of her throat. "Won't you, honey?"

"Yes," answered Lindsay. She hated the husky sound of her voice but could do nothing to control it. She reacted to Catlin's presence, his touch, his heat—even though she knew it was all an act. The pragmatic side of her mind consoled her with the fact that the throaty, sandbagged-by-passion voice added immeasurably to what otherwise might be an unconvincing performance on her own part.

Catlin smiled and caressed Lindsay's bottom lip with his thumb, bringing a stain of color to her clear cheeks. "That's my honey cat. With you, I'll never be cheated or surprised, will I?"

Mutely, Lindsay shook her head because she didn't trust herself to open her mouth. She didn't know whether she would answer Catlin's rhetorical question or bite his caressing thumb;

and if she did bite, she didn't know if it would be in retaliation or in sensual provocation.

If she had thought Catlin were simply teasing her for the sake of watching her response, she would have walked away and left him standing there. But he wasn't enjoying teasing her. There was neither laughter nor cruelty in his eyes, simply the cold calculation of a man who had learned to survive in hell.

A good teacher. The best. She had no complaints coming.

Lindsay's head came up with new determination. She gave Jackie the kind of look usually reserved for dubious art. "I've promised Catlin his charioteer," Lindsay said simply. "I'll remember anyone who helps me."

Catlin shot Lindsay a sideways glance, hearing the ring of certainty in her voice. His expression changed subtly, shifting from approving lover to just plain approval. Do unto others. Period.

"That's what attracted me to Lindsay," said Catlin, slanting her a very male smile. "She gives as good as she gets."

Both Malloy and Wang looked at Lindsay with new interest, for there was no mistaking the fact that her lover was obviously satisfied. That kind of satisfaction raised interesting sexual speculations in other men.

"I'll remember that if I ever need anyone to vet my bronzes," Malloy said, smiling meaningfully at the small blond woman who had been standing silently, patiently, by his side throughout the entire conversation.

"Don't count on it," Catlin said, his voice cool. "The service I get from Lindsay is exclusive."

"Does that work both ways?" asked Jackie, smiling innocently up at him.

"Yes," said Lindsay, before Catlin could answer.

"Well." Jackie shrugged, looking at Lindsay. "I can see you haven't changed *that* much. You still have a high opinion of yourself." She lifted her hand from Catlin's sleeve as she turned back toward him. "I have some bronze harness pieces that are either Warring States or Qin. Would you be interested?"

"I'm always interested in good bronzes."

Jackie smiled. "Ten o'clock tomorrow?"

"Fine."

"Where are you staying?"

"Lindsay's place."

There was a fractional pause. "Oh. In that case, just tell the cab driver to—"

"That's all right," Lindsay interrupted smoothly. "I know the way. That is, unless the harness pieces are displayed in your home?"

"It's settled, then," Jackie said brightly, ignoring Lindsay's rather sarcastic question. "I'll see you at my shop at ten."

Catlin turned to Wang. "Will you be there? I'd like to talk more about bronzes with you. It's been a few years since I've actively collected. Frankly," he added, smiling, "all that lured me out of retirement was the chance of getting one of Qin's bronze charioteers."

"Unfortunately, I'm going back to the Coast tomorrow, but—" Wang turned toward Lindsay. A smile transformed his face from merely handsome into the kind of riveting male beauty that was distinctly Eurasian, flawless without being in the least feminine. "Are you going to be out my way anytime soon? I just received two animals from the Hsing-p'ing district of Shaanxi that are quite remarkable. I'm sure Mr. Catlin would like to see them."

"Third century?" asked Lindsay, answering the charming smile with one of her own. "Inlaid?"

Wang nodded. "I wouldn't bother a woman of your taste with anything less."

She blinked, hardly able to believe that Wang was sending out seductive signals to her. The last time she had met him, he had been impeccably polite, no more. If it hadn't been for Jackie's suddenly narrowed gray eyes, Lindsay would have thought she was being overly sensitive. Then Catlin's hand settled heavily on the nape of her neck, underlining the accuracy of her judgment. The handsome Mr. Wang was definitely on the make. But did he want her, or simply an entrée into Catlin's wallet? Did Wang feel that if one man controlled her with sex, so could another?

"Lovely," murmured Lindsay. She tilted her head toward Catlin. "Will we be going out to the Coast soon, darling?"

"I'll go wherever I can find good bronzes," he said flatly.

"Then I can safely say that I'll be seeing you," Wang said, holding out his hand first to Lindsay, then Catlin. "The best bronzes pass through Vancouver or San Francisco." He smiled. "I have shops in both cities." He turned, dropped a casual kiss on Jackie's beautifully outlined lips and said, "I have to run. My plane leaves at an ungodly hour."

After Wang left, the group around Jackie fragmented. Catlin and Lindsay drifted off to find new dealers, announce their new status as lovers and seekers of a Qin charioteer, and move on again. The pattern was repeated until after midnight, when Lindsay finally drew Catlin aside.

"I think we've done enough damage to my reputation and feet for one night," she muttered.

"Home?"

"Home."

As soon as they were outside, Lindsay glanced around to see if they were alone. Catlin saw the gesture, understood and pulled her very close to his side.

"Questions?" he said very softly.

"I know that for the sake of appearances we have to stay together, but why are we using my place instead of yours?"

"I have maid service."

"So?"

"So anyone who's interested can slip her a ten and find out if we slept in the same bed."

"Oh."

"Yeah. Oh. Unless you have a maid, too?" asked Catlin.

"Uh, no."

"Figures. No maid and the world's shortest, lumpiest couch." He made a disgusted sound. "Flip you for the bed?"

Lindsay gave Catlin a sideways look. "With what, a two-headed coin?"

Catlin's smile was as dark as the night around him. "No, with half a coin. That way nobody wins and everybody loses."

"What?"

There was no answer.

A few hours before, Lindsay would have asked the question again. In the small hours of night, she did not. She was learning very quickly.

As Catlin's fingers closed around the mutilated coin in his pocket, he hoped that very quickly was fast enough.

9

*THE SHADOWS came again, rising out of a
black well as deep as time. But the shadows
themselves weren't black. They were a sticky, glistening red.
They poured through her hands endlessly, yet still more shadows rose out of the well, a red tide lapping up over her feet, her
knees, her hips, her waist, rising, rising, while red poured hotly
through her cold fingers. She couldn't stem the deadly tide, she
couldn't run, she couldn't hide, she couldn't breathe, she was
choking, no air, red strangling her until—*

Lindsay sat up in bed with a smothered cry.

The irrational part of her mind wanted to scream in fear as
primal as the bloody shadows waiting to claim her when she
slept again. The rational part of her mind knew instantly that
she was safe, it was just the dream again, the nightmare that
always came in times of stress and had come so frequently since
her mother had died.

With fumbling fingers, Lindsay turned toward her bedside
light. In the instant before she screamed, she realized that the
shadow standing in the doorway was black, not red.

"Bad dreams, Lindsay?"

She swallowed the scream clawing at her throat as she recognized Catlin's deep voice. Numbly she searched for the light
switch.

"Yes. The dream. Again." Her voice was tight, a stranger's
voice. The light came on and Lindsay wished she had screamed
while she had had the excuse of the nightmare.

Catlin was naked but for the blue-steel shine of the gun in his
right hand. There was nothing seductive about the muscles
shifting and coiling beneath his skin with each movement of his
body as he walked toward her, nor was there seduction in the
controlled intensity of his yellow eyes watching her. He was a

predator, not a lover, and as deadly as the gun gleaming in his hand.

Catlin's glance went automatically around the room. He found what he had expected to find since he had heard Lindsay's choked cry—a nightmare rather than an attacker. He flicked on the gun's safety with a casual gesture that spoke of long experience with weapons.

"Want to talk?" he asked matter-of-factly.

Lindsay made a guttural sound that could have been laughter or despair. "With a naked man carrying a loaded pistol? My God in heaven, Catlin, where did the FBI find you!"

"They didn't." He walked out of the room, reappearing a moment later. His hands were empty and he was wearing a pair of comfortably faded jeans. "Better?" he asked.

She let out a long breath. "I think so."

For an instant Lindsay was tempted to ask if he owned a shirt, too, something to cover the dark invitation of the hair curling across his chest and arrowing down below his narrow waist. She closed her eyes and her mouth, knowing that was one question she would not ask. Now was definitely not the moment to let her thoughts wander. She was too vulnerable. She was also too proud to seduce a man who wanted nothing more from her than an act.

And she had no doubt that an act was all that Catlin wanted. The instant the door had closed behind them that night, his loving touches and indulgent smiles had vanished. He had made her stand just inside the apartment while he checked out each room. He had refused her offer of a nightcap and politely waited while she used the apartment's sole bathroom to get ready for bed. Feeling self-conscious and uneasy, she had emerged from the bathroom in a simple burgundy silk nightgown, which was the only nightwear she owned that wasn't nearly transparent. Even so, she knew that the gown clung to her breasts and hips and made her skin glow as though lit from within.

If she had any doubts whether Catlin found her as attractive as she found him, they had died when she walked past him in the narrow hall. He had looked at her as though she were a piece of furniture. It was as if they had been together so long that there was nothing left between them, not even good memories. The moment reminded her all too painfully of the man she had married in the full flush of hopeful youth, and had been divorced by five years later, when neither one of them could think of any reason to stay together, good or bad.

"Lindsay?" asked Catlin, his voice gritty with the aftermath of the adrenaline that had yanked him from sleep when she had cried out. "Are you sure you're all right?"

Slowly she opened her eyes, preferring the difficult, uncertain present to the irretrievable certainty of the past. Besides, if she were lucky, the nightmare wouldn't come again. Not tonight. Maybe even not tomorrow night.

And if it did, then she would get through the nights as she always had. Alone.

"Fine," she said hollowly. "The nightmare always comes when I'm under unusual stress."

Catlin said nothing for the simple reason that there was little he could say. The stress Lindsay was under would get worse, not better, but there was no point in telling her that at three in the morning, when emotion screamed that dawn was too far away to be believed. He knew all about the dark hours of the soul and the unbridgeable gap between fear and sunrise.

"What do you do for it?" he asked, his tone low, soothing.

"The stress?"

"Yes."

She shrugged. "I work a little harder at my *tai chi chuan* in the morning and try to tell my subconscious that I'm thirty, not seven, and China is far, far away, over and beyond the curve of the earth."

"Do you talk with anyone?"

"Once in a while. Larry never understood."

Catlin knew who Larry was but he asked the question anyway, for Lindsay knew nothing of the file locked in Catlin's safe. "Larry?"

"My first and last husband." Lindsay's mouth turned down at the corner. "Poor Larry. He thought he was marrying a respectable Lutheran missionary child who would love, honor and obey in silence no matter what a jerk he was."

Catlin's laughter made Lindsay wish that they were what they were supposed to be. Lovers. She would have given a great deal to curl up in his arms, to touch the roughly curling hair on his chest with her lips, to fall asleep hearing his heart beat beneath her cheek.

It was more than the comfort Catlin could offer her that made Lindsay want to lie next to him. She had had the nightmare many times in the past, and sometimes there had been a man beside her in bed. Illusory comfort. She would have been better off alone. No one had understood that a platitude and a pat on the head enraged rather than eased her. Because her would-be comforters had seen nothing of sudden, inexplicable, violent death, they had assumed that it existed only in her mind and could be exorcised by a condescending shrink at one hundred dollars an hour.

She had learned not to hope for comfort from men. Yet somewhere, at a level as deep as the nightmare itself, Lindsay sensed that Catlin was different. He understood that horror was real. He understood that it could cast a shadow across time and distance, consuming both, leaving only horror itself. Horror was something that you lived with every day.

And sometimes at night you dreamed.

"Thank you," said Lindsay, lying back with a sigh, feeling the last of the shadows slide back down into the bottomless well of the past.

"For what?" Catlin asked.

"For not patronizing me. For knowing that horror is real." Lindsay smiled crookedly. "For being an understanding kind of genuine bastard, I guess."

"But still a genuine bastard?" he asked softly, his voice as dark as the night beyond the curtained window.

"Oh, yes. You taught me that very well, Catlin," Lindsay said, her smile fading as she remembered the ease with which he had aroused her and then had turned away from her, all business, a candle burning in ice, brilliance without warmth. "I'll try not to forget. I don't think my pride could take another lesson like that."

"Lindsay," Catlin said urgently, "I didn't want to hurt you. It was—"

"I know," she interrupted, reaching for the bedside light again. "It was necessary. Good night, Catlin."

Lindsay didn't know how long he stood in her bedroom doorway, not moving, not speaking. She wondered what he was thinking, what he was feeling, but she fell asleep before dawn revealed his expression.

She slept deeply, awakening to the fragrance of coffee steaming at her bedside table. Catlin was leaning casually on the doorframe as though he had spent the night there, thinking of just the right question to ask to explode her sleepy contentment.

"Are you on the pill?"

"What?"

"Contraceptives," he said, sipping from the mug he held in his hand. "Or would you leave it to your lover to take care of that little detail?"

"Only if he could get pregnant instead of me," Lindsay retorted instantly.

Catlin's mustache shifted over his faint smile. "I thought you'd feel that way about it, but I couldn't find any contraceptives in your bathroom. Do you keep them in the bedside table?"

Lindsay took a slow breath and reminded herself that she was always volatile in the first few moments of waking. It was as though her intelligence woke up more slowly than her visceral responses, which at the moment were telling her to yell at Catlin that it was none of his damned business what she did or did not have in the way of contraceptives.

"At the moment, I don't need contraceptives," she pointed out reasonably.

"We're the only ones who know that. Let's keep it that way."

"Catlin, that's ridiculous!" she exploded.

"So is wearing a seat belt—until the day your luck goes sour."

Lindsay's mouth opened, then snapped shut. He was the teacher. She was the student. And this was supposed to be a guided tour of the lower regions.

"Right," she said through her teeth. "I'll take care of it."

"Today."

"Right," she snarled. "Today! Any other little thing on your devilish mind?"

"Do you always wake up sassy?" he asked, smiling faintly as he took another sip of coffee.

"Do you always wake up insufferable?"

Catlin sipped his coffee for a moment, then gave up and laughed, shaking his head. "Never an unspoken thought. It could be addictive, that kind of honesty. And dangerous as hell."

"The door is closed, remember?" she muttered. "I don't have to act like a moonstruck teenager." She took a cautious sip of coffee. Strong but not bitter, with a flavor to break her heart. He had found her secret cache of gourmet coffee and put it to marvelous use. She took another sip and smiled in pure sensual pleasure. "I forgive you. For this coffee, I would forgive the devil himself."

"I'll remember that. Stone called."

"Speaking of the devil, right?" Lindsay glanced at the bedside clock. Seven thirty-eight. "Early bird, isn't he?"

"With a mouthful of worms."

"Ugh. Catlin, please. What an awful image."

His smile flashed again beneath his black mustache. "He wants to talk to you after we see Jackie."

"Just me?"

"Just you," said Catlin. What he didn't say was that he suspected that the topic under discussion would be Catlin himself. He didn't mind. The questions Lindsay asked him when she came back would tell him what the FBI knew, what they didn't know and what they wanted to know. "I've got an appointment over at the Senate, anyway."

She opened her mouth to ask the obvious questions—who and why. Then she remembered that she wasn't supposed to ask questions. With a stifled curse she went back to appreciating the unexpected gift of good coffee served to her in bed. From the corner of her eye she caught Catlin's small, approving nod.

"Am I permitted to ask when you'll be back?" she murmured.

"You just did," pointed out Catlin. "Where do you want to have lunch?"

"I don't eat lunch."

"You do today. We're going to stroll hand in hand through some of the more public bronze exhibits."

"Wh—Damn! Oh, to hell with it!" she said in exasperation, tired of stifling her very active curiosity before she was even fully awake. "Why?"

Catlin laughed softly, shaking his head. "To see who follows us, naturally."

Abruptly Lindsay felt her irritation replaced by sudden uneasiness. "Why would anyone follow us?" she asked before she could stop herself.

"To see where we're going."

"Thank you," she said gravely. "Thank you all to bloody hell."

"Anytime, honey cat," he said, amused and approving at the same time. "Anytime at all."

A frisson rippled through Lindsay at the endearment, for there was nothing patronizing about Catlin's manner this morning. "The door is closed, Catlin," she pointed out, subduing the natural huskiness of her voice with an effort.

"Yeah. I kept reminding myself of that fact the whole time I watched you sleep. Wish to hell you were another kind of woman, Lindsay. The casual kind." Catlin drained the rest of his coffee with a quick movement. When he spoke again, his tone was as controlled as the line of his mouth. "How do you like your eggs?"

"Without shell."

"I think I can manage that. How long do you take in the shower?"

"Ten minutes."

"Breakfast in eleven."

"Fifteen," Lindsay said firmly. "I don't want to drip on my toast."

"Who said anything about toast?"

"I did. I refuse to face naked eggs. Now vanish so that I can get out of bed."

Slowly Catlin shook his head. "We're supposed to be lovers, remember?"

"Only when the door is open."

Catlin sighed. "Look, Lindsay, this act of ours isn't going to have a sinner's chance in hell if your deepest reflex is away from rather than toward intimacy."

"What do you mean?"

"Christ," hissed Catlin between his teeth. "Half the time you flinch when I touch you. You touch me reluctantly, if at all. You're as wary as a stray cat. You act like you've never been in a bedroom with a man in your life."

"And you act like you've been in too many bedrooms with too many women. You call that intimate?" Lindsay made a sound of disgust. "A man your age should know the difference between intimacy and getting his ashes hauled."

She threw aside the covers and came to her feet in a single motion. Wine-colored silk swirled down her thighs in a shimmer of color. Without a word or a look, she stalked past Catlin into the hall.

Catlin's silence followed Lindsay into the shower, fading only beneath the thunder of water against lime-green tile. When she came out feeling refreshed if not renewed, the smell of sourdough toast tempted her palate. Hurriedly she put on her underwear and a short terrycloth robe. As she walked into the kitchen, Catlin looked up from the scrambled eggs he was spooning out of the frying pan onto two plates.

"See, I'm good for something," he said.

Lindsay looked at Catlin quickly, wondering if he were angry at her for her remark about the difference between intimacy and casual sex. His expression gave away little, but she was learning to read him. He was amused rather than angry with her, for the line of his mouth beneath the black mustache was relaxed, curling up slightly at the left corner. She had the distinct feeling that she was a novelty to Catlin, that most people walked very lightly around him when they couldn't avoid him entirely.

"Catlin," she said huskily. "I'm sure you're good for many, many things. But one of them isn't me, is it?"

Catlin's breath came in hard as Lindsay's honesty went through him like a razor, slicing away everything but pain and the truth. "No," he agreed, "one of them isn't you."

Lindsay looked at Catlin's yellow eyes and felt as though she had just stepped into the same black well from which her nightmares emerged. Except it was day, not night, and Catlin lived within those shadows all the time. Shadows weren't a transient dream state with him. They were the kind of reality that made him come out of deep sleep with a loaded gun in his hand when other men would still be lying in a daze, wondering if they were awake or asleep.

But those men would be dead before the answer came, and Catlin would be alive.

Lindsay looked at Catlin, really looked at him, knowing and accepting that he had lived with violence and survived by violence. With acceptance came the thought that it was a pity her uncle hadn't been more like Catlin. Then her uncle wouldn't have trusted the wrong person at the wrong time. Betrayal and death. That was what she had always wanted to ask her mother and had never found the nerve: *Do you know who betrayed Uncle Matt?*

"Jam?" asked Catlin, holding out a jar.

Lindsay looked at the strawberry preserves, shuddered and sat down. With an effort she dragged her mind away from the past that kept getting tangled in nightmares, a dark red tide of shadows rising. "No, thanks."

Catlin was content to eat in silence, grateful that Lindsay wasn't one of those people who had to be talking all the time in order to know that she was alive. Silence was a commodity that most Americans and almost all Chinese simply didn't appreciate. With Americans it was electronic noise. With Chinese it was the endless uproar of the extended family.

The comfortable silence held until Catlin and Lindsay went out into the street. While Washington wasn't as noisy as Manhattan, it was still a city, complete with competing horns and sidewalk construction.

The hushed, air-conditioned elegance of Jackie's small shop was located on Connecticut Avenue between the Mayflower Hotel and Dupont Circle. A gilt sign on the shop door advised that admittance was by appointment only, but Jackie's assistant let them in before Catlin's finger touched the buzzer.

They were taken to Jackie's office in a genteel rush that made it impossible to linger over the eclectic selections of Chinese objets d'art that were carefully displayed throughout the showroom. The carpet on the floor was luxuriant, absorbing every sound, and elegant porcelain glowed within ebony cabinets. The air smelled of furniture polish and the fresh roses that were Jackie's trademark.

As Catlin and Lindsay approached the office, his hand settled on the nape of her neck in a casual caress. She felt a sudden, involuntary change in her heartbeat and told herself again that she was a fool. Her mind agreed. Her body ignored everything but the warmth radiating through her from the rough palm gently stroking her nape, urging her closer to Catlin's body with each movement.

For a moment Lindsay almost stopped walking, not knowing how to deal with her own reaction. *What would I do if we were really lovers and I didn't give a damn who knew it?* she asked herself harshly, trying to still the conflict between her intelligence telling her to pull away from Catlin and her body telling her to get close, closer, closer still.

There was no answer except the obvious, dangerous one. The longer she was with Catlin, the more he intrigued her, and she was too honest not to admit it to herself. She had never known a man whose mind was so complex and yet so utterly pragmatic, a man whose reflexes were those of a hunter and yet whose touch was both sensitive and exquisitely erotic. Wryly she admitted to herself that if Catlin were truly her lover, chances were that she wouldn't be walking around right now. She'd be in bed, welcoming him into her body, moving with him, wanting him as she'd never wanted another man, knowing him as she longed to know him—intimately.

Which was precisely the response that the act required.

Gradually Lindsay gave in to the sensuality that she usually kept well under the control of her practical mind. She turned her head slowly from side to side, increasing the pressure of Catlin's palm on her neck, caressing him in turn as her hair slid over his hand. She sensed the instant of surprise, the almost imperceptible hesitation of his hand, and then the caress came back to her redoubled. His long fingers eased through her hair, seeking the warmth of her scalp, rubbing slowly until she shivered and turned toward him with lips parted in silent invitation.

"Catlin, Lindsay, how good of you to be on time," said Jackie, walking briskly out of her office to meet them. She glanced at Catlin's expression and the stain of color on Lindsay's cheeks, and added dryly, "Didn't get you out of bed, did I? You really ought to set your alarm earlier. That way you have time for, um, everything."

"We did," murmured Catlin, smiling down at Lindsay before he turned toward Jackie. "Haven't you ever wanted seconds?"

Jackie smiled. "Will you settle for coffee?" she asked, gesturing them ahead of her into the office. She tipped a crimson-nailed hand toward an ebony table heaped with various pastries. "I can recommend the croissants and the scones. After that you're on your own, although Sam swears by those sticky buns oozing with jam."

"We've eaten, thanks," Lindsay said.

"I'll bet you have," muttered Jackie, smiling as she slanted a sideways look at Catlin. "Coffee?"

"Not now, thanks. We're on a tight schedule," Catlin said, returning Jackie's smile with interest.

Lindsay noticed that the smile went no farther than Catlin's teeth. He was in what she had come to think of as his "work mode." Fully involved, fully alert, fully ruthless, a hunter hidden beneath a white cotton shirt, fawn slacks and a linen jacket cut so that it wouldn't tent over the gun in the small of his back.

Catlin glanced beyond Jackie to a table covered by a rich black velvet cloth. Various bronze artifacts had been set out. All of them were in hues of blue-green, wordless testimony to the passage of time etched deeply into bronze that had been buried in water-soaked earth. Slowly, thoroughly, Catlin began to evaluate the artifacts.

"Sorry to seem rude," he said without looking up from his study, "but I'm expected on the Hill in an hour."

"Then I'll leave you and Lindsay to it," said Jackie, walking toward the door with the alacrity of a good salesman who knows that no further pitch is required. "If you have any questions, I'll be in the back."

Catlin nodded. Still without taking his eyes from the bronzes, he held out his hand to Lindsay. After a very slight hesitation, she took it. He drew her to his side, leaned down and brushed his lips caressingly from her cheekbone to the curve of her ear.

"The door is still open," he said, looking intently at her to make sure that she understood. His voice was a bare thread of sound that carried less distance than a whisper but was easier to understand. "The whole shop is on closed-circuit TV."

Lindsay turned her face into Catlin's neck and tried to imitate his very soft voice. "I know."

He nodded, released her and went back to looking at the bronzes as though they were the only thing on his mind.

Lindsay stood beside Catlin patiently, not knowing whether the bronzes truly interested him. There was nothing on the table that she would recommend to a serious collector of third century B.C. Chinese bronzes, except perhaps some of the small

harness pieces at the end of the table. Even that recommenda-
tion was doubtful until she had a chance to examine them very
closely, which was what Catlin was doing now.

In fact, the only piece that truly interested Lindsay was a
kuei, a deep circular food dish with a graceful foot-ring and
spreading lip. Two handles in the shape of sinuous, exotic animals were set vertically on opposite sides of the bowl. At some
point in the bowl's history it had been broken and repaired. The
work had been done expertly, with every attempt made to
match the color and texture of the repaired surface to the rest
of the patina. But even the delicate, expert use of various
chemicals to induce rapid corrosion in the newer bronze hadn't
wholly concealed the seam that ran diagonally through the
bowl.

The fact that the vessel had been repaired made it much less
valuable as an objet d'art in a market where intact bronze bowls
were not difficult to find. Most collectors would have passed
over the *kuei* without a second look. But Lindsay was caught
by an indefinable quality of the bowl that transcended its battered history. The shape of the vessel itself was superbly executed, capturing the sense of a belly rounded with good food
and plentiful harvests. The aura of repletion about the bronze
was almost smug, a curving proclamation through the ages that
the bowl embodied the very idea of nourishment rather than
merely holding food until the moment of serving.

Somewhere between concept and execution, the bronze *kuei*
had slipped over that very elusive yet unmistakable boundary
between artifact and art. To Lindsay that was more important
than the marks left on the bowl during its remarkable odyssey
of survival through China's violent history.

"Lindsay."

"Yes?" she answered, looking up from the sinuous, ab-
stract dragon designs that wrapped the bowl, proclaiming that
its creators lived in very late Chou or early Han times. Or perhaps even in the dynasty between. Qin's dynasty.

"What do you think of this one?" asked Catlin, extending
his hand toward her.

Reluctantly Lindsay set aside the bowl and went to Catlin. Nestled between the base of his thumb and the curious ridge of callus at the edge of his palm was a roughly circular object. The circle was made by the body of an animal whose head was touching its tail, making an unbroken ring. The result was an object used either for personal adornment or for decorating a horse's harness.

"May I?" asked Lindsay, reaching for the small bronze ornament.

"Anytime," Catlin said immediately, smiling and running his fingertips down the inside of her wrist as she lifted the tiny bronze from his palm.

The distracting caress almost made Lindsay drop the bronze. "Catlin," she said warningly.

He smiled as he withdrew his hand, but his eyes were opaque, unflinching. He had decided that it was time to push Lindsay hard. If she blew up in his hands now, no one would die of it. Especially her.

"I'll be good," he promised.

"That's the problem," she retorted, looking at the small circular bronze. "You're too good already."

"Am I?" he asked, his voice deep. "Then I guess I'll just have to be bad, won't I?" He bent over and fastened his teeth delicately on the rim of her ear. "Very, very bad."

"The mind falters," she muttered.

Catlin laughed softly, another kind of caress. His hand slid up Lindsay's arm and closed on her breast with the assured sensuality of a lover. Instantly he found her nipple, drawing forth a response that was all too clear against the thin cotton of her dress.

"Catlin!" said Lindsay, caught between shock and reaction to his wholly unexpected caress.

"I know," he said, tracing her stunned mouth with the tip of his tongue even as his fingers teased her breast skillfully. "This isn't the time or the place." His tone was rough, thick, the voice of a man whose blood was running heavily, hotly. "But damn it, you're driving me crazy teasing me like this."

The injustice of the accusation robbed Lindsay of words. It was just as well, for she had forgotten about any watchers who might be monitoring a TV screen in a hidden room. Her whole body tightened as Catlin's hand teased the erect tip of her breast. Her breath came out in a rush that was almost a moan.

"You b—" she began, only to have her words overridden.

"Yes," he said thickly. "Me. All over you, licking up all that warm, wild honey."

Catlin's hands moved repeatedly, urgently, from Lindsay's shoulders to her hips. He kissed her with a force that left her stunned. All that kept her from striking out at him in rebellion was the knowledge that the door was open and she had a role to play.

And even more compelling was the evidence of Catlin's own desire pressing against the confinement of his fawn slacks. The knowledge that she wasn't alone in the sudden flaring of passion swept over Lindsay, catching her up in the act as thoroughly as Catlin himself. She thrust her fingers into his thick black hair and let him mold her body to his, giving back a kiss as hot as the one she was receiving.

"God, I don't know if I can wait until tonight," he growled, lifting his head and looking at her reddened lips with hungry intent.

For an instant Lindsay believed the hunger of Catlin's mouth poised over hers, the intensity of his eyes as he searched for signs of her response. He was the picture of a man passionately involved in a woman. She wanted the act to be true. She wanted it with a force that pulled her apart.

What frightened her was that he seemed to want it, too.

"Enough," she whispered, because she could barely breathe, much less speak aloud, "I can't take any more right now."

Catlin looked into Lindsay's eyes. They were dilated with emotion until they were more black than blue. He felt the involuntary shiver that went through her when his hips shifted against her body.

Too honest, he thought angrily. *Wrong woman. Wrong time. Wrong place. Everything wrong. Except the act. It's intact. She didn't blow up—she just came apart in my hands as though she had been created for me.*

Catlin swore beneath his breath and released Lindsay. "Back to the bronzes?" he asked roughly.

Lindsay closed her hand over the small, circular ornament until the age-roughened edges bit into her soft skin. "Back to the bronzes," she agreed in a voice that was too strained to be her own.

"What do you think of them?" he asked a few moments later.

"Which one?" she asked, wishing she had one-tenth the control Catlin had, angry with him for being such an accomplished actor when she was merely an accomplished fool.

"Pick one," he said sardonically. "Any one. Hey, how about the one in your hand?"

"Catlin, Jacob MacArthur, G.B.," retorted Lindsay.

He smiled with a warmth that surprised her. "Hold the good thought, honey cat."

Lindsay opened her hand, hating the fact that her fingers were trembling but unable to conceal it. "You have a good eye," she said. "It's the best of the lot. The design is still clear, the proportions are pleasing, and it's genuine."

As Lindsay talked about the familiar subject, she felt control returning. Even so, she was very careful not to look into Catlin's eyes. If she had seen a residue of passion in those amber depths she would have been shaken all over again. If she had seen only calculation she would have been furious. She could afford to be neither, so she confined her attention to the ancient bronze disc lying coolly on her palm.

"But?" he prodded, hearing the hesitation in her voice. "What's wrong with it?"

"Like all Ordos artifacts, this would be very hard to date with any real accuracy," said Lindsay. "The coiled beast motif used in this manner is both very ancient and remarkably persistent. It existed essentially unchanged in China from the fifth century B.C. to at least the fifth century A.D."

"If you had to guess, where would you place this one?"

"I wouldn't. Not without a great deal of research, including detailed comparisons with existing Ordos artifacts whose dates were determined in situ."

Catlin leaned forward until his lips were very close to Lindsay's ear. "Should we buy it just as a calling card to let people know we've got cash to burn and are willing to burn it?"

Thoughtfully Lindsay weighed the ornament before returning it to the black velvet.

"In that case," she said, turning toward the *kuei*, "I'd recommend that you consider this piece."

Catlin ran his fingertip lightly down the vague line of the bowl's old wound. With a nod, Lindsay told him that she had already seen the scar.

"Why?" he asked, lifting the vessel.

Lindsay hesitated, wondering if he would understand the distinction between old bronze and ancient bronze art. Then she remembered the sensitivity he had shown to the other bronzes he had handled.

"This bowl is an exquisite example of form both revealing and transcending function," she said simply.

"In a word, art."

"Yes."

"And the scar?" he asked, running his fingertip over the bowl in a long diagonal.

"It greatly diminishes the *kuei*'s value as an investment," Lindsay said bluntly. "A museum might overlook the flaw if the bowl were needed to fill a specific didactic function within a collection. Most knowledgeable private collectors wouldn't touch the *kuei*."

"But you would."

"Yes."

"Why?" asked Catlin, looking at Lindsay suddenly.

Once again Lindsay felt as though she had stepped into a spotlight, frozen like a wild animal within a blinding scrutiny. "I don't collect for investment," she said finally.

"What do you collect for?"

"I don't know if I can describe it," she said. "Most collectors are searching for absolutes. The best preserved, the rarest, the oldest, the—" She shrugged. "You get the idea. I can appreciate those things, but they don't compel me as a collector."

"What does?" asked Catlin.

Lindsay made a helpless gesture, telling Catlin that she had never put into words precisely what she sought in the bronzes that flowed ceaselessly through her hands. He waited silently, patiently, his whole body poised. She knew then that he would wait until he had the answers he wanted.

"Survival," she said finally. "Survival with grace and power. Art endures. Spirit endures. Flesh does not. That's why I hate frauds. They corrode man's soul, keeping him from knowing all that is beautiful and enduring of the human psyche. Frauds cheapen everything they touch. They are a betrayal of all that is best in humanity."

With an unconscious reverence Lindsay ran her fingertips over the *kuei*. "This is part of the human spirit cast in enduring bronze. Next to that fact, what is that faint diagonal line but a testament to the ultimate resilience of the human soul?"

Lindsay looked up at the man who watched her so quietly, focusing on her with an intensity that would have been frightening if she hadn't been focused on him in exactly the same way. Suddenly she wanted to make him understand things she had never articulated, even to herself. Her eyes as they met his were dark and yet brilliant, unflinching.

"I don't worship perfection, Catlin. I don't even like it very much. Everything is perfect until it breaks. Only in the mending do you know true quality. This bowl could have ten scars, a hundred, and still its essential power would radiate through, overwhelming the superficial perfection of things that have never been tested, never been broken, never been healed, never survived with grace and power."

"Are you talking about people or art?" he asked softly.

For a moment Lindsay was too surprised to speak.

"Both," she whispered at last, understanding something about herself that she had never realized before that instant. "Art and humanity are inseparable. One would die without the other. That's a truth older than Chinese bronzes, older than culture and civilization, older than mankind as we know it. The Neanderthals buried their dead with garlands of flowers, and their successors painted the spirits of animals on cave walls. Art isn't a luxury or an investment. It's the soul of humanity made tangible."

"Not always pretty, though," said Catlin, remembering just how accurately art could reflect the darker side of the human soul.

"No," agreed Lindsay. "But art is real in a world where too much else is false."

"And you'll take true darkness over false light," Catlin said softly, statement not question.

"Every time."

Catlin's fingertips touched Lindsay's cheek in a fleeting brush of warmth. "No matter what happens, the scarred bowl is yours."

10

"ARE YOU ACHIEVING progress, dragon?" asked Yi, inhaling sharply.

Catlin shrugged, closing his apartment door behind him. "Not with the very available Jackie. What she's offering doesn't interest me. What about you?"

"My comrades are feeling better. They wish to have a meeting with you. Tomorrow."

"Why don't you just paint Property of the PRC on my forehead?" Catlin asked sardonically. "Much quicker. Cheaper, too. Saves all that plane fare between coasts."

"The meeting will seem accidental. No one will suspect."

Catlin made a disgusted sound. "If you say so. It probably doesn't matter. If there are thieves, they're wired into your government. At this point in the game, your dear comrades are my second choice for nomination as those very same thieves—assuming that the bronzes have been stolen. And that," he added blandly, "is a very tricky assumption. There is no way in hell those bronzes could have been offered for sale in secret. No way, Yi. Word of a charioteer would go through the cognoscenti like fire through gasoline. There have been no solid rumors. Therefore, no bronzes have made it to America."

Yi grunted. "Who is your first choice as a thief?" he asked, ignoring Catlin's implicit question as to whether or not the bronzes had ever been stolen.

"You."

"Ah!" Smoke curled up from Chen Yi's thin-knuckled hand. There was no expression on his face, no clue as to whether he was insulted or amused or totally unmoved by Catlin's words. "The meeting with my comrades will occur at a private sale of third century B.C. Chinese bronzes. I believe you have already received an invitation."

"I have?" asked Catlin. His left eyebrow arched in an expression that could have been curiosity or disbelief.

"From the honorable Mr. Samuel Wang. Last night."

"So he belongs to you. I wondered."

"Wonder is a useful thing." Yi sent his spent cigarette in a flat arc that ended in Catlin's fireplace. "If Wang were mine, I would have no need of you, would I?"

"Really?" Catlin asked neutrally. "Then I'll give you a bit of advice. Whoever fishes with that particular cormorant better keep a damn tight string on him."

Yi made a curt gesture with his hand, dismissing the subject of Samuel Wang. "When can you leave for San Francisco?"

"When is the private sale?" countered Catlin.

"Tell Miss Danner to call Mr. Wang."

"What about Lindsay? Is she going?"

"Miss Danner will be traveling with you. The Museum of the Asias is interested in expanding its collection of third century bronzes."

"Convenient," grunted Catlin. "And just a bit pat."

"Please?"

"Too convenient to be convincing," Catlin explained.

"Yet the museum's needs are quite real and have been known by sellers and buyers of bronze for many months. That is, after all, why Miss Danner was hired."

"The word must have gone out about the time your Xi'an bronzes turned up missing," Catlin said with a thin smile. "Assuming they're missing of course."

There was a long silence that ended with the metallic click of a lighter being opened. Flame flared, turning Yi's lean cheeks a ruddy gold. The metal top of the lighter snapped back into place as Yi expelled a burst of smoke.

"To use the Museum of the Asias would have required much foresight, much planning. You have a devious mind, dragon."

"I have a survivor's mind."

Yi nodded slowly, plucked a bit of tobacco from his tongue, and said, "See that Miss Danner benefits from that mind, as well as from your more obvious physical gifts."

"My, my, gossip travels fast in this town, doesn't it?" Catlin said. "We must have made quite an impression at the dinner good old L. Stephen so conveniently missed. Or was Jackie's office wired into the local cable TV channel?"

Yi looked faintly amused. "Would it have been arousing to watch?"

Catlin felt a sudden, surprising shaft of anger. With the ease of long experience he controlled it, showing nothing on his face. "I didn't know voyeurism was approved by the Party. Next time I'll send out invitations."

Smoke sighed out with Yi's breath. "With any other man I would worry about distraction. With you—" Yi shrugged. "You are not as other men. The usual temptations are behind you. You have accepted being a bird with one wing. You have lived unmatched for so long that you have forgotten that your tortured spirals are not true flight. All that is ahead for you is survival and, ultimately, death. Ah!"

Yi drew quickly on his cigarette as he searched Catlin's face. Yellow dragon's eyes watched Yi in return, calm, predatory, patient. Catlin was familiar with the old Chinese saying that man is born a bird with one wing and thereafter spends his life searching for the woman who is his other half, his missing wing, for only with her will true flight be possible. A very romantic idea for a race of pragmatists. But then, the Chinese knew that many searched for and only very few ever found their missing wing.

"Do you believe that, Yi?"

"I am Chinese." He drew twice in succession on the cigarette. "If you have to give me information," continued Yi, "or there is something unforeseen, call this number. Use the name Rousseau. The message will come to me."

"How long will it take to reach you?"

There was no answer.

After noting the San Francisco area code, Catlin memorized the whole phone number. He held out his hand without looking up from the paper. Yi dropped the Zippo onto his palm. Flint sparked. Impaled on flame, the paper writhed for a moment before becoming no more than ash smeared across Catlin's callused palm. He flipped the lighter back to Yi. Without a word Yi pocketed the lighter and walked out of the apartment. Catlin didn't bother to go to the window to watch Yi's exit. He had obviously learned to leave via the less public routes.

Catlin waited a few minutes, went down to the lobby of the apartment building where there was a public phone and punched in the number he had just memorized. From long habit he shielded the phone's numeral pad with his body, making it impossible for anyone to see the number he was calling. He fed in coins, listened to the ringing sound, and heard the much more subtle sound of the call being forwarded to another number. After the first ring an answering machine broke in. A recorded voice told him to leave his message after he heard the tone sound.

The voice was Yi's, speaking Mandarin.

Catlin hung up. He hadn't really expected Yi to be so careless as to leave an easy trail, but at the same time it had been necessary to try. Catlin had seen more men die from overlooking the obvious than from being taken in by the devious.

He punched in another number, fed coins, and waited. The phone rang, was switched, rang and was switched again to a third number. As soon as a voice answered, Catlin gave Yi's number in San Francisco, speaking in a tone that carried no farther than the receiver.

"See who it's billed to," finished Catlin.

"Is it a rush?" asked the technician.

"Yes."

Patiently, Catlin waited while a distant computer crunched its way through a staggering amount of information.

"Second Home Phone and Mail Service, San Francisco, California," the technician said when he came back on the line. "Sounds like some kind of high class cheesebox operation. I'll see what I can do. Don't hold your breath, though. Last time I took on one of these puppies, I put in three solid days and all it led to was an answering machine in a room rented by someone who paid a month in advance by mail, no return address, no fingerprints, no way, no how."

"I'll check back from time to time."

Without waiting for an answer Catlin broke the connection. As he turned around he noted the man standing patiently behind him, change for a phone call held ostentatiously on his palm. Catlin didn't recognize the man until he turned aside; it was a profile Catlin had seen in the Sichuan Garden four tables away.

"Say hello to the boys for me," Catlin murmured as he walked past the stranger.

The man ignored everything but the phone in front of him until Catlin disappeared up the service stairs to his fifth floor apartment. He rarely took elevators if they could be avoided. It was too easy to wait in front of an elevator door until it opened, and then hold down the trigger until the clip was empty. Elevators were traps.

"Subject going back to apartment," said the man quietly, flipping up his suit coat collar to speak into a tiny microphone.

The message was passed along the line of command until it was brought to Stone's desk by a cheerful O'Donnel.

"They just tucked him back into bed."

Stone grunted. "It would be too much to ask him to stay there. Yi still with him?"

"No. He took the back way out. Should be in his hotel room by now."

Stone grunted again. "Any luck on the years missing from Catlin's file?"

"We rode it all the way up to the Oval Office."

"And?"

"Still missing. Likely to stay that way. I'm afraid Catlin's ass is well and truly covered from that direction."

"Keep trying."

"Yes, sir. You want Miss Danner yet?"

With a grimace, Stone flicked his blunt fingers over the file on his desk. "I was hoping to have more on Catlin before I talked to her."

"Maybe she can tell you something. From what I've seen, they got real close, real fast."

Stone smiled cynically. "In that case, what makes you think they wasted their time talking? Besides, the hot-and-heavy routine is part of their cover."

"Hell of an act," muttered O'Donnel. "From what I heard, he had her in such a sweat that she was lucky to tell wine from cheese at that dinner."

"Catlin has lived undercover. Way under. He's a goddam chameleon. He could fool God."

"She didn't strike me as a chameleon."

"Hell, Terry. She's a woman, isn't she?" Stone made an impatient sound. "Bring her in here. Let's see if Catlin is the kind who gets loose-lipped in bed."

O'Donnel didn't bother to hide his laugh. "Are you a betting man?"

"Yeah. I'll bet that when it comes to tight lips he could give a clam a run for its money—in bed, out of bed and anywhere in between." Stone's blunt fingers rolled a pen back and forth, back and forth across the top of his desk, making a thin metallic sound. "Knew a man like Catlin a long time ago. Korea. They beat the shit out of him trying to get him to talk."

"Ever break?"

Stone gave the younger man a cold, amused look. "You've been reading too many comic books, Terry. Everybody breaks if you torture them long enough. This guy held out a long time, but finally he broke, too. He told them whatever Commie claptrap they wanted to hear. And then he went back into his cell and he healed up and the next time they wanted him to play the 'I love communism game' he refused again. It took them just as long to break him the second time. And the third. And the sixth."

The pen rolled back and forth, back and forth. Stone's eyes were unfocused as he remembered the past.

"Hell of a man," Stone said finally. "In the end he managed to kill his guard and four more, and lead the rest of us on a long walk home." Stone's eyes focused suddenly on O'Donnel. "Professionally, I don't like Catlin worth a damn, because I can't control him and I can't be sure whose side he's on. But if I had a war to win, I'd fight in his shadow any day of the week. Don't ever underestimate him, Terry. Kill him if you have to—if you can—but never take him prisoner."

Stone paused, smiling unpleasantly. "You see, Chen has himself a genuine, A-number-one twenty-four karat, fully grown, he-male tiger by the tail. And you know what? I hope the tricky old bastard loses his grip and gets eaten."

The pen snapped solidly against the desk. Stone picked up the files and locked them in a drawer. "Bring her in. And hold my calls. If she's really in bed with Catlin, my sales pitch is going to need all the help it can get."

"Want me to try a little counterseduction?" O'Donnel offered, smiling ingenuously.

"The Bureau doesn't sink that low." Stone's mouth made a cynical curve. "Especially when it won't do any damn good. Or did she come on to you?"

"I didn't really try."

Stone grunted. "Pull the other one, Terry. I've known you since you were in fourth grade, sneaking kisses from sixth-grade cuties."

O'Donnel grinned. "I'm willing to give my all for my country, Brad. You know that."

"Keep your 'all' zipped for now," Stone said dryly.

Laughing, O'Donnel left the office and returned in a few moments with Lindsay.

"Please sit down, Lindsay," said Stone, standing up as she walked in. "It was good of you to come with so little notice. Steve tells me he's kept you quite busy since his father decided a few months ago to upgrade the museum's Chinese collection."

"Mr. White told me that I was essentially your employee until further notice," Lindsay said. She paused, then smiled widely. "Does this mean that I bill the FBI for any third century bronzes I purchase?"

"You can try," Stone said, smiling in return, "but don't buy anything your museum can't use."

"And I had such high hopes for a shot at the government wallet," she said, laughing lightly.

Lindsay sat in a dark leather chair that faced Stone's desk and watched him with an expectant expression, waiting for him to speak. Discreetly, O'Donnel withdrew. Stone picked up the pen again. He studied it as though he were seeing it for the first time while he wondered what would be the most effective way to recruit Lindsay. Then he remembered Catlin's approach— the kind of honesty that made you wince. But it had been effective. Given that fact, Stone doubted that an elliptical approach would work with Lindsay. This was a command performance and she knew it.

Besides, from what he had seen of her so far, she wasn't the kind of person who appreciated doing laps around the bush for the hell of it.

"How are you and Catlin getting along?" Stone asked neutrally.

"Fine," said Lindsay, hoping that any color in her face would be written off as a residual effect of the temperature outside. Memories of Catlin's sensuality simmered in her blood, but not as strongly as the intensity of him as he had listened to her, really *listened*, and then had promised her the scarred bowl. She had never felt so close to anyone in her life as she had to him in that instant.

"Fine," repeated Stone with a stifled sigh. He snapped down the pen. He hated one-word answers. "No problems?"

"Nothing that can't be worked out."

"Such as?"

"I'm not much of an actress, Mr. Stone."

"Brad."

"Brad," she repeated dutifully, wondering if she would ever feel at ease with the erect, silver-haired man who sat across the desk from her. "So far Catlin has managed to cover my dropped lines, as it were. I'm glad the Bureau found such a good teacher. He even—"

"We didn't," interrupted Stone.

"I beg your pardon?"

"Catlin isn't one of ours," Stone said bluntly.

Lindsay stared for a long moment, too surprised to speak, remembering that Catlin had said something similar. "Then where did he come from?"

"Pacific Rim Institute. A think tank on the West Coast," Stone added, doubting that Lindsay would be familiar with the deliberately low-profile operation that Catlin ran.

"Yes, he told me that. But he agreed to help you, didn't he, like I did?"

Stone shook his head. "Catlin isn't one of ours. He belongs to the People's Republic."

"I don't understand."

"I know. That's why I asked you to come in. There's a certain amount of risk in having you seen with the FBI, but I felt that what I had to say would be more understandable to you in person." He leaned back in his big leather chair, running his fingers over the cool body of the pen. "Coffee?"

"Coffee?" Lindsay laughed abruptly. "Forgive me, but I feel like Alice on the way down the rabbit hole. What risk?"

Smiling, Stone sat forward again. "Believe me, I won't offer you pieces of magic mushroom. The Drug Enforcement Administration would have my butt in a sling if I even thought of it."

Lindsay smiled in return, but her watchful eyes told him that she hadn't forgotten the word *risk*.

"The situation is a little complicated," Stone said, frowning. He fiddled with the pen.

"Don't worry about it," Lindsay said dryly. "It can't be much more complex than my doctoral dissertation on the evolution of symbol and design in Chinese bronzes."

Stone's head came up with an abrupt motion. He had forgotten that the attractive woman sitting opposite him was both intelligent and highly trained in her own field. It wasn't the first time in the past few years that a woman's sleek exterior had misled him. He still had trouble accepting the fact that some of the young women he passed in the hall not only carried guns, but had used them. With a muffled sigh, he ran his hand over his immaculate silver hair and wished he had been born either earlier or later in the century. Living in transition times was hell.

"You have a reputation for honesty," he said finally.

Lindsay waited.

"What I'm going to tell you is literally labeled Top Secret," continued Stone. "I'm taking a chance that you'll keep it that way. Will you?"

"Yes."

After a brief hesitation, Stone began speaking in a flat voice. "Chen Yi was a spy in the past, and almost certainly is on an intelligence gathering mission right now."

For a moment Lindsay was too surprised to speak. Disappointment washed over her, numbing her. "You mean there aren't any stolen bronzes from Xi'an?"

Stone made an impatient movement with his hand, sending the pen on his desk sliding against the ashtray with a distinct sound. As though reminded, he pulled a cigarette from the pack on his desk, lit up and turned back toward Lindsay.

"Maybe some stuff is missing from Xi'an, maybe not," he said. "What matters is that while we're looking for bronzes here and the CIA is looking for them overseas, Chen Yi is watching every move we make. He's going to learn a hell of a lot about how we operate, how efficient we are, how deeply we've penetrated Asian communities here and abroad. Information, Lindsay. That's all intelligence is. Gathering information. Chen Yi's good at it. Too damn good. His family has been doing it for centuries, near as we can tell."

As Stone pushed away from the desk, his glance went restlessly around the room, noting all the framed pictures, mementos of an easier past when enemies were named and numbered and known.

"When it comes to survival, the Chen family wrote the book," said Stone, looking at Lindsay again. "From emperors to the PRC, the Chen family has always kept at least one finger in China's governmental pie. Chen's family has tentacles all over the damn Asian continent, and in the West, too." Stone's tone was ambiguous, divided between admiration for the family's toughness and dislike for an old enemy. "There are cousins and cousins of cousins until hell won't have it. Chens are bankers and traders and teachers, prostitutes and pimps and pushers. But they all have one thing in common. They're all spies. They gather information and funnel it back up the line."

Lindsay nodded slowly.

"You don't look surprised," said Stone. "Did Catlin tell you about Chen Yi?"

"No. Catlin hasn't said anything about him."

Stone grunted. "That I believe."

"But what you've described isn't surprising. It's simply very Chinese." She looked at Stone, wondering what his background was, if his schooling had been in history or business. "For thousands of years the Chinese have survived because of the flexibility and sheer tenacity of family ties. For that reason, families command a loyalty that no government can," she explained.

"Then you understand how powerful the Chen clan is."

"Yes."

There was a moment of silence while Stone watched smoke curling up from the cigarette between his fingers. "Did Catlin tell you that Chen Yi is under suspicion by his own government?"

Lindsay's eyes widened. "No. Why?"

Stone didn't bother to stifle his sigh. It seemed that Catlin hadn't told Lindsay one damn thing worth knowing. "Who knows why one Communist suspects another?" Stone asked irritably. "It seems to be a national pastime over there. Hell, maybe Chen's been funneling bronzes over here so that he can cash out and run, and his government finally is catching on."

"Do you believe that?"

"I have an open mind," Stone said neutrally. "I do know that Chen Yi specifically asked me to keep you under wraps."

"What?"

"His comrades aren't to know that you're working with the FBI or with him," Stone said bluntly.

"Did he say why?"

Stone snorted. "Hell, no."

"Is it because of the risk to me?" She saw immediately that Stone didn't understand her question. "The risk you mentioned earlier, about me being seen with the FBI."

Unwillingly Stone smiled. "Bringing you here wasn't all that risky. Nobody's following you yet but us."

"Am I supposed to be comforted?" she asked, her eyebrows raised in disbelief. "Why are you following me in the first place?" As soon as the words were out, she remembered Catlin's response to a similar question. "No, don't tell me. Let me guess. You're following me to see if anyone's following me."

Pale blue eyes gleamed against Stone's ruddy face as he chuckled. "You'll do all right, Lindsay. You're quick."

"I have a hell of a teacher."

"Catlin?"

"Catlin," she agreed.

Stone muttered something beneath his breath, took a hard drag on his cigarette and stubbed it out in the ashtray. When he looked up again at Lindsay, his eyes were as pale as ice.

"Catlin's a big part of the problem. Chen Yi has hired him to help find the bronzes. Near as we can tell, Catlin is Chen's expert in this deal the same way you're ours. Except Catlin is probably getting paid, one way or another."

"That's a problem?"

"When a person is paid by a foreign government, we call them foreign agents."

There was a long silence while Lindsay weighed Stone's words. "Are you saying that Catlin is some kind of spy for the People's Republic?" she asked.

"I'm saying that's a possibility."

"How big a possibility?" she asked bluntly.

"That's hard to say."

"Try it one syllable at a time."

"Take my word for it," said Stone impatiently.

"I'd love to, but in the past forty-eight hours I've learned not to take anybody's word for anything."

"Catlin," muttered Stone, making the word an epithet. He rolled the pen back and forth with small motions of his hand, wondering how much he could tell Lindsay. Abruptly, he decided. Whatever he would tell her, Catlin already knew. And Chen Yi, too, most likely. "Catlin worked for the CIA in Indochina. Covert operations. Then all of a sudden he disappeared. He reappeared in Monterey a few years back, when he bought out the owners of the Pacific Rim Institute and began to put it on the map with the kind of information that only a man like Catlin would have access to."

"He sold Top-Secret information—is that what you're saying?" asked Lindsay.

"He used it to draw conclusions and to give advice."

"Is that illegal?"

Stone made an impatient sound. "Not precisely. It skates right out there on the edge, though."

"Then why is he not only permitted to operate, but invited to the Hill to give expert testimony?" she demanded.

"Because his information is solid and the conclusions he draws from it are nothing short of brilliant," Stone said, looking at Lindsay coolly. "He's a very intelligent man. And all the more dangerous for it."

"I know," she whispered, understanding that fact very well. For her, Catlin's mind was as compelling as his sensuality and his powerful body combined.

"He's not cooperating with us," continued Stone. "He won't answer our questions about his past or about Chen, either."

"Is that why you think he's spying for Yi? For China?"

"He sure as hell isn't spying for us," Stone said curtly. "Don't trust him, Lindsay. He's good at manipulating people. That's his genius. He finds out what they want, what they'll believe, what they need, and then he uses it against them. He's as ruthless as they come.''

Hands laced in her lap, Lindsay sat very quietly, wanting to protest, yet knowing that there was truth in what Stone said. Catlin was intelligent. He was dangerous. He was ruthless.

But was he a Chinese spy?

''What do you want me to do?'' she asked after a time, her voice strained.

''Work for us,'' Stone answered promptly.

''I thought I was.''

''Find out about Catlin and Chen Yi, and then tell us. We'll know what to do with the information.''

''Spy on them,'' she said flatly.

Stone shrugged. ''If that's how you want to put it, yes.''

Lindsay didn't bother to ask how Stone would have put it. She simply shook her head. ''I can't.''

''You mean you won't,'' Stone snapped, his voice cold. ''I guess Terry was right. Catlin got in your pants but good.''

Color left Lindsay's face, only to return in a flood. When she spoke, her voice was unnaturally calm.

''I'm glad our act is so convincing. That's all it is. An act. Without Catlin, there would be no act at all. I've said it before, Mr. Stone, and I'll say it again: I am not an actress. What you're asking me to do is impossible. I can't speak out of both sides of my mouth and simultaneously believe three other contradictory things in my mind.'' She closed her eyes, then opened them to give Stone an unflinching look. ''Even if I could, Catlin would see right through me,'' she said bleakly. ''He is frighteningly perceptive. I'm no match for him.''

Without hesitation, Stone cut his losses. ''I'm sorry. I didn't mean to be crude. I'm aware that this is difficult for you. If it helps, I'm taking a lot of heat over this Chen Yi affair myself. We have to cooperate with China, even though we know damn good and well we can't trust them.'' He smiled encouragingly. ''All I really want you to do is to keep in mind that you might find out things that we don't know—just as we've found out a few things about Catlin and Chen Yi that you didn't know,''

Stone added smoothly, coming to his feet. "If you happen on to something in San Francisco, give us a call."

"Am I going to San Francisco?" she asked, standing.

Stone nodded. "Remember, Lindsay. We're on the same side."

"And Catlin isn't?" she asked.

The outer door opened before Stone could answer. O'Donnel came in to show Lindsay out of the building.

Only later, safe in her own apartment, did she realize that O'Donnel must have been listening in on the whole conversation between herself and Stone. The thought sent a wave of anger and impatience through her.

"What a bloody mess," she said aloud, pacing her apartment like a caged cat. "The right hand doesn't know what the left is doing—and if it does, they both lie about it!"

Her brooding gaze roamed the apartment, coming to rest finally on the scarred *kuei* Catlin had purchased that morning and then given to her as he put her in a cab. Amid all the lies and half-truths, the bowl stood forth as the spirit of man made tangible. The blue-green curves held sinuous traces of dragons, and the bowl itself was replete with time and truth.

Slowly her fingertip traced the pale diagonal scar as she remembered Catlin's intensity while he had watched her, listened to her, understood her. Had that all been an act, too? Had he lied to her with his body after promising not to lie to her with words?

The doorbell rang, startling Lindsay from her silent absorption in the ancient bowl. Even before she peered through the spy hole, she knew who would be there.

Catlin.

She opened the door and stood back, allowing him in without a word.

"I see Stone has been sowing seeds of love and happiness," Catlin said after a brief look at Lindsay's face.

Lindsay opened her mouth to ask a question, then realized it was futile. How do you ask a man if he's a foreign spy? And having asked, how do you believe the answer?

"Are we going to San Francisco?" she asked politely.

"Looks that way," said Catlin.

"Nice of you to tell me."

"That's what I told Yi an hour ago."

"Oh." Automatically Lindsay shut and locked the door behind Catlin. "Did Yi tell you why we're going to San Francisco?"

"Sam Wang invited us."

"He did?"

"Last night."

"The bronze animals he mentioned?"

"Yeah. And a bunch more besides. He's laying on a private sale of third century B.C. Chinese bronzes."

"That's very, er, nice of him," said Lindsay, choosing her words carefully.

"Isn't it just," Catlin said, his voice flat. "You'll be meeting other people at the sale. One of them will be Chen Yi." Catlin paused, then said quietly, "You haven't met him before."

Adrenaline poured through Lindsay suddenly, making her hands tremble. She balled the betraying fingers into fists. *Was Stone right? Was Catlin spying for Chen Yi?*

The thought burst through her with such force that for an instant she was afraid she had spoken aloud. But Catlin was still watching her without expression, his eyes seeing her turmoil far too clearly.

"I haven't met Chen Yi," Lindsay repeated slowly. Then, almost helplessly, "I haven't?"

"You haven't. You also haven't met any of the FBI types who will doubtless be hanging around like white on rice."

There was a pause. "Have I met you?" she asked politely.

"I'm hurt," he retorted.

"And I'm a *kuei*," she shot back, tired of all the wheels within wheels, deceptions within lies.

Catlin laughed, shaking his head. "I hope whoever is listening for the FBI knows his Chinese artifacts."

"Listening in?"

"Yeah. If not this instant, then certainly by the time we come back. From now on, unless I get the room for us and vet it regularly, we'll have to assume it's wired for sound. All phones that aren't public are presumed to be tapped, taped and generally very public indeed."

Lindsay's breath came out in a harsh sound. She felt hunted, trapped, besieged. Suddenly she remembered Catlin's words: *Before this is over with, you're going to need somebody you think you can trust.*

"Catlin," she breathed, afraid to put in words what she was thinking: Was it him? Could she trust him?

"I'm here, Lindsay. Night or day, for better or for worse, I'm right beside you. You don't go anywhere without me anymore. No exceptions. No arguments. Dress rehearsal is over."

11

"UNCLE WU!" said Lindsay, her voice husky with surprise and pleasure as she saw the small Chinese man bent over one of Sam Wang's bronzes.

The man straightened and turned around. He smiled and bowed very slightly in the same movement, then took Lindsay's hand in both of his and smiled.

"It is as the beauty of the autumn moon for my humble eyes to see you once again, cherished daughter," said Wu. "Please take my softest wishes for the easing of your grief at the death of your most honorable mother. Surely our magnificent and most powerful God has taken up to Christian heaven the most beautiful, humble and dutiful of all his daughters."

Blinking back sudden tears, Lindsay squeezed Wu's hand. Catlin watched, listening to the odd rhythms of Mandarin thoughts translated directly into English. Apparently Wu's adaptation to America had ended with learning the language. Like Yi, Wu retained the Chinese order of his names, last name first. Unlike Yi, Wu hadn't changed the patterns of his thinking to match the culture whose language he had learned. Wu's English was as florid, self-effacing and evocative as the man himself was physically restrained. He didn't hug Lindsay as a Western man would have in the same circumstances; instead, he let his words caress her.

"Please accept this lowly daughter's most humble thanks, most honorable Uncle Wu," Lindsay murmured in Mandarin, bowing her head slightly, suiting her speech to the Chinese man who was inches smaller than she was in her high heels. "As always, your exquisite words are the sweetest of music to sad ears accustomed to the unadorned rhythms of English speech."

Wu smiled and caressed Lindsay's hand again, a public gesture of affection that was rare for a native Chinese. It told

Catlin more than any words could have. Wu felt the same complex—and to Western eyes ambiguous—affection for Lindsay that he would have felt for his own daughter. The ambiguity existed only in the Western mind, where women were valued more highly than in the Eastern culture. Wu had no doubt of his love for Lindsay, and neither did she.

She turned toward Catlin. "Uncle Wu, this is Mr. Jacob Catlin," she said, reverting to English. "Catlin, please meet the most honorable Mr. Hsiang Wu."

Lindsay's speech told Catlin two things. The first was that Stone hadn't told Lindsay that Catlin spoke Mandarin as well as she did. The second was that Wu had considerable status within the Chinese community of San Francisco—the designation "most honorable" was a normal part of the way people addressed him. That was surprising. Most of San Francisco's Chinese immigrants were from the south of China, not the north. Cantonese rather than Mandarin was by far the dialect of choice. For a northern Chinese to have power in San Francisco's Chinatown was unusual.

As he accepted the frail hand that Wu held out, Catlin bowed slightly, acknowledging Wu's status.

"It's an honor to meet you," said Catlin.

Wu bowed very slightly in return. "I am but the most humble of Lindsay's old friends," he said, so softly that it was difficult to hear his words.

"As I am but the most humble of her new ones," Catlin said smoothly.

Very shrewd black eyes fixed on Catlin for a long moment. Wu nodded once, as though agreeing with an inner thought. "I am pleased to see at last with my own humble eyes the man who is both intelligent and powerful enough to make my sometimes lamentably willful daughter acknowledge her proper place within history and culture."

"That's well beneath man, preferably chained to a steaming wok," Lindsay explained to Catlin, her voice rich with amusement over what was obviously an old argument. "Ah, Uncle Wu, it's good to be lectured by you once again."

"It is an unrelenting and stern duty that this most humble uncle pursues in the sad absence of your true father," acknowledged Wu, his eyes sparkling with suppressed humor.

"Barefoot and pregnant, hmmm?" asked Catlin, running his fingertip along the line of Lindsay's jaw. "The idea has possibilities."

Lindsay felt color climbing up her cheeks, but she didn't withdraw from Catlin's touch. Instead she turned her head slowly, an act that both increased the pressure of the caress and allowed her to face him fully. "Don't get any ideas, Catlin."

"Not new ones, certainly," Catlin agreed with a wicked smile. "Men have been having those kinds of ideas since the first time one of them figured out it was the only way to keep women from taking over the world."

There was a bark of laughter and an approving look from Wu that told Lindsay her old friend had accepted Catlin. It didn't surprise her. Wu had the traditional Chinese appreciation for intelligence, as well as the equally traditional appreciation for strength and sheer male presence. Catlin had more than his fair share of all three.

Lindsay sighed dramatically and shook her head. "I'm surrounded by traditionalists."

"Surely that is to be expected, daughter," murmured Wu. "You have returned to stand in the glorious reflection of China, the greatest of all traditions." His voice changed, showing for a moment all the emotions of an exile from a beloved land. "It is a terrible thing to know that men who have less honor than dogs stand astride the bleeding body of the most subtle and magnificent culture the world has ever known."

In Wu's voice Catlin heard resonances of grief and regret, hatred and grudging acceptance. Obviously Hsiang Wu had not greeted with enthusiasm the revolution that had transformed one of the oldest empires on earth into one of the younger Communist countries.

"But that is only the babbling of a thoughtless old man who has never learned that living in memory is a beggar's substitute for the unfolding glories of a new day," Wu said, dismissing his complaint with a wave of his hand. "Come, daughter of one of my oldest and most honored friends. Indulge the whims of a humble old man who would know what young eyes see in these most venerable and ancient of bronzes."

Lindsay hesitated, then slipped into Mandarin for a moment, not wanting Wu to lose face in front of Catlin. "Honorable uncle," she murmured, "Tonight I am the most humble servant of the respected Mr. Jacob Catlin, as well as the undeserving employee of the most honorable Museum of the Asias. I cannot tell you anything that would diminish the interests of the honorable Mr. Catlin or those of the museum. But when I find out which of the bronzes Mr. Catlin might wish to purchase, and whether there are any the museum should have, I will be most honored to discuss all other bronzes with you."

For an instant Wu's black eyes fixed on Catlin as though the Chinese expected a response from him despite the fact that Mandarin had been spoken. When none came, Wu looked back to Lindsay, understanding that she believed their conversation to be a private one that excluded Catlin.

"Ah! Forgive the clumsiness of an eager old man," Wu said in Mandarin. "I would do nothing to cast shadows on your honor and the honor of your esteemed family."

Catlin waited impassively, doing nothing that would reveal his knowledge of Mandarin.

Lindsay threw him a quick, appealing look, "I'm sorry to be rude, but—"

"No problem," Catlin said, interrupting her apology for speaking in a language she believed he didn't understand.

Lindsay resumed her outpouring of effusive Mandarin, apologizing in many different ways for her inability to help Wu. He accepted her apologies with more apologies of his own until the ritualized politeness was complete on both sides. Then, with a few more graceful phrases, Wu withdrew to study another of the bronzes that Sam Wang had arranged so artfully throughout the room.

Catlin pulled Lindsay close. "Problems?" he asked too softly to be overheard.

"I explained that I was your expert and couldn't help him with any of the bronzes," Lindsay said in a very low voice.

"Would you usually?"

"Of course. He's a very old friend. And he returns the favor. Some of the best bronzes the Museum of the Asias owns came to me originally through Uncle Wu."

"Convenient," murmured Catlin.

"What does that mean?" whispered Lindsay.

"It's always convenient to have well-placed friends."

"It's what the Harvard types call the 'old boy network,'" Lindsay said softly, but her smile was very hard. "The Chinese invented it about the time Europeans wore badly cured furs and carried clubs."

Laughing softly, Catlin bent and brushed Lindsay's mouth with his own. "Do you suppose Wu has heard about a bronze charioteer?"

"No."

"So quick. So sure." Though Catlin said nothing more, the question was implicit in his words and in his watchful eyes.

Lindsay shrugged. After a moment's hesitation she leaned toward him like a woman enjoying the warmth and strength of her lover's presence. "Uncle Wu's family is in exile," she whispered, her voice barely above the threshold of hearing. "The Hsiang family supported the wrong side of the revolution. They fought on for a time after Mao was in control, but finally they were forced to flee."

"So?"

"So whoever has the Xi'an bronzes also has an in with the Chinese government," Lindsay murmured impatiently, pointing out the obvious. "There would be no other way to get the bronzes out of the ground, out of the province and out of the country."

"Is that what Stone told you?" Catlin asked softly.

"He didn't have to. Anyone who knows anything at all about Xi'an and China would figure that out for himself."

"Do me a favor," Catlin breathed, caressing Lindsay's cheek with his hand. "Don't mention your conclusions about China's government and stolen bronzes to anyone but me. Okay? Not everyone knows China as well as you do."

"What about Stone? Can I tell him?"

Catlin's only answer was the movement of his palm over her smooth skin.

"But—"

Catlin's hand tightened subtly, warningly, on Lindsay's chin, reminding her that the place for arguments was not in public.

"I—all right," said Lindsay, her voice low, husky. And in her mind Stone's words echoed, describing Yi as a Chinese spy and Catlin as little, if any, better. She wondered if Catlin would be willing to discuss the matter when they were alone.

"Anyone else in the room that you know?" Catlin asked.

She blinked at the sudden change of subject and glanced quickly around. The living room of Sam Wang's hillside home in Marin County was large, about the size of two average living rooms put together. Any similarity to an ordinary home ended there, however. The carpet was scarlet, with a thick plush-cut pile that deadened sound. Woven throughout the rich red wool were dragon designs in a gold material that had the unmistakable shine of raw silk.

The carpet's synthesis of East and West was repeated throughout the room's appointments. The furniture was ebony, but patterned after Scandinavian rather than Oriental designs. The only exception was a stunning carved ebony screen where dragons tangled in an intricate, quintessentially Chinese display. Beyond the living room, a wall of glass revealed the setting sun and the seething magenta surface of San Francisco Bay. The city itself lay across the water, tier upon tier of buildings rising from the darkening land in sunset shades that went from scarlet to gold.

There were few people in the room. Sam Wang had staggered the invitations to allow guests to file past the bronzes. Lindsay's quick glance revealed no one else who looked familiar, although two of the men huddled around a bronze showed the unconcealed enthusiasm of avid collectors rather than the more restrained appreciation of scholars or connoisseurs.

Lindsay shook her head, silently telling Catlin that no one else was known to her.

"All right," he said softly, smoothing his hand over the shining thickness of her hair. "Let's take a run at the bronzes."

"Wait," she whispered urgently, putting her hand on his upper arm.

The hardness of the underlying flesh surprised her. In his handmade suit coat and slacks, Catlin looked too civilized to be so powerful. *Wolf in sheep's clothing,* she thought to herself, divided between wariness and amusement. *Thank God I'm not wearing a curly white coat and baa-ing for mama.*

Catlin arched his left eyebrow in wordless query even as he covered Lindsay's fingers with his own.

With her hand pressed caressingly between his hard palm and equally hard biceps, Lindsay felt her thoughts unraveling into sensual speculation.

"Are we supposed to buy something tonight?" she asked a little desperately, hating the effect that Catlin had on her when she had so little effect on him.

"If the bronzes are good, yes. We'll buy spectacularly. It will get the word out as nothing else could."

Lindsay nodded, knowing that Catlin was right. Word of a new, aggressive collector would go through the grapevine like wildfire through dry grass.

"Are we buying for you? The museum? The government?" she asked.

"The check won't bounce," Catlin murmured dryly, thinking of the Hong Kong account that had been opened in his name, "if that's what's bothering you."

She shook her head, then saw the tiny expansion of his nostrils as perfume drifted up from her hair. She saw his eyes dilate suddenly, and knew in that instant that he was as intensely aware of her as she was of him. The knowledge was both exciting and oddly comforting.

"But what if you and the museum both want the same piece?" she asked softly.

Catlin smiled as he bent down and kissed Lindsay slowly, ignoring the people hovering over the bronzes. "You tell me, honey cat," he murmured, lifting his head.

"You," said Lindsay, her voice both soft and tight, her heart beating too quickly, "are a—"

He kissed her again, cutting off her words. "Just call me G.B.," he whispered. "That way if anyone overhears he won't wonder why you're calling your lover a genuine bastard."

"In other words, you get what you want and the museum takes what's left over," she whispered, her eyes bleak as she realized the implications. Tonight the cream of the bronze connoisseurs, buyers and scholars would be treated to a first-class example of a museum employee overlooking the interests of her employer in favor of the interests of her very obvious lover.

Catlin shrugged. "You're assuming I leave something." He looked at her, his amber eyes gleaming with reflections of the elegant track lights overhead. Slowly he pulled her close against his body and whispered softly in her ear. "I don't leave much behind. Ask anyone who knows me. When I'm finished all that's left are memories, and damn few of those. Remember that, Lindsay. And remember what I told you last week in D.C."

The voice was hushed but the words were like razors cutting her. She remembered what he had told her. And she also remembered her own blithe words: *I won't say you didn't tell me if you won't say I told you so.*

For a moment Lindsay stayed frozen within Catlin's arms; then she deliberately returned his apparent hug. She was getting better at the act, although she had forgotten the ramifications for a moment. In the week that Catlin had lived with her, she had become accustomed to his presence. She had fielded Sherry's envious queries as to Catlin's prowess in bed. She had learned to smile at Jackie's probing questions as to Catlin's "needs." She had even held her tongue when L. Stephen's propositions had gone from tasteless to crude. But tonight it was Hsiang Wu she would disappoint. Hsiang Wu, who was the bulwark of the Chinese refugee community she had grown up in and loved. Hsiang Wu, who knew everyone and honored her by calling her daughter.

For the first time, Lindsay was glad that her mother was dead.

"I remember," Lindsay said raggedly against Catlin's skin.

Catlin closed his eyes, hearing bleakness where laughter and music had formerly been in Lindsay's voice. He knew with the understanding that came only from experience that she was tasting the bitterness of betraying old friends. He had tried to prepare her for this. And he had known that there was no preparation for betrayal.

Welcome to undercover life, Lindsay, he thought. *Welcome to the outer ring of hell. Step right this way. The next ring awaits, and the next, and the next, until nothing is left and hell is everything that ever was or ever will be.*

Abruptly he released her. "Let's give it a fast once-over to see if there's anything new to add to my collection."

"You came to the wrong place if you want something new," said Lindsay, keeping her voice even with an effort. "The newest piece in this room is twenty-two centuries old. Or should be, if Wang's bronzes are as advertised."

Catlin smiled at Lindsay's small joke and ignored the signs of strain around her eyes and mouth as he led her toward the black, lacquered cube that supported one of Sam Wang's third century bronzes.

As soon as Lindsay bent over the bronze she forgot her inner turmoil in the rising excitement of seeing something that was both ancient and exquisitely made. She looked up at Catlin and nodded, knowing that his first question would be whether or not the piece was genuine.

"It's a very fine wine vessel," she said, looking at the cylindrical bronze that had been made to hold an individual portion of wine.

Slowly Catlin walked around the piece. The vessel was just over six inches high and three inches in diameter. It stood on three vaguely clawed feet and had once been inlaid with gold, silver and turquoise. Some of the precious metal still shone forth from grooves that had been created during the casting process itself, rather than incised afterward. Here and there a few chips of turquoise remained, adding a blue-green accent that complemented the vessel's fine patina.

Lindsay knew before Catlin looked up that he admired the bronze but wasn't going to bid on it. It was there in his expression, in the way he appreciated the piece without any trace of possessiveness. A week ago she wouldn't have noticed the extremely subtle clues as to his thoughts, and she doubted that many other people would notice those clues under any circumstances. She was simply attuned to Catlin's responses, to the way he looked at and touched the objects around him.

"Why not?" she asked quietly.

He glanced up, startled. "I'll have to brush up on my poker face," he said. "How did you know?"

She opened her mouth to answer, then realized that there was no way to explain that somehow she read him accurately even when he gave no overt clues. "I just knew."

Catlin's amber eyes weighed Lindsay for a long moment. No one had ever read him easily, not Susie, the childhood sweetheart he had married, not even Mei, the woman who had almost killed him. Catlin had learned young that it was too dangerous to be open to another person's mind, for the simple reason that people betrayed you. And you betrayed them. Trust simply wasn't a survival attribute. Not that Susie had meant to betray him. She had simply been too young and too lonely to wait for her high school hero to come home from the war to her. It had been different with Mei. Mei had meant to betray him from the beginning, for that was the job given to her by her pimp and occasional paramour, Lee Tran. Mei had let nothing stop her, not even her own unexpected emotion for the man she had been assigned to kill.

And Lindsay, who had never betrayed anyone, was being taught how to by an expert.

"I have a wine vessel like this already," Catlin said, his voice as emotionless as his eyes. "The design on this one is slightly more ornate, but the inlay on mine is intact, even to the turquoise. The patina on mine is richer, more even. Superior, in a word."

Lindsay stared at Catlin, absorbing the fact that at one time he must have been a very serious collector indeed. The wine vessel in front of her was of museum quality, a work of art as well as a piece of history. If he had one in his collection that was better, he had a treasure.

"I would like to see your collection," she said distinctly.

"So would I," Catlin said, his mouth turning up in something less than a smile.

For Catlin, leaving his bronzes in a Hong Kong vault had been the most difficult part of ending his old life and beginning the new one. It had also been very necessary. If Catlin were to survive, his undercover identity as Rousseau must end. Completely. And so his "death" had been arranged.

But Rousseau didn't die, did he? Catlin asked himself bitterly. *Not completely. Chen Yi resurrected him from the hell of the past with half of an old coin. And now I'm dragging someone down into that hell with me, someone who has done nothing to earn it, someone who deserves much better than what I'll bring to her.*

Lindsay watched Catlin's dark face and wondered what thoughts were turning within the desolate amber depths of his eyes. From what little she knew about his past, she could guess that his memories weren't the sort to be trivialized on rose-tinted greeting cards. The realization didn't disturb her. Some of her own memories were less than cheerful, too.

For once Lindsay was glad of the role she had to play. It gave her an excuse to take Catlin's grim face between her hands and kiss him gently. His mouth was unresponsive. His hands covered hers, removing them abruptly.

"Save it for later," he said in a carrying tone. "I want to look at the bronzes." He smiled as he spoke, but there was no emotion in his eyes, nothing but the chill she had instinctively attempted to warm.

The rejection was complete and unexpected. For an instant Lindsay stared at Catlin, seeing from the corner of her eye the smiles of two collectors before they looked away from the small incident. Humiliation and anger rose in her cheeks. Deliberately she smiled at him, showing all her lovely white teeth.

"Later? I don't think so," she said, her voice much softer than his had been. "Unless *later* is another word for never." She leaned closer to him, smoothing his tie with her fingertips. When she spoke, her voice carried no farther than his ears. "I'm supposed to be infatuated, not rock stupid. You made the touchy-feely rules, Catlin, and now you will damn well play by them. Or else we can have a lovely, very public little spat and you can get another hotel room"

Lindsay smiled suddenly, a real smile, for the knowledge that tonight she would have to share Catlin's bed in reality rather than simply appearing to share it had been undermining her composure at odd moments. And share it she would. There was no help for it; the hotel maid would know very quickly if two beds had been slept in. What the hotel maid knew, other people could buy from her.

"Yes I like the idea of two rooms," Lindsay murmured. "It has real possibilities. Why didn't I think of it sooner?"

Humor flickered for a moment, changing the grim lines of Catlin's face. But it was only for a moment. "Don't push it, honey," he said very softly. "If you do, I'll make you blush down to your toenails."

Lindsay understood the warning very clearly—play the game his way or undergo a very public bout of lovemaking. "You really are my very own G.B., aren't you?" she whispered, smiling brittlely.

"Remember that," he answered with equal softness. "It will save us both a lot of trouble."

She stared up at him for a moment, her face as expressionless as his.

In the sudden silence came the sound of an old-fashioned lighter's metal top snapping shut. Catlin looked up just in time to see Yi return the lighter to his pocket and expel a stream of pungent smoke. Yi's glance passed over Catlin and Lindsay without pausing, as though they were strangers.

"Remember, too," murmured Catlin, "that you have never seen Chen Yi."

Lindsay nodded and carefully disengaged herself from Catlin's embrace. "Shall we look at some bronzes?" she asked, her expression tight, closed.

"What a clever idea," he said ironically. "I wish I'd thought of that myself."

"I'm just full of clever ideas," said Lindsay. Her voice was husky, as though she were referring to joint bedroom acrobatics. "Remember?"

Then she realized that Wu was watching her from the corner of his eye. Undoubtedly her old friend had been treated to a full view of a teasing woman being brought to heel by her man. She couldn't prevent the flush that heated her face as she realized what the very conservative Wu must think of her.

Catlin, too, had noticed Wu's discreet scrutiny. When Lindsay's eyes lifted to Catlin in silent apology for the blush she couldn't control, he took her arm and led her toward the next bronze. He wanted to tell her that the blush didn't diminish her role one bit. In fact, it helped to validate the act as little else could have. She was the perfect picture of a woman caught in a blazing affair, doing things that she would never do otherwise, embarrassed but helpless to resist because she was caught in the grip of a passion that simply overwhelmed her normal scruples. He wanted to tell Lindsay those things, reassuring her, but Wu was too close, too curious.

The next bronze was a superbly executed mirror with interlocking geometric designs and copper inlays that had turned a uniform blue-green. Lindsay had seen similar mirrors, which was just as well, for her mind was still seething. Beyond the fact that the piece was genuine, she could think of little else to say to Catlin about it. He walked around the mirror several times and moved on without comment.

It was the same for the next three pieces, ritual vessels inlaid with gold and silver. The workmanship was of a high order, but that was the hallmark of bronzes made from 500 B.C. to 206 A.D., the beginning of the Han dynasty. Karlgren, a famous bronze scholar, had designated the bronzes created in this period as the Huai style. It was the final, and greatest, of the three styles of Chinese bronzes. The pieces that Wang had collected for tonight had been cast midway through the Huai style—or were said to have been.

"Something wrong?" Catlin asked softly, seeing the vague frown on Lindsay's face.

"Nothing major. A matter of taste, you might say."

"Meaning?"

"Meaning that I think this food canister is closer to Han than to third century B.C."

"But genuine?"

"Oh, yes. It will make a very nice addition to the museum's collection," she said, walking slowly around the piece. "We don't have a—"

"No," Catlin said smoothly.

"What?" asked Lindsay, startled out of her concentration on the bronze.

"Just that. No. I want this bronze."

As Catlin was making no particular effort to lower his voice, it carried quite clearly to anyone who was interested in listening.

"But it was my name on the invitation tonight," Lindsay said automatically, "and the museum always has first call on my—"

"Don't go all technical on me," interrupted Catlin, smiling as he caressed Lindsay's arm. "Buy something else for the museum. Bid on this one for me."

"Catlin—"

"Do it, honey cat. For me."

Although the words were coaxing, the pressure of his hand on her arm was very firm, as though he expected her to bolt. She smiled weakly at him, realizing what he was doing and why. What she hadn't realized before this instant was how very hard it was going to be for her.

"I—" Lindsay's voice fragmented into silence. She took another breath and tried to smile up at the golden-eyed dragon who was watching her so intently. "All right. Darling. Just this once."

Catlin bent and kissed Lindsay's unconvincing smile, concealing it. Then he quickly led her around the corner of the L-shaped room to the display that had been out of sight until that moment. Lindsay stopped without warning. The bronze she was facing wiped everything from her mind but a sense of wild astonishment and discovery followed by a piercing stroke of regret.

At the end of the room was an ebony table big enough to seat four. Crouched in the center of the table was an extraordinary bronze dragon. In it the realism that was the highest development of the Huai style had reached a magnificent level. Sinuous, powerful, mysterious, the dragon watched the world with eyes of beaten gold. The gold was repeated in a scrollwork of designs that both defined and enhanced every muscular line of the dragon's body. Traces of silver showed in tarnished teeth and in claws.

In absolute silence Catlin and Lindsay studied the dragon. After several long minutes he looked up, reluctant to ask whether the beast were genuine art or a powerful fraud. She met his eyes and didn't know what to say.

"Tell me," he said flatly.

"I—oh, Catlin," she said, her voice low, sad, "I'm afraid it's a fraud."

Catlin's breath came out with a harsh sound. "Are you sure?"

"I—"

He waited, seeing both her distress and her confusion. "Lindsay?" he asked finally, softly.

Almost wildly she looked away from Catlin, back toward the magnificent dragon who watched her in return. "I want it to be genuine," she said raggedly. "It's magnificent," she whispered. "Just . . . magnificent. I would never have believed that a fraud could be so compelling, so alive."

"But you're sure it's a fraud?"

Slowly, sadly, Lindsay nodded.

"Why? What's wrong with it?" he demanded.

She spread her hands helplessly.

"The designs are right for the period," said Catlin. He wasn't asking for her opinion. He knew.

Again, Lindsay nodded. "They're very like the rhinoceros."

"What?"

"A bronze found in Hsing-p'ing. Extraordinary. The same dense, sinuous designs worked in gold. The same profound realism in the details of anatomy. Unmistakable. Very powerful. Very masculine. The rhinoceros was by far the most stunning piece of bronze I'd ever seen—until today."

"Go on," said Catlin.

"But unlike the rhinoceros, there were no models in real life to take this dragon from. This came out of man's mind, a creation from whole cloth based on thousands of years of tradition. And that's just it. The style of the dragon is wrong for the third century B.C. In Huai times, the dragon motif was little more than sinuous lines and two eyes staring outward. The Huai style worshipped a reality that was as solid and magnificent and tangible as a rhinoceros with its head thrown up to test the wind for danger. Dragons are not tangible. They're symbolic."

Lindsay sighed and brushed her fingertips over the bunched muscles of the dragon's neck. Absurdly she felt tears burn behind her eyes.

"Whoever made this was an artist of incredible skill and power," she said when she was sure of her own self-control once more. "He knew that dragons weren't real, that they lived only in the mind of man. And he knew that for that very reason, dragons are more real than anything else, because reality is what we make of it rather than what it makes of us."

Lindsay looked up suddenly, feeling Catlin's intensity as he listened to her. "Whoever created this dragon was modern," she said. "He looked at the world through the eyes of a man who has discovered that ancient Taoism and modern particle physics are one and the same pursuit, that the more closely man investigates physical reality, the more metaphysical reality becomes. That is a very modern point of view. And to me, very compelling. This art is from my own time, my own world, my own beliefs. That's why it's so incredibly moving to me.''

Lindsay shook her head, still unable to believe that the fraudulent bronze could hold her mind and emotions so completely. "I should hate this dragon. I hate all fakes. Why don't I hate this one?"

"Because the dragon isn't a fraud. Only this is," said Catlin, flicking his fingernail against the card that stated: "Hsing-p'ing district, Shaanxi province, about third century B.C."

There was a long moment of silence before Lindsay let out her breath and said, "I would like to believe that this bronze was created out of a need to express the nature of reality and dragons, rather than a desire to pull money out of gullible pockets. In fact, I choose to believe it."

"Reality is what we make of it, is that it?" said Catlin, repeating her words like a man turning a familiar, complex object in his hands, examining it from all perspectives.

"Up to a certain point, yes," Lindsay said firmly.

"You mean that no matter how hard you try, you can't make sand out to be wine," he said, smiling suddenly.

She laughed, feeling the last of her sadness slide away, a melancholy that had come when she had realized that the magnificent dragon was less than it seemed. And it was also more. "Exactly. Although I'm told that some people have lived who can drink sand wine."

"Do you believe that?"

With a graceful shrug, Lindsay returned her attention to the dragon. "It doesn't matter, because I know that I'm not one of them."

"How about you, Wang?" said Catlin, turning smoothly. "Can you drink sand wine?"

Startled, Lindsay looked over her shoulder. Her breath came in sharply. Sam Wang was standing not four feet away. Next to him was Chen Yi and his two Chinese comrades. From the look on Wang's face it was clear that he had overheard the discussion of his expensive, beautifully wrought and almost certainly fraudulent dragon.

12

FOR A MOMENT all Lindsay could do was
stare at Sam Wang's handsome, utterly controlled face and wish that she had heard him come up behind
her as Catlin so obviously had. Everything that she had said
about the dragon returned to her in a rush.

Because it would have been rude to do otherwise, Wang introduced the three Chinese to Catlin and Lindsay. The woman
was Mrs. Zhu. Her counterpart was Mr. Pao. Like Yi, they
spoke Mandarin. Unlike Yi, they didn't understand or speak
English; or if they did, they kept it to themselves. When introduced, they gave Lindsay the exaggerated facial responses of
people who have no other means of communicating. Although Zhu and Pao were introduced as Yi's secretary and assistant respectively, they stood elbow to elbow with Yi, silently
proclaiming that they were his equals. Lindsay thought that
odd; despite the carefully enforced equalities of the modern
People's Republic, nuances of position and power were ad-
hered to with a cultural tenacity that was the result of five
thousand years of obsession with face. No matter what role Pao
and Zhu were playing, they would not position themselves as
Yi's equals unless they were.

With the directness possible only to a nonnative Chinese,
Wang raised the subject of the dragon as soon as the introductions were complete.

"So you don't like my dragon?" he asked Lindsay, but there
was no real doubt in Wang's voice. Obviously he had overheard more than he had wanted to.

"I like it very much," countered Lindsay.

"But not as a Huai bronze?"

"It's every bit as finely crafted as a Huai," she said, wishing that the subject would be closed.

"But it's not a Huai?" pressed Wang.

Lindsay sighed. "Mr. Wang—" she began.

"Sam," he corrected, glancing approvingly at the picture Lindsay made in her simple black dress and unusual ivory jewelry. "In California, only enemies and outlanders use last names."

She smiled unwillingly, appreciating both Wang's quickness and his approval of her as a woman. "I can't be positive without tests, of course, but there is something about the dragon that is very modern. At least to me," she amended.

"Certainly not the patina," retorted Wang.

"It's an excellent patina," Lindsay agreed, looking again at the rare cinnamon finish and wondering what new process had been discovered that could chemically age bronze to that color.

"It shows the marks of being cast by the *cire perdu* method, as all Huai bronzes were," pointed out Wang.

With a sense of being led into a trap, Lindsay nodded. She, too, had noted the very subtle marks of the lost wax casting process. As with the best of such bronzes, the casting marks had been incorporated into the design itself, enhancing rather than detracting from the final result.

"The clay core that the dragon was cast around passed the thermoluminescence test. Third century B.C., plus or minus a century," Wang continued. He waited half a beat and added smoothly, "Would you like to see the lab report?"

Even though she was watching Wang, Lindsay felt Catlin's sudden scrutiny. She knew what he was thinking. The thermoluminescence test was the benchmark of authenticity for all articles made of fired clay. The test was based on the fact that tiny crystals within the clay absorbed background radiation at a known rate. When heated by firing, the crystals gave up all their stored radiation in tiny flashes of light. Then the crystals began storing radiation all over again. When a sample of clay was reheated centuries later in a modern lab, the crystals once more gave up their stored energy. The energy that was released was measured, compared to a time scale and a date was assigned to the clay used in creating the objet d'art.

"Was a thin section of the bronze put under a microscope to see whether the patina has penetrated the bronze itself rather than simply being applied to the surface of the metal?" Lindsay asked quietly. It was the one test that men hadn't learned how to get around. Only time could root the patina deeply in the bronze itself.

Wang shrugged. "Why bother? The test I used is the standard in the field."

"For fired clay, yes," agreed Lindsay, her voice both pleasant and firm. "But a modern clay object can be irradiated until it will appear to be old on a thermoluminescence test."

"But you'd need very expensive X-ray equipment and a really thorough knowledge of modern testing to pull that off," objected Wang.

"It's been done," Catlin said dryly, entering the conversation for the first time. "Caused quite a stir, if I remember correctly. A museum participated in the X-raying just as a way to prove that copies and forgeries couldn't make it past their experts."

Wang shot Catlin a single look, then returned his attention to Lindsay.

"I can give you the name of two labs that specialize in testing the age of metal artifacts," Lindsay offered.

"Hell, that would take weeks," muttered Wang, shaking his head. Then he circled back on the argument from another angle. "Why would someone buy hundreds of thousands of dollars worth of X-ray equipment just to irradiate a bronze?"

"Is that how much it costs to fake a bronze?" Catlin asked, raising his eyebrows.

Wang's mouth thinned to a flat line at the implication.

"The why of it is simple," Lindsay said quickly, wanting to keep the discussion as pleasant as possible under the circumstances. "If the dragon is Huai, it's automatically placed in a very old, very valuable artistic tradition. On the other hand, if the dragon is modern, in terms of the marketplace its value is problematical. There is no definable market for a modern Chinese bronze, no matter how exquisitely made and artistically superb that bronze might be. Put another way, a modern bronze is worth whatever someone will pay for it."

Surprisingly, Wang's expression softened for an instant. He looked at the dragon. "Artistically superb, huh? So you liked it?"

"Very much," said Lindsay, hearing the wistfulness in her own husky voice. "But I won't bid on the dragon for the museum, Catlin, or myself. Not as long as the bronze is being sold as third century."

Silence stretched while Wang brooded over the crouching dragon. Then he pulled a pen from his pocket, turned over the card that proclaimed the dragon was more than two thousand years old and printed NFS neatly across the back of the card. Not For Sale. He propped the card up against the dragon's long, curving claws.

"That isn't necessary," Lindsay said softly, knowing that the gesture was costing Sam Wang a literal fortune. "I wouldn't have said anything to anyone who didn't ask. And if someone did ask, I would tell them exactly what I'm telling you—I could be wrong. That dragon could be as old as it is magnificent."

Wang gave her a sideways look. "It could be, but the damage is done either way. When Mr. Chen discovered that you were one of the people here tonight, he asked to meet you. Your reputation has preceded you, as they say. We overheard what you said." As Wang shrugged, his smile turned down at the corners. "What's that old saw about eavesdroppers never hearing good news? Well, it's true in this case. Until I get a test run on that dragon's patina, I don't have a chance in hell of getting a decent price for it."

"I'm sorry," Lindsay said quietly. "Not for my opinion, but that you would suffer a loss because of it."

"The dragon's on consignment from Vancouver," Wang said carelessly, "so I'm not out more than the cost of insurance and shipping. Besides, I suppose it was worth it to see you at work. I've heard about your feel for bronzes, but frankly, I didn't believe it. Chen Yi was right. You're the best."

When Lindsay glanced at Yi, he bowed slightly, acknowledging her status as a respected expert.

"You do me great honor," murmured Lindsay, bowing her head in the Chinese fashion.

Mrs. Zhu burst into rapid Mandarin, asking Chen Yi what was being said.

Lindsay started to answer in Mandarin, then realized that just as she was supposed to pretend that she had never before met Yi, perhaps she shouldn't reveal her knowledge of Mandarin, either. The thought of such concealment was so foreign to her that she literally froze. In the end she waited silently, eyes downcast, trying to reassure herself that by not speaking she was actually being polite. The questions, after all, had been addressed to Yi, not to her; he was the respected male, while she was merely the foreign female whose status, no matter how great, could not equal that of any Chinese man, no matter how humble.

Catlin put his hand in the small of Lindsay's back. "If you will excuse us?" he asked politely, looking from Wang to the three Chinese. "There are other bronzes we should look at before the auction begins."

As they walked away Lindsay could feel the glances of the Chinese following her and Catlin. When they turned the corner and went back into the larger part of the L-shaped room, she made a sound of relief.

"Yeah," Catlin said into her ear. "Comrade Zhu could stare holes in bronze."

Lindsay sighed and relaxed against the warm hand that was guiding her. "Women rather like her must have sat in public squares knitting caps while the guillotine sliced its way through the French aristocracy," whispered Lindsay.

"Don't underestimate good old Comrade Pao at chopping time," Catlin said in an equally discreet tone. "I suspect he understands English quite well."

"Really?"

"When you and Sam were talking, Pao's eyes followed the conversation, not the speaker," explained Catlin. "When Sam was arguing about patina, Pao looked at the dragon. When Sam was arguing about thermoluminescence tests, Pao looked at you for your reaction.''

"You mean Pao already knew I'd tagged the dragon as modern? He didn't have to wait for Yi's translation?"

Catlin nodded. ''They had been standing there for nearly all of our conversation about the dragon. As none of them said a word to each other until I turned around and said hello to Wang, there was no opportunity for Yi to translate your words for his comrades.''

"Oh. Suddenly I feel better about not translating for the good Mrs. Zhu,'' Lindsay murmured. She glanced up, catching Catlin's eye. ''Should I let on that I speak Mandarin?''

"Why not?" he said softly against her hair as they bent over a bronze. ''Your background as a child in China is part of your value as an appraiser, so your knowledge of the language is hardly a secret. Go ahead and speak Mandarin. You have enough lies to keep straight without worrying about that.''

"Well, at least these aren't among the lies,'' muttered Lindsay, gesturing to the inlaid bronze ovals resting on a black velvet cloth.

Like the oval harness pieces that Jackie Merriman had shown to Catlin, these bronzes were Ordos. Some were in the Coiled Beast motif, others were in the Animal Combat motif, with two animals locked together to make the obligatory circle. The inlay work was unusually well done, and unusually well preserved.

"Does your collection have similar pieces?'' asked Lindsay.

Catlin made a sound that could have signified interest, disinterest or anything between. It was the sort of all-purpose noise collectors and connoisseurs used when they didn't want to be disturbed in their study of an objet d'art. Without irritation, Lindsay took the hint and stepped slightly to one side, allowing Catlin free access to the small table.

The long decorator mirror hanging on the wall in front of the table reflected not only the bronzes, but also Catlin's features as he moved from side to side in his study of the small oval pieces. Lindsay watched the shadows change on his face as he turned, the midnight shine of hair and mustache, the steeply arched eyebrows, the metallic glint of gold as light pooled in eyes surrounded by a thick frame of black lashes. It was not a peaceful face. The line of cheekbone, nose and jaw was too hard, too unforgiving. It was, however, an arresting face, a study in masculine planes and strength relieved only by the unexpected sensuality of full, sharply defined lips beneath the midnight gleam of mustache.

Gradually Lindsay became aware that she was not the only person studying Catlin's face in the mirror. On the other side of the table, at the same angle as she was but ten feet farther back, an Asian man stared at Catlin's reflection like someone who was confronting his imminent death. The man's skin was pale, glistening with sweat, and his mouth was slack. He turned away suddenly and retreated straight across the room, brushing by people and bronzes as he went.

Moving aside slightly to change her angle of view, Lindsay kept the man in sight as he reached the far end of the long room. He went straight to a group of Asian men, one of whom was Hsiang Wu. Lindsay couldn't hear the conversation, but from the agitated gestures of the man's hands and the startled turning of heads, it was clear that Catlin was the subject.

"Do you recognize anyone in the group besides Wu?" asked Catlin in a quiet voice. Then, harshly, "No. Don't look at me. Just answer."

Lindsay would have sworn that Catlin hadn't looked up from the bronzes, but his words made it clear that he had seen at least as much in the mirror as she had.

"They're too far away for me to tell, unless I study them openly. I could find out later from Wu if you like," she added, wondering how important it was.

"I don't think so," murmured Catlin, picking up and handing to her one of the small bronze ovals. "Yi will find out for us if we can't wangle an introduction from Sam."

"At least one of them won't need an introduction to you," Lindsay said, her voice low. She looked at the bronze Catlin had put on her palm, but it was the man's shocked, terrified face she was seeing. "He knows you, Catlin," she said flatly. "And he's scared."

Catlin's mouth curved into a small, chilling smile as he turned the bronze over on her palm.

"Do you recognize him?" Lindsay asked tightly.

Catlin took the bronze again, replaced it on the velvet and guided her to the next table, which lay in the direction of the man who had taken several long looks at Catlin and then fled as though hell had opened up before him.

Lindsay bit her lip against the temptation to repeat the question. She had seen fear too often in the past not to recognize it on the man's face now. That kind of fear was contagious at some primal level, making her heart beat faster. With each step closer that Catlin came, the man flinched and subtly drew back, putting more of the group between him and Catlin.

"What do you think of this one?" asked Catlin, bending over a bronze rice bowl.

"Genuine," Lindsay said in a clipped tone. "Like you."

"G.B.?" he asked, flashing her a smile and a glance from clear amber eyes.

"The rope pattern is done very well," she said grudgingly, giving the bronze her whole attention. "It looks strong enough to hang someone with."

Laughing softly, Catlin pulled Lindsay on to the next bronze display, a move that brought them closer to the man who was trying very hard to fade into the silk wallpaper. The pieces on display were three spearheads. They were very slender, with elongated, leaflike shapes. The design was both elegant and deadly, for the graceful contours of the spearheads concealed the architectural strength given to the weapon by the powerful central rib and harshly beveled edges. The sockets were decorated, and from each depended a small loop which could have carried a decorative silk tassel or a feathered plume.

"These," murmured Catlin, "I will buy."

Lindsay was grateful that the Museum of the Asias had a fine and extensive collection of bronze spearheads, for she knew she didn't have a chance of talking Catlin out of these. Part of her admired the clean lines of the weapons; the rest of her would rather the artist had expended his skill on something other than death.

"Without them, there would have been no Qin, no unified China, no Xi'an, no Mount Li, no history but barbarism," said Catlin, accurately reading Lindsay's expression. "Civilizations didn't just happen. They came at spear point."

"And they went the same way," she pointed out crisply.

Catlin's laugh was both startling and warm, as unexpected as the dragon crouched around the corner, out of sight but not out of mind.

"No argument there," he said. "But I still want those spearheads." Without changing his expression at all, Catlin asked, "Is he gone?"

It took Lindsay a moment to realize what Catlin meant. Discreetly she looked a bit to the right, where the group stood about ten feet behind Catlin.

"Yes."

"Recognize any of the others now that we're closer?"

There was a silence while Lindsay bent over the spearheads and simultaneously studied the group of men through the screen of her lowered eyelashes.

"Maybe. One of them might be a collector from Japan. Another could be a Korean collector I saw up in Vancouver just before I met you." Lindsay made a hidden, dismissing motion with her hand. "It's hard for me to say. They weren't clients or competitors when I first saw them, so I really didn't pay much attention."

"Have you seen anyone here who is a curator for any museum?" asked Catlin.

As he ran a fingertip along a spearhead that was surprisingly sharp, he heard Lindsay's breath come in and sensed her sudden intense scrutiny of the faces around her. The room was comfortably full but not crowded. People milled slowly, looking at bronzes and greeting associates.

"That's odd," Lindsay muttered.

"What?"

"There aren't any curators, yet I know of at least seven museums that would give a hefty portion of their acquisition funds for some of these bronzes. Sam Wang must know that, too." Lindsay frowned and looked around the room again. "Maybe the other museum curators came earlier, or will be coming in later."

Catlin made a neutral sound and continued looking at the spearheads. Lindsay's words had confirmed what he had already suspected—tonight was a roll call of potential bidders on Qin's charioteer. There wouldn't be any legitimate curators present tonight. No museum employee would bid hundreds of thousands of dollars for acquisitions that might have to be turned back over to the rightful owner amid a huge scandal.

Private collectors, however, were under no constraint to display their acquisitions publicly and thus risk discovery. If the provenance were doubtful, the bronze would simply vanish into a vault or a very well-guarded home. If inquiries were made later, a bill of sale could be produced showing that the bronze in question had been resold and shipped to Switzerland. The trail would end there, for Switzerland was the great burial ground for any hopes of recovering stolen art. In Switzerland there was no restriction or tax imposed on imported art. As a result, anything that could be smuggled into the country was home free as far as the Swiss authorities were concerned. It could be legitimately and openly exported from Switzerland— after a hefty export tax was paid, of course.

The fact that the art obviously hadn't originated in Switzerland and quite probably had been stolen and smuggled across international borders was of no interest to Swiss officials. Nor were the export forms the Swiss required very useful to someone tracing stolen goods. "Ancient Chinese bronze," was a rather broad category. A museum full of dubious goods could be concealed under that heading.

In matters of private wealth and profit, the Swiss were, as ever, accommodating.

"What do you think, Catlin?" asked Lindsay.

He glanced casually around the room. "I think we missed a row of tables."

She started to say that she had been asking about missing curators rather than missing bronzes, but after a look at Catlin's profile she pressed her lips shut and followed him. She confined her comments to the bronzes, unbending only to admire a particularly fine rectangular wine vessel. The combination of silver and malachite inlay brought the vessel's *t'ao-t'ieh* motif into stark reality. Full-faced, complex, the beast mask stared outward into the centuries, a dark shadow cast by a human soul.

The thought did not reassure Lindsay. It was one thing to understand intellectually that art reflected all that was human—good, bad and neutral. It was quite another to look at art and see your own midnight fears looking back at you. Even so, she knew that the wine vessel was worthy of a position in any museum's collection. Next to the food canister, the wine vessel was the most outstanding ancient bronze in Sam Wang's collection.

With a half-hidden sideways glance, Lindsay watched Catlin, trying to decide whether he intended to have her bid on the bronze for him, or whether he would be satisfied with the food canister he had chosen.

"Relax. I have one similar to it," he said.

Startled, Lindsay faced him fully. "Stop doing that."

"What?"

"Reading my mind!"

Catlin's slow smile made Lindsay's pulse quicken in the instant before she reminded herself that it was an act, all of it, the touches and kisses and sexy smiles. Lies.

Suddenly all the rest of the lies crowded in on Lindsay, making the room seem too small, too hot, too tight. The bidding would begin soon, and then Wu would watch while his protégée tossed away a lifetime of scruples for a man who was at best simply a temporary lover and at worst a con artist using her for his own ends. But Lindsay couldn't do anything to change the act or its ramifications. She could only watch Wu's face and silently cry out that she hadn't changed, that she was still worthy of respect, that her fall from grace was just a deception to conceal a deeper, more worthy truth.

But Wu wouldn't hear her inner cry. He wouldn't know. He would see the lie and call it truth. And then he would turn away from her.

"Don't think about it," Catlin said, taking Lindsay's hand.

"About what?" she whispered, looking at her slender fingers enveloped within his harder, darker flesh.

He put his other hand under her chin and forced her to look into his eyes.

"About tonight," Catlin said very quietly, his words going no farther than her ears. "About the bidding. About what people will think when you buy that food canister for your lover instead of your employer. About the sideways looks and hidden smiles. About disappointment and regret. About Hsiang Wu."

A tiny shudder rippled through Lindsay. "How did you know?" she whispered.

"I'm the tour guide, remember? I've been to all these places before. And then I went on to other places, carefully selected areas of hell I hope you never have to see. Think about that, Lindsay. No matter what happens, I've been there, too. I'll help you if I can, if you'll let me."

"Why?" she asked, searching the golden brown eyes that were so close to hers. "Because it's your job?"

"Does it matter?"

"Yes," she whispered.

"It shouldn't," he said bluntly. His voice was low, urgent. "My motivations aren't part of the act. Only the act matters. Only the act will get you what you wanted badly enough that you sold your soul for it—a chance to see Emperor Qin's bronzes."

"That wasn't the only reason," whispered Lindsay.

"It should have been," Catlin said in a low, gritty voice. His fingers tightened almost painfully on her chin. "Leaving the world a better place than you found it is a dream for fools."

"You can't believe that," she breathed.

"Can't I?"

"No!"

"*Yes.* Welcome to hell, Lindsay Danner."

She stared into Catlin's savage eyes for a long moment, then looked away.

Silently Catlin watched Lindsay's profile. When she controlled the tears that had given a silver sheen to her dark blue eyes, he allowed himself to relax slightly for the first time since he had realized that Hsiang Wu would be present for Lindsay's debut as an unscrupulous curator of Chinese bronzes.

"It will be easier the next time," murmured Catlin, running the back of his finger lightly down Lindsay's cheekbone. "The lies won't seem as unbearable."

"I'm not sure that comforts me," she said in a strained whisper.

Catlin's mouth thinned as he wished urgently, futilely, that Lindsay were a different kind of woman. Less intelligent. Less perceptive. Less sensitive. Less honest. The last most of all. She saw the ramifications of what she was doing, what she had yet to do; and she was too honest with herself to lie and say it would all turn out just fine. She saw too many ways it could go wrong, too many people who would never trust her again.

And she didn't even see the half of it.

Silently, bitterly, Catlin consigned Chen Yi to the inmost circle of the complex hell he had drawn Lindsay into. With a firm hand at her back, Catlin guided her to the adjoining room where delicacies from all over Asia had been set out to refresh guests who had already assessed the bronzes. Lindsay wanted to refuse the morsels Catlin offered her. One of his cool, subtly goading looks changed her mind. She ate succulent tidbits of seafood and sipped the elegant French and California wines that Sam Wang had put out.

At first Lindsay thought that her stomach would rebel. She closed her eyes and tried to summon up some of the mental discipline of *tai chi chuan.* The ancient Chinese combination of meditation, exercise, philosophy and self-defense had helped her even as a child, when days of tension and nights of churning, violent dreams had left her frayed and nervous. She had learned to look forward to the early morning *tai chi chuan* sessions when everyone in the compound would follow the stately, subtly powerful movements of the compound's oldest male. As she had grown older herself, her interest in *tai chi chuan* had deepened. Even today, half a world removed, she continued to spend an hour a day pursuing the ancient discipline. Though she had never spoken the thought aloud, she often felt that the requirements and rewards of *tai chi chuan* were more suited to her than the stringent form of Christianity her parents had gone to China to spread.

"Lindsay?" Catlin's voice was low, concerned.

She breathed deeply in a way that was supposed to fill her mind with serenity and her body with energy. It didn't work completely, but it did allow her to control her exterior responses. That was all she asked—an improvement on the impossible. She had meant it when she told Catlin that she wasn't interested in perfection.

"I'll be all right," she said quietly, opening her eyes. "Not perfect. Just all right."

He searched the shadowed indigo of her eyes and saw that, as always, she was telling him the truth. He nodded slowly and turned the conversation to the bronzes they had just seen.

By the time the auction began, Lindsay had herself under control once more. She managed to smile at Catlin, neither flinching from nor responding too greatly to his touch, and brushed against him with the casual assurance of a woman who was intimate with a certain man. She thought about nothing but the act, focusing her attention on it with the same intensity and intelligence that she had always brought to the study of *tai chi chuan* and Chinese bronzes.

If Lindsay's smile was too quick, too brittle, and her eyes were too shadowed, too evasive, Catlin didn't complain. He sensed the cost of her act with an acuity that disturbed him. It was necessary for him to be attuned to her, because then he could step in and take over if the demands of the act confused or overwhelmed her. It was not necessary for him to sense her distress to the point that he, too, felt like a wolf with its paw in a trap, forced to choose between self-mutilation and death.

Yet he couldn't help feeling that way. His insight into people had always been unusually good. It had saved his life more than once. But this was different, an awareness of Lindsay that was both unexpected and uncanny, shafts of understanding illuminating her and himself, instants both painful and compelling. It was distracting. Even worse, it was dangerous. He could afford to feel no emotions at all while he lived in hell. Not a single emotion. Nothing. That was the only truth in hell; and it was that truth which had finally driven him out of hell into a wider, more gentle world.

Then Chen Yi had come, holding in his hand half a coin from a dead man's eyes.

Grimly Catlin forced himself to concentrate on the progress of the auction rather than on old mistakes. Eyes narrowed, he watched the bidders shift and change with each moment. The bidding was aggressive and generous. Despite the careful informality of the auction—the object under bid was simply pointed to by an assistant during the bidding, as no catalog had been presented or expected—the auctioneer was a professional of the highest skill. He joked in English and Mandarin, repeated bids in each language as increments of ten thousand American dollars were passed, and kept the bids coming with deceptive ease. His assistant was a stunning Eurasian woman with black hair to her hips, a scarlet silk wraparound that wasn't much longer, and a linguistic repertoire consisting of Japanese, Cantonese and British-accented English.

The first purchase Lindsay made was quite simple. The assistant's elegantly sculptured nails touched the spearheads; Lindsay listened to the bids for a moment or two, then quietly entered with a bid that was high enough to discourage any but truly avid collectors.

"Twelve thousand dollars."

"Thirteen thousand," said a man on the other side of the room.

"Eighteen," Lindsay said calmly.

There was no counteroffer.

"Sold," said the auctioneer.

"Well done," Catlin said, smiling at Lindsay as the assistant took down his name as the new owner of the spear points.

"Hardly a bargain," she muttered, "but I did what I could to keep the price reasonable."

"One good, sobering jump rather than a bunch of little bids that sneak up. Keeps auction fever to a minimum," summarized Catlin.

She threw him a speculative glance. "Sounds like you've done it before."

"Once or twice," he agreed dryly.

They listened while Hsiang Wu went head-to-head with a Korean collector over a gold-and-silver-inlaid bowl. Lindsay was happy that the Museum of the Asias didn't want that particular item, because both Wu and the Korean were intent on owning it. In the end Wu was forced to bow out at sixteen thousand dollars. He was a seller, not a collector. If he bid any higher there would be no profit for him in a resale.

Lindsay ignored the tension rising in her each time the auction moved to another bronze. None of the pieces had been numbered, so she had no indication when the food canister that Catlin wanted would come up for bid. It was probably just as well. She had no desire to know the exact moment she would open her mouth and ruin her own reputation.

The bowl disappeared from the auction table, only to be replaced by the rectangular wine vessel and lid that Lindsay wanted for the museum. The presence of a lid was very rare, making the vessel enormously attractive. She listened to the bidding for a moment and knew there would be no hope of preempting. The bids were rising in thousand-dollar increments. When two of the bidders dropped out, she entered her first bid.

"Twenty thousand," said Lindsay.

"Twenty-one," countered the Korean who had outbid Wu.

"Twenty-two," Lindsay said.

Another bidder entered. The bidding resumed. By the time the price reached thirty-one thousand, only the Korean and Lindsay remained.

The Korean hesitated, then shrugged, signaling his withdrawal. The Museum of the Asias was thirty-five thousand dollars poorer, but its bronze collection had been enriched by a much-needed example of Huai inlay artistry.

"Congratulations," Catlin said softly. "It's a bowl I wouldn't mind owning. Not a bad price, either. Especially for this crowd."

Lindsay's eyes widened. When she spoke, she kept her voice low in what was becoming an automatic reflex against being overheard. "I thought you said you already had a bowl like that one."

"Did I?" he murmured. "Wonder what I was thinking of."

Suddenly Lindsay realized that Catlin had let her buy the richly inlaid bowl for her museum while keeping the somewhat less spectacular food canister for himself. Buying either bronze for him would serve to ruin her reputation; yet this way she could at least have the private satisfaction of knowing that the museum had gained the more valuable of the two bronzes. It was small comfort, but then, hell wasn't known for its comforts.

And Catlin knew it.

"Thank you," Lindsay whispered, touching his hand.

His fingers closed around hers in a grip that was just short of pain. She didn't object. She, too, had seen the vessel Sam Wang was carrying up to the auction table. It was the food canister she must buy for Catlin—the downfall of her reputation cast in bronze, with fragments of inlay clinging to it like tattered, worn truths.

13

"Do I HEAR TEN THOUSAND?" asked the auctioneer, opening the bidding. "Ten. Do I hear ten?"

"Thirty thousand dollars," Lindsay said tightly.

The preemptive bid brought a few startled murmurs from the crowd. Lindsay ignored them. She wanted to get the whole sordid thing over with as quickly as possible.

"Thirty-one."

The bid came from a place just a few feet to Lindsay's right. When she recognized Wu's high, calm voice, she felt a sense of relief. He wouldn't bid for the canister as long or as fervently as a collector, because Wu had to have a margin for profit on resale.

"Thirty-three," said Lindsay.

Sideways glances registered surprise as the crowd heard the bid. With the same calm voice, Wu topped Lindsay's bid again and then again. She countered each time, sending the price higher and higher, knowing that Wu would have to stop soon. He should have stopped at thirty-three. He was a businessman, not a collector in the full flush of obsession. For him, the canister simply wasn't worth the money that was being bid on it now.

"Forty thousand dollars," Wu said.

Lindsay turned and stared at him, unable to believe her ears. What should have been a brief auction was turning into the kind of bidding match that would send waves of electric curiosity through the elite community of bronze fanciers.

Wu watched Lindsay in return, his face impassive, his eyes black and clear.

In that instant she knew what Wu was doing. He was going to drive the price of the canister up so high that Catlin would walk away from the bronze, and in doing so, save Lindsay's reputation as a woman of scrupulous honesty. Wu was trying to prevent her from reaping the bitter harvest of regret that would come if she betrayed her own principles.

Almost desperately Lindsay looked toward Catlin, not caring that she was the center of avid interest among the gathering.

"It isn't worth—" she began.

"Buy it."

The flat command went through Lindsay like a shock wave. People murmured and shifted, straining forward to better see the curator of bronzes who was taking orders from a lover rather than an employer. Lindsay barely noticed the increased interest on the part of the crowd. All she wanted to do was get the bidding over with, no longer to be the center of speculative glances and gossiping tongues, to have this first step in the destruction of her reputation concluded so that she could walk out into the night and be free of the act for just a few minutes.

"Forty-one thousand," Lindsay said in a stranger's voice.

"Forty-five," said Wu.

She didn't need to look to Catlin for advice. He couldn't have made himself more clear. Money wasn't the object, nor was the canister.

"Fifty thousand," she said.

"Fifty-fi—"

"Sixty," Lindsay interrupted flatly, not waiting for Wu to finish his bid.

It was much more than the canister was worth.

There was a long silence during which Lindsay looked at nothing but the canister.

"Sixty thousand dollars American," said the auctioneer. "Going once. Going twice. Sold to Miss Danner." He smiled at her, a gesture that failed to entirely conceal his curiosity. "May I be the first to congratulate the Museum of the Asias on an unusually fine acquisition?"

"It's mine," Catlin said clearly, "not the museum's."

There was a slight pause before the auctioneer recovered. "You have excellent taste, sir. I've heard of only two other inlaid canisters like this, and one of them is in the Beijing Museum. Have you been collecting long?"

"Thank you," said Catlin carelessly, ignoring the question with a bland, amber stare that made the auctioneer shift his attention quickly back to his work.

The remaining auction was a blur to Lindsay. She began to focus only when they were on the point of leaving. Catlin was saying all the polite, necessary, meaningless things to Sam Wang as they stood in front of the open door.

"I'll forward the papers to the museum," Wang concluded, smiling first at Catlin and then at Lindsay. Any anger Wang might have had over the bronze dragon had been offset by the outrageously high price the canister had brought.

"Don't bother," said Catlin. "Papers mean nothing to me. What I buy I keep, no matter who owned it before me. Besides, most of the papers you get in this business literally aren't worth the ink that went into them."

Wang's smile was a cynical curve that had little to do with humor. He turned to Lindsay. "How about you?"

"Send the papers on the wine vessel," she said tightly. "The museum can't afford to ignore the question of provenance."

"It can, however, afford to be charitable about interpreting that provenance," Wang said smoothly. "Can't it?"

Lindsay felt the silent demand radiating from Catlin. She knew what Wang was suggesting—for a very fine piece like the wine vessel she had purchased, the museum could afford to just take the papers at face value and not ask potentially embarrassing questions.

"My museum's policy toward gift horses is the same as any other legitimate museum's," Lindsay said tightly.

Wang laughed. "Hell, I know that, Lindsay. I just didn't think you did. Ciao, you two. I'll give you a call the next time I have something good."

His words echoed in Lindsay's brain, hinting at aspects of the Museum of the Asias that she really didn't want to know about.

Reflexively she opened her mouth to object that the museum she worked for was honest. Catlin's arm closed across her shoulder, turning her around with a concealed strength that was as shocking in its way as the implications of Wang's words.

Before she could speak, she was being swept down the long, beautifully lit walkway that descended gracefully to street level where Catlin's car was parked. The hillside was flawlessly landscaped, a multilevel garden that was lighted as carefully as a museum exhibition. Dark, graceful pines burned like black, windblown flames against the lighter shade of ebony that was the night sky. A cool breeze flowed along the hill, playing hide-and-seek among the fragrant evergreen needles.

Relief swept through Lindsay, a feeling of wild freedom. There was no one to watch, to listen, to judge. The act was over for now.

But as the afterimage of the brilliant rectangle of light thrown by Wang's open door faded, Lindsay saw a slight figure standing fifteen feet down the walkway. Spotlights at ground level silhouetted the man without revealing his features. Lindsay didn't need to see the man's face to identify him. The silver-headed cane Wu used when outdoors gleamed like a fallen star.

Wang's casual insinuations about provenance and the Museum of the Asias echoed again in Lindsay's mind. Words carried very clearly in the crisp, damp air. Wu must have overheard. Now he would believe that Lindsay had put her lover's interests ahead of her employer's; and worse, that she had also tacitly agreed to accept bronzes of dubious provenance for her museum. The former act might be forgivable, a hormonal foolishness that a woman might succumb to once in her life. The latter was not. It was a compromising of principles that had no excuse.

"I'm glad we caught up with you, Mr. Hsiang," said Catlin, recognizing the silhouette as quickly as Lindsay had. "The night has barely begun. Lindsay and I were just going to celebrate the canister over some fine cognac. We'd be delighted if you joined us."

Illuminated from below, Wu's face looked like a stranger's, enigmatic, almost sinister. "It is most kind of you to include this humble person in your celebration," he said. His soft voice carried clearly in the damp air. "I am heavy with regrets that I am unable to accept your most generous invitation. The night is indeed only a child, but I am in the autumn of my years. Forgive an old man his much-needed rest."

"Of course," Catlin said, tightening his fingers warningly on Lindsay's waist, silently telling her not to speak. "Lunch, then. Tomorrow? Lindsay tells me you have some wonderful things in your shop."

Wu bowed very slightly. "It is always an honor to serve a notable collector of bronzes such as yourself, Mr. Catlin. My small and humble shop is open six days a week. Whenever you find time to visit, you are sure to find something of interest to entertain your hours. Now, if you will please be so gracious as to excuse this unworthy old man, I find that the chill of evening makes my ancient bones complain and my mind dream softly of fragrant tea and the small comforts of my home."

"I hope we can see you soon," said Catlin, acting as though he were oblivious to the currents of evasion and withdrawal that swirled through Wu's very polite phrases. "Lindsay is always talking about you."

"Catlin, don't," Lindsay whispered, ignoring the painful pressure of his fingers digging into her waist.

"She is most kind to remember a worthless old man," Wu said, speaking effortlessly over Lindsay's subdued protest. "I would not presume upon the friendships of the past by expecting her to resume them in full enthusiasm when her present overflows with new people and experiences. For her to display such kindness and generosity of spirit toward my worthless person would be unthinkable."

In aching silence Lindsay watched Wu retreat through the thick shadows and shafts of light that criss-crossed the walkway. She didn't trust herself to speak. The damp air would have amplified even the softest voice until it rang through the night like a cry for help.

Catlin gave her a hooded look, stretched his arms above his head and then draped them loosely over her shoulders. "Where do you want to celebrate?" he asked in a normal tone.

Lindsay turned and looked at him, saying nothing.

"Jet lag?" Catlin asked sympathetically. "C'mon," he said, tugging her down the path again. "I know just the thing."

"Good," she said flatly. "I need it, whatever it is."

He laughed and kissed her lips briefly. "Carte blanche is a dangerous thing to give me, honey cat."

"Don't I know it," she retorted, trying to conceal the bitterness in her voice.

Lindsay reminded herself that none of what had happened was Catlin's fault. He had warned her. She had believed him. But she hadn't believed that Wu would be the first to turn away from her, the first to lead the chorus of withdrawal and disdain. In her heart she hadn't believed that he would turn away from her at all. She had assumed that somehow he of all people would magically believe that she had good and worthy reasons for whatever she did, however unworthy those actions might appear on the surface.

"First we'll go to the hotel," Catlin said cheerfully, pulling Lindsay along in his wake with a strength that wasn't nearly as jovial as his voice. "A long, hot shower and two fingers of cognac for starters. Then I'll give you a rubdown that will unravel every nerve in that sexy body."

"Wonderful," said Lindsay, wincing at the rawness of her own voice.

She hoped that anyone overhearing the conversation would assume that it was passion rather than tears thickening her throat. Even as the thought came, rebellion flared suddenly, wildly, within her. She was so tired of monitoring each word, each intonation, of being on stage every minute of every day. The strain of it was like acid eating into her will, dissolving it. Dissolving her.

And there would be no peace back at the hotel room. There a different round of lies would begin while she tried to conceal her attraction to Catlin and tried not to remember all the small

touches and hot caresses they had shared during their time on-
stage. Concealing and forgetting her response had become more
and more difficult with each night she had spent talking to him,
laughing with him, learning from him, sharing her thoughts
with him in the hours before he had curled up on her lumpy
couch and slept until dawn.

She knew that he wanted her. She knew that he wouldn't take
her, because she wasn't a casual kind of woman and he was a
man who started nothing he couldn't finish. Even though he
might call her a fool for putting herself at risk over something
as ephemeral and intangible as the relationship between two
nations, she knew that he liked her and respected her intelligence. Just as he must know that she respected and liked him,
no matter what his past might have been. Those kinds of mutual discoveries were unavoidable between people who literally
lived in each other's pockets.

It would have been easier if she had liked him less each day.
As it was, the enforced mental intimacy of the offstage hours
made Catlin's careful avoidance of any physical intimacy during those same offstage hours all the more obvious, all the more
telling—and all the more difficult, almost to the point of impossibility.

Living with Catlin, living a lie when the truth of her feelings
was screaming silently within her, made for the kind of loneliness that eroded Lindsay's soul. Now there would be no space
remaining for anything but lies. She would have to share the
same bed with Catlin, listen to him breathing, feel his warmth
radiating out to her. So close, and never more far away than in
the hours between darkness and dawn. A second act, harder
than the first, more relentless.

Impossible. She couldn't do it. She simply couldn't. The realization made her draw a ragged breath. She fought to control her thoughts before they spiraled any further down into
darkness and despair.

"Come here," Catlin said huskily.

He pulled Lindsay into the shadow that lay thickly behind the
landscape lights. For an instant there was only the rigidity of

her resisting body, then she made a small sound and leaned against him, shuddering silently. His hands hesitated before moving soothingly over her hair and back as he gathered her closer.

Goddamn you to hell, Chen Yi! And goddamn me for helping you!

Nothing of Catlin's savage thoughts showed on his face or in his touch or in the bleak eyes searching light and shadows for any sign of watchers. For the moment there was no one close enough to tell the difference between passion and compassion as he held her.

"Try not to cry," he breathed against Lindsay's ear. "And be damn sure not to cry once we're in the car. It's probably bugged by now," he added grimly.

Or, to be precise, he had to assume it was bugged, because it was too dangerous to assume anything else. The Asian man who had fled the auction after recognizing Catlin was fully capable of getting and using electronic surveillance equipment, as well as other more deadly devices.

"Wait until we're back at the hotel," Catlin continued very softly. "Then I'll turn the shower on full and shut the door and you can cry until hell won't have it if that's what you want. But not now, Lindsay. Not now. We're sure to meet someone between here and the car. It would be hard to explain why you're crying when we should be celebrating getting our hands on that spectacular canister."

Catlin's words swirled around Lindsay like dark leaves borne on a cold wind. She didn't want to hear them, didn't want to feel the coolness of rationality on her skin. She wanted to scream and claw and curse in a searing release of all that had been building inside her since her mother had died and a dragon called Catlin had walked into her life, turning it upside down.

He felt the rigidity of Lindsay's body as she fought to control the emotions ripping through her. He knew what she was going through, knew the trapped feeling that came when your adrenaline was pouring and your body was clamoring for physical release—and your icy mind knew that to make one sound, one move, was to die. There was no physical outlet, so you turned against yourself and you raged in silence, pulling yourself apart.

He couldn't let that happen to her.

Deliberately Catlin shifted his hands, arching Lindsay against his body as he had earlier. He gave her no chance to resist effectively. Her arms were pinned against his chest, her head held in place with his hand gripping her hair. As she opened her lips in surprise, he took her mouth, filling her before she could make a sound.

For a moment she continued to fight him, twisting wildly against his superior strength and knowledge. And then the inchoate angers of the past few weeks focused in a soundless explosion of passion as she accepted the outlet that he was offering. Hands that had been futile fists became fingers searching beneath his suit coat, digging into his hard flesh with a force that would have been painful if he hadn't been as angry as she was beneath the cold necessities of the act.

There was as much rage as there was desire in Lindsay's response. Catlin knew it, encouraged it with hoarse words as her nails sank into the fabric of his shirt and raked over his chest. The feel of his flexed strength raced through her, making her moan deep in her throat. It was the only sound possible to her, because her mouth was wholly involved with his in a way that was utterly new to her. She had never felt a man's textures with such violent clarity—the hard smoothness and primitive serrations of his teeth as he captured her lower lip, the sensual roughness and surprising smoothness of his tongue, the unique heat and taste of his mouth biting into her. With a small sound she tried to get even closer to him, burning him as she was being burned.

Catlin felt the change in Lindsay's body as she went from conflicting emotions to focused desire. She fitted against him perfectly. Her body was a taut, supple curve burning him from his knees to his mouth mated with hers in a hot promise he knew he should not keep. Hunger exploded him, the hunger that had never ceased prowling since he had seen her through a two-way mirror. A wave of heavy, wild heat surged in his blood, pulsing in time with his increased heartbeat, making him want to groan with pleasure and need.

For a few minutes Catlin knew nothing but Lindsay's heat and his own hunger. After the first shock wave of desire ripped through him, he told his hands to stop kneading her resilient body, to stop rocking her hips against his violently aroused flesh. Finally he forced his hands to slide slowly up to her back, but even then the primitive, provocative caress of her hips moving against him didn't stop. He groaned and his hands swept down, clenching into her, holding her against his hardened body with a strength that was just short of bruising. She flowed closer, and then closer still. Her tongue matched the primal rhythms of her hips as her mouth drank from his as though she would never get enough.

"Sweet Jesus," groaned Catlin, tearing himself away from Lindsay. "No more. You're burning me alive."

Lindsay stood swaying, bracing herself against his powerful arms, dazed by a consuming desire she had never before known.

"Catlin?" she whispered. She saw his face drawn with the same sexual tension that had made his body so incredibly alluring to her. Then she realized what she had done. In her own need for an outlet, any outlet, she had inadvertently punished Catlin for the painful role she had to play, a role she had chosen to play in spite of his blunt warnings. "Oh, Catlin, I'm sorry," she said wretchedly. "I don't know what—"

His hard hand over her mouth stilled the incautious words. He let out an explosive breath, counted to twenty and smiled ruefully down at her. Reluctantly he removed his hand, because the heat and softness of her mouth were burning through necessity's cold resolutions, tempting him unbearably.

"It's all right," he said, his voice the thinnest thread of sound. "I asked for it. I just didn't have any idea how much you could deliver." Abruptly he closed his eyes for a few moments, because it was a lot easier to keep his hands off Lindsay if he couldn't see her breasts stirring with each of her too-quick breaths. "Think you can keep it together long enough to get to the hotel?"

The sound she made could have been an inarticulate protest or harshly suppressed laughter. She followed Catlin's lead, closing her eyes and taking a long, raking breath. She didn't know what to do with the wildness singing in her own blood, her own body, a consuming heat that was equaled in the man whose hard hands were even now supporting her. Nothing in her experiences with men had prepared her for the elemental sensuality that now prowled through her on unsheathed claws. The violence of her feelings shattered her. It was as though she had spent a lifetime waiting for a man to release and then match her passion.

"Lindsay, move."

The whisper was a raw demand, as hot as the male breath searing her temple. Without a word she turned away from Catlin, stepped back out onto the pathway and began walking toward the car. The emotions that had driven her first to the edge of raging tears and then to the brink of irretrievable passion still seethed within her, but she was no longer on the breaking point of explosion. She could take a few deep breaths and face the rest of the demands of the act until she was in the privacy of the hotel shower with water pouring over her, drowning out everything, washing it all away.

Catlin caught up within two steps. When he heard a group of people coming up from behind, he took Lindsay's hand. He felt the subtle shiver that went over her at his touch, and he cursed the sensuality that was as much a part of her as her indigo eyes. He would never have guessed her sensuality from reading her file, which meant that under normal circumstances, she kept herself very tightly wrapped. But living undercover was hardly normal. It had a way of eroding even the most strongly held habits of civilization. He wondered if she had realized that yet.

Then he wondered if it would help her when she did realize it.

Understanding the psychological dynamics of undercover living hadn't helped him. Not at first. He hadn't believed that the emotions and philosophies he had thought so deeply embedded in himself could be swept away in the primitive demands of sheer survival. Living undercover peeled you down to the enduring core of your mind—and if there were no core, no center, you simply were peeled until nothing was left but a vacuum waiting to be filled. At that moment you became the ultimate actor, a human chameleon with no more morals than your reptilian namesake.

That hadn't happened to Catlin, but it had been a long, cruel descent to the central core of personal reality. For others he had known, the trip had been even more cruel, for there had been nothing waiting at the center but the terrible knowledge of emptiness.

"Wait," Catlin said, pulling Lindsay to a halt on the last curve of the path before the road was revealed between the thickly grown trees. "No matter what happens, don't go to the car until I come back for you."

The tempered edge of his voice brought Lindsay out of her inner turmoil. She looked up to see the same primal aspect of Catlin that had surfaced the night she had called out in her sleep and he had appeared in her doorway naked but for the gun in his hand. Catlin the hunter, the predator, the man who radiated both violence and restraint.

He bent over her, murmuring words that barely reached her ear. "If you hear anything odd, run like hell for Wang's house and then call the number Stone gave you."

"How did you know about the number?" whispered Lindsay, for it was easier to ask questions than to try to comprehend the sudden change in Catlin.

"It's what I would have done if you were my agent," he said, his tone neutral, just above the threshold of hearing. "Remember. Don't come until you see me and you're sure that I'm alone." His fingers tightened suddenly on her arms. "Promise me."

Helplessly she nodded, not understanding.

"Good," he murmured, releasing her.

Without another word Catlin turned and walked sound-lessly down the path, keeping to the deepest shadows. He had already picked out his vantage point earlier in the evening, on the way up the trail. He eased between two large pines, letting the fallen needles cushion the sound of his footsteps. The low branches broke up his silhouette, transforming his wine-colored shirt, black jacket and charcoal slacks into just a few more tints of darkness among the thickly layered shadows.

In front of him the hill sloped steeply to the street. Without moving anything but his eyes, Catlin looked to the left, where he had parked his car down the street and across the dark pavement, within the circle of golden light thrown by a corner street lamp. There was no car parked close to his. Nor was anyone walking nearby. Two limousines were parked farther up the street. Their drivers leaned against the fender of the nearer limo and talked, their clearly pitched Cantonese speech expanding into the night like the sharp, invisible smoke from the cigarettes both men held between their fingers.

The FBI escort was reasonably discreet. The car was parked downhill from the walkway. The driver had adjusted the mirrors so that he could check on both the path and Catlin's car without turning to look over his shoulder.

Catlin would have given a great deal to be able to have a radio connection with the FBI agent. There were a few questions Catlin urgently wanted to ask. Had the Asian man who had bolted earlier from Wang's house gone into one of those dark-windowed limousines? Was he sitting in there right now, waiting with a highly illegal, highly lethal Uzi in his lap, hoping that Catlin would carelessly appear and let him finish something that had started many years and thousands of miles away? Would Lee Tran expect Catlin to appear on the walkway with a woman whose pale hair would show up like a beacon in the dark?

If so, Tran would be surprised. Catlin was alone. He stepped out of the enfolding pines and walked quickly to the street. He gave his car a very fast once-over, sensitive fingertips searching for wires that could be connected to bombs that peeled flesh from life with devastating ease. He didn't really expect to find anything this early in the game, especially on a car parked under a street lamp in full view of an FBI escort. On the other hand, he was still alive because he trusted no one to cover his ass for him.

There were no wires, no scratched paint or other subtle signs of forced entry, nothing but wet metal surfaces where the bay's rich air had condensed like the exhalations of a gigantic, invisible beast. Catlin sensed the interest of the other men on the street as a primal tightening of the skin at the base of his neck. He ignored it. He didn't care if they thought his actions strange.

There had been at least three men at the gathering tonight who had been expecting to hear a name other than Catlin when he had been introduced. One or all of those men could have slipped away and made a call, summoning other men. Anyone who knew Catlin's past identity as Rousseau would understand immediately why he was running his fingertips over the trunk lid and hood and doors, opening each slowly in turn, a man feeling in the dark for rattlesnakes, holding his breath for fear that he really would find one.

Nothing had been added to the car but the increasing chill of night.

With a long breath of relief, Catlin crossed the street and went up the path with swift, soundless strides. He noted the adrenaline riding his veins and smiled crookedly. Once he had felt a fierce elation at the sleeting chemical storm that danger brought to him. Unfortunately, somewhere through the years he had lost his taste for the adrenaline of danger. It had been a hell of a lot more exciting to run his hands over Lindsay than the car, and a damned sight more pleasant.

"Ready?" asked Catlin, holding out his hand to Lindsay as though it had been her idea rather than his that she wait there.

"I don't know. Am I?" she asked. She had used the minutes by herself to try to call up some of the calmness that she knew in theory waited deep within her mind. The result, however, was less than satisfactory. She couldn't remember ever feeling this off balance, this besieged.

"You'll do fine," said Catlin. His smile flashed as he stepped around her so that he could take her right hand.

Lindsay wanted to ask him what he had been doing while he was gone, but knew that she shouldn't. So she said the first thing that came to her mind, knowing that anything was better than the heavy silence that had nearly suffocated her while she waited to hear sounds of violence that she didn't want to hear.

"I don't have warts on my left hand," Lindsay said, "and even if I did, it's an old wives' tale that they're contagious. I'd think that a man of your erudition and, er, more practical education would know that."

Catlin shot her a sideways look. "Is there a question buried somewhere in that outrageous observation?"

"How did you guess?"

He laughed and shook his head. "You were born asking questions, honey cat."

A frisson moved over Lindsay at the provocative endearment. She wondered why he called her honey cat. It was another question she wouldn't ask, shouldn't ask, didn't even want to know because the answer had nothing to do with the undercover act.

"Why don't you ever hold my left hand?" she asked.

For a moment Lindsay thought Catlin wasn't going to answer. Then he smiled strangely, bending over her, snuggling her body close to his as he whispered.

"Because, little innocent, I'm a much better shot with my right hand than my left." He watched her reaction as the meaning of his words sank in, the widening of her eyes and the slight parting of her lips around a silent exclamation. "Sorry you asked?"

She nodded, feeling too numb to speak.

"Don't be," he murmured. "It's a good thing to remember. Stay on my left side. Always. We'll both be safer that way."

Catlin stepped away from Lindsay, held on to her right hand and resumed walking. She followed him, all thought of conversation abandoned. Numbness settled over her, a distancing of herself from reality that she had never before experienced.

It wasn't even relief, because relief was an emotion and she felt nothing at all. As Catlin tucked her into the car she realized that she was exhausted. It was a kind of fatigue that was as new to her, like being suspended within thick, absolutely clear glass. Too much had happened. Too many new emotions. Too many forbidden words, forbidden thoughts.

Too many lies.

She leaned her head against the upholstery and closed her eyes, wondering how people survived a life undercover. She wasn't meant to live like this, exposed, every word monitored, every thought skating over a thin ice of unreality. Yet there was no alternative. Not any more. She had made her choices in Washington, D.C. Now all that remained was to live with them any way she could.

Catlin looked at Lindsay's pale, still profile and swore silently. He remembered how it felt to come down off an adrenaline jag, to feel energy bleeding out of you like air out of a flawed balloon until nothing was left but a deflation that was as close to narcosis as he ever wanted to come. Eventually that stage passed, as did the extreme high of adrenaline. Until then, it was life on a chemical roller coaster.

It wasn't a life Catlin wanted anymore. It was a life he had worked hard to leave behind. He had learned that violence was a reflex, not an emotion. He had learned that too much violence first numbed and then destroyed whatever it was in man that separated him from sharks in a feeding frenzy. He had learned, he had left, and now he was back in it, the violence and the adrenaline and the slow stripping away of humanity. Even worse, so was Lindsay. He could see the layers peeling down, more and more, faster and faster until she was spinning helplessly. He could see it.

But he couldn't do a damn thing to stop it.

14

CATLIN STOOD by the bathroom door, looking at the object that he had taken from beneath the toilet tank. After a few moments he flipped the tiny transmitter like a coin, caught it and flushed it down the toilet. He sensed the question on Lindsay's lips and shook his head. She nodded and leaned against the wall, eyes closed, outwardly indifferent while he finished his circuit of the hotel suite. He found two more bugs, one in the mouthpiece of the phone and one in a phony wall socket. He flushed those bugs, as well, and turned back to Lindsay.

"Let's get that nightcap downstairs."

She didn't object. She was too tired, and the knowledge that someone had been bugging their hotel room in their absence made the idea of staying there unnerving.

The piano bar was noisy enough to ensure that they weren't likely to be overheard. The cocktail waitress took their order, returned with two glasses of cognac and left again. Catlin waited until the waitress was well beyond hearing range before he put his arm around Lindsay and pulled her close to him. The padded booth surrounding them gave a sense of privacy that he knew could be deceptive.

Lindsay accepted the embrace without objection. She leaned against Catlin, inhaling deeply. The clean, subtly masculine smell of him was reassuring, as was the soft texture of his lightweight French wool sport coat. Her breath came out in a ragged sigh as she felt his warmth seep into her.

"Sorry," he breathed against her ear, "but I can't guarantee I found all the bugs. Until I say otherwise, we'll have to assume we're always on stage."

She nodded, not even caring. With a vast sense of weariness she realized that she was on stage all the time lately, one way or another. Touch Catlin in public. Don't touch him in private. Believe what he said in private. Don't believe him in public. The dualism was too much to juggle along with all the rest of the demands and lies tearing at her emotions. It would be easier to have just one part to play, just one series of words to monitor, just one category of thoughts to suppress. From now on she would know that she could touch Catlin all the time—and believe him none of the time.

Except for moments like this, when he spoke too softly for anyone else to hear. And even then, could she be sure? Was he simply saying what had to be said and doing what had to be done in order to keep her intact long enough to go back on stage again?

Does it matter? Lindsay asked herself. *It shouldn't. Remember that. Take what you need and don't ask why he gives it to you.*

"No questions?" Catlin asked softly.

Lindsay shrugged because she hadn't the energy to speak. It didn't matter. None of it mattered except getting the job done, finishing it, going back to a world where every thought, every touch, every glance wasn't a lie.

Unease moved over Catlin as he looked at Lindsay's pale, drawn face. Her passivity was unexpected, unprecedented. She should be demanding to know who had placed the bugs and why. She should be furious at the new intrusion into her privacy. As he watched, her eyes closed, revealing lavender-blue shadows that owed nothing to makeup and everything to emotional exhaustion. Thick, honey-colored eyelashes quivered against her cheeks, casting long shadows in the bar's side light. She looked fragile, bruised, spent, and she was resting against him as though her own body could no longer support her.

Swearing silently, Catlin drew Lindsay closer, wishing he could give her some of his own strength to throw off the aftereffects of an adrenaline jag. With repeated experiences she would learn to moderate her reaction, both on the upswing and the down. Until then, it was adrenaline and depression in exhausting sequence.

It wasn't a life he wanted anymore. It was a life he had worked hard to leave behind. But at least he had the experience to cope when he was thrown unexpectedly back into the world of pure lies and dangerous truths. Lindsay had neither the temperament nor the experience to help her handle the unique mental and physical demands of this life, most especially the reality of an isolation that went all the way to the soul, first chilling and then freezing the ability to feel.

At least that was how it had finally become with him. He had discovered that living undercover was a game for young players. Only the young had the kind of reflexive faith in themselves and in life that permitted them to survive in a world where true emotion was the only tabu. Catlin was no longer young. Not like that. He had gotten out of the game, taking nothing of the past with him but too many memories, too much understanding of the man-shark continuum, and one half of an old coin.

Lindsay stirred, but only to relax more fully against Catlin. His hand smoothed over her arm, feeling the chill on her skin.

"Cold?" he asked.

There was no answer.

Catlin took off his jacket, wrapped it around Lindsay and pulled her back against his chest.

"Here," he said, tipping the brandy snifter against her pale mouth. "Sip."

Obediently her lips parted. He watched the amber liquid move slowly toward her mouth, saw the pinkness of her tongue as it touched the potent drink, felt her small shiver as cognac slid down her throat.

"Better?" he asked.

Lindsay nodded and burrowed even closer to his abundant warmth.

Catlin smoothed back the shining hair that had drifted forward over Lindsay's cheek. Without realizing it he rocked her slowly while he spoke, trying to comfort her with his body, for he knew there would be no comfort in his words.

"I know you don't want to talk about it, but this is probably our safest time," he whispered against her hair. The scent
of her perfume drifted up, as subtle as the rocking motions he
was using to reassure her. He inhaled slowly, wondering what
scent she was wearing. "The bugs were probably FBI, a hurry-
up job just to let me know they care. They'll get serious about
it real soon. That's why we can't assume that the room is safe
anymore."

Lindsay's lashes opened, revealing the indigo depths of her
eyes. She said nothing, simply accepted what Catlin had said.
He had the feeling that if he had told her that little green men
from another galaxy had bugged the suite he would have gotten the same response.

"The FBI don't trust me," he continued. "They don't really trust anyone who isn't FBI. That includes you, although
I'm sure Stone would be the first to say that the bugs are a way
of protecting you. He may even believe it."

Lindsay said nothing, did nothing.

"Are you listening?" Catlin whispered, his breath stirring
her hair.

"Yes."

It was as much a tired sigh as a word. Catlin didn't object or
insist on a greater show of attention. He simply kept talking,
telling Lindsay things she didn't want to hear.

"I could have kept the bugs in place, ignored them, but they
were planted in such obvious ways that it would have been like
ignoring turds in buttermilk. No point in it."

He didn't add that one of the bugs had been in the wall
socket right beside the bed. That had been the one that had
decided him. Lindsay had sacrificed a lot already for the U.S.
government and her own ideas of what was right; she should be
able to turn over in her sleep without triggering an eavesdrop-
per's gamey speculations as to what each shift of weight and
rustle of sheets might mean.

"As we get closer to the bronzes, there might be more bugs—
FBI, PRC or what are termed 'other interested parties.'"

That penetrated Lindsay's indifference. The thought of more factors to juggle was appalling.

"Why?" she asked tiredly.

Catlin's arm tightened around her. His mouth turned down in wry acknowledgment of the fact that he would have preferred her passive, unquestioning state to last just a few minutes longer. He wondered how much more she could take tonight before she fractured more deeply than eight hours of sleep could heal.

Across the room the piano bar singer returned from her break. The woman had hair that fell like dark water down to the small of her back. She moved well, a woman on display, soaking up each particle of the audience reaction. Her costume was a sleek cascade of hot pink. In her feline self-assurance, she reminded Catlin of another woman long ago.

He watched and listened with a fraction of his attention as she began to sing. Her voice was clear, high, supple. It, too, reminded him of Mei, and Mei reminded him of too many ways to die and none to live.

"There are people out of my past," Catlin said finally, turning his full attention to Lindsay, bending over until he could speak against her ear. "People who may or may not be involved in the missing bronzes. People who get very nervous around me."

"The man at the auction," said Lindsay, stirring against Catlin's chest.

"He's one of them. There are others."

"Why?"

When Catlin didn't answer, Lindsay tilted her head back until she could see his eyes. She wished she hadn't moved. Nothing she saw there comforted her. Yet even as that thought came she realized that it had to be worse for him. She was only visiting in hell. He lived there.

"I'm sorry," she said, touching his black eyebrows with her fingertips, trying to smooth away the harsh lines. "I shouldn't have asked. It's none of my business."

He gathered her fingertips and brushed his lips across them. "I'm afraid it is, now. I tried to warn Yi about this possibility, but—" Catlin shrugged and didn't finish the sentence. The facts spoke for themselves. He and his past were now endangering Lindsay, as well as the success of Yi's plan, whatever that plan might ultimately be.

The warmth of Catlin's breath caressed Lindsay's fingertips, making her realize how cold she was, a chill that went all the way to her soul. She wanted to draw him closer to her, to absorb his heat as though he were a fire burning against a winter night. She realized at that instant that Catlin had been right. In the midst of all the lies and half-truths, plots and counterplots, she needed someone she could trust. She needed that the way she needed oxygen, for without it she would suffocate beneath the torrent of deceptions. That was why she didn't want to ask the next question. She needed him.

And that was why she must ask.

"Why don't you trust the FBI? Is it because you're Yi's man—a Chinese agent?"

There was no answer except for a subtle tightening of Catlin's body. His hands closed over Lindsay's upper arms. With a swiftness and ease she found shocking, he lifted and turned her in the booth until she was lying half across his lap, facing him. In the muted light his eyes were tarnished gold, impenetrable. He looked at her for a long, long time while the sounds of the piano bar singer swirled around them, crying for an unfaithful love.

"Is that what you believe?" Catlin asked finally, softly.

Lindsay touched his mouth with a fingertip that trembled. "Is that your answer?" she whispered.

Catlin's eyes closed. He hadn't wanted to add anything more to Lindsay's problems for the night, but she was leaving him no choice. If he refused to answer, she wouldn't trust him. And if he did answer, she would have one more thing to worry about. Either way it would be hard on her.

"Yi doesn't trust his comrades," said Catlin. "He hasn't told them about you, and he asked that Stone not mention you either. If Stone decides to exceed his direct orders and play divide and conquer with the Chinese, then he'll grab a translator and start telling the good comrades that you're working for the FBI. If they're just what they seem to be—dutiful bureaucrats—that won't matter.

"But," added Catlin, "if the comrades are also the crooks, Stone could put you right on the firing line. So as a precaution, I'm trying to make sure that there's no communication between the FBI and Yi's comrades. That's why I flushed the bugs. It's the old need-to-know game. Right now the FBI doesn't need to know a goddamn thing that Yi doesn't tell them up front. When and if that changes, I'll be the first to get on the phone and start spilling state secrets."

"Oh, God," sighed Lindsay. Her forehead tilted down until it rested heavily on Catlin's shoulder, silently telling him that she was too tired to even hold up her own head anymore. "Do you trust Yi?"

"On a scale of one to ten?"

Lindsay shuddered. "Catlin," she said raggedly, "trust doesn't come that way!"

"The hell it doesn't. I don't trust anyone worth a ten. Or even a nine." But as he said it, he realized that it wasn't true. He laughed softly, ruefully, shaking his head. "Except you, Lindsay. Sweet innocence. You don't lie very well. It's such hard work for you that your body language gives you away every time."

"Then I'm a fool and a liability to everyone involved in this," said Lindsay, her voice as pale as her skin. "I'm trying, Catlin. I really am." She shuddered and took a deep breath, fighting for control. "It's just when I saw Wu's face and knew that he was thinking I was a slut and a liar, I—" She made a helpless gesture as her voice broke. "And yet I know that I'm not good enough at lying, that I could blow the whole thing to hell and it would all be for nothing and—"

Catlin's kiss stopped the tumbling words with a gentleness that made Lindsay want to cry. With an inarticulate sound she clung to him, needing him as he had said she would, needing him in ways she couldn't even name.

"You're doing fine," he said gently, holding her close, reassuring her. "If things go to hell, it won't be because of you. You've done better than anyone could have expected."

As Catlin looked down into the darkness of Lindsay's eyes, he silently raged at what was being asked of her. It was one thing to dress a wolf like a sheep and turn him loose on the world. Politicians and reporters did it all the time. But to dress a lamb like a wolf and throw her into the wilds was to ask a hell of a lot of the lamb.

Stone either had assumed that Lindsay was strong enough to do what he asked of her, or he hadn't cared. Yi had improved his chances of success by using Catlin as a wolf to guard the lamb in drag.

Too bad no one thought of protecting the lamb's mind, as well as her body, Catlin thought bitterly. *But it's too late now. There's nothing to do except what I'm doing now—holding her.*

So little. Words, touches, warmth.

Catlin hoped it would be enough. It never had been enough in the past, though. Susie, Mei and all the nameless others, a feminine cascade rushing through his life. He had drunk from the beautiful, mysterious stream, bathed in its wild pleasures and watched it flow inevitably by, sliding from his present down and down into the dark sea of the past, silver heat and laughter and passion running through his fingers until nothing was left but his empty hands glistening with memories and cold with betrayals.

The chanteuse's song of faithless love ended, only to be replaced by a lament about true love discovered too late. Catlin listened with only a fragment of his attention. With gentle hands he settled Lindsay more comfortably against him, supporting her weight as he looked past her shimmering hair to the room beyond.

There was nothing remarkable about the two men sitting three tables to the right, waiting to be served, but Catlin noted them instantly. The FBI had made a religion out of being unremarkable. To the left there was a table of mixed Anglo and Oriental people who had just entered the piano bar. There were other Chinese scattered throughout the room. Catlin marked the new arrivals, looking for anyone who was overly interested in the couple sitting in the booth.

If he had been alone, he would have walked out into the night and seen who noticed, who followed, who had been able to set up outside surveillance in advance. The FBI, certainly. The PRC, probably, but which side? Yi's men? The thieves' men? Both? Or were Yi and the thieves the same?

Alone, Catlin might have been able to answer a few of those questions. He could have lured a tail into one of Chinatown's midnight alleys and twisted some information from him. But not tonight. Not with Lindsay along.

"More cognac?" he asked, bending his head to her shining hair once more.

She shook her head. Silky strands whispered over his lips. Her hair was cool, haunted by perfume.

"Sure?" he whispered. "It will help you to relax."

She made an odd, abrupt sound that could have been laughter. "I'm having enough trouble sorting out truth and lies right now," she said in a tired voice. "Alcohol won't help."

"Can you sleep?" he asked bluntly.

With you two inches away? Not very damn likely, Catlin!

But the words went no farther than Lindsay's mind. Yelling at him wouldn't help. It wasn't his fault that she found him frighteningly attractive.

"Lindsay," whispered Catlin against her hair, feeling her sudden tension, understanding its source. "I'm sorry, but we have to sleep in the same bed. The maid—"

"Yes," Lindsay said quickly, her lips all but touching his ear as she spoke. "I understand. Part of the act. That's all. Just an act."

She tried to sit up but found it impossible. She was trapped between the table and Catlin's body. With the same swift power that had surprised her once before, he lifted her from his lap and returned her to the bench seat beside him.

"I hate to be unchivalrous," he muttered, "but I'm going to need my jacket back before we leave."

Surprised, Lindsay shrugged out of the soft wool and handed it over to him. She watched as he put it on with the same smooth coordination that he did everything. When his body turned to receive the coat, she saw the dark gleam of metal in the small of his back and realized that he was wearing a gun. The thought shocked her before common sense took over, reminding her that Catlin was always armed, always dangerous, a man fully suited for the hell he was guiding her through.

With a suppressed shudder Lindsay slid out of the booth and stood by herself in the smoky bar. She remained alone only for an instant. Catlin was right behind her, his hand resting lightly just above her waist as he eased her through the press of people surrounding the bar. The men he had pegged as FBI agents stayed at their table. They didn't glance up as Lindsay passed, but Catlin's instincts told him that the men took a good look at his back.

A couple stood in front of the bank of elevators, waiting for a car to arrive. As he and Lindsay approached, doors slid aside. The couple walked in and politely held the doors open until Lindsay and Catlin could enter. He hesitated reflexively, assessing the possibilities of an ambush. Then he mentally shrugged. There was a limit to how many shadows you could check behind, how many conspiracies you could assume. In the end you had to go with the odds or go crazy, and the odds said that Lee Tran hadn't had enough time to plan and execute an assassination in the lobby of one of San Francisco's major hotels.

Catlin waited until the well-dressed couple had pushed the button for the tenth floor. As the man stepped aside, Catlin took the room key out of his pocket and gave it to Lindsay.

"Sixteen, honey," he said, pressing the key into her hand.

Lindsay started to object that their room was on the eighteenth floor. A single look from Catlin's eyes froze the words on her lips. She inserted the key into the slot that activated the upper bank of buttons, the higher floors that were off limits to people without the proper room keys. Silently she pushed the button marked sixteen.

As Lindsay stepped away, the woman took a key from her purse and inserted it into the emergency override lock on the elevator, bringing the car to a halt between floors. Simultaneously her partner's hand went into his suit coat.

Catlin spun, sweeping Lindsay behind him with his left hand even as the blunt, lethal shape of a gun appeared in his right. As he completed the spin, his left elbow rammed into the man's diaphragm. With a grunt, the man slammed against the elevator wall and slumped down to the floor, fighting futilely for breath. Catlin's left hand shot out and closed around the woman's arm just as she reached for her purse. He squeezed the delicate, vulnerable wrist bones. The purse dropped from her numbed fingers as he shoved her against the wall and held her immobile beneath the impact of his body.

"FBI!" she gasped as the gun's barrel sank into the soft skin beneath the jaw.

Catlin smiled. "Probably," he agreed. "That's why you're both still alive."

The woman simply stared at him, unable to speak for the weapon digging into her neck.

"Lindsay," Catlin said calmly, not looking away from the woman's wide brown eyes. "Check this little beauty's purse. If it doesn't have a leather folder and an FBI shield, let me know."

Lindsay looked from Catlin's expressionless face to the frightened eyes of the woman who stood absolutely still within his grasp. The dark barrel of the gun was hard against the woman's throat, leaving her barely enough room to breathe. A thready groan rose from the floor of the elevator. Startled, Lindsay looked down.

"Don't worry about him," said Catlin. "He won't be doing much but trying to suck in air for a few minutes. The purse, Lindsay."

She stepped forward, realized that she was coming up from Catlin's right side, his gun side, and hastily moved to his left.

He caught the change of direction from the corner of his eye. His smile changed subtly, approving rather than predatory.

"It's a pleasure to work with a fast learner," he said softly, but his eyes never left his captive's face.

The feeling of disbelief that had settled around Lindsay never seemed stronger than when she opened the dazzling gold-mesh evening purse and found a lipstick, a comb and a blue-steel gun. Numbly she searched beneath the gun, fishing out a leather folder. As she opened it, the blue-and-gold shield of the FBI gleamed in the elevator's fluorescent lights.

"FBI," said Lindsay, her voice hoarse. "Special Agent Nancy Conner."

The sound of the safety being clicked into place on Catlin's gun was very loud in the elevator's confined space. He stepped away from the woman and returned the gun to its holster in the same motion.

"Pleased to meet you, Agent Conner," said Catlin. "You have five seconds to pass on your message."

"But—" she began. Then she realized that Catlin meant it. "Leave the bugs in place. They're for your safety."

"Bullshit."

Catlin's tone was as cold as the gun he had just held to her throat. She looked from him to her partner, who was struggling to his feet.

"You okay, Ted?" she asked.

"The PRC can kill this son of a bitch for all of me," her partner said harshly, rubbing his aching diaphragm.

Catlin turned swiftly. "Listen, cowboy," he said, his voice low and hard. "You want to talk to me, call me up and say that Freddie Black has a bronze for me to look at. I'll walk to the nearest pay phone and call the local office. That way nobody will get hurt. Because the next time I'm ambushed, I'm going to slip the leash and go hunting for real. Hear me?"

The agent stood very still, hearing exactly what was being said. He knew the controlled blow to the diaphragm that had paralyzed him for a few moments could have been much harder. Lethal. Catlin had the skill and the power to kill with no more weapon than his hands. The agent had been told that before he had walked into the elevator, but he hadn't believed it. He believed it now.

"Freddie Black. A bronze to look at," the agent re-peated.

"Good. You can bug everything but the bedroom. I find FBI eavesdropping gear in there and the first agent I get my hands on will spend the next week shitting high tech."

The two agents looked at each other. The woman sighed.

"Show him, Ted."

The male agent hesitated, shrugged, and said, "All right if I get something out of my pocket?"

Catlin nodded.

The agent reached into his suit coat and pulled out a flat aluminum box that could have held lures for fishing. He opened the box, revealing matchbook-sized transmitters nestled in specially cut nests in the sponge that filled the box. He pointed to two of the bugs.

"These are for the—"

"Phone," interrupted Catlin, recognizing the shapes that both replaced standard parts of the telephone receiver and at the same time rendered conversation in the room anything but private. He took the box, closed it and slipped it into his pocket. "If you aren't getting signals within an hour, have 'Freddie' give me a call. I'll take the bugs with me if we change hotels and install them wherever we go. Got that?"

The agent nodded.

"Remember it," said Catlin. With bleak amber eyes he looked at first one FBI agent and then at the other. "From now on it's open season on uninvited guests. Pass the word."

"You can't just—"

"Like hell I can't."

Before anyone could object, Catlin's hand flashed out to the control panel. He jerked out the override key and slipped it into his pocket. The elevator continued on to the tenth floor. Neither agent asked for the override key to be returned, for it was obvious that Catlin intended to keep it. Without a word both

agents got off as soon as the doors opened. The doors closed
and the elevator went on toward the sixteenth floor.

"You all right?" Catlin asked softly. He knew that the sudden violence had shocked Lindsay, but he didn't know how
much.

"All right?" Lindsay stifled an impulse to laugh, knowing
that it was hysteria rather than humor tightening her throat. It
had happened so quickly, so unexpectedly, a man down and a
woman with a gun buried in her throat. Both people could have
died so easily. And without Catlin, Lindsay knew that she
would have been helpless. She hadn't even known something
was wrong until it was over. "I'm fine. Just fine," she said, her
voice empty.

"Bloody wonderful," muttered Catlin. "Can you do two
flights of stairs?"

"I can do whatever I have to," she said hollowly.

With the swift grace that could be so unexpected, so lethal,
Catlin knelt and removed Lindsay's elegant high heels. He
rubbed the red indentations that the leather strap had left on
her high arch.

"Hell of a thing to do in the name of style," he said.

Lindsay looked at Catlin's sleek black hair and gentle hands
and felt as though she had well and truly fallen down the rabbit hole. "You would have killed that woman," Lindsay said
huskily, fighting absurd laughter, "and now you're worried
about a welt on my foot!"

He smiled up at her crookedly, relieved that she was responding with something more than the dead voice and lifeless
eyes she had shown him a few minutes ago. "Such a pretty
foot," he murmured, rubbing out the red mark with his fingers.

"You spent too long in China."

It took an instant for Catlin to understand what Lindsay was
implying. When he did, he laughed aloud and released her foot,
standing again in a surge of power.

"Not that long. I'm not a foot fetishist," he said, holding her shoes in his hand.

Lindsay laughed. She couldn't help it. She didn't even want to.

Catlin listened to her clear, beautiful laughter and smiled, knowing that she was getting herself under control again. It had been a hard night for her. Too hard. Despite his efforts to shield her when he could, tonight she had been pushed to the point that she had to either give up and withdraw or accept the new reality and go forward.

Not only had she accepted, she was still able to laugh.

"You're quite a woman, Lindsay Danner," Catlin said, leading her out of the elevator. "Was your mother like you?"

"Like me?" Lindsay repeated, thinking of the small, tenacious, lavender-scented woman who had walked through her childhood and still glided through her dreams.

"Gutsy," explained Catlin.

"Dad used to say that mother would charge hell with a bucket of water."

Reflexively Catlin checked that the stairwell was empty before he allowed Lindsay to enter it.

"Like I said. Gutsy," murmured Catlin.

"Crazy," Lindsay amended, shaking her head. "It wasn't that mother didn't believe in evil. It was just that she believed so passionately in good."

"And you think that's crazy?" asked Catlin, knowing that Lindsay believed in good in exactly the same way, whether she realized it or not. It was the only possible explanation for why she was here with him now, walking down into hell with a man she didn't know and yet followed with such shattering trust.

"Don't you?"

"I think your mother was frighteningly sane," Catlin said, automatically listening for the sound of other footsteps, doors opening or closing, the click-click of a gun being cocked. "To believe only in evil is to give yourself to it."

Lindsay heard the flat certainty in Catlin's voice and felt a chill sweep down her spine. "Is that what happened to you?" she whispered.

For several moments there was no sound but that of Lindsay's nylon-sheathed feet meeting the stairs. Catlin made no noise at all. The movements of his body were utterly controlled. There was no careless slap of leather soles against concrete as he climbed the stairs. It was like walking next to a wolf, except that there weren't even the tiny sounds of claws being drawn over stone. Such a small thing, silence, yet it drove deeply into Lindsay, telling her just how long and how deeply Catlin had lived as both predator and prey. It was in his every motion, his every breath, his eyes constantly searching roof lines and shadows, doorways and passing cars, every sense alert for the first threatening movement.

"It was close," Catlin said finally, answering Lindsay's questions as he took the room key from her. A single glance told him that the nearly invisible sliver of transparent tape he had placed across the top of the door hadn't been disturbed. "I realized what was happening in time," he added, pulling her into the room, locking and bolting the door behind. "That's why I got out."

"Out?" she whispered. "You call this 'out'?"

"No. Why don't you shower while I set up the bugs?"

Lindsay opened her mouth. After a moment she turned away without saying anything. There was nothing to say except the obvious: *Then why are you here, back in the hell you know all too well and so obviously hate?* But that was the question Catlin had refused to answer, even for the FBI. There was no reason to think he would answer it for her.

Catlin watched Lindsay walk into the bedroom and begin pulling things from her suitcase. He knew what she had wanted to ask, and he knew why she had kept silent. She needed to trust someone. Him. It was vital to her. Without it she could become irretrievably lost in the maze of lies, no signposts to guide her, no enduring truth shining in the darkness to comfort her.

It would have been different if she had been drawn to undercover work by some aspect of her own personality, her own psychic needs; then the lure of the adrenaline would have been reward enough for the demands of the game. But that wasn't the case with her. She had been drawn by innocence and idealism into a game that had no room for either. What she was doing now went against her grain in ways that abraded her psyche until she was raw.

Catlin knew, because it was rather like that for him. The lure of the game was gone, leaving only the lies. And Lindsay, tangled among lies like light in darkness.

The thought still disturbed Catlin late that night, when he awakened to Lindsay's quiet, incoherent cries. Even as his fingers closed around the cold grip of his gun he realized that there was no danger in the room. Not for him. It was Lindsay whose body moved restlessly, turning and twisting in slow motion, trying to escape nightmare. As he returned the gun to the end table he wondered whether it was the past or the present that haunted her dreams, causing the whimpers that cut into him like tiny knives.

"It's all right," he murmured, stroking her tangled hair from her face. "You're safe. Shhhhh. You're safe, Lindsay. I won't let anyone hurt you. Shhhhh."

The soft words and slow, soothing strokes of Catlin's hand penetrated the nightmare. Lindsay half awoke, her eyes dazed, unseeing. With a choked sound she turned toward the source of the comforting words and touches.

"What is it, honey?" he asked softly. "Can you talk about it?"

"I never—remember," she said raggedly. "I just—wake up."

Catlin gathered Lindsay along his body, stroking her back and hair, talking softly to her, trying to draw out the cause of her fear. She pressed even closer, instinctively seeking the safety he promised.

Desire exploded through him as her soft, resilient body fitted itself to his contours. He ignored the sudden, sweet heaviness of his own arousal. He didn't want to take in physical hunger what she would offer him out of psychic need. That would be another kind of lie, a wounding kind, the game sweeping past all barriers until only the game was real—and therefore everything was lies. He didn't want to do that to her. She was too vulnerable. She didn't know that she was drawn to him because she sensed that he was safety in a world of danger.

But he knew it. He had felt all the instant, almost overwhelming urgencies that were just one of the hazards of the adrenaline roller coaster. If she had been a different kind of woman, or if she had known the rules and lures of the game, he would have taken her without hesitation. He wanted her. He wanted her husky voice crying for him, her warmth sheathing him until cold was only a fading memory. He wanted to bury himself in her tight satin heat, letting the rest of the chill world slide away while he knew what it was like to be fully alive again.

And it would be like that with her—hot, vivid, vital. He knew it, and it made him ache to be complete with her.

Hearing his own thoughts made Catlin smile grimly. He should know better by now. The pleasures of sex were intense but transient. The emotional emptiness sex tried to fill was permanent, the legacy of too many years in hell. He was alive. Period. That was more than most men he had worked with could say. That was more than any of his enemies could say.

Except for the one enemy who was still alive. Lee Tran, Mei's pimp, the man who had tried to buy Catlin's death at the delicate hands of the woman he had loved years ago because he needed love too badly then to question its source.

Like Lindsay now, asleep in his arms. He knew what would happen unless the bronzes were found and found very soon. The urgencies of adrenaline and survival would undermine her judgment. The role she played would become the only reality. And on that day she would look up at him and see the love that she needed to survive.

He hoped that when that moment came he would be strong enough to turn away from her, protecting her in the only way he could.

15

STONE MOVED RESTLESSLY through the hotel room that had been turned into an FBI command post. Field reports were scattered about, coffee pooled coldly in smudged cups that left rings on unusually expensive hotel furniture, and the sheets lay in a snarl at the foot of the bed because he had refused to allow the maid into the room. With a tired curse he smoothed his palm over his short hair.

"And he kept the goddamn key?" Stone snarled, shooting O'Donnel a narrow glance.

The younger man nodded. "Given the circumstances, there wasn't anything the agents could do. Catlin is very quick and not at all careless."

Stone grunted. "I could have told them that. Hell, I did! Did they believe me?" He made a sound of complete disgust. "For this I'm told to camp in California and run this operation. I could have run this farce by phone. I should have!"

"Yes, sir," said O'Donnel. He knew as well as Stone did that there had been no real choice in the matter. When the director said follow it to California, you followed it to California. It would have been the same if the moon were the destination. "Catlin kept his word. The bugs are in the suite."

"Except the bedroom."

"Except the bedroom," agreed O'Donnel, smiling slightly. "Wonder why he dug in over that? Maybe he and sweet Lindsay have something going after all."

"Ask him," retorted Stone.

"Thanks, but I'll pass," O'Donnel said cheerfully. "I saw the bruises on Nancy Conner's wrist. Not to mention the beauty below Ted Marsh's breastbone. Catlin doesn't pull his punches. I pity the guy who has to install the bedbug."

"There won't be one."

O'Donnel gave his boss a swift look. "But none of the bugs we used are sensitive enough to cover the bedroom. Hell, we weren't expecting him to be hostile. We figured he'd see the bugs, know they were friendly and not worry about it."

"You think Catlin was bluffing about open season, don't you?" Stone asked.

The younger man shrugged. "He knows we're following him. He knows we're not going to trash him. Why would he trash us? It would put him in a world of hurt and not help him at all."

"Suppose you had to take a walk through a dark alley," said Stone. "Suppose you knew that some sort of friendlies might follow you down the alley, and some real enemies would try to kill you there, and there was no way to tell them apart in the dark. What would you do?"

"Shoot the first thing that moved."

Stone nodded. "Catlin was sporting about it, though. He warned us first. Somebody gets shot, it's because we didn't listen."

O'Donnel stared, hardly able to believe what he was hearing. "Are you saying that we accept his shit with a grin and a shuffle?"

Without answering, Stone lit a cigarette and accepted the ashtray that O'Donnel brought to him. He gave the young agent a long, measuring look, wondering how to make the point. That was the trouble with young men. They hadn't been around long enough to know the difference between a threat and a promise. Stone had.

"If I thought it would do any good," Stone said, blowing out a harsh stream of smoke, "I'd let you try to administer the attitude adjustment that you think Catlin needs." Stone looked at the glowing end of his cigarette. "Of course, it wouldn't be Catlin's attitude that got adjusted. It would be yours. And then I'd be mad as hell and probably do something stupid, because you're as close to a son as I've got."

O'Donnel's eyes narrowed but he said nothing.

"You're out for blood because Catlin roughed up two agents who tried to show how cute they were by blind-siding him in an elevator,'' continued Stone. "This is one guy who isn't going to be blind-sided, but try and tell that to these California hotshots. They'll argue with you over the color of the sky. They could have gotten a message to Catlin in a hundred other ways, but they're used to rousting rubber check artists. They thought he'd have heart failure when they stopped the elevator.'' Stone shrugged. "April fool, baby. At the cost of a few bruises they learned how easy it is to misjudge a man and die. Valuable lesson, that.''

"He didn't have to be so hard on the woman,'' O'Donnel said flatly.

"God Bless America,'' muttered Stone, looking at his cigarette as though it were burning rubber. "A woman will kill you as quick as a man. Quicker, because you don't expect it. Ask any grunt who fought in Asia. It's the last thing some of those kids learned. Not that I blame them,'' he added honestly, settling onto the couch. "I still haven't learned it, not all the way to the bone.''

Stone looked at O'Donnel's expression and knew that the young agent wasn't satisfied.

"Catlin's living in an undeclared war zone, waiting to be killed,'' said Stone. "He doesn't have time to sort out enemies and friendlies, not if he wants to survive. He learned that a long time ago. He survived. Think about it, Terry. You're standing there telling yourself that you're good enough, you can take him; and if you can't, he'll recognize you and stop before he kills you.'' Stone shook his head slowly. "Forget it. The fact that Catlin knows your face is no protection if you try to blindside him. Catlin's known a lot of men. Some of them betrayed him. He'll kill you and send flowers to your funeral if any apologies are called for.''

There was a silence followed by a muttered curse. "I'd still like to teach him some manners.''

"Try him at the gym on Powell and Stoner tomorrow,'' offered Stone, smiling thinly. "Before Chen recruited Catlin, he worked out there regularly.''

"Weights,'' O'Donnel said scornfully.

"Does he move like a body builder?" retorted Stone.

"Boxing?" O'Donnel asked, curiosity in his voice.

"Full contact karate."

Stone watched that idea penetrate O'Donnel's youthful arrogance. Demonstration karate was one thing. An outright battle wearing only a few pads was another. As a dangerous entertainment, full contact karate ranked just below Russian roulette.

"All the same..." muttered O'Donnel. He swore beneath his breath as he scooped up a handful of papers. He squared the edges automatically before replacing the sheets in the file folder. "What about this Tom Lee, alias Lee Tran? Did the CIA have anything on him?"

"About four hundred pages. The Bureau had quite a file on him, too."

"Anything we can use?"

"Not in the States. We ship his ass back to Vietnam, though, and a whole lot of people will line up to say hello. Seems Lee liked to sell people and information on both sides during the war. Heroin, too. Still does. Works out of Hong Kong and San Francisco now."

O'Donnel's hands stopped for a moment, then continued their work of straightening up the small dining table that Stone had been using as a desk. "Why is Lee afraid of Catlin?"

"Lee once duped an assassin into Catlin. Would have gotten him, too, if someone hadn't walked in and turned her into wallpaper."

"Her?"

"Yeah. The hit man was a woman. Catlin's mistress, apparently. He damn near died in the saddle."

O'Donnel gave a harsh laugh and shook his head. "That would be enough to throw a man off his stride. How long had she been his mistress?"

"It wasn't some Saturday night pickup."

"No wonder he's hard on women," muttered O'Donnel. "So where does Lee fit into Chen and Catlin and the bronzes?"

"Hard to say. Officially, Lee is a political refugee, which means we're stuck with him until Ho Chi Minh City turns back into Saigon or hell freezes over, whichever comes sooner."

"Lee was one of the Boat People?" O'Donnel asked skeptically, thinking of the poor, ragged, half-starved Vietnamese and ethnic Chinese Vietnamese citizens who had fled to the U.S. after Saigon fell.

"That's what it says in his file." Stone's mouth flattened in a cynical smile. "Bet his damn boat had a solid gold keel. He hit San Francisco and started buying into the local power structure. Chinatown, not the city. Chinese benevolent associations, Chinese neighborhood committees, that sort of thing. What he couldn't buy he killed, and he was mean enough to make it stick. They don't like him much here, but they've learned to live with him."

"Sweet guy."

"Yeah. Lee could give lessons to the Sicilians. Not that some of the people he killed didn't have it coming, from what our local agents say." Stone stubbed out his cigarette. "Anyway, he's dug in real good here. Gives money to Chinese charities, scholarship funds, churches and cultural preservation societies. Pillar of the community, as long as you don't ask where all that money comes from."

"Buying his way into respectability?"

"He's giving it the old college try," agreed Stone. "He's turned the slavery and dope trade over to his sons. Now he spends his money buying ancient Chinese bronzes, classical Chinese calligraphy and ten-year-old boys."

O'Donnel grimaced. "The things we put up with in the name of fighting communism. Christ. Do you think Lee's smuggling in the bronzes from China along with heroin?"

"What bronzes?" Stone retorted bitterly. "All we have is Chen's word for it that the damn things even exist. You want to know how much I think Chen's word is worth?" Stone didn't wait for the younger man to answer. "Lee has the money and the contacts to get those bronzes smuggled out of China, as near as we can tell. He's got a heroin smuggling apparatus in place to handle the transport. Whether or not he's actually lifted the bronzes is another question."

"What does Chen think?"

"Damned if I know," Stone said in a clipped voice. "When I asked him if he had ever heard about Tom Lee, a.k.a. Lee Tran, Chen said he would 'make inquiries.'" Stone took a sip of cold coffee from his cup, made a sound of disgust and put the cup down with a thump. "That stuff is bad enough when it's hot." He looked at his watch. "Bring me up to speed on Catlin and Lindsay."

O'Donnel checked his own watch, pulled a spiral notebook from his breast pocket, and began running down the list. "Five in the morning, someone flushed, brushed and showered. Someone else brushed and flushed. Silence for about ten minutes, then some odd sounds and a lot of heavy breathing. Just when the guys listening were getting all excited, she starts talking to Catlin about *tai chi chuan.*" O'Donnel looked up from the notebook. "Some kind of Chinese aerobics, I guess."

Stone nodded and tried not to yawn.

"She showered at 5:22. No conversation other than the rye-toast-or-white variety. He called room service. They delivered breakfast at 6:04. Bellboy was legitimate; he's worked here for ten months. She drank tomato juice, Catlin had orange. Eggs poached and over easy, side of potatoes and ham."

O'Donnel yawned and flipped to the next page. Stone closed his eyes and wondered why jet lag got worse as he got older. The three hours between D.C. and San Francisco were killing him.

"Six twenty-three, she called Steve Waters and told him about a bronze she bought last night for the museum," continued O'Donnel. "Six-thirty, she called a D.C. dentist and canceled an appointment."

Stone smiled faintly. "Conscientious thing, isn't she? At least now she can't say we never did anything for her."

The younger man laughed in agreement, then continued. "Six thirty-seven. Conversation about going to see her aunt in San Francisco. Six forty-four, Lindsay calls and discovers that said aunt left early for her annual tour of the Orient. Lindsay says, 'Thank God.'" O'Donnel looked up. "Guess she doesn't get along with her aunt."

Stone shrugged, unimpressed. There was a world full of people he didn't get along with.

"Lindsay reminisces about what it was like to go home every summer to Hong Kong," continued O'Donnel. "Seven-oh-four, Catlin goes downstairs and uses public phones to make two calls."

"Did we pick up anything?" Stone demanded, suddenly alert.

O'Donnel shook his head. "We can't cover every pay phone in town with a pen register, boss."

"In other words, we don't know who he called." Stone rubbed his palm over his hair and sighed. "I should have expected it. Catlin learned to play the game from experts. Anything else?"

"Short of bugging every public phone within walking distance . . ." O'Donnel's voice trailed off.

"Dream on," Stone said sarcastically. "The attorney general would faint if he even suspected what you were thinking. Public phones? No way, and we both know it."

With a grunt O'Donnel returned to his notebook. "Catlin came back at 7:18. Together they compiled a list of bronze dealers."

Stone looked interested again.

"We ran the names," continued O'Donnel.

"Anything?"

O'Donnel shrugged. "Not a whole lot of information comes out of Chinatown, apparently. The few Chinese agents we have are all third-generation Americans. They don't speak anything but English—Bureau had to send them to language school so they could work in Chinatown. Can you believe it?"

"Your grandparents were immigrants. How's your Gaelic?" Stone asked dryly.

"Nonexistent." O'Donnel smiled unwillingly, seeing Stone's point. "Anyway, none of our Chinese-American agents have family ties in any of the refugee communities—not Tai-wanese, mainland Chinese, or ethnic Chinese from the late, unlamented Southeast Asian war.''

"Damn!"

"Yeah. I gave a duplicate list of the people Lindsay mentioned to Customs. So far only Tom Lee's name caused a hic-cup in their computer. The rest are either legitimate export-import types or haven't gotten caught yet. Same for the Drug Enforcement Administration. Only Lee's name rang their chimes.''

"Catlin's going to visit Lee?" asked Stone, disregarding everything but the one surprising fact. "Didn't he recognize Lee at the auction?''

"If he did, he didn't say anything. We had an agent at the auction, but he saw no sign that Catlin knew Lee." O'Donnel smiled suddenly. "Hell," he said, looking over his notebook again. "Let them run into each other in the dark. Lee is a real badass. Maybe he can teach Catlin some manners.''

"Don't hold your breath. If the surveillance team is correct, Lee looked like a bat coming out of hell when he left Wang's party. Hardly the act of a man eager for combat.''

Without comment O'Donnel turned another page and re-sumed his recitation of Catlin's and Lindsay's activities since morning. "They spent an hour having coffee with the Chinese Christian Benevolent Society. Apparently Lindsay's mother found immigration sponsors for half the membership at one time or another. Some of them have been over here for a long time. Long enough to be powerful, anyway.''

He looked up as Stone lit a cigarette.

"Apparently the recent emigrees are giving the locals a run for their money, power-wise," O'Donnel said. "Like Lee. Beg, borrow, earn or steal money, and then use it to buy your way to power and respectability.''

"Face," Stone said succinctly. He rubbed his jaw, testing the length of the stubble. "The Chinese didn't invent that method of getting ahead," he pointed out. "Every immigrant group has done pretty much the same thing. Including the Irish.''

O'Donnel grinned. "Yeah. Old Joe Kennedy didn't do bad for himself, did he?"

"A president, an attorney general, a senator and enough money that he didn't have to count it anymore. No, old Joe didn't do bad at all." Stone yawned and checked his watch again.

"After the benevolent society reunion," continued O'Donnel, "Lindsay and Catlin went to Asian-American Imports. Two hours, more or less. They didn't buy anything."

"Did they meet anyone?"

O'Donnel made a frustrated sound. "We don't think so, but we can't be sure. Once they get off the tourist track, they're damn hard to tail."

"I'd think they would stand out."

"So do the tails, and you told us to be very sure not to tip any watchers that Lindsay is being followed."

Stone sighed and took a hard drag on his cigarette. A pretty problem, hiding a round-eye surveillance team in Chinatown. Not that Lindsay or Catlin needed to be fooled, but any surveillance by the opposition was another matter altogether. "Don't any of the local Bureau boys blend in?"

"Most of the ones who do are undercover already, working on organized crime. If we pull them, we jeopardize their cases."

"I'll talk to the director. We've got to have people who can go into Chinatown and not stick out like clams on rice."

O'Donnel carefully kept his face expressionless. The San Francisco Bureau was already unhappy about its turf being invaded by D.C. brass who explained themselves only within the most stringent need-to-know rules. If Stone started yanking local agents out of cover to work on a case that had all the earmarks of becoming a no-win political hot potato, there would be real hell to pay. But then, Stone knew that better than anyone else. If he were even considering it, the director must be camped on Stone's ass—and the President must be similarly camped on the director.

"They had lunch at a no-name Sichuan place. Or if it had a name, the tail sure as hell couldn't read it." O'Donnel looked over the notebook. "The agent who was working in close said he'd never eaten better Chinese in his life."

Stone put out his cigarette and thought of the congealed hotel food that had been his last meal. "Wonder if they do a takeout business," he muttered.

Smiling, O'Donnel continued his recital. "Nobody approached Lindsay or Catlin. Of course, they could have given their life stories to the waiter and we wouldn't have been the wiser," O'Donnel said, scanning the page quickly. "Not speaking Chinese can be a real handicap in this part of America." He began to laugh. "Oh, Jesus, I'd forgotten about that. The poor son of a bitch."

Stone listened to O'Donnel's laughter for a moment and then said, "Who?"

"The agent who was working in close. He no more speaks Chinese than I speak Gaelic. So his helpful non-English-speaking Chinese waiter goes over to Lindsay's table and enlists the pretty blonde's aid. She goes over, translates the menu for the agent and then goes back to her own table."

Throwing back his head, Stone laughed, knowing just how uncomfortable the agent must have been.

"I'll bet Catlin nearly busted something keeping a straight face," said O'Donnel, snickering.

"Lord, what a mess. I'll bet that agent—" Stone stopped, struck by something. "Lindsay did the talking? Not Catlin?" Stone asked, remembering that Catlin spoke fluent Mandarin.

"Nope. She ordered for Catlin, too. Why?"

"He speaks Mandarin as well as Chen does."

O'Donnel was still for a moment. "Interesting," he murmured. "Wonder if Lindsay knows that?"

"Let's save it for now," Stone said thoughtfully. "We can always use it if undercover fever gets to her and she forgets who she's reporting to. That lady doesn't take kindly to being misled."

"Yeah. A more unlikely undercover agent God never made." O'Donnel shrugged. "But she volunteered." He flipped over another page. "After lunch they went to Tien Sung's Garden of Serenity—that's one of those fancy import shops that looks like a museum and is priced like God's back teeth. Again, they could have talked about the overthrow of the American government for all the tails could figure out. Every so often Lindsay gave Catlin an English update. I guess the tail did everything but crawl in Catlin's shorts trying to overhear."

"I told them not to—"

"Relax, they switched off outside the restaurant. A woman did the close work for the import shop. She came on to Catlin like she was trying to pick him up."

"Maybe we'd do better wiring Catlin for sound."

"Hell of an idea, boss. Who gets to bell the cat?"

Stone grimaced. Even if Catlin stood still for it—very doubtful—wiring someone was an overrated way of eavesdropping on conversations. Half the time only garbage was transmitted. When it came down to making the final buy, maybe wiring someone would be worth the trouble. Until then it was easier to trust Lindsay to pass the word if anything useful were discovered. They weren't trying to build a case for a courtroom, after all. They were just trying to pacify the President and the Chinese government without giving away every FBI counterintelligence agent and informant between D.C. and San Francisco.

After a moment O'Donnel continued his recital. He summarized visits to three more shops, looked at his watch and said, "They should be going into Hsiang Wu's China Dream about now. Next report isn't due for an hour."

Without a word Stone looked at his watch. He wondered if the next hour would provide anything more useful than the past twenty-four.

STONE WASN'T THE ONLY ONE wondering, but none of Catlin's impatience showed beneath his calm exterior as he walked Lindsay toward her former mentor's store. Dragged her would have been a more accurate description. After Wu's polite, devastating evasions of the previous night, she had not wanted to impose herself on him.

"I'm sure Wu has the message about my newly fallen status," Lindsay muttered rebelliously. "What good does my coming here do?"

"Wu sells bronzes, doesn't he?"

"Not the kind we're looking for!"

"You mean he doesn't touch third century inlaid—"

"You know what I meant," interrupted Lindsay, her voice low and hard.

"Is Wu known for his bronzes?"

"Of course he is! He's—"

"Then it would appear odd if we avoided him, wouldn't it?" Catlin countered. "Especially when you're so demonstrably eager to please your new lover," he added smoothly. He opened the door for Lindsay and gestured her into the shop. "After you."

Lindsay looked into the yellow-brown eyes that watched her without flinching. "Damn you," she whispered. "Do you know what this will be like for me?"

"Yes."

Catlin didn't say another word. Nor did he have to. Lindsay remembered what she had said to him in D.C.: *I won't say you didn't warn me if you don't say I told you so.*

The blithe words out of her past turned in Lindsay's mind like broken glass, cutting her. She wanted to object that she hadn't known what it would be like, that no words could have prepared her; but that was exactly what Catlin had told her in Washington. He had flatly stated that she was volunteering for a tour of hell. She hadn't believed him. Not really. She hadn't known that she would feel as though her life were being peeled away from her layer by layer. First her mother's death, then the nightmares, then the relentless demands of a double life she had neither the experience nor the temperament to handle gracefully.

She had hoped it would become easier, that she would adjust to the necessities of living a lie. It was getting harder, not easier. Watching Wu's reactions had been like sitting at her mother's deathbed and watching life fade with each ragged breath. In many ways Wu had been Lindsay's father, elder brother, uncle. He had taken her eager, untrained mind and shown it the fantastic world of ancient bronzes. Her gift for recognizing genuine bronzes had both amazed and oddly amused him. He had all but adopted her, arranging with her aunt for Lindsay to come and go from his home and shop as she pleased.

For Lindsay, Wu's house had been like a stable island in a stormy sea of change. When the pressures of adjusting to a new culture, a new home and a new life in America had eroded her sense of reality, she had slipped from her aunt's home to the seething, exciting, familiar sounds and smells of San Francisco's Chinatown.

She had been an exotic creature there, a white teenager who spoke Mandarin and had the protection of some of Chinatown's most powerful immigrants through her affiliation with the Chinese Christian Benevolent Society. Though she never became wholly a part of the lives around her, she had been accepted into them. That, too, was familiar, a continuation of her childhood in China.

Now Lindsay had to appear to disdain all the guidance, affection and patience that Hsiang Wu had given to her. She had to seem ungrateful and uncaring, a person to whom the sensual moment was more important than the enduring ties of loyalty and family. To a Chinese there could be no greater betrayal.

Without a word Lindsay walked past Catlin into Wu's shop.

As the bell shivered on the doorframe, announcing Lindsay's arrival, the scents and textures of her teenage years reached out to welcome her—ginseng and the imagined dust of the ages, the crisp aroma of ginger and the satin finish of ebony furniture, framed examples of calligraphy like black lightning dancing across a white silk sky. And above all there were the gracious shades of blue and green and bronze itself, ritual vessels condensed out of time and silence and man's hunger for continuity.

A young girl was washing the glass-fronted cases where the most expensive bronzes were displayed. From the back of the building came the high-pitched conversation of two young men struggling to uncrate a bulky shipment. There were several people in the store, either customers or friends of Wu, or both. One of Wu's daughters was showing a fine collection of bronze spearheads to a well-dressed man. She looked up, saw Lindsay, hesitated and then spoke rapidly to the man.

As the girl turned and vanished into the private area of the store, Lindsay tried to hide the clammy wave of sickness that was sweeping through her. May was the youngest of Wu's many daughters, too young to have been close to Lindsay. Even so, the girl's precipitate flight was like a slap in the face.

"Wu should be along soon," Catlin said, his voice low but not so soft as to ensure complete privacy.

Lindsay felt Catlin's strong fingers lacing through her own in silent reassurance that she wouldn't be alone when she confronted Wu. Unconsciously she squeezed Catlin's hand in return, accepting what small comfort his presence could bring. He turned and smiled down at her. Very carefully she avoided looking at his eyes, not wanting to see them empty of all but calculation. She needed the act, the pretense of caring and passion. It was the only warmth left in her world. She smiled blindly up at him, her eyes unfocused, unseeing. His fingers tightened almost painfully over hers.

Behind them the street door opened, making the bell shiver musically. Catlin turned, saw the casually dressed white man and looked away. Catlin had seen the same man once before, when the FBI woman had handed Catlin off half an hour ago. He was relieved that Stone was changing tails frequently, for they were highly visible; and more than once Catlin had sensed that he was being watched by someone other than the FBI. If he had been alone he would have quickly found out whether he had more than one set of tails. But he wasn't alone.

If he were right about the new watchers, he couldn't leave Lindsay by herself long enough to flush the surveillance. The game within a game had frozen him on center stage. He couldn't exit long enough to find out if the watchers belonged to Lee Tran or some unknown player.

As Catlin heard Wu's voice from the back of the shop, his hand tightened protectively on Lindsay for a moment before he tipped her face up to his and smiled like a lover into her haunted indigo eyes.

"Ready?" he murmured, nuzzling the corner of her mouth.

Lindsay took a ragged breath and nodded.

"Then smile," he breathed. "You're happy, remember? Passionately involved with me. Can you pretend that, or—" his hand slid up and stopped just below her breast "—do I have to go back to reasoning with your body instead of your mind?"

The warning reached through Lindsay's misery. She didn't bother to protest, because she knew that Catlin would do whatever he had to in order to get to the missing bronzes. If that meant stripping her and taking her on Wu's ebony desk, then that was what would happen.

Catlin felt Lindsay tighten beneath his hands as his words sank into her. "Don't tell me, I already know. I've known for years," he whispered. "I'm a ruthless bastard."

The bleak words went into Lindsay like slivers of ice. Her eyes focused on Catlin's. The raw desolation she saw there made her breath stop. She realized that he no more wanted her to confront Wu than she did. For a moment she felt dizzy, disoriented, as though reality had shifted unexpectedly. Catlin hated what he was doing as much as she did, but he accepted the necessity without flinching.

Abruptly she remembered what Chen Yi had called Catlin, a word that was both simple warning and complex description. "Dragon," she whispered.

And then she stood on tiptoe and kissed him.

16

CATLIN LET THE effusive Mandarin flow past him like a moonlit river, each polite apology and each polite denial of inconvenience a separate current curling darkly, creating emotional eddies that turned and gleamed in blackness. He kept his face blank, revealing nothing of his understanding of the language. But even if he had not known a single word of the exchange between Wu and Lindsay, he would have known that she was distressed. Did Wu know? Did he sense the raw misery that lay beneath her welcoming smile?

Without thinking, Catlin smoothed his fingertips slowly down Lindsay's spine, stroking her gently, trying to tell her that he understood what she was going through, that he would rather be anywhere else than right here, right now, watching her unravel the delicate fabric of memory and affection that bound her to Hsiang Wu.

It will get worse, Lindsay, Catlin thought grimly. *But you don't think that it can and I'm damned if I'm going to be the bearer of more bad news. Unless it's necessary. I'll do it if I have to. And you know it.* Then, relentlessly, came the question that he couldn't ask her because it wasn't part of the act they must play. *Why did you kiss me? At the moment I was pushing you the hardest, why did you turn to me as though I—not you—were being dragged to the fire?*

There was no answer but the tactile memory of her warm lips against his, the sweetness of her breath in his mouth. If she had turned on him in confusion and rage as she had last night, he would have understood it. He had expected it. What he had not expected was the baffling tenderness of her kiss. It had gone through his defenses like light through darkness, swiftly, wildly, illuminating parts of himself that he thought had died long ago.

"We're in luck, darling."

Lindsay's words penetrated Catlin's fierce inner concentration. He wondered if her fluent Mandarin apologies had softened Wu's impeccably, cruelly polite treatment of the woman he had called daughter.

"We are?" Catlin asked.

The look in his amber eyes made Lindsay pause. "Yes. Wu just got in a shipment of Huai-style bronzes."

Catlin smiled.

Lindsay flinched subtly. "If you've seen enough bronzes for today," she said, "we can come back some other time. Wu won't mind. He understands the necessities of business." What Lindsay didn't add was that it was obviously business rather than affection that kept Wu standing nearby, watching the interchange between her and Catlin. She didn't have to say it; Catlin knew that brutal truth as well as she did.

"Honey cat," said Catlin, tracing the line of Lindsay's mouth with his fingertip, "have you ever known me to turn down a chance to look at good Huai?"

"No," she said, her voice dry, thin. "I never have."

"And you never will."

Catlin looked from the sensual curve of her lower lip to the shrewd eyes of Hsiang Wu. Not for the first time, Catlin wondered what Wu was thinking, if he loathed Catlin as much as most men in Wu's position would have. If Wu felt resentment, it didn't show on his face; not by so much as a flicker of his eyelids did he reveal that the conversation meant any more to him than the distant barking of dogs.

Smiling, Catlin nodded to Wu and said very clearly. "Thank you, I'd be delighted to see what you have in the back room. And it will be in the back room, won't it? All shops like yours have them."

"Catlin!"

At Lindsay's low, scandalized cry, Catlin turned toward her. "C'mon, Lindsay," he said, his voice a careful mixture of amusement and exasperation. "You act like back rooms are a big secret. Hell, everyone has them. Have you ever been in a Chinatown shop that didn't have at least one?''

Lindsay swallowed and shook her head. It wasn't Catlin's words she had objected to as much as the baiting tone of his voice. It was as though he were angry at Wu for something. Quickly she turned toward Wu, apologetic Mandarin pouring from her lips in an invisible torrent.

"Forgive me, honorable Uncle Wu. My American client does not have the fine understanding of the Chinese in these matters. He did not mean to denigrate your esteemed bronzes."

"It is as nothing to this humble self. Be at ease, and permit your servant to direct your discerning eye toward objects of vast antiquity and beauty."

Wu's polite rejoinders faded into the small sounds he made as he led them to the back of his shop. In silence Catlin followed the shadow-thin Wu until he put a key in the lock of a door and ushered his clients inside. The room reminded Catlin of the Museum of the Asias basement workshop, except for the closed-circuit TV cameras set inconspicuously at opposite corners of the dropped ceiling. The furniture was hardy, scarred by use, and scattered with various tools. The lighting was harsh, relentless, not at all like the flattering light of the public display room. Packing cases bearing Chinese ideographs, U.S. Customs forms and official stamps from both countries lined the walls.

Two assistants were unpacking a large crate. They looked up as Wu entered. An invisible signal must have passed among the Chinese, for the assistants bowed briefly and disappeared through a different door, leaving Wu and his clients alone. Catlin watched the assistants leave and wondered what Wu was keeping back there that he didn't want his own men to see.

Wu went to a long, coffin-sized packing case. He picked up a pry-bar and began to work on the tightly nailed lid. After a moment it became apparent that his strength wasn't quite sufficient to the task.

"Allow me," said Catlin, taking the bar from Wu with a feral smile.

The Chinese looked up, startled. Catlin ignored him. With quick, controlled motions he jammed the leading edge of the bar between lid and case and levered down sharply. Nails pulled free with high, shrieking sounds, for the wood was green. Catlin sensed Wu watching him with assessing eyes, measuring the power of the male who had corrupted Lindsay. Whatever conclusions Wu reached about Catlin didn't show in Wu's opaque black eyes or in the narrow, erect body.

Catlin levered up the last row of nails and carefully removed the lid. Nails glittered in the hard light like warped steel fangs. He propped the lid against the wall, nails inward. Even as he positioned the lid, he felt disappointment replace his initial rush of excitement. The box wasn't from Xi'an. The packing material was twentieth-century Styrofoam chips, not the tangled mounds of vegetable fiber that the PRC still used.

"Does the honorable Mr. Hsiang do a lot of business with Taiwan?" asked Catlin. His words were for Lindsay, but his eyes watched Wu.

The Chinese nodded once, very slightly, and answered before Lindsay could. "The most esteemed and honorable government-in-exile understands the needs of the overseas Chinese to share in the cultural history of their lost land."

It was the first time that day that Wu had deigned to speak English. His voice was papery, wispy, yet oddly sharp.

Catlin smiled crookedly. He knew that as General Chiang had retreated across the face of China, freighter after freighter had been loaded full of China's art and shipped to the island of Taiwan. There Chiang had made his last, ambivalently triumphant, stand. The generalissimo had vainly resisted the tide of communism that had wiped out thousands of years of Chinese political tradition in much the same way as Emperor Qin's revolutionary ideas had remade China's government long, long ago. Like the feudal nobles of Qin's time caught in their beleaguered cities, the exiled Chinese Nationalists of the present sat on their fortified island and tried to deny that their time had passed. Even worse, they tried to deny that their future consisted of bare survival dependent on the generosity of the U.S., an ally who looked covetously toward the far more massive, lucrative markets of mainland China.

"It's not surprising that you're renowned for the quality of your bronzes," said Catlin, inclining his head toward Wu in a brief nod. "It's well known that the generalissimo had excellent taste in national treasure."

Wu's head came up fractionally, proudly. "It is most kind of you to hint that this miserable self is connected to such lofty personages as the courageous and honorable leaders of the true China. However, such dazzling connections are far beyond my mundane possibilities. The unworthy objects that fill my store come from people like myself, who have found that the world of yesterday is not the world of today, and who burn much incense in the hope of a better world tomorrow."

"Exiles," summarized Catlin.

"Just so." Wu's voice was soft, almost hissing, hinting at barely restrained anger.

Lindsay made a small movement, silent protest against the currents of hostility flowing between the two men.

Wu turned away and removed a bronze from the long case. Catlin watched in silence, his only movement that of his hand smoothing Lindsay's bright hair. The motion was unconscious, an attempt to both soothe and silence her, to protect her as much as possible both from Wu's disappointment in her and his ire at Catlin.

Uneasily Lindsay glanced aside at the powerful man standing so close to her. She wondered why he was needling Wu so openly. She couldn't ask Catlin what he was doing, though. Wu was too close. She couldn't even plead with Catlin to walk more gently around the proud old man. Then she felt the sudden tightening of Catlin's hand on the back of her neck as the first bronze was revealed. She turned, and discovery pulsed softly through her body.

The mirror was exquisite, in superb condition. Its burnished bronze face was the exact color of Lindsay's hair. The surrounding rim was worked in geometric designs that sinuously suggested dragons with glowing eyes and long, deadly tails. The patina on the mirror's rim had been allowed to develop into a textured blue-green that made a sensual contrast to the polished face of the mirror itself.

Wu braced one edge of the mirror on the table and deftly reversed the oval bronze. The reverse side of the mirror was gracefully worked in the dragon motif, with inlays of copper, silver, gold and malachite. The metal inlays were intact. Both the silver and the copper were untarnished, yet showed the mellow surface that only came with age and long, loving care. The malachite inlays had a few gaps. The imperfections reassured rather than distressed Lindsay, for she had a well-developed suspicion of artifacts in flawless condition. Given the care that Chinese families lavished on their ancestral treasures, such perfection might be possible; however, it wasn't very probable.

Catlin looked away from the mirror long enough to catch Lindsay's eye. She nodded. Though Wu's expression didn't change, Catlin knew that he had caught the silent communication that assured Catlin the bronze was genuine.

"May I?" Catlin asked, reaching for the heavy mirror.

Wu relinquished it and went to a nearby cupboard. He removed a thick towel, shook it out and laid it on the table. He glanced toward Catlin. After another long look at the polished face of the mirror, Catlin lifted the bronze and very gently laid it facedown on the towel. With the changed angle of the lighting, inlays leaped to life like streamers of colored fire licking over the ancient metal. The workmanship was breathtaking, the design utterly balanced and the result fit to grace the chambers of Emperor Qin himself.

"Nice piece," said Catlin.

Neither his tone nor his face gave away what he thought of the bronze. He glanced from the mirror to the box in a hint that Wu would have to have been dead to have missed. Lindsay hoped that her own poker face was intact, but doubted it. She had no doubt that the mirror was a treasure and was sure that Wu knew it, too.

"Is the mirror sold?" Lindsay asked.

She knew that Wu had standing orders with various overseas bronze dealers. The mirror could easily be the result of a long search for one of his many special customers. She hoped that was not the case. The mirror would be a splendid addition to the museum's collection. It would also be priced just this side of outright extortion. She hoped that L. Stephen had meant it when he had turned her loose to build the museum's bronzes into the most extensive and excellent collection in the United States.

"This is not held in the name of any of my clients," said Wu. "It is but one of many excellent pieces to be surrendered to the market as the true China's fortunes are eclipsed by the rise of the mainland gangsters."

The sudden spareness of Wu's English told Catlin that the old exile was displeased by the prospect of America's deepening alliance with the People's Republic. Catlin didn't blame Wu. Taiwan was small. China was vast. Politics was the art of the possible. It was no longer possible for America to deny the massive reality of the People's Republic. That didn't make the process of adjustment any more pleasant for aging refugees like Wu, who prayed daily that they would live long enough to be buried in a China free of communism.

Catlin wondered if Wu realized that the new government of China was trying very hard to lure its skilled, English-speaking, refugee businessmen back home. Unfortunately, many of those very same businessmen were pragmatic enough to distrust the shifting ideological enthusiasms of China's government.

Silently Wu unwrapped and put on the table five more bronzes. All had various types of inlay. All were well preserved. All were of museum quality. Lindsay watched incredulously as piece after piece was unveiled. Usually such truly fine bronzes came onto the market only rarely. She wondered what disaster had struck a collector in Taiwan that so many magnificent pieces should appear all at once on the market. When word of this went out, every collector of any stature at all would descend on Wu's shop and demand a chance to bid. She herself wanted to bid on at least four of the bronzes for the Museum of the Asias.

The eighth and ninth bronzes set off tiny warnings along Lindsay's nerve endings. There was something subtly wrong with them. She couldn't have put her instinctive response into words, but she knew that the vessels were far more modern than the others lined up on the long table.

Catlin had been watching Lindsay closely. He knew instantly that she hadn't liked the eighth and ninth bronzes. He wondered if Wu had noticed, too. Or did he already know that the bronzes were false? Had the shrewd dealer simply slipped some dross among the gold in hopes that the deception would pass unnoticed? It was an old ploy in the antiquities trade, and it was still used because it still worked.

"Are these on consignment?" Catlin asked casually, flicking three of the bronzes with his fingertip. Two of the three he indicated were the ones Lindsay had subtly rejected.

"No."

To Lindsay, the bare word was like a red flag thrown among the previous Mandarin effusions. If those two bronzes turned out to be false, it would be Wu who suffered, not the former owner, for Wu had bought the bronzes rather than simply accepting a brokerage fee for selling them. Miserably she wished that she had been born with any other talent than that of discerning genuine from false. She didn't want to have to be the one to tell Wu that he had spent thousands and thousands of dollars on two bronzes that weren't worth anything but a small curiosity value as part of a scholarly exhibit on frauds.

"If you will excuse me," murmured Wu, "my unworthy presence is required elsewhere for a short time. Please stay and bask in the reflected glory of China's ancestral greatness. If any of these honorable and humble vessels pleases your discriminating eye, I will be most grateful to discuss a possible transference into your keeping."

Catlin lifted his hand indifferently, letting Lindsay take care of the polite protestations of unworthiness and gratitude. As the door shut behind Wu, Catlin's arm snaked out and pulled

Lindsay very tightly to his body. His lips nuzzled hers, making speech impossible. When he was certain that he had her attention, he nibbled his way to her ear.

"Wired for sound."

The words were barely audible, but Lindsay caught their meaning very quickly. She eased her fingers into Catlin's hair and rubbed her cheek against his.

"Here?" she murmured, smiling slowly, acting as though he had just whispered a deliciously provocative invitation in her ear. "I don't think so, darling."

"Trust me," he shot back, his arms tightening around her warningly.

Her eyes were very dark as they searched his. "All right," she whispered.

Catlin went very still for an instant before he released Lindsay. "In that case, honey cat, I'll wait." He turned toward the bronzes but all he saw for a moment was the soft invitation of Lindsay's parted lips. Blood beat hotly, pouring through his body in primal rhythms of hunger and sensuality. When he spoke again his voice was rough with restraint. "I want this," he said, indicating the mirror. "And these."

Unhappily, Lindsay looked at the two pieces resting beneath Catlin's light touch. The eighth and ninth bronzes. The frauds.

"The mirror is superb," she said softly. "Have you considered this one?" she asked, passing over the bronzes until she came to the food dish that had caught her eye. "It's—"

"No," Catlin said savagely, interrupting her. "The three I pointed out." His eyes narrowed. "What's the matter? Don't you like these two?"

Lindsay closed her eyes. "No," she said, her voice thin. "I'm afraid they're not what they seem."

Catlin turned and studied the suspect bronzes for a long time. "I see." His laugh was soft, but there was no humor in it. "So your old mentor got stung. Badly."

With puzzled eyes Lindsay watched Catlin. She didn't know what was going on, but she sensed very clearly that Catlin was playing to a hidden audience—or thought he was.

"I'm afraid so."

"No problem," Catlin said, shrugging. "If they're fake, they're so good that I'll bet only three people know—the forger, you and me. With your reputation, all you have to do is say that those bronzes are kosher. Presto. Two kosher bronzes. If the forger ever finds out, he sure as hell won't complain."

"Are you suggesting that—"

Impatiently, Catlin cut across Lindsay's instinctive protest. "I want those two bronzes. They fit a gap in my collection I thought would never get filled. If I buy them, my whole collection damn near doubles in value. Besides, everyone makes mistakes. Even you. So just give these beauties the benefit of the doubt and put your stamp of approval on them."

"No," Lindsay said tightly. "Anything else you want but not that. I won't lie about the bronzes. Don't you see? I can't! Bronzes are my life! Don't ask me to—" Her voice broke as she searched his cheerless eyes, "Catlin?"

With a very male smile, Catlin pulled Lindsay against the length of his body. "I'm your life now, honey cat." He kissed her almost roughly before he buried his lips in her hair. "Don't give in," he breathed. As he lifted his head he said clearly, "And I want those bronzes."

"Then buy them yourself," Lindsay retorted, her voice strained by conflicting currents of confusion, anger and relief.

"No. If you buy them for me, everyone will know that they're genuine."

"Catlin, I won't do it. Not even for you. And if you cared at all for me you wouldn't ask me to compromise myself that way!"

Lindsay's low, shaking words traveled to every corner of the room. Catlin let the silence gather for several moments before he swore explosively and rocked her in his arms.

"Hell, honey, don't get upset. I was just trying to improve my collection and do Wu a favor at the same time. You know he's going to take a bath on those two pieces."

Numbly Lindsay nodded. "I know. But it's got to be that way," she said. "And I've got to be the one to tell him. He would be mortified if anyone else knew that he had inadvertently sold fraudulent bronzes to his longtime customers. Maybe—maybe Wu will be able to recoup at least part of the money from the man who sold him the bronzes in the first place."

"Not likely," Catlin said succinctly. "Caveat emptor."

"Yes." The word came out as an unhappy sigh.

Catlin looked covetously at the eighth and ninth bronzes again. "You're sure?" he asked, his voice harsh.

"I won't lie about—"

"I know, I know," he interrupted. "What I meant was are you sure that they're fake?"

"As sure as I can be without a lab test."

"You want to spend a little more time looking at them?"

Lindsay shrugged and went to the two bronzes. As she picked them up in turn, Catlin noted her tiny signs of distaste, the almost invisible tightening of her lips as though it were all she could do not to snarl at the three-dimensional lies. She didn't handle them carelessly, but there was none of the reverent, almost caressing quality in her touch that Catlin had first noticed through a one-way mirror in Washington.

"They're quite well made," she said grudgingly.

"Like the dragon last night?"

She gave him a startled look. "Yes and no. That is, the actual bronze craftsmanship is excellent in both cases, but the dragon was an original, a unique work of art. I'll bet that these are copies of originals hidden away in someone's very private collection."

Catlin grunted. "Wonder how many of them have gone out to the market before these two?"

With a frown Lindsay picked up the second suspect bronze. She didn't like to think of Wu being used as a conduit for all-but-undetectable frauds. He was a very proud man. He would lose much face if it were known that he had been so thoroughly fooled.

"I don't know," she said softly. "I'll have to tell him not to buy from this particular source anymore."

Catlin started to say something, then decided against it as the door opened again. One of Wu's assistants came into the room and with many bows and apologies asked for Lindsay to accompany him to the rooms of Mrs. Hsiang. Lindsay listened, answered quickly and turned to Catlin.

"He says that Aunt Tian is ill and would like to see me before we leave. Since she's in bed, I would have to visit her alone," Lindsay added.

"You know I don't like being away from you," said Catlin. It was the truth. He didn't like the idea of Lindsay being beyond the reach of his physical protection.

"This is different," she said firmly. When she saw that he was going to object, she added, "Catlin, this woman practically raised me when I came to San Francisco. It would be unforgivable not to see her if she requests it."

Catlin suspected that it was Wu who wanted Lindsay alone, not his wife. But there was no way to point that out at the moment, so Catlin shrugged and gave in.

"If you're gone more than ten minutes, I'm going hunting for you," he said, his voice teasing and his eyes as hard as amber crystal. "Understand me?"

Memories of the brief, vicious fight in the elevator swept over Lindsay. She swallowed suddenly. "Yes," she said in a husky voice. "I understand. I won't be long, darling."

Catlin pulled her close for a quick, hard kiss. "Don't let me down," he whispered urgently. Then he added very clearly as he released her, "Ten minutes and counting."

Even as the door shut behind Lindsay, she glanced at her watch. She had no doubt that Catlin had meant every word. She followed the silent assistant to private quarters that took up the third and fourth story of Wu's building. The assistant opened a door for her, bowed, and gestured her into a room. The door closed behind her with an almost soundless click.

There was no one in the room but Wu. Before Lindsay could speak her surprise, he pointed toward a chair.

"Sit, daughter," he said in clipped English. "I would speak to you as your father would speak if he were still alive. I am a man who is older and wiser than you, a man who has some small reputation for sagacity and discrimination, and a man who has seen much more of the world and of the kinds of men who inhabit it than you have."

With a sinking heart Lindsay lowered herself into the bare wooden chair, bowed her head and prepared to hear an unpleasant lecture from a man she respected and loved as a second father. She wanted to defend herself but knew she could not. There was nothing she could do but endure the well-meant words.

"Yes, honorable Uncle Wu," she said softly. "I know you are a man both wise and generous. You have always been kind to me, most revered uncle."

There was a charged silence as Lindsay's indirect plea for mercy registered on Wu. The stern look on his face didn't soften, nor did the ice in his voice melt.

"What are you doing with dog spittle such as Jacques-Pierre Rousseau?" demanded Wu.

Lindsay's head snapped up in surprise. "Who?"

There was another moment of silence while Wu measured Lindsay's honest shock. "It is as I feared," he muttered. "You do not even know the true nature of the dishonorable dog whose hands travel over you with the confidence of a husband's."

Dazed, Lindsay could only stare at Wu.

"Ah, foolish daughter," he said, sighing harshly. "You have been blinded by lust. The man you know as Jacob MacArthur Catlin is really Jacques-Pierre Rousseau. He is not fit to carry your night soil to the kitchen garden."

"Uncle Wu—"

"Silence! Do you have so little respect for the man who has called you daughter that you would interrupt him as though he were no more than a quacking duck?"

"Forgive me," whispered Lindsay. Her interlaced fingers tightened until her knuckles were white. "Forgive me, honorable Uncle Wu. I meant no—"

"What you meant or did not mean does not change what is," he interrupted coldly. "You have become the whore of a man who was known throughout Asia for many terrible acts, but most of all for the buying and selling of lives using opium as currency."

Lindsay made a choked sound of disbelief. She wanted to speak, to defend herself, yet knew that if she protested she would only anger Wu more. And he sounded so certain, so absolutely and unalterably confident. She tried not to think of Bradford Stone, who distrusted Catlin, and Chen Yi, who had hired Catlin. Chen Yi, who apparently did not have the trust of his own comrades.

"Rousseau profited greatly from his immorality, as such men always do for a time," Wu continued, not knowing that his words were swirling around Lindsay like the wind, sound without meaning. "His power grew enormously. People came to him to kowtow and pay tribute. Part of that tribute went into acquiring a collection of ancient bronzes." Grudgingly Wu added, "He had a fine eye for value. He was also known from Hong Kong to the Golden Triangle for being as ruthless as Emperor Qin himself. He dealt very harshly with people who brought less to him than they had promised, whether it was information, bronzes or opium. No one who cheated Rousseau survived to cheat him again."

Lindsay's head came up as her eyes searched Wu's closed, harsh face. She saw only his belief in the words he was speaking.

"His name is Jacob MacArthur Catlin," she said desperately, but even as she spoke, doubt was spreading through her. Wu was so certain, his eyes blazing with contempt, his words cutting through her. Stone had been the same way, so certain that something was very wrong with Catlin. All those missing years. Was that what he had done? Had he gone renegade and lived as a gangster in a land torn by intrigue and violence? "His name is Catlin!"

"His name is Satan," hissed Wu. "He is corrupt. He has corrupted others. Do not let him corrupt you. Tell him that you will see him no more. Tell him in Mandarin, daughter. It is a language he speaks as well as I do!''

For an instant Lindsay thought of confessing, of admitting that she and Catlin weren't lovers, that she still had maintained the high principles of her childhood. The words were crowding into her mouth when other words came to her, Catlin's words: *It's the people you respect who will tear the guts out of you. You have to deceive them, too. All of them. All the way to the wall. No hedging, no flinching, no secret winks, no hand signals. And no exceptions.* She also remembered his urgent warning just a few moments before: *Don't let me down.*

Lindsay knew that the act transcended what Catlin was or was not, what he had been or had not been. She had volunteered for this charade. Now she must play it as she had agreed to; as Stone had asked her to; as she had promised Chen Yi she would, and Catlin, her tour guide in hell.

"I can't do that," she whispered, not knowing whether her words were for Wu or Catlin or herself.

Wu had no such doubts. "Are you so besotted with his sexuality that you have no honor? Do you want to become one more in the multitude of foolish, immoral women he has used as whores, taking information from them and then sending them into the alleys to suck more information from other men? He paid them in opium and sex, and when they were too diseased to be of any further use he gutted them like fish."

"No!" The word was harsh, ragged, a denial torn from Lindsay's soul. She wasn't hearing what Wu said so much as she was hearing his conviction that Catlin was evil. She didn't believe that. She couldn't. "He is Catlin, not Rousseau!"

"You are no different than the other worthless sluts who have presented their ripe channels for him to rut upon," Wu said in disgust as he turned and walked to the door. "Tonight I will burn incense to thank God that your parents did not live to see their only daughter permit a dog to piss into the sacred vessel of their honor."

"Uncle Wu!"

It was too late. The door had shut behind him.

Lindsay sat huddled in the chair for a moment, unable to move, unable even to cry. Slowly she dragged herself to her feet, Wu's words ringing terribly in her mind: *Rousseau. Opium. Satan. Sexuality. Catlin. Opium. Rousseau.* She didn't realize that she had stumbled downstairs and back into the workroom until she heard Catlin's voice calling her name.

"Lindsay? What's wrong? Lindsay!"

Hard fingers bit into her shoulders, shaking her.

"Lindsay, what the hell is going on?" Catlin demanded, his voice harsh.

The pain almost felt good. It proved to her that she was still alive, that Wu's contempt hadn't killed her.

"Rousseau. You once called yourself Jacques-Pierre Rousseau, didn't you?" she whispered in Mandarin. She saw the instant of shock on Catlin's face as he comprehended her words, and she felt as though a knife had ripped through her. Catlin understood Mandarin. Wu had been right. All of it. Rousseau and the opium and the women. And now she was one of them. She had responded to him as she had to no other man. She shuddered horribly. "Don't touch me," Lindsay said in English. "Don't ever touch me again."

"What kind of lies has Wu been telling you?" demanded Catlin.

"He wouldn't lie to me," Lindsay said hollowly. "But you would, wouldn't you? *Rousseau.*"

Catlin didn't try to argue with Lindsay. It would have been too dangerous, the outcome too uncertain. He slammed the door shut behind her with one hand, and with the other he pulled her against him, using enough force to send the air from her lungs. His right hand moved up her throat to her jaw, holding her head immobile even as his body flattened her against the workshop wall. His left thumb slid inside her lips to the back of her jaw, opening her mouth for the savage intimacy of his tongue.

There was no possibility of withdrawal, no way for Lindsay to resist. Catlin jerked her off balance, ruthlessly using his superior strength and skill. Suddenly there was no floor beneath her feet, no wall at her back, nothing but the shocking strength of his arms holding her suspended between lie and truth, despair and hunger, the unknown past and the agonizing present. Her fingers moved convulsively, digging into his biceps as she braced herself against his power. There was nothing sexual in her response. She hung on to Catlin because at some elemental level she knew that if she let go she would never find her way out of hell with the seeds of a better future in her hands.

Catlin felt the change in Lindsay's body and knew that she had remembered the role she must play. Wu had shocked her, had savaged her cruelly and had told her God knows what lies and even more devastating truths about a man called Rousseau. But Lindsay was still game. She would be able to go on with the act and with Chen Yi's many-sided quest. Catlin knew that he could release her from his harsh grasp now, let her slide like heavy, warm satin down his body until she was standing on her own again. He knew, but his arms didn't shift. Only his mouth did, rocking gently as his tongue caressed Lindsay, coaxing her, filling the soft heat of her mouth with his own presence.

Slowly Lindsay's fingers relaxed until they no longer dug fiercely into Catlin's flexed strength. Her hands caressed him in the same slow rhythms as his kiss, stroking his shoulders and neck and finally sliding deeply into the warm midnight of his hair. He felt Lindsay shiver as her fingernails delicately scraped his scalp and the sensitive rim of his ear. The caress was returned to her with exquisite restraint as his teeth sank into her lower lip.

Lindsay's eyes opened slowly. He saw desire in their depths, and unshed tears, and the darkness that had increased with every new level of hell he had led her down into.

"Uncle Wu wouldn't lie to me," she said, her voice husky, her lips trembling.

"Neither would I," said Catlin. In slow motion he let her slide back down his body, making no effort to hide the thrusting evidence of his own arousal. "Does that feel like a lie?" he asked softly, savagely against her mouth. "Does it?"

"No," Lindsay breathed, closing her eyes, unable to bear looking into Catlin's any longer. "No..."

Tears infused her lashes and seeped down her cheeks in hot silver drops. She started to speak, but he took her mouth again and then again until all she could say was his name between kisses, his name a litany on her lips as she clung to him, forgetting everything except him.

Only then did Catlin release Lindsay, sheltering her face against his body as he looked over her head into the flat eye of the television camera and smiled.

17

"YOU KNOW SOMETHING?" Stone said in disgust, turning away from an unbroken view of San Francisco and the cobalt blue water of the bay. "The director assured me that this would be a really quick one. 'Just on the edge of breaking open,' he said. 'It could happen any minute and I want you to be there. The Bureau has worked hard for this one. Don't let the CIA take the credit.' So what happens? Nothing. Nearly a week I spend in this crummy hotel room and not one damn thing happens."

O'Donnel's lips flattened into an unhumorous line as he looked around the luxurious suite with its commanding view of city and sea. "Oh, I wouldn't say that, boss. Lindsay has taken us on a grand tour of Chinatown. We've seen every import shop, Christian mission and Chinese clip joint within twenty miles. Though I have to tell you, that lady's fortunes sure have fallen lately. From the Chinese Christian Benevolent Society to Chinese Cutthroats Anonymous. Well, not so anonymous, actually. Most of them have a whole section to themselves in our local office's computer."

"Imported whores, interstate hits and China white for local heroin addicts only. I care about counterintelligence, not the Ten Most Wanted assholes in Chinatown," Stone muttered as he lit a cigarette.

"Look at it this way," O'Donnel offered with deadpan cheer, nudging an ashtray toward his boss as he sat down. "Our men have learned to eat soup with chopsticks. Not a dead loss at all."

Stone smiled unwillingly. "I knew there was a reason I put up with you." He tossed his lighter on the table and shook his head in rueful admiration. "Soup with chopsticks. Hell, Terry, that about sums up this farce."

"You're just out of practice," chided O'Donnel. "You've forgotten how boring most undercover operations are right up until the instant when you pull out the shotguns and the handcuffs. It's a lot like fishing. You spend ninety-eight percent of your time scratching your balls and waiting for a bite."

Stone grunted. "I'd rather be fishing." He ran his palm over his hair and sighed. "All right. Give me the most recent condensation of useless crap."

With an automatic motion O'Donnel retrieved a notebook from his breast pocket. With narrowed eyes he skimmed the pages quickly. "Okay. Here we go. Do you want it all, or just the stuff since Lindsay last called you?"

"Any discrepancies?" Stone asked in a bored voice.

"Nope. The stuff she gives us agrees right down the line with what the other agents have picked up."

"That's one bright spot," Stone said, flicking ashes in the direction of a huge crystal ashtray. "After our little chat in D.C., I was afraid she wouldn't cooperate."

"Chen Yi's been straight, too," O'Donnel pointed out. "His updates on what Catlin and Lindsay are doing have matched our information to the last detail."

"Why does that make me nervous?" Stone asked rhetorically.

"Because none of them have mentioned Catlin's past as a CIA undercover called Rousseau?" retorted O'Donnel. "Including the CIA itself?"

Stone's smile was like an unsheathed knife. It still rankled that the CIA refused to fill in the gaps in Catlin's file. "Maybe Lindsay doesn't know what he used to do."

"Maybe she does, and doesn't think it matters. Or maybe Catlin's forcing her to be quiet. Remember, he's always in the room when she calls," said O'Donnel.

Grimacing, Stone took a drag on his cigarette. "If I had to guess, I'd say she doesn't know. Catlin is probably keeping her in the dark to avoid scaring her to death. Unfortunately, she could get herself blown up and never know the reason why. And neither would we. If the stakeout team at Wang's auction hadn't caught Tom Lee's hit man wiring Catlin's car, the whole operation could have been blown to hell and we'd have blamed it on the damn bronzes, not on Catlin's stint as Rousseau in Indochina.''

O'Donnel shrugged. Catlin was a big boy. He had played hardball with the pros for nearly all of his adult life. If he bought it, no one would cry. "The stakeout team seemed to think Catlin would have found the bomb himself. He checked the car pretty thoroughly.''

O'Donnel flipped through the pages of his notebook, checking the entries that had come after Lindsay's last call.

"The room bugs show the same pattern," he said. "Lindsay got up in the middle of the night and took a long shower. Alone." He shook his head and muttered, "Fifth night in a row, too. Hell of a time to solo in the shower. She must not be sleeping worth a damn. Both of them got up at the same time in the morning, early, and she did her *tai chi chuan.* So did he.''

O'Donnel looked up for a moment. "You were right about that gym and full contact karate, by the way. The agent who had the watch on Catlin yesterday morning said he hadn't seen anything like it since the early Chuck Norris movies. Catlin and some big Vietnamese were going at it like hell on fire. Agent said it was a wonder nobody was killed. Is that stuff legal?''

Stone shrugged. "Between consenting adults, it is.''

O'Donnel flipped to another page. "Damn few phone calls. Her San Francisco friends have gotten the word, I guess. No more invitations to lunch or tea or brunch or Sunday School.''

A grunt was Stone's only answer.

"Some flaky art dealer they met in D.C. is in town. He invited them to dinner beginning—'' O'Donnel looked at his watch ''—twenty minutes ago. There may be something strange going on there. One of our surveillance team said it looks like they've picked up an extra tail, a Chinese. He latched on to Catlin at the hotel. Now he's hanging around inside a grocery store across the street, watching the front of the restaurant.''

Stone's pale blue eyes narrowed. He straightened up on the couch with his first display of real interest. "Another one of Tom Lee's hit men?"

"Impossible to tell right now," admitted O'Donnel. "The local field office has a snitch inside Lee's organization, but they haven't been able to get anything definite. The snitch says Lee is sweating bullets over Rousseau coming back from the dead, but that doesn't mean Lee has authorized a move on him. Beyond the bomb, of course, and that could have been kind of a little 'hello, welcome back to the pros,' to see if Catlin had lost his edge."

Swearing tiredly, Stone stubbed out his cigarette. "What's your best guess, Terry? Does Lee have the bronzes?"

"Could be. He's certainly got the smuggling apparatus to bring them in."

"So do half the gangsters in Chinatown," muttered Stone, "and more than a few of the Christian missionary groups, too. Christ. What the hell are Customs and Immigration and DEA doing while all this garbage comes in under their noses? Dope, antiques, every kind of contraband you can think of, including human beings. I'll bet half the new arrivals in Chinatown are illegal aliens. If I were a federal agent in San Francisco, I'd be so embarrassed I couldn't look at myself in the mirror long enough to shave."

"Maybe that's why everybody in DEA has a beard," replied O'Donnel.

Stone sighed. "Okay, so Lindsay and Catlin have picked up a new tail. Who's on the countersurveillance when they leave the hotel?"

"I am."

"Getting bored holding my hand?" Stone asked dryly.

O'Donnel laughed. "Nope. I just wanted a chance to stretch my legs. But don't worry, boss. Like Catlin, I haven't lost my touch after a stint at desk work."

Stone frowned and fiddled with a pen, ignoring the cigarette still smoking in the ashtray. "Okay, you've got the counter-surveillance. But let's play it safe. Pull the primary surveillance off Catlin and Lindsay. It's going to get too crowded, otherwise. Just keep your eye on the Chinese shadow in the grocery store. Let him do his thing, unless he moves in too close. Take him down if he becomes a threat, but I'd really like to know who he is and who he works for. See if you can get any kind of ID without spooking him.''

"Right," said O'Donnel, coming to his feet with barely disguised eagerness. He headed for the door.

"And Terry . . ."

O'Donnel turned back and saw Stone's pale, hard eyes. The look reminded O'Donnel that his boss hadn't gotten to the top of the FBI heap by being a nice guy.

"Don't lose 'em and don't get burned," Stone said succinctly.

"In which order, sir?"

"Whichever order you think would do your career the most good or the least harm."

"Gotcha."

O'Donnel shut the door quietly behind himself.

THE SMILE ON LINDSAY'S FACE felt like a porcelain mock-up of the Cheshire cat. Her cheeks ached. The meal was a disaster in all ways. Every time she or Catlin tried to talk about bronzes, Mitch Malloy offered to put them onto a hot real estate investment.

"I don't need a condo in Miami or Houston or Malibu," Catlin said finally. "I don't collect condos. I collect third century B.C. inlaid Chinese bronzes. You said you had some to sell. Do you?"

Malloy drained his glass of wine and poured another. "Depends on what you want and how long you'll wait to get it— know what I mean?"

Beneath the black mustache, Catlin's mouth lifted slightly at one corner. "Not long enough for you to make one," he said bluntly.

Malloy barked with laughter and reached for another piece of sourdough bread. The movement brought him closer to

Lindsay, which was what he had in mind. He pushed his thigh against hers as he leaned into her.

"Your boyfriend has a great sense of humor—know what I mean?" said Malloy, stretching his arm across Lindsay's shoulders and letting it rest there. "Did I ever tell you that?"

"In the last minute? Not more than once," Lindsay said, trusting her cramped mouth to hold its brittle smile as she leaned forward in a futile attempt to evade Malloy.

"Great!" he said, laughing. "That's just great, babe. I like a girl with brains."

"Really?" murmured Lindsay, carefully not looking at the female who was on the other side of Catlin. If Malloy's date, who had been introduced simply as "Missy," had a brain, it was moldering unnoticed beneath the bleached-blond haystack that passed for her hair.

Lindsay's glance switched to her plate. She wondered if the dinner would ever end. Malloy and Missy had trapped Catlin and Lindsay between them in the forced intimacy of a booth. Lindsay had retreated by increments from Malloy's coarse presence, but could move no farther without crawling right into Catlin's lap. The only escape was a trip to the powder room, but she had already left the table twice.

"How long?" Catlin asked.

Lindsay's head snapped up, wondering if he had read her mind. Then she realized that he was baiting Malloy, daring him to produce some bronzes.

"Well," said Malloy, leaning back expansively. He stretched his arms across the back of the booth and crowded Lindsay even more. "It all depends on what you order. If it's the kind of thing that never comes on the market, it might take a while to, uh, persuade the owner to sell. And the harder it is to get my hands on the bronze, the more it costs. Know what I mean?"

Catlin nodded curtly.

"Figured you would," Malloy said, idly stroking Lindsay's shoulder with his forefinger. He seemed utterly oblivious to her discomfort. "After all, the guy who can hustle Lindsay is no dummy. You know, babe, you really had them going in D.C.

They thought you wouldn't say shit if your mouth was full of it." He laughed. "God, were they ever wrong! You're just plain folks, like the rest of us." He pulled Lindsay against him in a hard hug. "A lotta people are gonna be real surprised when I tell them just how folksy you are—know what I mean?"

Lindsay closed her eyes and tried to block out Malloy's presence. It didn't work.

"How long would it take you to get your hands on a bronze charioteer from Xi'an?" Catlin asked blandly.

Malloy stared for a moment, then gave a forced laugh. "Great kidder, aren't you?"

"No." Catlin's eyes were narrowed, as opaque as hammered gold. "I don't have any sense of humor at all. Know what I mean?"

With a nervous laugh, Malloy lifted his wineglass and drank heavily. "Well, I'd like to help you," he said, licking his lips as he put down his glass, "but I'm fresh out of bronze soldiers this week."

"I'll wait."

"Shit, man," Malloy said in disgust. "I've been trying to get my hands on one of those bronzes for three years. About six months ago I heard a really hot rumor."

"And?"

"It wasn't so hot, after all." Malloy looked at his wineglass to avoid Catlin's hard eyes.

"What have you heard lately?"

Malloy swirled the red wine and watched the greasy rim of his glass with heavy-lidded eyes. The cast of his face became frankly sullen. "Nothing worth mentioning. Not like six months ago. I had it wired, but my connection stiffed me. Said the shipment was ripped off on the other end. But that's what they always say when they can't deliver. Jerk-offs."

Catlin tilted his head to one side and studied Malloy openly. There was a good chance that Malloy was just another spotted toad trying to sing with the bullfrogs. On the other hand, there was a very small chance that he might actually have information. Catlin doubted that Malloy was a major outlet, but he might be able to pull off a good score once in a while. Malloy was the kind of dealer who was only as crooked as he had to be, but if he stumbled across a rich prize, he never looked back. Raiders like him were a regular part of the art underworld.

And there had been rumors linking Mitch Malloy to a load of bronzes that had been stolen on order, then stolen again en route to their destination. Malloy didn't have the brains to set up the original theft, but he had all the qualities needed to steal from the people who had. Six months ago, had he somehow stumbled onto someone who was trying to ship stolen bronzes out of Xi'an's Mount Li?

"Go on," Catlin said quietly.

"Nowhere to go." Malloy finished his wine, reached to pour himself more and discovered that the bottle was empty. "I don't have a damn thing from Xi'an."

"Were you on a direct line to the charioteer or were you a raider?"

Malloy stared at Catlin for a moment. "Hey, I'm an honest businessman trying to—"

"Save it for someone who cares," Catlin interrupted in a bored tone. "I know all about the Cellador bronzes."

Malloy swallowed visibly. "You *are* Rousseau, aren't you?" he asked in a dry voice.

Catlin waited silently, staring at Malloy out of predatory yellow eyes.

"All right, yeah, I do a little raiding," said Malloy. "But never from friendlies. I don't mind dumping on the Commies when I get the chance—know what I mean?"

"Who had the pipeline to Xi'an?"

Malloy shook his head. "Uh-uh. No way, no how. I'm gonna live long enough to sponge off my kids."

"Bullshit, Malloy. I heard you were planning to steal the charioteer from the dealer who smuggled it in. The word was all over the street."

"Not the dealer," Malloy denied quickly. "I may be crazy but I ain't stupid! I was gonna lift it from his customer. But the deal never went down."

"What was the dealer asking for the charioteer?"

"Half a million."

"I'll pay twice that."

Malloy let out an explosive breath. "Shit, man, I'd give my left nut to broker that deal, but I don't have the goods."

"Get them."

"Can't be done."

"Then introduce me to someone who can do it. I'll make it worth your while."

"How much?"

"Three points of the final deal."

"Five."

"Three."

Malloy studied Catlin, shrugged and said, "Three."

"How long?"

"As long as it takes. I'm not exactly in the man's family—know what I mean?"

"One week. After that you lose a point a week."

"Hey, that's hardly—"

"Take it or leave it," Catlin said, turning back to his meal.

There was a moment of silence followed by Malloy's forced laugh. "You're on." He fiddled with his empty wineglass, adding more greasy fingerprints to the ones already there. "Well now, this calls for a celebration. How about a little champagne? We're gonna have a great night. You won't regret it—will he, Missy?"

Malloy read Missy's wide, damp smile as agreement all around. He signaled a waiter, ordered a bottle of "the best goddamn champagne in the house" and then settled back into the booth with a satisfied smile. Under the table his thigh rested heavily against Lindsay's. He began jigging his knee, rubbing away at her leg as though he were a boy scout with two sticks and a cold night ahead.

"Isn't it exciting?" offered Missy, looking up into Catlin's eyes. "Oh, I just love helping Mitch with business. I'm going to look forward to seeing more of you. A whole lot more."

Catlin's smile was not encouraging, but subtleties eluded Missy. She snuggled her abundant breasts against his arm as she walked her fingers up and down his tie, counting the stripes. When the tie-fiddling failed to elicit a reaction, she managed to lose one of her diamond clip earrings between Catlin's legs. She shrieked in mock dismay, then giggled and began to grope around industriously, missing no possible hiding place, however unlikely that place might have been. As she explored Catlin, she apologized in a breathy little voice that became a squeak when she looked up and saw the boredom and contempt on his face.

"It isn't going to happen with you," Catlin said flatly. "Ever."

Malloy's hand had joined in the campaign on Lindsay's thigh. Suddenly she felt nauseated enough to make another trip to the rest room seem inevitable. She had managed to sit down to dinner with maggots, but she hadn't yet learned not to gag.

"Let me out," Lindsay said, turning toward Malloy without meeting his eyes. "I have to—"

The sentence was never finished because Malloy was standing up and pulling Lindsay out of the booth.

"Me too, babe," he said, sliding his arm around her waist, digging his fingers into her hip. "C'mon," he said against her ear. "I know a place where the sheets are hot and the movies are in color—know what I mean? And don't worry about Catlin. Once Missy goes to work, he won't even know you're gone."

Lindsay's control snapped. She made a choked sound and tried to push free of the drunken art dealer. It didn't work. He was taller than she was, thick bodied, strong.

"Malloy." Catlin's voice was oddly toneless. When Malloy glanced over, Catlin smiled. "Come here, Lindsay-love," Catlin said softly.

For an instant Lindsay was too shocked to move. It wasn't the endearment Catlin had used that paralyzed her, it was the smile he directed at Malloy. She had never seen such a naked promise of violence.

Malloy had seen it, too. He let go of Lindsay and stepped back quickly. Catlin slid out of the booth and stood with predatory grace.

"Hey, man, I was just kidding," Malloy said quickly, holding up his hands as though to show that he was weaponless, no threat at all.

"I told you once before. I don't have a sense of humor. I've never had to tell anyone a third time. Know what I mean?"

Malloy knew exactly what Catlin meant.

Catlin held out his left hand. Lindsay came to him instantly, pressing against the hard length of his body as though that could wipe away even the memory of Malloy's grasping fingers. Dimly she realized that she was trembling.

"I don't—" Lindsay said, but her voice thinned until it broke. She closed her eyes and desperately willed herself to be calm. She had come this far. All she had to do was get out of the restaurant without going to pieces. "I don't feel very well, Catlin," she said carefully. "Too many late nights, I guess." Her smile was as pale as her face. "Would you mind very much if we skipped dessert?"

"You're all the dessert I ever need," he said softly, smiling down at her.

It was a real smile, promising comfort rather than violence. Lindsay tried to smile in return. Catlin's arm squeezed gently. He bent down and brushed his lips over her hair.

"Hang on," he breathed against her ear.

Her only answer was the painful tightening of her fingers on his wrist.

"Call me when you have something to sell," Catlin said over his shoulder.

He didn't wait for an answer. He simply picked up Lindsay's cape and led her out of the restaurant and into San Francisco's crisp, damp summer night. He felt her shoulders shake with each deep, almost desperate breath she took and he felt the fine trembling of her body as he settled the black wool cape around her.

Part of Catlin's mind wondered almost dispassionately whether the bronzes would be found before Lindsay shattered into useless fragments. She was sleeping no more than four hours a night, and she spent part of that time deep in nightmare, crying out for a childhood long dead.

Not that Catlin was doing much better. He wasn't crying out for the past, but he lay awake cursing the present with a rage that grew greater each time Lindsay returned from her midnight shower and crawled into bed next to him. He hadn't needed to turn on the light to know that her eyes were swollen from crying. Spent tears clogged her breathing and made her movements clumsy. It had been all he could do not to gather her up and warm her with his body, to breathe reassurance and peace into her until she slept deeply within his arms.

But he had neither reassurance nor peace within himself, so how could he give either to her? And without that, how could she survive long enough to do what must be done?

Is that what Chen Yi meant when he told me to protect Lindsay? Catlin asked silently, savagely. *Am I somehow supposed to protect her from herself? Because sure as hell I can't protect her from anything else. Not from Wu's righteous cruelty. Not from Malloy's clumsy slobbering. Not even from Stone's constant, subtle pressure to turn informer. What Lindsay really needs is a massive dose of tender loving care—and nobody ever accused me of being tender or loving.*

So what the hell good am I to her?

Lindsay shivered, drawing Catlin out of his bleak thoughts.

"Cold?" he asked, the only thing he could say because there were too many people around them.

"Just tired."

"Want to get a taxi instead of walking these hills?"

"No. I like being outside. It makes me feel ... free. Clean." She laughed. The sound was as brittle as her smile. "What a silly thing to say. Must be the wine."

Absently Lindsay rubbed her hands up and down her arms, both warming herself and enjoying the softness of the wool jersey cape.

Catlin unbuttoned his suit coat, preparing to give it to her in addition to the cape.

"No," Lindsay said quickly. "Your gun will show."

"So what? Everyone who matters knows that I'm always armed."

"You? Or Rousseau?" Then, quickly, "Never mind. It doesn't matter. They're the same man."

Once Catlin would have agreed with her. Now he wasn't sure. The man called Rousseau would not have had rage turning in his gut like molten steel every time he thought of the pressures being brought to bear on a woman whose only fault was in being more gentle than the world around her. Rousseau would have done what he could and not lost any sleep over the results.

But the man called Catlin wasn't sleeping very well lately.

"I'm sorry," whispered Lindsay. "I have no right to—"

Her words were cut off as he stepped in front of her and wrapped her close. Even as his body registered her softness and warmth, his half-closed eyes looked past her, seeking the FBI surveillance team that had been behind him now for a week.

They were nowhere in sight.

After a moment, Catlin led Lindsay slowly down the street. He stopped to admire a display in a store window, drawing her to a halt beside him. After he looked at the fall clothing on the half dozen mannequins, he glanced back down the street casually. Still none of the shadowy, anonymous figures who had become familiar in the past week.

But there was a new shadow, a wiry Chinese man who was all the more remarkable for his loitering outside a restaurant that was blocks from Chinatown.

"We've got company," Catlin murmured.

"We always have company," Lindsay said, trying and failing to control a ripple of fear. That, too, was part of her nightmare. She had been followed like this before, shadows sliding soundlessly behind her as she ran toward something, driven by a child's heedless anticipation of a gift. Lindsay knew one thing with a certainty that transcended rational memory: as a child, she had been followed and then something horrifying had happened, something that had been her fault. She knew that, too, even though she remembered only in nightmare what the incident was.

"This one's new," muttered Catlin.

Lindsay put her arms around him, resting against him for the space of a long breath. "Is that good or bad?"

"How are your feet?"

"Same way yours would be if you spent eight hours a day on tiptoe," she said, looking down at her high heels.

"Are you up to taking the long way home?"

"Catlin, I'll take any way home that will get me there," she said flatly.

"That's my honey cat," he said, smiling and kissing Lindsay's mouth softly. "Equal parts of claws and sweetness. Ready?"

Lindsay tried to ignore the sensations of heat sliding through her blood as Catlin smiled down at her and nuzzled her lips with his own. It was just an act, and Catlin-Rousseau was a consummate actor.

"Ready for what?" she asked.

"I want you to get a good look at the Chinese who's following us. No. Not yet," Catlin said, holding Lindsay's face immobile against his chest. "He's hanging way back. We're going to turn at the next corner, find a shop with a foyer and wait to see who comes looking for us. The man we want is about five feet six. He's wearing a dark, long-sleeved zipper jacket with no logo and dark slacks."

"Won't he know he's been discovered?"

"If you walked past a couple who had ducked out of the light for a bit of heavy breathing, would you worry about attracting their attention?"

Catlin kissed Lindsay swiftly before he turned and took her hand, kissed it and then kissed it again. As they walked along, he brought her hand to his lips many times, nibbled teasingly on her fingers and tested the softness of her inner wrist with his teeth, playing at being the impatient lover.

The instant they turned the corner, Catlin's legs stretched out in a fast, smooth stride, making for a doorway halfway down the block. He quickly discovered that the spot was even better than he had hoped. The sidewalk was illuminated from two sides—from the store itself and from the streetlight nearby. He pulled Lindsay close.

"Catlin?"

"Yes?" he whispered, sliding his hand deeply into the silky warmth of Lindsay's hair.

Lindsay wondered how to voice her fears without revealing too much to him. Then she realized with a rising sense of panic that it no longer mattered. All that mattered was the act—and surviving it. "If you really kiss me, I won't be able to concentrate on the man who's following us," she said flatly.

Catlin's hand tightened in Lindsay's hair as the implications of her words went through him in a hot wave of desire.

"Close your eyes almost all the way," he whispered. "Just keep them open enough to catch a quick glimpse."

Long, thick lashes lowered over Lindsay's dark eyes. Catlin had to peer closely to be sure that she was looking at him.

"Like this?" she asked.

"Can you see?"

"Yes."

"Then it's perfect."

In the side light from the street, Lindsay's lashes threw mysterious shadows across her cheeks. Catlin looked at her for a long moment before he turned her, pulled her back against his chest and thrust his left hand through the overlapping front of her cape. He felt her silent gasp as his palm smoothed deliberately up the front of her body, shaping her thighs and stomach, coming to rest finally just below her breasts. The startled sound Lindsay made was muffled as his right hand settled firmly over her mouth, tilting her head back against his chest, subtly arching her body, holding her in place for his touch. He bent and closed his teeth on the rim of her ear.

"Easy, honey cat," he breathed against her ear. "This is the only way I'll be able to see him, too."

Catlin felt the wild beating of Lindsay's heart beneath his hand and knew her trembling came from more than fear. He swept aside the knowledge, because the demands of the act were more important; he needed to identify the Chinese man who should be turning the corner at any moment, his black eyes seeking the silhouette of two lovers strolling up the street. But the man would see nothing. That would worry him. He would hurry ahead, checking all the shadows, forgetting to conceal himself in his driving need to find the lovers he was following. As he stepped into the streetlight's revealing golden pool, he would see two people tangled together in the recessed doorway. He would hesitate, peering into the darkness, trying to see whether the couple was the same one he had been following.

That was when Catlin knew he would get a good look at the Chinese shadow, when the man stood impaled between the dual illumination of store and streetlight.

Almost absently Catlin caressed the fragrant softness of Lindsay's throat, delicately savoring the too-rapid beat of her pulse. At the edge of his vision he could see the shadow of her eyelashes trembling across her cheek.

"Can you see the street?" breathed Catlin, his voice a bare thread of sound.

"Y-yes."

The catch in Lindsay's husky voice sent a hot burst of desire through Catlin. It shocked him even as he ignored it, concentrating only on the street, ruthlessly dividing his mind from his emotions in the way that he had learned to do long ago.

He had also learned that such a division would ultimately destroy him. But that didn't matter, either. Not now. Now the world and everything in it was focused on one narrow slice of darkness from which the nameless Chinese would soon emerge.

18

"OUR CHINESE SHADOW will be along any second," breathed Catlin, nuzzling Lindsay's neck. "Remember. You're supposed to be a woman so hot for her man that she doesn't know the difference between an alley and the honeymoon suite at the Ritz."

Lindsay made an odd sound that could have been laughter. Her head tilted back as her hand reached up and behind her, curling around the back of Catlin's head, bringing him even closer to her. Slender fingers kneaded through his hair, and her free hand found his wrist beneath the concealing cape. She guided his palm down her torso while she moved against him like a cat, caressing him with her whole body. She had the satisfaction of hearing his breath hiss in and feeling his fingers flex against her taut stomach in a reflex that was as primitive and revealing as the sudden hardening of his body against her hip.

"Sweet God, woman," Catlin whispered hoarsely, biting the nape of Lindsay's neck. "Have a little mercy."

"Do you?"

His hand slid up to her mouth, covering it. "Okay, I asked for it," he said softly. "I keep forgetting what you're like when all the prim and proper is peeled away. My fault, not yours. Next time I'll—"

The words stopped abruptly as Catlin spotted a shadow figure gliding silently into view from the right. He could tell from the sudden tension in Lindsay that she could see the man, too. Discreetly Catlin moved his right hand closer to the gun in the small of his back, knowing that the Chinese shadow wouldn't be able to see the small motion.

Catlin waited for a moment, timed the man's footsteps, and then gave a soft, husky groan, like a lover caught within a hot vise of unsatisfied need. Startled, the Chinese stopped for an instant, illuminated from two sides as he peered into the black shadows of the recessed door.

Lindsay stiffened. Her breath came in with an audible hiss. It could have been passion, but it was not. She suddenly felt as though she had been hurled down a long, spinning tunnel, sucked back through time to a moment when as a child she had stood frozen beneath wind-whipped trees. She had sensed someone following her and had turned suddenly. For a moment she had seen her black-clad pursuer, his face divided between light pouring from a window and the endless darkness of night.

It was the same man who watched her now.

Even as the thought came, the rational part of Lindsay's mind rejected it. This wasn't her nightmare come to life. The man who was even now gliding beyond range of the streetlight was in his twenties. It was impossible that he had been the one to follow her nearly a quarter century ago in China. She had just been caught by the similarity of their predatory expressions.

Even so, Lindsay knew that she would never forget the face of the man she had just seen. It was engraved on her memory as surely as the nightmare was, another link binding the darkness of the past to the uncertain light of the present.

"Not yet," breathed Catlin, tightening his hold on Lindsay when she would have moved. "He may go by again on the opposite side of the street. See? There he goes, heading for the far corner of the block."

Lindsay sagged against Catlin, feeling chills move over her. She realized suddenly how deeply she hated to be followed, to be spied upon, to be *used*. The vehemence of the emotion shocked her, for she sensed that it came from more than the tension of the present. She sensed long roots of fear stretching down into the past, a dark plant unfurling, growing through the years, blooming blackly in the nightmares of the present.

"I'll be damned," Catlin growled in a voice that barely reached Lindsay's ears. "That's O'Donnel following our Chinese. I didn't know the FBI allowed their agents to own running shoes, much less to wear them on the job. Bet he's got at least five more men working with him.''

Lindsay laughed weakly, a sound that carried no farther than Catlin's bent head. ''Must be getting crowded out there,'' she whispered.

''Yeah.'' His hand slid out of her cape. ''We'd better break the logjam before O'Donnel gets burned.''

Silently Catlin wished that he were alone. He hated having to trust someone else's abilities. But he had no choice. He had to stay with Lindsay rather than take off on his own, shake the Chinese shadow, and then turn the tables and follow the shadow back to its owner.

''Let's go,'' whispered Catlin.

Arm in arm, he and Lindsay strolled back to the hotel, talking in clear voices, making a show of their desire for a private night alone. The Chinese shadow fell back as they approached the steep climb to the hotel. O'Donnel was nowhere to be seen, nor were the agents who were backing him up. At least Catlin hoped there were more agents. It took more than one man to safely follow another one through city streets at night.

Lindsay walked tiredly through the lobby of the hotel and into the elevator, letting Catlin support her with his arm. He keyed into the upper bank of buttons and punched the twelfth floor.

''Why do you do that?'' Lindsay asked as the doors closed. She had wanted to ask each time it happened, but had always held her tongue. Tonight she was too tired to watch every word, every impulse, every question.

''Do what?''

''Pick a different floor to get off at each time,'' explained Lindsay.

''Makes it much harder for a man with a gun to know where to wait for me.''

It took a moment for Lindsay to absorb the implications of Catlin's matter-of-fact statement. ''Tom Lee?'' she asked, her voice thin. ''Is he still after you?''

"Stone must have been real chatty the last time you talked," Catlin said curtly. He hadn't wanted Lindsay to worry about Lee Tran, alias Tom Lee.

"At least now I know why we're taking taxis," she said.

"And knowing doesn't make you feel a damn bit better, does it?"

"What did you do to Tom Lee?"

"It's more like what Lee Tran tried to do to Rousseau," retorted Catlin. "Hold still."

Instantly Lindsay froze, not knowing what would happen next and wondering what had gone wrong. When Catlin knelt and removed her high heels she let out her breath in a long sigh. The contradictions in him kept her off balance and intensely aware of him. In one breath he was talking about someone who had planted a bomb in his car. In the next he was removing her shoes as though he knew how much her feet ached—and he cared.

Was caring part of the act, too?

But that was the one question Lindsay knew she would not ask, because the answer should not matter. It must not. She couldn't live any longer balanced on the crumbling edge of her ability to pretend and to recognize pretense in others. She had been reduced to emotion, reflex and an exhaustion that was numbing, layer after layer of reality peeling away from her until she didn't know what was act and what was not.

Nor did she care. She felt as though she were empty all the way to her core.

"Lindsay?"

Without answering, she began climbing the stairs.

Silently Catlin followed. A quick inspection revealed that the door had not been opened in their absence. When they were inside he shot the bolt and went to the phone, dialing quickly.

"Stone?" asked Catlin. "Then get him. It's Catlin."

Lindsay went into the bedroom and took off her clothes. Though it was rather early to go to bed, she pulled her nightgown from the closet. The soft, sheer folds of cotton settled around her body in a rosy cloud. She didn't notice. She wanted nothing more than to crawl into bed and not wake up until the act was over and forgotten, but she knew she would dream long before that and, in dreaming, awaken choked by fear and grief.

With a long sigh she pulled the covers up to her chin and lay motionlessly, watching Catlin through the open door, putting off the moment when she would fall asleep and, in sleeping, dream.

"Stone?"

"What is it, Catlin?" demanded Stone. "Is something wrong with Lindsay?"

"No, she's fine. Just tired. This game is hell on honest people."

"That shouldn't bother you."

"Or you," Catlin said curtly. "We both got a look at a Chinese man who was following us. Last I saw, O'Donnel was following him."

"Good. When Terry checks in we'll know who's interested in you."

"Maybe. Tailing someone on foot at night is damn tricky. Luck counts as much as skill."

"Terry knows what he's doing, and he has a squad with him."

"Our Chinese shadow was no slouch, either," Catlin said dryly. "But that's not what I called about. Lindsay and I need some mug books from your local bureau's files. If our tail was Tom Lee's man, chances are you've got pictures somewhere. But don't limit the mug shots to known or suspected organized crime figures. Bring in all the stuff you have on the various Chinese benevolent societies."

"What stuff?" Stone asked blandly.

"Tell it to the newspapers," snarled Catlin, suddenly impatient with all the lies. "I know damn good and well which branch of the FBI you work for, Stone. Counterintelligence. Among other jobs, your boys keep tabs on every ethnic group that might serve as a cover for introducing foreign agents into the U.S. The national and international Chinese benevolent societies make one hell of a spy pipeline, and we both know it. So cut the crap and get the mug shots to us."

There was a long silence followed by "I'll see what I can do."

"You do that, Stone. And you do it goddamn quick, because Lindsay won't last much longer in this business. Maggots just aren't her style."

Catlin dumped the receiver back into its cradle and swore silently, savagely. He knew that he shouldn't have lost his temper with Stone. On the other hand, that was better than giving in to the idea that had been tantalizing Catlin since dinner—taking Mitch Malloy, holding him over a wine bucket and slitting his throat.

For a long time Catlin stood motionlessly by the phone, flexing his hands, staring at them, thinking, remembering. He had been drawn into covert operations by a combination of idealism and the thrill that came from adrenaline coursing through his blood. Adrenaline had lost its allure. He had thought that idealism had, too. It hadn't. It had simply lain dormant beneath layers of cynicism and survival reflexes. At his core he still wanted to protect the weaker from the stronger, the hopeful innocents from the immoral power brokers, and the would-be good from the accomplished bad.

So what am I doing now? Throwing a lamb to the wolves, that's what. Nice going, Catlin. Hell of a way to live up to your buried ideals.

Abruptly his hands became fists. Watching Lindsay's demoralization had been the most difficult thing he had ever done in his hard, unsheltered life. He knew that she teetered on the edge of self-discovery now, and that whatever her discovery ultimately was, it would never be as comforting as her innocence had been.

There was no help for it, though. There never was. That was how you knew you had finally arrived in hell. Only the best intentions led there.

Noiselessly Catlin walked across the room and stood in the bedroom doorway. Lindsay was asleep or hiding by pretending to sleep. Either way, he wouldn't disturb what peace she could find. There was little enough comfort in the hell he had led her down into, and less peace.

Catlin undressed, positioned his gun on the night table and crawled into bed next to Lindsay. She didn't move. He reached to turn out the bedside lamp, then decided against it, knowing that sooner or later she would wake up disoriented and afraid. The light would help her in the first terrifying instants when she was still gripped by nightmare. Light would also help her when she walked to the bathroom and turned on the shower full force so that the hidden bug couldn't pick up the sound of her crying. Then, eventually, the light would help her when she dragged herself back to bed and lay awake until dawn.

He would be awake, too, telling himself all the reasons why the development of normal relations between two countries was worth dragging a good woman down into hell. He would also be telling himself all the reasons why he shouldn't stretch his arm across the space separating Lindsay from himself, why he should not pull her against his naked body and give her a few moments of warmth to balance against the demands of a game she hadn't the coldness to play without destroying herself.

Catlin was still awake listing reasons when Lindsay began to move restlessly. Her motions were tiny, abrupt—unmistakable echoes of the nightmare that she had refused to talk about with him, the nightmare that no amount of showering and tears had been able to exorcise. Muffled whimpers came from her lips, tearing at him in ways that he could neither name nor understand.

As he had all the other nights, Catlin stroked Lindsay's hair very gently, trying to calm her without waking her. After a few moments she turned toward him as though she sensed at some unconscious level that he was safety in the midst of her terrifying dream. Even as he told himself not to be a fool, that he was too vulnerable tonight to trust his own control, he eased her lightly into his arms, hoping that she would be reassured and sleep more deeply. He told himself that he had to do it, that she was on the ragged edge of breaking and that she had to have sleep; for without it, she wouldn't last longer than a few more days.

And it was true. It was also true that Lindsay's breath was a rhythmic warmth bathing Catlin's skin, and the weight of her breasts sent the sweet heaviness of desire surging through him. He concentrated on breathing evenly, deeply, soundlessly, focusing his mind on anything but the unleashed hunger pulsing through his body.

As before, Lindsay calmed for a time in Catlin's arms; but then the dream returned redoubled, and she fled through a terrible black landscape, pursued by horrors that she either could not or would not speak aloud. When she began to move abruptly, uttering shattered, incoherent words, he knew that she would be waking soon. Then she would ease herself from his arms while he pretended to sleep. She would walk to the bathroom, her steps clumsy with the remnants of fear, and she would stand beneath pouring water until her skin was all but raw.

And he would lie in bed, feeling rage eat into his soul because he was the one guiding her deeper and deeper into hell.

Lindsay came awake in a frightened rush. She stiffened in the instant before she realized where she was and what had happened. The nightmare had come again, only worse. This time the man pursuing her had had two faces, one old, one new, both terrifying.

For a moment Lindsay lay utterly still, her cheeks wet with tears, her body tense as she fought to control her breathing. With each deep breath, the warm male scent of Catlin reassured her in an elemental way that she neither understood nor questioned. There was nothing rational about the feeling; it simply existed, a fact like sunrise and the turning of the earth, inevitable, unstoppable. She wanted to curl more closely to him, to draw him around her like a living blanket, to fill her senses with him.

But she would not. She remembered too well the night in D.C. when she had cried, *What do you want from me?* and he had answered *An act. That's all. Just an act.*

As on the previous nights, Lindsay moved cautiously onto her own side of the bed, trying to disengage from Catlin's loose embrace without awakening him. But tonight it didn't work. Tonight his arms tightened, refusing to let her go.

"No," Catlin said gently, stroking her hair. "Water torture hasn't been doing you any good, Lindsay-love."

"What?"

"The showers," he murmured, kissing her temple, her wet eyelashes, the tear-streaked hollow of her cheek. "If the nightmare could be washed away, it would have been gone by now. Believe me. Water just doesn't get it done."

"Then what does?" she asked bleakly.

"Fire."

The hand that had been smoothing Lindsay's hair slipped down to her throat, tilting her head back along Catlin's arm. Delicately he found the most sensitive nerves on her neck and teased them into shivering life.

"Catlin . . . ?"

Her husky, unfinished question made desire rip through him, but he controlled it with no more sign than a fractional tightening of his hands as his lips covered hers. The tip of his tongue caressed the generous curves of her mouth, probed gently at the corners and delicately tasted the inner softness of her lips until her breath caught.

She turned her head, trying to capture his sweet, caressing mouth for the harder, deeper kiss that she suddenly realized she must have. He laughed softly and evaded her sensual seeking while he brushed her lips again and again. Her breath came out in a ragged sigh. She caught his face between her hands, holding his mouth still for the kiss she needed more than she had ever needed anything in her life.

When Catlin's mouth opened beneath Lindsay's, she made a soft sound. The taste of him went through her in a shock wave of pleasure. She savored all his textures—the sliding roughness of his tongue and the smoothness hidden beneath, the tiny serrations of his teeth and the resilience of his lips, the intriguing curves and salt-sweetness of his mouth. She felt herself savored in turn, tasted, enjoyed, responded to with an honesty that was as compelling as the kiss itself. She gave herself to it and to him, letting nightmare fade beneath the sudden, overwhelming heat rushing through her, flushing her skin with passion.

Catlin felt the change in Lindsay, the hunger that not only permitted but demanded that their mouths join deeply in a prelude to the hotter, even deeper joining to come. The rhythmic mating of their tongues made Catlin's whole body tighten like a drawn bow. In a sensual reflex as old as passion he pulled her closer, holding her hips against his while his body matched the primitive movements of their mouths. She shivered and made a tiny, wild sound that went through him like chain lightning, burning away his self-control.

Even as he stripped off her soft nightgown, he tried to slow down, to leash the primitive male sensuality that had always been his greatest vulnerability. The sight of her creamy breasts did nothing to help his control. Her nipples were deep rose, tight with hunger for his touch. He forced himself to wait, to trace the line of her body with his fingertips from her smooth shoulder to the curve of her waist and the shadowy dimple just below.

Lindsay's breath caught when the tip of Catlin's little finger filled the sensitive hollow of her navel and moved slowly, gently, finding nerve endings she hadn't known she had. Heat uncurled deep within her body, expanding outward in rhythmic rings of sensation that made her want to twist slowly beneath his touch.

He saw the tiny, revealing motions and stifled a groan of need. He wanted to stroke the curve of her thighs, to tangle his fingers in the burnt gold hair at the apex of her legs, to explore the textures and hunger of her. But he was afraid that the instant he found her hidden softness, his control would evaporate; then he would open her legs and sheath himself in her satin heat until years of cold were burned away in a fire so hot that not even ash would remain.

Knowing that he shouldn't, feeling his control slipping away by hot increments, Catlin bent and touched Lindsay's rose-tipped breast with his tongue. He sensed the sudden change in her heartbeat, heard the break in her breathing, felt the wild tightening of her nipple as his lips closed around it. With a groan he took her deeply into his mouth, tugging on her rhythmically, shaping her to his intimate demands.

Heat pulsed through Lindsay with each sweet movement of Catlin's tongue. She heard a moan and knew that it was hers, just as the growing pressure of hunger demanding to be re-leased was hers. She tried to tell him, but her breath wedged in her throat when she felt the warmth of his hand sliding down her body. Her hips shifted, seeking his touch with sinuous movements that were as graceful and as elemental as fire itself.

Catlin's fingers shook as he shaped the firm curve of Lind-say's thigh, stilling her, trying to slow himself down. With a broken sigh she turned toward him. The movement shifted his fingers to the smooth warmth of her inner thighs. His breath shortened as he accepted her wordless invitation. He traced her layered softness, teasing her until she shivered and melted, opening for him, asking for a deeper caress.

Eyes closed, fighting for control, he delicately touched her humid softness again and again. It wasn't enough. He wanted to feel her around him, clinging to him, moving with him. He wanted it with a violence that shocked him. And he knew that she wanted it, too. It was there in her heat, in the incredible softness of her, in the way she moved against him, promising a joining that would be both hot and perfect.

With a throttled groan Catlin withdrew his touch, no longer trusting himself. He took Lindsay's mouth as he longed to take the hot center of her body. Her hands moved restlessly, hun-grily over him, finding and combing through the rough silk wedge of male hair that covered his chest. The flat, smooth circle of his nipple was another texture, as intriguing to her as the tiny, hard center that rose to her touch. Her nails scraped lightly over his nipple. The husky groan of his response made her hand drift lower, searching for even more sensitive masculine flesh, finding it.

In the next instant Lindsay found herself flat on her back, pinned beneath the sensual weight of Catlin's body. He caught her hands and brought them alongside her head, lacing his fingers deeply through hers.

"Don't you want me to—" began Lindsay, only to have the words cut off by the force of Catlin's kiss.

"Yes, I want you to touch me," he said finally, lifting his mouth. His voice was gritty and his pupils were so dilated with passion that only a golden rim of color remained to his eyes. "I want those sweet hands all over me, and I'd kill to feel your mouth in the same way." He closed his eyes and took a shuddering breath. "But I'm nearly out of control right now. If you touch me," he said, biting her lips and neck and breasts with barely leashed hunger, "it will be all over. I'll bury myself in you until the only thing I know is your softness, your heat."

"Yes," she said huskily. "That's what I want. You. Inside me." Her body arched into his, openly pleading for him, demanding him. "Please, Catlin," she moaned. "Now!"

"Christ, Lindsay," he grated, "we'll burn down the night."

He sheathed himself deep inside her with a single powerful movement of his hips. The sweet shock of him sliding into her made her cry out raggedly. He filled her until she overflowed with pleasure, sending heat spilling between them. He moved again, slowly, slowly, and drank the tiny cries that were torn from her. He shook with the effort of holding back. He wanted to feel her come apart beneath him first. He needed to know that she would feel the same shattering release that was clawing at him even now. He wanted that wild release for her as fiercely as he wanted it for himself; yet each time he moved within her, control slipped further away from him.

With a distant sense of shock Catlin realized that Lindsay's gliding, sliding heat had burned through his will, leaving only an elemental hunger for her that could no longer be leashed. He caught her hips with one arm and arched heavily into her again and again, trying to bury himself in her so deeply that the pleasure exploding through him would never stop. Her name caught in his throat, coming out as a broken groan echoing the pulses of his release.

The sound of her name breaking on Catlin's lips hurled Lindsay into ecstasy. He felt the tiny convulsions begin deep inside her, closing around his rigid flesh, caressing him with the intimate rhythms of her climax. Suddenly, impossibly, fire burst within him once more, spreading up from their joined bodies, sending him over the edge again with a sweet violence that was like nothing he had ever experienced, hot and untamed and endless, destroying him, creating him.

Lindsay clung to Catlin, absorbing the shock waves of his ecstasy into herself, knowing only the sensual weight of him covering her, the salty taste of his sweat as she kissed his skin, and the wild, shivering aftermath of his climax. For a long, long time there was no sound but that of broken, gradually slowing breathing. When he finally stirred and moved as though to roll aside, she made a small sound of protest and clung to him.

"I'm crushing you," he said, kissing the slightly swollen curve of her mouth.

"Don't leave me yet," whispered Lindsay. She moved against Catlin, bringing down even more of his weight on her, holding him with a reflexive movement deep inside her body. "You feel so good like this. So right. Just a few moments more. Unless you're uncomfortable?"

Catlin looked down into Lindsay's eyes, half closed, midnight blue, luminous with sensuality. The reality of her swept through him in another kind of shock wave, near pain and savage pleasure combined. She had taken him into her body with a sweet and searing generosity that had twice undone him. She had played no games, expected no rewards beyond the intimate moments she shared with him; and now she was asking nothing but that those moments be a few more before she returned to the cold world that had been tearing her apart.

"Uncomfortable?" Catlin's laugh was husky, ragged, almost broken. "Sweet God, Lindsay. You fit me perfectly. Can't you tell?"

If she gave an answer, it was lost as he bent and took her mouth in a slow, savoring kiss. His arms surrounded her, lifting her with him as he rolled onto his side without separating himself from her. She returned the kiss even as she shifted languidly, burrowing closer to his muscular warmth. With long, slow sweeps of his hands he caressed her, taking pleasure in the smooth texture of her skin, the elegant line of her spine and the warm weight of her resting against his body. The feel of Catlin's hard palms and sensitive fingertips stroking her made Lindsay murmur contentedly against his shoulder. She flexed her hands, enjoying the heat of him radiating up through the damp, musky wedge of hair covering his chest.

Catlin tilted Lindsay's face up to his so that he could brush his lips over hers once, twice, and then a third time, hungry for her in a way that had nothing to do with unappeased desire. She had satisfied him all the way to his soul.

Yet he still wanted her.

He wanted to absorb her into himself as honestly as she had absorbed him, to teach her that ecstasy could be simultaneously savage and endlessly sweet, that it could be brilliant torrents of life pouring through her, destroying her, creating her. He didn't think that she knew ecstasy in that way. He hadn't known it himself until tonight.

"Stay here," Catlin murmured, kissing Lindsay deeply as he slowly separated himself from her.

Other than making a muffled sound as Catlin left her body, Lindsay didn't object.

"I'll be back," he said, smiling, caressing her cheek with a gentle fingertip.

Catlin went into the bathroom, filled a glass of water and poured it slowly into the toilet. He flushed, then lifted off the back of the tank very carefully and set it aside during the height of the flushing noises. As the tank refilled, he took his comb and jammed the shut-off mechanism, ensuring that water would run continuously into the tank. Because the bug had been placed just below the tank, whatever was said in the bathroom from now on would be blurred by the noise of running water. When he added the pounding roar of the shower to the background sounds, Stone's eavesdroppers would think they had been dropped over Niagara Falls.

Lindsay watched Catlin coming back toward her through the semidarkness of the bedroom. As always, he moved smoothly, displaying a feline certainty of his own coordination and strength that fascinated her. She looked at him openly, honestly, letting him see her appreciation of the powerful interplay of tendon and sinew, of the masculine strength revealed in the flex and flow of muscles beneath his skin and of the potency she had so recently enjoyed.

"You're like the dragon we saw at Wang's auction," she said, her voice husky, intimate. "Sensual. Powerful. And very, very male."

Catlin saw the approval in Lindsay's indigo eyes, heard it in her words, felt it as he stood by the bed and she traced the center line of his body until she cupped him warmly in her hand. Smiling, he bent and eased the sheets down her body, looking at her as completely as she had looked at him. He kissed the curve of her neck, the tips of her breasts, and then dipped his tongue into her shadowed navel.

"I'm glad you like what you see," Catlin whispered, smiling as he took tiny, loving bites of Lindsay, "because I think you're the most perfect maiden ever sacrificed to a needy dragon."

"I'm hardly a maiden," she murmured, allowing him to pull her out of bed and into his arms.

"Thank God," he said almost roughly. "The things you make me want to do would horrify a virgin." His teeth raked lightly along Lindsay's shoulder, finding and caressing unexpected nerves, making her shiver suddenly as her eyes widened with surprise and returning desire. "Come on," he muttered, taking her hand and pulling her after him toward the bathroom. "Stone expects you to take a shower in the middle of the night. We wouldn't want to disappoint him, would we?"

As soon as Catlin was in the bathroom he grabbed a bath towel. Deftly he scooped up Lindsay's hair and wrapped the towel around it. He opened the glass door to the tiled shower, turned the faucet on full, tested the temperature and tugged Lindsay in after him. The big enclosure began to fill with steam. As soon as Lindsay was wet, Catlin turned his back to the force of the water, creating a sheltered place for her to stand.

Without a word Catlin began lathering Lindsay from her chin to her toes. The feel of his strong hands sliding over her body made her breath catch with pleasure. She closed her eyes and simply enjoyed his touch, twisting and turning very slowly, savoring being stroked with an honesty that drew a smile from Catlin's hard mouth.

Lindsay opened her eyes in time to see the sensual curve of his lips beneath the black mustache. She followed his glance down to her breasts, where foam glittered and gathered with each breath she took. She ran her hands over herself, scooping up lather. Smiling, she spread the slippery foam over Catlin's shoulders and torso, weaving ragged ribbons of white through the thick mat of black hair covering his body.

Catlin's hands slid lower, tantalizing Lindsay's sensitive navel before he spread his fingers wide over the taut swell of her hips. He tested the resilience of her buttocks with open pleasure, letting her fill his hands and then flexing his fingers slowly into her flesh. Lindsay's dark blue eyes widened in surprise as sensations speared through her, making muscles deep inside her body contract as though she were still trying to keep him within her. Catlin saw the reflexive, quintessentially feminine response and wanted to laugh with sheer triumph.

"What are you smiling—" she began to ask, only to have her voice break as his hands clenched again and pleasure lanced through her.

"It's you, honey cat," he said, catching her mouth beneath his, opening her lips with a slow thrust of his tongue. "Didn't you know?"

"Know what?" she asked softly when he freed her mouth.

"You. You're as much woman as I've ever had my hands on." Catlin's voice caught as he filled his hands with her again, and felt again her uncontrollable feminine reflex. "Oh, God," he breathed, lowering his mouth to hers. "I've never known a woman as honestly sensual as you."

"But I'm not—" she began, remembering other times, other men. Words and memories spun away suddenly and her voice splintered into a moan as his hands flexed once more.

Catlin laughed deep in his throat. "Tell me about it," he encouraged, biting gently into Lindsay's mouth with his own, savoring the passionate shivering of her body. "Tell me everything you feel."

But Lindsay couldn't speak because Catlin had taken her mouth again, making it his own. By the time he released her, she had forgotten everything but his taste, the feel of his powerful body beneath her hands. Slowly he turned her in his arms, letting warm water pour over her. Streamers of lather slid down her body, following each indentation and curve with a fluid perfection that sent sensations of heat and heaviness coursing through Catlin. With one hand he pushed the shower head away, sending water pouring over tile instead of flesh.

"I—" Lindsay closed her eyes, suddenly unable to bear the golden dragon eyes watching her with such sensual intensity. "I usually take longer in the shower," she said in a husky voice. "That is, if we're trying to fool Stone?"

"I know. I wanted to allow plenty of time to dry off that lovely body of yours."

"That won't take long," whispered Lindsay, opening her eyes as she reached up and unwrapped the towel from her head.

"The way I'm going to do it, it might just take the rest of the night."

Catlin tugged the towel from Lindsay's hands and dropped it to the wet tile. His head bent toward her with a slow inevitability that made her tremble in anticipation. She felt the warmth of his breath and then the heat of his mouth as he licked drops of water from her face with tiny strokes of his tongue.

His name came from her lips in a small rush of sound. He licked up that, too, wanting nothing of her response to escape him. The taste of her was more potent than cognac, sweeter than anything he had ever had on his tongue. With a soft groan he pulled his mouth from hers and moved on, smoothing water from the taut curve of her neck and sucking up bright drops gathered in the hollow of her throat, counting the wild beats of her heart in the pulse racing beneath his lips.

The swelling promise of her breasts lured him lower. He stole warm drops from her skin in a slowly diminishing spiral that led finally to the ruby peak. This time she couldn't whisper his name, for the sweet burst of sensation took even her voice. She braced herself on his arms as she felt the world begin to slide away, leaving her suspended within his primal sensuality.

Catlin made a thick sound of satisfaction as he felt Lindsay sag against his strength. He turned to her other breast, slowly brushing his mouth from side to side. The coarse silk texture of his mustache electrified her, making her nipple tighten wildly. When he pulled the peak into his mouth and caressed her with the hot, slow rhythms of increasing desire, she began to tremble all over again. Smiling, he slid down her body, caressing her with his hands, licking up water, tasting her, enjoying her with all his senses. He bit softly at her inner thigh, then less gently, sucking on the creamy skin with enough force to leave a loving mark.

The tiny pain sent a sunburst of sensation through Lindsay. Her head tilted back against the tile and she moaned softly, a sound that was all but lost in the pouring of the water down the far side of the shower. Catlin heard the small cry and felt fire burst through him. His hands slid up to the very top of her thighs, seeking and finding the twin creases where torso and legs joined. His thumbs caressed the tendons before his hands flexed deeply. With a helpless moan she arched toward him, bracing her legs wide apart because she could support herself no other way.

He nuzzled aside the dark bronze hair, revealing her to his caressing mouth. Delicately he traced the hot flesh, feeling her tremble beneath his hands and his intimate kiss. When his tongue found and stroked the tight knot of nerves hidden between layers of softness, she moaned again. A wild pleasure coursed through her repeatedly, tightening her body. He laughed against her and his teeth closed with exquisite care around the violently sensitive nub of flesh, isolating it for his teasing tongue.

Lindsay's fingers locked on Catlin's shoulders and her nails bit into his flesh as his name was torn from her lips. He drank the small pain of her nails just as he drank the shivers coursing through her, giving her to him.

"Honey cat," he said thickly. "Sweetness and claws."

With a cry Lindsay arched against him, twisting slowly in the flames called by his wild caresses, shaking with the force of the ecstasy consuming her. Catlin kissed and stroked and gently bit her sweet flesh again and again, unwilling to release her even though he knew that he would have more from her tonight. He would have everything. He had just begun to explore her shimmering sensuality.

Finally, reluctantly, Catlin came to his feet once again, holding Lindsay against his body because she could barely stand alone. With quick motions of his hand he shut off the shower before he lifted her, carried her to the bed and lay down between her legs. Slowly be began caressing her all over again.

"Catlin—" Her husky voice broke. "I can't!"

"Yes, you can," he said, kissing her gently, loving her with his mouth, all of her. "And you will. Tonight you're going to learn what you taught me. There's no end to me, to you."

He smiled at her, and her breath caught with the certainty in his untamed golden eyes.

"Yes," he said huskily, seeing her expression change. "I'm going to absorb you into me, all of you, just as you absorbed me."

Catlin knew that with a certainty that was both calming and infinitely exciting. It let him come to Lindsay with a slow, consuming sensuality that was as new to him as it was to her. His touch unraveled her, stripping her of inhibitions as she responded to his husky, urgent words and primal touch. She held back nothing of her response or her need or herself, letting him teach her the secrets of her body and his own until neither he nor she knew which one touched and which one was touched, which one wept and which one tasted tears, which one cried out and which one drank the cry.

When he finally became a part of her, she flowed over him like a wild river of fire, and together they were consumed by that fire while the night burned down around them.

19

THE FIRST HARSH RING of the phone brought
Catlin from a sound sleep to full wakeful-
ness in less than a heartbeat. In the instant before his hand
brought the receiver to his ear, his body registered the warm
impact of Lindsay curled along his side, and his mind filled
with a rush of recent memory. He didn't know whether to laugh
or swear when he hardened almost violently in response to the
sensual images.

"Yes," Catlin said curtly into the phone.

"Your toilet's running."

Catlin glanced at the bedside clock. "You called me at six-
thirty in the morning to tell me that? What's the matter—Stone
turn you into a plumber?"

"No, but the boys sure are tired of listening to your toilet
leak," said O'Donnel.

"I'll see what I can do."

Catlin yawned and stretched hugely as he sat up and propped
his naked back against the padded headboard. Lindsay stirred
restlessly, still asleep, missing Catlin's warmth. His free hand
smoothed over her hair and then slid beneath the sheet, savoring the warm, womanly body that turned toward his touch. The
bone-deep honesty of her response both fascinated and aroused
him.

"Did Stone come through with those mug shots?" continued Catlin.

"I'll check. He's on the other phone yelling at someone."

"Take your time," Catlin offered, easing the sheet down
Lindsay's body.

She lay on her side with one hand under her head. The other
hand was drawn up between her breasts and tucked beneath her
chin. One of her breasts nestled in the crook of her arm. She

looked altogether too edible for Catlin's peace of mind. He circled her breast with sensitive fingertips, enjoying the changing texture from silk to nubby satin. The nipple rose to a taut peak that grew even more erect as he tugged gently at the ruby tip.

Lindsay's eyes opened slowly, a blue so dark that it was like a midnight sea. Half asleep, half awake, wholly a creature of her senses, she stretched languidly in response to the gentle streamers of sensation radiating from Catlin's touch. His breath shortened as her breast pressed against his palm and the sheet slithered down her body to reveal a golden triangle of hair. He put his palm over the receiver, making sure that no sound would be transmitted.

"Come here, honey cat," Catlin said. "I've been waiting a long time to kiss you good-morning."

"I thought the phone just rang a minute ago," Lindsay murmured, her voice husky. She sighed and rubbed her cheek against Catlin's chest. Her eyelids lowered as she slid back into the warm, sensual world of near sleep.

"Yes," Catlin said, almost groaning as he felt Lindsay shape herself to his body. "That's a long, long time to wait."

Eyes closed, Lindsay smiled and reached for Catlin even as he drew her across his chest. His tongue swept into her mouth, filling her. She made a small sound, remembering the long, wild hours before dawn. Nothing in her experience had prepared her for a man of Catlin's uninhibited sexuality. He had consumed her and then laughed with sheer pleasure as he drank the cries pouring from her. She had responded to his searching, soothing, inciting caresses as she had to no other lover, letting him strip away years of hesitation and mistrust, peeling her down to her sensual core and then rebuilding her layer by layer with his own body as he gave himself to her without restraint or calculation.

An honest man.

"Catlin? Catlin! Did you go back to sleep?"

The sound of O'Donnel's voice yelling close to Catlin's ear made him reluctantly release Lindsay's mouth. As he uncovered the receiver, Lindsay snuggled against him, exploring him sleepily with her mouth. The texture of his chest hair intrigued her, tickling her lips as it had in her dreams. She tugged experimentally, unsure whether she were waking or dreaming, and not really caring. Wherever she was, it was warm and musky and sensually gratifying.

"I'm here," Catlin said, his eyes darkening as tiny slivers of pleasure pierced him with each movement of Lindsay's lips.

"You sound half asleep," complained O'Donnel.

Catlin smiled down at the bronze hair that was lying across his chest. As Lindsay's head turned he could see the pink tip of her tongue searching for his nipple, finding it. He controlled his breathing even as he buried his free hand in Lindsay's hair. He thought he was going to pull her away from his chest, but then he felt himself moving her head slowly from side to side, encouraging her to rub her mouth across his sensitive flesh. The contrast between the heat of her tongue and the coolness of the room brought every one of his senses into sharp focus.

"I'm waking up," Catlin said into the phone.

Teeth closed on his small, erect nipple, tugging at him with a lazy sensuality that made him ache. He gave up any thought of pulling Lindsay away. It felt much too good to have her tongue stroking him, tasting him. His fingers worked through her hair to her scalp, holding her against his erect nipple, caressing her.

"If you can manage to stay awake a few more minutes," O'Donnel said tartly, "Stone wants to talk to you."

"I'll try," Catlin said, smoothing the ball of his thumb down Lindsay's spine. "Did you run down that Chinese tail you were after last night?"

There was a silence, then a startled laugh. "For a second there I thought you were talking about a piece of ass," explained O'Donnel, "and I was wondering how the hell you knew that I'd picked up a little honey who—"

"I'm too old to be interested in a piece of ass," interrupted Catlin, yawning again, "and if you aren't, you ought to be."

"Too old for sex?" O'Donnel taunted.

"No. Too old for ass. There's a difference."

"There is?" O'Donnel asked cynically.

Catlin's laugh was a low, rough-edged sound of pleasure as Lindsay's hands kneaded down his torso as though she were a sleepy, contented cat. Her fingernails raked lightly over the long muscles. He knew as surely as if she had spoken aloud that she was savoring the warmth and power of his body, just as he had savored the warmth and softness of hers last night. They were perfectly matched as lovers. No games, no secrets, just the endless hot honesty of their mutual response. Susie hadn't been like that. They had been too inexperienced in too many ways. Nor had Mei been like Lindsay. With Mei there had been wild heat but no light, no honesty. She had given him the least important part of herself. He had been too young to realize it at the time—and it had almost cost him his life.

"There's all the difference in the world," Catlin said softly into the phone as his fingers tightened in Lindsay's hair. "Is this a roundabout way of telling me that you screwed up and lost the Chinese shadow who was following us?"

"No, it's a roundabout way of distracting you until Stone can get to the phone."

Lindsay's mouth opened as she bit a ridge of muscle on Catlin's torso with dreamy deliberation, testing his resilience. His deep voice was little more to her than a soothing vibration beneath her cheek, a purring background to the sensual dream enfolding her. She had wanted to do this last night, to know him as intimately, as completely, as he had known her. But before she could follow her impulse they had fallen asleep in each other's arms, their bodies still joined, still slick with sweat, utterly spent.

"Who was he?" asked Catlin.

"Who was who?" O'Donnel said innocently.

Catlin's expression shifted from gentle indulgence to the kind of hardness that people associated with the name of Rousseau.

"If I don't hear a name in thirty seconds," Catlin said very quietly, not wanting to disturb Lindsay's sleepy, sensual explorations, "I'm going to lock Lindsay in the room and take a little walk. First I'll shake the local Bureau boys. Then I'll take whichever Chinese shadow has morning duty on a tour of Golden Gate Park. After we've done a few laps I'm going to come up from behind and run right up his ass. By the time I get back here I'll be all alone, and I'll know who's getting fucked and who's paying the pimp."

There was a long silence.

Catlin's hand found Lindsay's breast as her weight shifted slowly, softly over his body. He caressed her with a gentle care that belied the harshness of his face. As he watched her expression of deep, dreamy sensuality, he realized that she was more asleep than awake, operating entirely on instinct . . . and her instinct was to touch him lovingly. He had never seen that expression on a woman's face. It pierced him like slender, transparent claws sinking sweetly, deeply, beneath his skin, reaching past the physical reality of his body to his mind, touching him in ways he could not name, only feel.

"The guy got into a car," O'Donnel said, his voice rough. "The car was registered to the Chinese Christian Benevolent Society."

"Not much help," grunted Catlin. "How many members? Two thousand?"

"Closer to ten. It's the biggest damn ethnic society in the U.S. and Canada."

"How many of the people at Wang's party belong?"

O'Donnel hesitated, then gave a throttled curse. "Everyone but you and Chen Yi, near as we can tell," he said in disgust.

"And Lindsay," Catlin amended dryly.

"Wrong. She's listed. So is her mother."

"How many people have access to the car?"

"We're working on that."

"Maybe I better work on a few laps around Golden Gate Park," Catlin shot back.

Lindsay moved restlessly, disturbed by the sharpness of Catlin's tone. He soothed her with a slow, caressing motion of his hand on her breast, tracing the hard nipple with his thumb.

Sighing with pleasure, she smoothed her hand over his torso and nuzzled her mouth against his waist, sinking back down into the sensual dream.

"Don't do it," said O'Donnel. "You could blow the whole thing to hell. We're not jerking you around. We just don't have any information yet."

Catlin's breath came in soundlessly as Lindsay's tongue probed at his navel. His hand tightened on her breast until she arched slowly into his palm. Her eyes were closed, her lips smiling, her body languid and uninhibited as it rubbed over his. In slow motion her hand moved beneath the sheet, dragging it down to his thighs. The soft sound of her approval as she discovered and caressed his erect flesh all but made Catlin groan.

"Catlin? Catlin, are you there?" O'Donnel demanded.

All there, Catlin thought ruefully. *And she's loving every bit of it.*

"I'm here," Catlin said, "but I'm losing patience." His voice caught. He drew a deep breath, trying to regain control of himself as Lindsay explored him. "Is Stone going to have those mug shots this morning?"

Lindsay's fingers moved caressingly, then nestled between Catlin's thighs, taking the twin weight of him into her hand, savoring all the different textures of his maleness. Catlin's fingers closed over hers gently, irresistibly, holding her hand still. She murmured something as she kissed his thigh, tracing with her tongue the border between warm skin and the intriguing thickness of his hair.

"Hold it. Stone's saying something to me," O'Donnel said.

Catlin waited in an agony of sensual suspense as he watched the pink tip of Lindsay's tongue. When she discovered the hot, blunt flesh rising eagerly to meet her, he knew he should stop her. He covered the receiver with a convulsive movement of his hand.

"Lindsay," he muttered, "you're going to—" The words ended in a thick sound as the soft heat of her mouth encircled him. Her nails flexed lightly, nipping him like tiny teeth. "God, woman," he groaned. "You're killing me."

He didn't know if she heard him. He didn't know if he even wanted her to. Her breath was warm, moist, another kind of caress. A wild, sweet heaviness claimed his body as his blood focused exclusively between his legs. A long shudder of desire racked his body. He closed his eyes because if he watched Lindsay caress him any longer he wouldn't be able to control anything, even his voice. But instead of pulling her away, his fingers were working deeply into her hair, holding her even closer to his body, wanting every hot, moist bit of her mouth. Her bronze hair spilled over him in a long, silky caress. He stirred beneath her hair with every hard beat of his heart.

"Catlin? You still there?" asked O'Donnel.

"Just a minute," Catlin said roughly. "Lindsay's trying to tell me something." He covered the receiver again. "If you don't stop," he said, turning Lindsay's head toward him with a steady pressure of his hand, "I'm going to pull you up and bury myself in you right here, right now, and let O'Donnel hear every one of the wild little cries I'll wring out of you!"

Lindsay tried to turn away, wanting to go back to the shimmering, sensual dream. Then Catlin's words echoed and reality came in a cold burst of understanding.

O'Donnel.

Lindsay blinked and shook her head as though she were disoriented. And she was. Catlin's initial lazy caresses had taken her from sleep into a sensuality that was so new to her that she had no way to control it, or herself. She stared at the phone and flushed deeply, realizing what she had been doing, what she had nearly done.

"I'm sorry," Lindsay whispered, pulling away from Catlin, retreating in an agony of embarrassment. "I don't know what I—I'm not like that. I've never done anything like—" Her voice broke and she stopped trying to explain what she didn't understand herself.

Catlin heard the truth in Lindsay's shaking voice, saw it in the red color staining her cheeks, felt in her confused withdrawal. She hadn't been teasing him just to watch him squirm; she had been as caught in the endless sensual instant as he was.

And now she was retreating, ashamed of the sensuality he had summoned out of her very core last night, revelling in it as much as she had.

Suddenly Catlin's arm swept out, dragging Lindsay up his hot body and pinning her as his mouth caught hers in a deep kiss.

"I know what got into you," he said against her ear. "Me. Last night. All night. And it's going to happen again. Come here, honey cat," he whispered urgently. "Sit on my lap while I tell O'Donnel to go to hell."

She shook her head, refusing to meet Catlin's hungry amber eyes.

"O'Donnel?" Catlin said into the phone. "We're keeping Lindsay awake. You've got until nine to get the mug shots here. Then I'm going hunting."

Catlin didn't bother to hang up. He simply pulled the jack out of the phone and dumped the instrument onto the floor.

"Catlin," Lindsay said in a strained voice, "I didn't mean—"

"I know," he said, pulling her over him like a warm, living blanket, ignoring her futile attempts to resist. "I know. You weren't even really awake, were you?" he asked, opening her mouth with his hungry tongue. "Can you imagine what it does to me to know that you want me even in your dreams? Do you know that I want you the same way?"

Lindsay's eyes opened, searching Catlin's face for the truth.

"Oh, it's true," he said, watching her. "Any other woman could have been all over me like a heat rash and I would have talked to O'Donnel until I was damn good and ready to hang up. But you—" Catlin shivered and moved his hips slowly, sensuously, sliding his fully aroused flesh against her thighs, feeling her satin warmth and the silken roughness of her hair. "You make me lose control," he said huskily. "I want your mouth again. I want to watch you loving me. Do you want that? Talk to me, honey cat. Tell me what you want."

Lindsay cried out as Catlin's teeth scored gently down her neck, silently demanding an answer.

"You," she said, her breath catching. "I want you."

"Then take me," he said, his voice deep, rough. "Any way you want. Every way. Because that's what I'm going to do to you. And when we've each had a turn we'll begin all over again, you taking me and me taking you until it's like last night, no beginning and no ending, just the two of us locked together, burning down the night. Take me, Lindsay. Take me into that sleek, hot body of yours."

She made a broken sound that could have been Catlin's name, then took him with a single, slow, sliding movement, giving herself to him at the same time. As he filled her completely she tried to say his name again, but could not. Her body no longer belonged to her alone. It belonged to him, to them, to what they created when they were so deeply joined that she could not say where he ended and she began. The realization sent tiny, exquisite pulses rippling through her. She melted hotly over him, burning through his own control, fusing them into a single being. With a hoarse sound he poured himself into her, giving himself to her and to the primal ecstasy they called from each other.

THE SECOND TIME Catlin awakened that morning, it was to the knocking of a heavy fist on the hall door.

"Room service!" came the call.

"And I'm the tooth fairy," Catlin muttered, looking at the clock. Eight fifty-five, and the voice had sounded rather like O'Donnel's. It was hard to tell, though. He'd never heard O'Donnel yell through two closed doors. "In a minute!" called Catlin.

The knocking stopped. Lindsay murmured sleepily. Smiling, remembering, he smoothed her hair.

"Time to get up, honey cat," he said softly.

"Breakfast?" she asked, stretching sleepily.

"More like show and tell, I'm afraid," said Catlin, pulling on his clothes.

Her eyebrows rose. "Show and tell?"

"Mug shots," Catlin said succinctly, zipping up his slacks.

"I'd rather have Eggs Benedict," she grumbled.

"Hungry?" he asked, smiling slowly.

Lindsay looked at his lips and remembered what it had felt like to have his mouth caressing every part of her. If the memories hadn't been enough, there were small, sensual aches in the secret places of her body to tell her that she had become the lover of a man whose sexuality would have been intimidating if he hadn't been as skillful as he was powerful.

Catlin saw the direction of Lindsay's glance and knew what she was thinking. His body stirred, wanting more of what it had discovered so recently. He wondered then whether he would ever be able to get enough of Lindsay. The thought disturbed him. He had been in the business long enough to know that relationships forged in the heat and complex stresses of undercover work ended when the job did. That was why he had tried to stay away from Lindsay in the first place.

But staying away simply hadn't been possible. He was a man, and all too human. She was human, and all too much a woman.

"Don't look at me like that," Catlin said, his voice gritty, half amused and half serious.

"Like what?"

"Like you were remembering how my mouth felt all over your body."

Lindsay couldn't control the shiver of response that coursed through her. Catlin saw it, swore softly and turned on his heel toward the bathroom. The pounding came again from the hall. He ignored it. He picked up the toilet tank cover from the floor, scraped the lid against the tank as though he were just removing it and fiddled with the tower. The comb came free, the toilet tank filled and the sound of running water stopped.

Catlin used the toilet, flushed and waited while the tank refilled. Everything worked normally. He replaced the cover with a generous amount of scraping and thumping, stuffed the slightly chewed comb into his pocket and, after a slight detour to the bedside table, went to answer the door.

"What's the breakfast special?" Catlin asked, standing to one side of the door.

"Eggs O'Donnel, sir," came the low, polite reply. "Chef Stone also highly recommends his own personal favorite— creamed Catlin on toast."

The words carried no farther than Catlin's ears. Smiling, he unbolted and unlocked the door; but he didn't step into the open and uncock the gun he held until O'Donnel came into the room alone, pushing a breakfast cart in front of him. Catlin shut, locked and bolted the door before he turned toward O'Donnel.

"If you fox the phone again," said O'Donnel, looking toward the closed bedroom door, "Stone will have your balls for breakfast."

"You look real nice in uniform," Catlin said gravely, eyeing O'Donnel's gaudy maroon-and-gold hotel livery. "Is that how you trolled up your no-class piece of ass last night?"

O'Donnel raised his middle finger.

Catlin laughed, then inhaled deeply as he lifted the silver lid on one of the containers and the spicy fragrance of *huevos rancheros* and *frijoles refritos* drifted up to his nostrils. He realized that he was hungry enough to eat snake—and enjoy it. The sudden, insistent growl of his stomach underscored his discovery.

"The mug shots are in the bottom of the cart," O'Donnel said. "Any change in your schedule today?"

Catlin shrugged. "Lindsay and I will get out of here long enough to let the maid clean up. Other than that, nothing's on the burner. We've seen every bronze in San Francisco except the ones we want. None of the rumors about bronzes coming through Seattle or Vancouver have panned out worth a damn. We're through eating out with scumbags like Malloy. There's no point in doing any more laps around the lowlife track. Either the thieves are satisfied with our cover by now or they won't ever be. All we can do is wait to be approached."

"Is that what Chen Yi wants to do?"

"Ask him."

"We don't have his phone number," O'Donnel said smoothly.

"He has yours. If he doesn't like the program, he'll be the first to tell you."

O'Donnel's mouth flattened. He looked at his watch. "I shouldn't stay any longer. We haven't seen anyone inside the hotel watching your room, but we can't be sure. They probably don't need a special guard. Most of the help here are Chinese." He glanced toward the bedroom. "Is Lindsay okay?"

"She's gutsy. She'll survive. But Wu was hard on her. And Malloy—" Catlin made a cutting gesture with his hand. "Malloy would gag a maggot."

O'Donnel winced, thinking of the midnight showers Lindsay had been taking. He wondered if she had managed to wash off the stink of the people she had been associating with. A look at Catlin's hard face kept O'Donnel from asking. "The lady really wasn't cut out for this life, was she?" asked O'Donnel. "Stone suggests that you take the day off after you look at the mug shots."

"Hell of an idea," Catlin said, yawning. "We could both use some more time in the sack."

"I'll be back in an hour for the cart. If the maid comes before then, don't let her in."

As soon as the door shut behind O'Donnel, Catlin locked and bolted it again. He went to the bedroom. As he opened the door, the sound of the shower came to him.

"Breakfast is here," he called, not trusting himself to go into the bathroom after Lindsay. The memories of sharing a shower with her were too new, too hot, too tempting.

Lindsay's muffled answer came, telling only that she had heard Catlin's words.

He went back to the living room, poured coffee and filled a plate for himself. He took it over to the small dining alcove. The only thing to indicate that day had dawned was a brilliant, very narrow stripe of blue-white light where the heavy green drapes failed to meet.

Although Catlin loved San Francisco's rare, incandescently clear mornings, he made no move to open the drapes. Too many people had died looking out of hotel windows while a sniper was looking in. Lee Tran knew that as well as Catlin did. Better, perhaps. He had lost more people to windows than Catlin had.

No more than half of Catlin's spicy eggs had disappeared before the bedroom door opened. Lindsay walked barefoot into the living room, her face flushed from the shower, her body elegant beneath the heavy silk robe that was the exact rosy color of her nipples when she was aroused. She looked good enough to eat, but Catlin kept the thought to himself—one of Stone's bugs was no more than six feet away.

"Sit down," offered Catlin. "I'll get your plate for you."

"Thanks," Lindsay said. "Usually I hate breakfast, but after—" Her words broke off as she remembered just why she was so unusually hungry today. She also remembered the bug that was behind the mass-produced oil painting of an English country scene.

"Yeah," Catlin said, smiling over his shoulder. "I know just what you mean. I didn't eat much dinner last night, either. Malloy is enough to take away anyone's appetite. God," continued Catlin in a disgusted voice, "the things Stone expects us to do in the hope of buying a Qin charioteer."

Catlin's eyes were anything but disgusted as he handed Lindsay her breakfast plate. When she took it he held on. She looked up, startled. Then she realized what he wanted. She stood on tiptoe and kissed him. What began as a simple brush of lips ended as something much deeper and more satisfying.

"Mmmm," she said after a long moment. "Firm. Spicy. Steamy. Exactly the way I like it."

He smiled slowly. "That quick little tongue is going to get you in trouble," he whispered against her ear. Then, in a normal tone he asked, "Coffee?"

"Please," she said, sitting down with her plate and taking her first bite of omelet. It was everything she had said it was. The thought made her smile.

They ate in a comfortable silence, enjoying the undemanding moment. While Catlin showered and changed, Lindsay lingered over her second cup of coffee. A feeling of well-being pervaded her mind. At first she thought that it was simply the profound sensual satisfaction Catlin had given to her, but as she sipped her coffee she realized that what she felt was more complex than simple satiation. She felt warm, cherished... safe. Yes, that was it. Safe.

The absurd thought made Lindsay laugh aloud. She was in a vortex of conspiracy and lies; she was being shunned by her former friends; she was the lover of a man who slept with a gun by his hand and awoke at the least noise with death in his eyes. Yet she felt safe for the first time since she could remember.

Lindsay hadn't heard Catlin come back into the room, but when she looked up he was there, watching her with shadows and concern in his beautiful dragon eyes. The shadows no longer disturbed her, nor did the knowledge that dragons could kill. She knew to the bottom of her soul that she had never been safer in her life than she was with Catlin.

"Ready?" he asked.

"For what?"

"Show and tell."

Lindsay's dark glance went from Catlin's short-sleeved rugby shirt to the faded jeans that faithfully showed every hard male line of his body.

"Sounds interesting. You first," she said in a husky voice.

Catlin smiled. His golden-brown eyes darkened as he read the approval in hers. "Let's do it together. The sooner we're done, the sooner we can play."

Wisely, Lindsay held her tongue. Her smile, however, said a great deal.

Catlin slid aside the metal door on the cart's lower level and pulled out two oversize ring-bound notebooks. Lindsay stacked the empty dishes on the cart, poured the last of the coffee and went back to sit at the small table.

"If you like anything you see," Catlin said, putting a pen and a small notebook on the table, "write down his number."

Lindsay opened the book and looked inside. A page of Oriental faces looked back at her. Some of the pictures had obviously been taken as part of routine police processing. Others were like snapshots taken by a paparazzo, slightly blurred because of movement or distance.

"Look at it this way," said Catlin, opening his own book. "We both have an advantage. We've lived in the Orient long enough to see subtle differences among these faces."

She looked up, surprised.

"It's true," he continued, not looking up. "The old saw about 'They all look alike,' is a literal fact for most people, no matter what race is being looked at. Ask any cop. He'd a hell of a lot rather take the word of a black man about what another black man looked like than that of a white man." Catlin turned a page slowly. "That's especially true with Orientals. They can tell a Korean from a Vietnamese a block away. Most Caucasians don't get past the epicanthic fold and broad facial structure."

Catlin turned another page, glancing over the pictures with a quick, practiced eye. Lindsay followed suit, but more slowly. Her first page yielded nothing. She turned the heavy sheet. More faces looked back at her. Oriental. Male. Between fifteen and fifty. No outstanding scars. There were gaps where pictures had been removed from the pages. She wondered if the men were in jail or dead. As her eye traveled down the third page, she made a startled sound.

"Something?" asked Catlin, watching Lindsay with intent yellow eyes.

"I know him. Not from last night, but from the Chinese Christian Benevolent Society. His name is Wo Feng. And this is his older brother. And his younger."

Lindsay's finger moved over the page, picking out relatives of Feng. As she turned other pages she recognized more men, people from her childhood in China, people from her lonely teenage years in San Francisco, people from her dealings as curator of ancient Chinese bronzes for the Museum of the Asias. But most of the faces were from her childhood, faces of men whom her parents had known, faces without bodies, faces pursuing her through years of restless sleep.

With each page turned, Lindsay felt herself sliding helplessly deeper and deeper into the past. *I've done this before. Pictures. Faces. When? Why?*

Uneasiness moved over her, making her shiver as though it were midnight, and her nightmare surged invincibly from the dark well of repressed memory. She tried to fight it, to hold back the unwanted tide of remembrance, but could not. She had fought it for too many years, winning only in the day, losing at night; and now it was neither night nor day, only an endless twilight of faces pouring over her, pursuing her.

Grimly she turned pages, wondering why she had fought off the past so long and so successfully, only to lose the battle at a time when she had felt so safe. And she was losing. She knew it. Felt it in the chill claiming her blood. Tasted it like brass on her tongue.

Fear.

She turned the page and saw him. She whimpered like a child as the past exploded over her.

20

"LINDSAY?"

As though from a great distance Lindsay heard Catlin's voice calling to her. She sensed him coming to stand behind her, looking over her shoulder at the faces welling terribly out of the open wound of her past.

"Yes," he agreed, pointing to a snapshot on the left-hand page. "That's the man."

The warmth of Catlin's hand caressing Lindsay's shoulder seeped through the chill that was making her shiver repeatedly. But the voice and the warmth were all wrong, and her body was wrong; she was a child, not a woman, and she had just killed her uncle. She saw him dying, choking, blood spurting from him over her hands as she frantically tried to push the bright life back into the hole in his chest. Uncle Mark was dead and she was seven and her father was holding her; and she was thirty and her lover was holding her and her father was dead.

"I'm going crazy."

Lindsay didn't know that she had spoken aloud until she felt herself lifted from the chair into Catlin's arms.

"Easy, honey cat, easy," he murmured, carrying her to the couch. He sat and held her, rocking her. "He's just a picture on a page. It's all right. He can't get to you as long as I'm here. It's all right, Lindsay. You're safe."

"I killed him. Can't you see? I killed him!"

Catlin looked into Lindsay's blank indigo eyes and saw the same thing he had seen too many times before. Nightmare.

"What are you seeing?" he asked gently.

It was the same question he had asked before, when she had awakened whimpering, wrapped in fear and nightmare. But this time she began to speak, because now she could see everything clearly. Too clearly. In a cold, tearing rush she knew what she had tried to avoid knowing for so long.

"I was supposed to stay in bed, but Ha's daughter had whispered to me that Uncle Mark was back. I couldn't wait until morning to see him. He always brought me candy, bright ribbons, laughter."

Catlin waited while Lindsay drew a long, ragged breath. He imagined her as a child—quick, intelligent, a creature of her senses, hungry for the small gifts and flashes of color that poverty made so rare and so precious.

"Go on," he said softly, brushing his lips over her forehead.

"Oh, Catlin," she said brokenly, turning her face into his chest. "I killed him."

"Tell me," Catlin coaxed. "Tell me and the nightmare will end."

Lindsay's hands closed convulsively, digging through the cotton knit of Catlin's shirt to the flesh beneath. He ignored the discomfort as his hand stroked her hair and her back. He spoke soothingly, murmuring words without meaning, sounds as reassuring as his touch and the slow rocking of her body against his chest.

"I—" Her voice broke. She swallowed and tried again. "I was staying with the family of Ha, the rice merchant. Mother and Dad had been called into the city to talk to some government official. I waited until my friend was asleep and then I tiptoed out the back way and went to my uncle's house. No one was there. I was scared. It was windy and the moon was full and cold. I went to the church. He wasn't there, either."

Catlin felt the tension building in Lindsay. His arms tightened but his hand never stopped its slow, soothing motion over her head and back.

"I kept feeling like I was being followed," Lindsay whispered. "I would stop and turn suddenly but no one would be there. The shadows were all wild and twisted beneath the trees—or is that my nightmare?" She shivered. "It's hard to tell the difference after all these years. Memory. Nightmare. But two things are true and always will be. Uncle Mark died, and I killed him.''

"You were only seven," Catlin murmured.

"How old does a judas goat have to be?" she asked bleakly.

Catlin's eyes closed for an instant. He could guess what was coming, and it enraged him. He could guess just how a young girl's trust could be twisted to an assassin's use, but it was for Lindsay to discover that and put her discovery into words. It was her truth, her nightmare, her mind that had been unable to fully accept an act that had occurred long ago and was still tearing her apart.

"I knew that there was a place where Uncle Mark sometimes met with other men," said Lindsay. Her voice was flat, raw, the voice of a woman again rather than a child. As she spoke, nightmare was receding slowly, but not horror. That would stay with her for the rest of her life. "I knew that it was supposed to be a secret. But I wasn't going to tell anyone. I was just going to surprise him with a visit. So I ran through the village to the meeting place at one of the outlying farms. He was there. So were four other men."

Lindsay began to tremble. She started to speak, failed and tried again. Catlin watched the tears streaming silently down her face and wished he could spare her whatever was to come. Yet he knew he must not. She needed the knowledge that she had both sought and denied through years of nightmares.

"The other men were angry with me, but not Uncle Mark," said Lindsay, words rushing out, leaving her no time to breathe, words demanding to be said. "He just held out his arms and hugged me and then there were shots and screams and he fell. I tried to push the blood back into his body—I tried and it just spurted through my fingers. He—he cried out a word and then he died and I ran and ran and ran."

"What did he say?" Catlin asked gently.

Lindsay closed her eyes, sending a veil of tears down her cheeks. "Betrayed."

"He didn't mean you," Catlin said, rocking her slowly. "You were too young to know that soldiers would follow you to the secret meeting place."

"I think—yes, I remember now—that's what my parents said to me when they found me the next day." Lindsay drew a shuddering breath. "They washed me, held me, and then—" Her eyes widened as she remembered. "They had me look at pictures. Like now. That's what brought back the nightmare. Faces and more faces, years of mother's snapshots pouring over me, picture after picture, face after face. 'Is this one of the men who shot your uncle? This one? This one?' And when I said, 'No! I killed him,' they held me and told me over and over that it wasn't my fault, that I didn't kill him." Lindsay closed her eyes. "But it was my fault. I was greedy for his presents, his laughter."

"You were a child, Lindsay," Catlin said, kissing her eyelids. "Just a child. Someone used you."

"If I hadn't been greedy—"

"If your uncle hadn't been up to his neck in politics," Catlin interrupted grimly, "he wouldn't have been shot."

Lindsay's eyes opened, surprise clear in their indigo depths. "How did you know about the soldiers and the politics? I didn't find out until just a few years ago, and even then all mother would say was that Uncle Mark was dead and times were changing, and it was better that the past die with him."

Catlin rubbed his cheek slowly against Lindsay's soft hair. "I knew because in those days in China, there wasn't much else besides soldiers and politics." He kissed her cheek gently, tasting tears that should have been cried years before. "Was your uncle a missionary?"

She nodded.

"Then he was probably involved with the Christian underground," said Catlin. He watched Lindsay, but saw no understanding on her face. "Various missionaries banded together and smuggled out their parishioners—particularly those who had fought against communism and lost and had been declared traitors to be executed on sight," he explained. "It took a lot of guts to hide those people, feed them, steal their families out from under armed guards and smuggle the whole lot out of China to a new life in Hong Kong or Taiwan or North America. It was the Church Militant in action. Quite impressive and quite dangerous, as subversive action is always dangerous."

"Subversive!" Lindsay said, startled. "My parents were missionaries, not revolutionaries. They didn't want to rule. All they cared about was God and their converts."

"The Communists viewed religion as dangerous political competition," pointed out Catlin, smiling crookedly. "Which it was, so long as politics were pursued with religious fervor. Mao didn't permit moral competition from anyone, even Christ. Since Mao's death, things have changed. Politics is slowly becoming a profession again, rather than a holy calling. That could change, though," Catlin admitted. "It could change in an instant. The balance is very precarious."

"Chen Yi," murmured Lindsay. "That's what he's afraid of, isn't it?"

"Partly. Like a lot of intelligent, educated Chinese, he didn't enjoy the Cultural Revolution, or any of China's recent stabs at creating its very own version of the Dark Ages."

"What happens if we don't find the bronzes?"

Catlin leaned back against the couch, pulling Lindsay with him, resettling her in his lap. "If no one else finds them, either, the prodevelopment element of China's government will probably manage to patch things up and continue dragging China into the twentieth century, trading in the people's Little Red Books for radios and refrigerators and leaving people's souls to priests rather than politicians."

"And if we do find the bronzes?"

"Chen Yi and his colleagues will have a little housecleaning to do," Catlin said. Then he added sardonically, "Assuming they manage to hang on to the broom and their own necks long enough, that is. Otherwise—" Catlin shrugged "—the isolationists and ideological purists will win. There will be another round of purges and withdrawal from the world, and once again millions of Chinese will starve while their rulers learn a simple truth: pure ideology is a piss poor guide to running a country."

"Chen Yi," Lindsay murmured again, resting her head on Catlin's chest. "He must hope we don't find the bronzes."

Catlin laughed softly. "Not quite. He's hoping we find the bronzes all right—but he's hoping they're frauds."

Lindsay sat up and fixed Catlin with an intent glance. "Why?"

"Then it would be America's face at risk, not China's. It would be a joke on greedy capitalists, not a slur on the morals of the Chinese race."

"Do you think the bronzes will be frauds?"

"If the bronzes exist at all, I could make arguments on either side of the question," said Catlin. "In the end, what I think doesn't matter. True Qin or recent fake, you'll know the difference. And when you tell us, we'll know. That's why the Chinese would have no one but you for the job. You have an unimpeachable reputation for knowing the truth about bronzes—and telling it, no matter whose ox is gored. Truth is a religion with you, and you're its shining missionary. Yi knows all about religions and missionaries." Catlin smiled sardonically. "Chen Yi is one shrewd son of a bitch."

Lindsay searched Catlin's golden eyes for a long time, feeling his words sink into her, wondering what he was trying to tell her that he wouldn't put into words. "And betrayal?" she asked. "Does he know all about betrayal?"

"He's Chinese. They wrote the book on loyalty and betrayal."

"But was he the one— Did he—?" Lindsay's voice broke.

"Is he the kind of man who would whisper Christmas in a child's ear so he could follow her to Santa Claus and kill him? Is that what you're asking me?"

Lindsay flinched but didn't look away. "Yes," she whispered, "that's what I'm asking."

"He could have," Catlin said flatly. "He would have, too, if he'd wanted to kill your uncle badly enough. But did he?"

Catlin shrugged. "I doubt it. The world is full of men like Chen Yi and your uncle, men passionately committed to opposing causes, men in the wrong place at the wrong time. I'd bet that Ha the rice merchant was one of them. I'd bet that he told his daughter to whisper in your ear and then watched from the shadows while you tiptoed out into the night."

Lindsay shuddered. "Oh, God," she whispered. "To be used like that, betrayed. *I hate lies.*"

"Then stop lying to yourself," Catlin said bluntly. He watched as Lindsay's head jerked up and she stared at him in surprise. "You didn't kill your uncle, Lindsay. Men with guns did. If you'd stayed on your little straw pallet that night, your uncle still would have been betrayed and murdered. There have been a lot of times and places in China when life just wasn't worth a handful of shit. Hell, I'm surprised your parents weren't killed, too. They were lucky to have been out of town when the hunters closed in for the kill." Catlin's hand tilted up her chin. "And you, honey cat." He kissed her wet eyelashes gently. "It's a miracle those men didn't kill you, too. The life of a girl child, especially a foreign devil, meant nothing at all."

Lindsay's arms went around Catlin abruptly, and she shuddered. "But the blood," she whispered. "The blood!"

"I know," he said softly, rocking her, remembering his own horror when blood had first spilled over his hands. "I know."

Catlin didn't tell Lindsay how he knew, for that wouldn't comfort her at all. He simply held her while she pulled herself back together, settling pieces of the past into new places, letting the ramifications of that resettlement ripple up into her present. It was a process without an end, the adult reassessing the child's view of reality. The new knowledge was painful but necessary, for while nightmare ruled, ignorance was not bliss. Ignorance had brought weakness, not strength; and she needed strength to face and survive the demands of the present.

"Thank you," Lindsay said finally, kissing the hard line of Catlin's jaw. "No one else ever understood. Not even my parents. They wanted me to give my fear to God and then forget it. All of it. Mother said that no good ever came of remembering the past. I tried to forget. I thought I had forgotten, but—"

"You dreamed," said Catlin, stroking her hair.

"I dreamed," she agreed, sighing.

"And you hated lies."

"Yes."

"And you trusted no one. Not really. Not completely. Not even God."

Lindsay looked up and saw herself reflected in Catlin's desolate amber eyes. She wondered who had betrayed him and who had died and if he had ever trusted anyone or anything again.

And then she realized that distrust, like the nightmare, like the man called Rousseau, was part of the past. She lived in the present. So did the man called Catlin. "I trust you," she whispered. "I feel safe with you. That's why I gave up fighting the nightmare. You were with me."

Pain clenched deep inside Catlin. He wanted to tell Lindsay not to trust him, that she wasn't safe with him, that he was the wrong man to be reflected in her dark, beautiful eyes. Yet even as denial sliced through him, he held her, kissed her and then kissed her again, because he knew that she must trust someone or become lost among the lies she was being forced to live. He had known that from the first.

But he had not known how much it would hurt to be the one she trusted.

"Will you be all right now?" Catlin asked.

Lindsay nodded and let herself relax against his hard, warm body. "I feel tired," she said softly, "but it's a different kind of tired. Almost...peaceful. Thank you, my dragon, my love," she whispered, sliding her arms around him again, holding him. "There's no one like you. There never has been."

Catlin closed his eyes for an instant as pain clenched again, wrenching his nerves, twisting along all the emotional pathways he had discovered last night and this morning with her. The cost of earning back half of a mutilated coin kept mounting, yet there was no way to stop, no way to go back, nowhere to go but forward.

Trust me if you must, Lindsay, he thought in agonized silence. *But don't fool yourself into calling it love. That's too high a price to pay—for both of us.*

Yet he held her for a moment longer, savoring the soft weight of her in his arms, cursing the game they both had volunteered to play. Then he kissed her tear-starred eyelashes and gently lifted her aside.

"I'd better call Stone," Catlin said, "and tell him that we identified the Chinese man who was following us."

Lindsay's only answer was to take Catlin's hand and press a soft kiss into his palm. He closed his eyes, feeling the caress in every cell of his body. He could not stop himself from taking her face between his hands and kissing her softly, as though she were a beautiful dream shimmering as it condensed out of darkness. When he lifted his head there were new tears glittering on her eyelashes. He caught the brilliant drops on his lips and felt pain twist through him, ripping apart his control. He knew then that he wanted to be loved by Lindsay, to dissolve away his years of suspicion and chill in her hot honesty, to be fully alive in a way that he had never been.

Grow up, Catlin, he told himself harshly. *You're no rookie to forget the difference between the act and reality. You know what being undercover is like, the wild adrenaline ride out and down to the frozen reaches of the human soul. When this is all over, Lindsay isn't going to want a reminder of her time in hell. She's going to want to forget as fast as she can. She certainly won't want her demon lover hanging around, reminding her with every look, every touch.*

"I have some other phone calls to make," Catlin said finally. "I can't make them from here. Bolt the door when I go. Don't leave the room. Don't let anybody but O'Donnel in while I'm gone."

Lindsay nodded.

"I mean it," Catlin said, trying unsuccessfully to stem the urgency in his voice.

"I know," she said, standing on tiptoe, brushing her mouth over his. "I won't leave. I won't let anyone but O'Donnel in."

Catlin felt the warmth of Lindsay's promise against his lips and drew back as though he had been burned. He turned and went to the table, memorized the ID number of the snapshot and left without looking back, pausing only long enough in the hallway to hear the sound of the dead bolt going home behind him.

Once outside the hotel he passed up the first two public phones he found. The third was inside a coffee shop. As soon as he began feeding in coins, a man came to stand in line behind him. Catlin had expected it, just as he had expected the two other men who had followed discreetly from the hotel; and the fourth man, a Chinese, who had hung back and looked in shop windows.

"Stone?" said Catlin into the receiver, making no effort to lower his voice.

"Speaking. Catlin?"

"Got a pencil?"

"Right here."

Catlin gave Stone the ID number, waited while it was read back to him, and then said, "That's the one who followed us. I'll hold the line while you get the information on him."

"It will take several hours—" Stone began.

"Bullshit," snapped Catlin.

"Look—"

"No, you look," Catlin said savagely. "There's a different tail this morning. Chinese. I can lead him down an alley and have the information I want in a New York minute. And that's just what I'm going to do if you don't quit cocking around."

There was a long silence. Catlin didn't mind. He knew that Stone had put down the phone, gone to another room and called the local Bureau office.

"His name is Joe Sheng," Stone said, picking up the phone again. "He's a free-lance, but he does a lot of leaning for one of the Chinese benevolent societies."

"Tom Lee's society?"

"Once or twice, but nothing regular. Lee's a crook, pure and simple. Mostly Sheng works for the Taiwanese faction. The True China Benevolent Society, or some such thing. Apparently the ideographs that make up the name can have several translations."

"Yes. Like poetry. What else?"

"Hell, Catlin, we're not miracle workers," Stone said angrily. "I'll have a list of the True China members soon, for what good it will do. We'll cross-match with people who had access to the Chinese Christian Benevolent Society car and maybe we'll come up with something meaningful and maybe we won't. Seems like everybody in Chinatown belongs to at least six societies."

Catlin couldn't argue with that for the simple reason that it was true. The various Chinese societies formed a maze of interlocking and overlapping interests that were religious, social personal and political. It was the societies that knit together the disparate goals and dreams of recent Chinese refugees and fifth generation, American-born ethnic Chinese.

"And," Stone continued, "ninety-five percent of the societies are absolutely legitimate."

"So send them a Presidential Citation for good citizenship," retorted Catlin. "Call me when you have a match on names. And it better be fast." He hung up and felt that subtle crowding of the FBI agent behind him as the man maneuvered for a view of the numeral pad. Catlin spun around suddenly, fed up with the game, fed up with being crowded down paths he had chosen to leave a long time ago.

"Back up," Catlin snarled.

The stranger read the barely suppressed violence in Catlin's stance. Slowly the man took a few steps backward. Catlin turned around again, shielded the numbers with his body and made another call. He listened while the call was switched and then switched again at least one more time. When the line was picked up, Catlin very softly repeated the number that Chen Yi had given him in New York. He was switched to another operator. He repeated Yi's number.

"Have any information on that number yet?" asked Catlin.

He waited, listening to the tiny, hollow sounds of computer keys being hit as the man on the other end of the line input the telephone number.

"Yeah. We finally cracked that puppy yesterday. It's an apartment complex owned by something called Consolidated Overseas Chinese. It's a limited partnership."

"Who are the main partners?" asked Catlin.

"Ling-Cheong Li, Martha Song-Min Chung and Samuel David Wang."

"Bingo," breathed Catlin. "What's the address?" He memorized the street and numbers as they were given, and then asked, "Anything more?"

"We ran those names on an off chance you might be interested."

"And?" Catlin asked, smiling at the frankly smug sound of the man's voice.

"That partnership does a lot of mainland Chinese business. They're building a big hotel in Shanghai and a steel mill farther inland, plus underwriting some small stuff for Chinese collectives. Ling-Cheong Li is a Hong Kong businessman who's been working very hard to get into the good graces of the mainland Chinese."

"Smart man. Mainland China will own Hong Kong in a few years."

"Yeah. They didn't wait that long for good old Ling-Cheong, though. They own him right now. His real name is Liu Zheng, and he's an agent of the PRC."

"What about the woman?" Catlin asked.

"A naturalized Canadian dragon lady. Owns a string of restaurants and small shopping centers in Vancouver, employs mostly illegal immigrants from the PRC. Canada hasn't answered our queries, but I'll bet that she smuggles in the help and that some of them turn out to be agents."

"Is the third partner one of them?"

"If he is, we can't prove it. Samuel David Wang is fourth generation American, with a grandmother who was as high

WASP as they get. He was educated at the Sorbonne. He's well left of center in his politics, but he's not one of the Che Guevara crazies. He's real friendly with the PRC, but then, so is the President. There's no law against doing business with the PRC or supporting various pro-PRC groups in America. Like they say, it's a free country.''

Catlin grunted. "Did you turn up anything connecting the three partners with Mitch Malloy, Hsiang Wu, Tom Lee a.k.a. Lee Tran, Chen Yi or L. Stephen White? Names spelled as follows.'' Catlin spelled the names rapidly, using the full-word alphabet developed by the military to avoid confusion among similar sounds. "Got that?''

"Every last one. Hang on."

Catlin waited while the operator ran the program that would pick out all words in the file that began with an upper case letter. Another search followed, this one to match with the names Catlin had given.

"No hits."

"Damn!" Catlin hesitated, then said, "Try some phonetic variations in the Chinese names. Substitute *o-o* for *u*, *e-e* for *i* or vice versa, and *X* for *H-s*. And try for the name Chen alone.''

"Running," the man said laconically, punching in the variations.

Catlin waited.

"There's a Chen Xiang Xi. He's the mainland contact for Consolidated.''

"Run his name."

"Running."

It seemed like a long time before the man came back onto the line.

"There are a hell of a lot of Chens in China, and some of them spell their name with a *Q* instead of a *C-h*.''

Catlin sighed. "Yeah, I know. Do we have anything on this particular one?''

"He's a member of an old trading family that walked real small during the Revolution and is just now making a comeback. Overseas family all around the Pacific Rim. No specifics. This is all just general background. The last entry before I made the Consolidated hit was three years ago, an obituary. We haven't caught them dirty at anything. From all that I can see, Chen Xiang Xi is just one more PRC government functionary assigned to make it easier for Chinese-American businessmen to spend dollars in the People's Republic.''

For a moment Catlin was silent. ''Run my original list of names through the open files. Cross-match each hit for proper names.''

''The open files,'' repeated the operator carefully. ''Shit. I was hoping to get some time off before Christmas.''

''I'll call back.''

''Do that, baby. In about a year.''

''An hour.''

''Save yourself a dime,'' the operator retorted. ''Make it a month.''

''A day. And it's twenty cents.''

''Huh?''

''Pull your head out of the computer,'' Catlin said, laughing. ''In California, it costs twenty cents to make a phone call.''

Catlin hung up very gently, cutting off the flow of cheerful invective. He fed in a few more coins, punched in the number Yi had given him and waited for the answering machine to kick in. Yi's recorded voice spoke in Mandarin. Catlin answered in the same language.

''This is Rousseau. I am going to separate myself from my shadows. Meet me at the house of Samuel David Wang at one o'clock. I will wait half an hour. If you do not arrive, I will assume that you have officially opened hunting season and I am on my own as regards protecting Lindsay Danner. In that case, I had better not see you, Chen Yi. You will be first on my hit list.''

Catlin hung up, dialed Sam Wang's import shop and asked to speak to Wang. Using Mandarin, Catlin worked his way through two functionaries before Wang came to the phone. In the background Catlin heard the sound of a receiver being lifted from the hook; someone in Wang's establishment was listening in.

"Do you still speak French?" Catlin asked in that language.

"Yes," responded Wang.

"You remember the dragon that isn't for sale?"

There was a hesitation. "I remember," said Wang, sticking to French.

"Is it still at your house?"

"Yes."

"I'll be there to look at it at one o'clock today," said Catlin. "I'm expecting someone else, as well. If you hope to continue your profitable relationship with the People's Republic, be sure your servants are either very loyal to you or have the afternoon off. Do you understand?"

"Who the hell do you think you—" began Wang in English, abandoning French in his anger.

"Do you understand?" Catlin repeated harshly in English.

"Yes, but—"

Catlin hung up. He dialed the hotel room. Lindsay answered on the second ring.

"Something has come up," said Catlin. "I'm going to be gone until three. Can you stay cooped up that long?"

"Yes."

Catlin let out a long breath. "No arguments? No questions? You're special, Lindsay Danner. I'll be back as soon as I can."

"I'll probably be asleep," she said, yawning.

"Then I'll call from the lobby so you'll know who's at the door," he promised. "Be there, honey cat. Promise me."

"Yes," she said, her voice husky.

Very gently, Catlin hung up.

21

CATLIN LOOKED at his watch and then wandered casually through the lobby to the hotel restaurant, acting like a man with food on his mind. Within seconds he was through the kitchen and out into the alley. Three doors down on the opposite side of the alley he ducked into the kitchen of another restaurant and then out the front door. Moving swiftly, discreetly, he wove through the sidewalk crowds until he could make an illegal, midblock entrance onto a passing trolley. He exited the same way, in midblock, and cut through a store to another alley. He repeated the evasive maneuvers three more times before he was certain that he was alone.

An hour later Catlin sat quietly in the back of a rented van parked along the only approach to Wang's house. The van's smoked windows prevented anyone from seeing into the interior easily, but didn't prevent Catlin from looking out. For the next two hours he watched the street. No one gave the van a second glance. No car drove past Wang's house more than once. None of the parked cars contained watchers.

Catlin was well and truly alone.

At 12:55 Catlin left the van and took the back way into Wang's house. He moved through the elaborate landscaping very quietly, arriving at the back door without warning. Gun drawn, he stood to the side and knocked once. The door opened a crack. Catlin didn't wait for a better invitation. He kicked the door open and shoved past the person standing behind it.

"You!" Wang said.

Wang regained his balance with a trained speed that Catlin noted even as he saw that Wang was unarmed. Catlin holstered his own gun in a smooth action.

"Me," he agreed, going past Wang into the kitchen. "Is Chen Yi here yet?"

"Is he supposed to be?" asked Wang, his face impassive.

"Pull the other one," Catlin said over his shoulder as he headed for the front of the house. "If Yi hadn't told you to let me in, you'd have met me at the back door with a gun."

Wang's dark eyes narrowed. He started to say something, then hurried to catch up with Catlin.

"What would have happened if I had?" Wang asked as they walked through the living room.

"Met me with a gun?"

Wang nodded.

Catlin smiled.

"Ah, dragon," said Chen Yi, stepping out from the alcove that had once concealed an extraordinary fraud. "Was it not you who explained to me the unwisdom of teasing tigers?"

"I'm trusting you to keep this one securely leashed," Catlin said in a sardonic tone. He turned to Wang. "You have a choice. You can stay and listen and know that if any part of this conversation leaks I will kill you. Or you can get in your fancy red Ferrari and drive around for an hour or two."

Wang turned to Chen Yi, who waited impassively, saying nothing, giving no clue as to what decision Wang should make.

"Yi won't make the choice for you," Catlin said flatly. "He can't. He doesn't control me."

Narrowed black eyes measured Catlin for a long moment. "I see why he calls you dragon," Wang said. "You don't heel worth a damn, do you?"

Catlin laughed, appreciating Wang even as he knew that he might have to kill him.

Wang nodded, both understanding and sharing Catlin's appreciation. With a sudden smile Wang looked over into the alcove. The dragon crouched there, sinuously alive, vibrant with the modern intelligence that had created him.

"And here I'd been hoping that Lindsay had changed her mind about the authenticity of my bronze dragon," Wang said, gesturing into the alcove.

"Oh, she thinks its authentic art, all right," Catlin retorted. "It's just not ancient."

"What do you think?" asked Wang.

"I think it's probably the most powerful piece of bronze art I've ever seen."

Wang looked at Catlin for a moment, nodded again, then bowed to Chen Yi and said, "It has been my pleasure to be of service to the honorable representative of the People's Republic of China. If you have no further need of my humble presence, I will withdraw."

Chen Yi nodded slightly, dismissing Wang.

Catlin waited until he heard the Ferrari retreating down the long, winding driveway before he turned to Chen Yi. The Chinese was watching him. Whatever anxieties or speculations he might have had were hidden beneath the impassive exterior of a politician or a spy.

"You are a taker of risks," Yi said, lighting a cigarette and exhaling sharply. "Mr. Wang might not have chosen to be gracious about our uninvited use of his home."

"When it comes to taking risks, I'm not a patch on you," Catlin said bluntly. "Teasing tigers is one thing. Recruiting and then teasing dragons is another thing entirely."

"Ah!" Yi inhaled hard, making the tip of the cigarette flare. "Continue, please. The teasing of dragons is a serious matter."

Catlin's eyes narrowed to dark amber lines. He weighed Yi quietly and then decided that the Chinese was being forthright rather than sarcastic. Not that it mattered; the outcome would be the same whether understanding or sarcasm were involved. If the dragon didn't get the information he wanted, Yi would have to get himself another dragon.

"I asked you once why you didn't use Sam Wang as your stalking horse. You said he wasn't yours to use. I'm asking you again, Chen Yi. Why didn't you use Wang?"

"Stalking horse? Ah! I remember the idiom now," said Yi, smiling faintly. "Yes. Stalking horse. Just so." Yi inhaled smoke, exhaled, inhaled again. "My reasons haven't changed. Mr. Wang isn't mine to use."

"Like hell he isn't. You're using the building he owns as part of your answering service. You made up a guest list for his auction and he invited every last person. One of his two partners in Consolidated Overseas Chinese is an agent of the PRC."

Catlin watched Yi but saw only a veil of smoke twisting between them.

"Then there's the fact that Wang has a reputation for coming up with some really astonishing ancient bronzes," Catlin continued. "People think he gets those bronzes because of his ties to the refugee communities. You know what I think? I think the bronzes are his pay, and his employer is the People's Republic of China. Very neat. Very clean. Untraceable. Just as the activities of the third partner in Consolidated are untraceable. She brings in Chinese agents mixed among the true refugees. Doubtless the agents are the ones carrying payoffs in the form of extraordinary ancient bronzes."

Yi's eyes were thin black lines, emotionless, watching.

"You didn't want to use Wang to find the missing bronzes because you didn't want to blow his cover," summarized Catlin. "You knew the counterintelligence boys at the FBI would vet anyone you picked right down to his toenails. Wang couldn't take that kind of scrutiny. I could."

The only sound in the room was the slight, breathy whisper of Yi inhaling pungent smoke.

"Like I said," muttered Catlin. "You took a real risk that whatever you found out about American counterintelligence operations wouldn't be offset by what America found out about yours."

The end of the cigarette glowed brightly. "Explain."

Catlin grimaced. "It's simple, Yi. Under Mao, the People's Republic cut itself off from the West and the twentieth century. Now China wants back into the global political game. But you have a real handicap in the game—lack of information. Without trade, without diplomacy, without even the ritualized intercourse that we call war, China hasn't had any reliable way to gather intelligence on the U.S. To the PRC, America was the Great Unknown, yet America was vital to China's hopes of staving off Russian dominance long enough for the People's Republic to hold its own in a highly technological world.

"China had a lot of catching up to do, and you had to do it very quickly. It's a hell of a lot easier to steal information than it is to go through the long process of research and development. Cheaper, too. The Russians found that out after World War II. Spies are the cheapest form of R & D. But for your spies to be successful, you have to know what the other side has in the way of counterintelligence. More specifically, Yi, you had to know how much trouble the CIA and the FBI could cause your men."

Yi said nothing, did nothing. Smoke curled silently into the air.

Catlin smiled again, and again the smile was ambivalent. "Emperor Qin's bronzes were a brilliant stroke, Chen Yi," Catlin said, bowing slightly. "The pursuit of them was the perfect 'open sesame' to the workings of America's counterintelligence community. But the bronzes were a little too brilliant, weren't they? What began as a whole-cloth fabrication by one of China's foremost intelligence officers was seized on by the Maoists who had lost the power struggle to Deng. Deng's enemies started using the 'missing' bronzes to beat his progressive policies to death. The Maoists and the isolationists screamed that China's face was being blackened by the impure pursuit of capitalism. The scheme you had devised to help bring China quickly and cheaply into the twentieth century was taken over by the antiprogressive fanatics and was being used to drag China further back into isolation and stagnation."

Laughing softly, shaking his head, Catlin asked, "Are you familiar with the English idiom, 'Hoist on your own petar'?"

There was no answer but the exhalation of smoke from Yi's nostrils.

"How about hanging yourself on your own rope? Have you heard of that?" Catlin asked sardonically. "You dreamed up the stolen Qin bronzes to use as a straight intelligence gathering scheme against the U.S. Suddenly your enemies have taken that scheme away from you and are using it against you and your supporters. Against Deng himself. Talk about all eggs being at risk when the nest is kicked over!'' The words ended in a hard laugh. "That's an understatement, Yi. You have hell's own omelet on your hands—and face."

Yi inhaled sharply, his expression impassive.

"You couldn't even cut your losses by saying, 'Hey, guys, it was all a joke—China hasn't lost face. Qin's bronzes are safe,'" Catlin continued. "You couldn't say that because there was no way that you could prove that the bronzes were safe and had always been safe. How do you prove that twelve square miles of buried artifacts are intact, untouched?"

Catlin's smile turned down at the corner as he watched Yi's unmoving face.

"You can't prove it," Catlin stated softly, "and the Maoists wouldn't have believed you even if you had confessed to the whole hoax. So you were stuck. You had to go through with the plan for gathering intelligence against the U.S. by using the excuse of stolen bronzes. There would be one minor change in your plan, though. Some bronzes actually had to appear in America, because only if and when you caught the crooks could you claim to have the situation under control. Only then could you say that China's soul was no longer being looted out from under Mount Li.

"That meant you had to find the right pipeline to get the 'stolen' bronzes to America. You screwed up once by trying to use dope runners and the kind of unsavory buyers who are preyed on by the likes of Mitch Malloy. You discovered your mistake before Malloy could raid you, and then you went looking for a better, safer pipeline."

There was no motion from Yi, nothing to indicate that Catlin was even speaking aloud.

"But it's still one hell of a risk you're taking, Yi. You're really riding a tiger. Fake bronzes are the only thing that will win the propaganda battle at home for you—yet I doubt that even you could commission, execute and chemically age Qin bronze copies in the time since Mitch Malloy showed you how dangerous it was to deal with true crooks. And," added Catlin, "even if it were physically possible for you to fake the bronzes, such creations couldn't be kept secret. Too many people would have to be involved. Too many eyes. Far too many tongues. The fakes would be traced to your people and you would be back in the toilet, treading water like crazy and trying to prove that the Maoists were wrong about Deng, capitalism and loss of face."

Catlin looked beyond Yi to the dragon crouched in self-contained magnificence on its black table.

"No," Catlin said very softly, as though to himself. "The bronzes that came to America would have to be real. Which leaves you with three hellish problems, the same problems any thief has. How to get them. How to move them. How to sell them."

Without looking at Yi, Catlin walked to the cinnamon magnificence of the dragon and ran his fingertips gently down the beast's scaled back. "I don't know how you solved the first two problems," he said. "I don't care. All that matters is how you're going to sell the bronzes. Because that's when Lindsay will be at risk. That's when it could all go from sugar to shit real fast, with raiders or Maoists or Christ knows what else crawling out of the woodwork."

There was a long silence enclosed by streamers of smoke. Catlin waited, studying the dragon with appreciative eyes and sensitive fingertips.

"Continue," Yi murmured at last. "To hear a fine Legalist mind at work is a rare pleasure."

"Then you should try thinking out loud," Catlin said matter-of-factly.

Yi laughed once, a sound of regret and pleasure combined. "Ah, dragon—you should have been my son!"

Catlin's mouth tugged up at one corner in a smile as ambivalent as Yi's laugh had been. "I doubt that either one of us would have survived the experience."

"Ah! You are probably correct."

Still smiling, Yi pitched the smoking remains of his cigarette into an ashtray.

"You have created such a beautiful design of pride and hope, treachery and betrayal," Yi said after another silence. "I hesitate to suggest any amendments. But, sadly, I must do just that."

"I'm listening."

Yi smiled suddenly, genuinely. "Yes. You are very good at that. You are even better at listening than at talking. A rare gift in men. A common attribute of dragons."

There was the sharp sound of a lighter opening, the rasp of flint and steel, and then the click of metal against metal as the lighter closed once more.

"I will neither protest nor embrace the conspiracy you have outlined," Yi said finally. "I will only say that if I were my own enemy—Maoists and isolationists, as you call them—I would have seized upon the rumor of stolen bronzes just as you suggested. But I would also have sought a true propaganda coup. I would seek to convince the unconvinced among China's government that capitalism is the great corrupter of Chinese morals. Ah!"

Yi inhaled, glanced at Catlin and continued. "If I were my own enemy, I would have bribed enough people to steal the Qin bronzes, to ship them and to sell them in the United States. If I were my own enemy, I would be thoroughly aware of the danger of fakes in undermining my plan, for there is no loss of face to China in selling fakes to greedy capitalists. Ah! So I would have moved to ensure that such fakes were neither cast nor shipped.

"If I were my own enemy," Yi continued, "I would ensure that whoever appraised the bronzes in America had a reputation that was unimpeachable, therefore proving beyond any doubt that the bronzes were indeed from Xi'an and that China's face therefore had been blackened by her contact with the running dogs of capitalism. If I were my own enemy, I would have chosen a man like you to 'help' me in America, a man like you who was once China's worst enemy, a ruthless man to whom the future of an old enemy meant little.

"If I were my own enemy, I would have built a cage for me from which there was no escaping. *Ah!*"

Catlin stared at the dragon's sinuous form. His fingertip traced the gold inlays that both enlivened the bronze and hinted at the history behind the dragon. After several minutes he looked up at Yi with eyes the exact color of the gold inlay gleaming from the ancient bronze.

"Are you telling me that your enemies have completely taken over the game you started?" Catlin asked. "That your enemies have stolen some Qin bronzes, are shipping them to the U.S. and are forcing you to go through with the charade of finding them? And that once found, the bronzes will result in your own undoing, and in Deng's, as well?"

The Chinese inhaled, expelled smoke and inhaled again without taking his eyes from Catlin's face. "I am telling you what I would do if I were my own enemy," Yi said calmly.

"Are you in control of the Qin bronzes, or are your enemies? Are you player or pawn?" Catlin asked bluntly.

With a weary gesture, Yi dropped his cigarette into an ashtray. "We are all pawns, dragon. Even you."

"God in heaven," breathed Catlin, realizing what Yi had just admitted. It was true. What had begun as a means of getting information out of the U.S. by claiming that Qin's tomb had been looted had become a naked grab for power by the Maoists who hated Deng.

"I was afraid of this," Catlin said harshly, "but it was the only probability that made sense. You shouldn't have wanted Lindsay in the first place, because then you couldn't even mount a decent whispering campaign saying that the bronzes you would find in America were fakes. With her reputation, you didn't want her anywhere near the Qin bronzes!"

Yi lit another cigarette without saying anything. He didn't have to. Catlin was understanding all of it, and not liking any of it.

"It was your idea to ruin Lindsay's reputation, wasn't it?" Catlin asked roughly. "You knew that smearing her wouldn't be necessary to lure the thieves to her, because the thieves would approach her, anyway. They had to. It was part of your enemies' plan. Your only hope of spoiling that plan was to impeach Lindsay's reputation. So you dropped an emetic into your comrades' drinks, came to D.C., and arranged for me to ruin Lindsay's reputation in order to save your own. Is it working, Yi?" Catlin demanded harshly. "Are you going to be able to go back to China and say that you can't trust Lindsay's word on the bronzes because she would say anything, do anything, just to please her demon lover?"

Yi smiled faintly at Catlin's description of himself. "But she did not lie about the bronzes she has seen thus far," Yi countered sadly. "She would not." He exhaled sharply. "That has already been tested and proven. Not once, but twice. Ah! You wanted to buy bronzes that she believed were fake. She would not approve of you buying them. Nor would she say that fake was real even to please her lover. She would not bend even to save the face of the man who once honored her as a daughter. When the question is bronzes, Lindsay Danner answers only the truth. That part of her reputation is, regrettably, very much intact!"

Catlin's eyes narrowed until all that showed were splinters of gold. "Does Wu know that somebody at his shop listens in for the People's Republic?"

Yi exhaled smoke and said nothing.

Catlin wasn't surprised. He hadn't really expected an answer. He watched the motionless bronze dragon and tried to control his rising rage. Lindsay's reputation had been ruined in pursuit of a cause that had been doomed long before Yi even came to America. Lindsay herself was being ground up in a political shoving match between ideologues living in a country that was half a world away.

"You were really grasping at straws, weren't you?" Catlin said finally.

"Straws and mud make excellent bricks. With bricks, a man can build . . . everything."

"*Shit!*" snarled Catlin. He stared at the dragon without seeing it as he weighed all that Yi had said. How much truth, how many lies, how to tell the difference, and how to explain the one thing that didn't add up. "Why me?" he asked. "You didn't need a translator, and even if you did, you wouldn't have chosen a man who has the experience to see past the blue smoke and mirrors to the lies beneath. You aren't a stupid man, Chen Yi. Neither are your enemies. Why did you come to me with half of a coin? Why did they let you?"

"My enemies chose you for me," Yi said.

Catlin sensed the satisfaction beneath the simple statement. "The way Stone chose Lindsay?" he retorted.

Yi smiled faintly. "They believed you to be my enemy. As you were, once, and may be yet again. But not while you earn back half of that coin."

"Why, Yi? Why did you want me?"

"You are a man of face," Yi said simply.

Catlin turned the statement over in his mind, viewing all the possibilities. "All right," he said, accepting it. "You knew I would honor the old debt. That meant you could trust me not to be frightened or bought out from under you. Even so, the original question remains: what could I possibly do for you that would compensate for the risk of having me unravel all your lies?"

"It is as I told you before. You are to protect Lindsay. No more. No less. You are uniquely suited for that purpose. You are a man of intelligence to help her when she becomes lost among all the conspiracies. You are a man of decision to know when to strike and when to hold back and ask questions as you are asking now. You are a man who, when he strikes, is deadly. Lindsay could be given no better man to guard her days and nights."

"Why do you care about Lindsay's health?" Catlin demanded bluntly. "You should be at the top of the list of people who want her dead and buried."

"I know that better than anyone alive!" retorted Yi. "Ah!" His cigarette glowed hotly, repeatedly, and then he began to speak from the shifting veil of smoke. "Twenty-five years ago a man and his son were ambushed and left for dead. They were found by a woman. She did not ask whether they were Communist or Nationalist, Buddhist or Christian or atheist. She took them into her home at great risk to herself and her family. She cared for them, giving them rice from her own bowl, tea from her own cup and bandaging them with strips of cloth torn from her own clothes."

Yi's eyes glittered blackly. His voice was oddly strained, almost brittle. "While the man and his son twisted in the grasp of fever and pain, she sat between their pallets and read to them, letting her voice soothe them. If they cried out in the night, she came to them carrying a candle, sat with them, read to them from the worn book she loved more than she loved her own life. In the night, in the darkness lit only by a single flame, her hair was a radiant golden river. She was an angel reading aloud about angels. And her voice—her voice—" Yi stopped, unable to speak.

"'Dreamed in shades of silver,'" Catlin finished softly, remembering what Yi had once said. "Lindsay's voice. Lindsay's hair. Lindsay's mother." Catlin paused, remembering other things about Lindsay and her past. "It was you who called her parents out of town the night Lindsay's uncle was slated for assassination."

"She healed us and never asked for anything," Yi said obliquely, "not even our names."

"And in doing so, she bound your family in the debt of her own family forever. A matter of face." Catlin shook his head slowly, sensing the designs of the past curling forward into the present, shaping it, face and pride and obligation passed from hand to hand like ritual bronzes. "Lindsay's mother didn't know that, Yi. She didn't want the burden of your gratitude. She would have refused it if she had known. She was simply honoring the teachings of her religion."

"As I am honoring my own beliefs," Yi said calmly. "I could not save her husband's life. Like his brother, her husband was a man of great courage and even greater foolishness. He refused all warnings. Eventually he came back to the People's Republic once too often."

"I thought he died on a trip to Taiwan."

"Many people believe that."

"Did Lindsay's mother?"

"Does it matter?" asked Yi, inhaling harshly. "She had the life she wanted. She lived and died among Chinese peasants, sharing their poverty and naive faith in an all-caring God. Yet in the end I believe she became wholly Chinese. I believe she died loving her lost China even more than she loved her European deity. I burn much incense in the hope that she passed that greater love on to her beautiful, *dutiful* daughter. And I have given to that daughter what few men and even fewer women will ever know—the protection of a dragon."

Catlin looked at his hands for a long, long moment, seeing the ridge of callus along each palm, the scars of past combat, the brute strength that had enabled him to survive when other equally ruthless men had not.

As though at a distance he heard Yi light another cigarette. When Catlin finally looked up from his hands, Yi was watching him. Yi, who was both spider and fly, caught in an intricate web that was only partially of his own making, a web that was still being spun in conflicting patterns. Yi, who was a man of intelligence and face. Yi, who was risking everything on the strength of a single gossamer thread that he hoped would stretch from mother to daughter, the past to the present, changing the course of lives and countries. The risk had been forced upon Yi, but he had grasped it and made it his own. Like a master of unarmed combat, Yi was trying to use his enemies' own strength and momentum as weapons against them.

Slowly Catlin bowed to Yi as a Chinese would bow to a respected opponent. "You are a man to learn from, Chen Yi."

Yi bowed in return. "I have learned from you, Jacob MacArthur Catlin."

Catlin ran his fingertips lovingly down the dragon's sinuous length. "Is there anything you can do to speed the delivery of the bronzes?" he asked finally.

"Is there anything you can do to ensure that Lindsay will make the right choice?" Yi returned smoothly.

With a swift, feral motion Catlin turned on Yi. "The only right choice is the one Lindsay can best live with. Because that's what she has to do when this is over—live with her memories and regrets and all the rest of it. I'm her protector, Chen Yi. All of her. Body *and* mind. That's the risk you took when you brought me the other half of the coin."

Yi didn't like what he heard, but he had expected it. After another tight silence, he accepted it.

"Bird with one wing," Yi murmured, remembering both the old saying and the faint outline of a swallow on the severed coin. "Do you fly better now with your other half?" Then, as though he didn't expect an answer, Yi continued. "I believe Qin's charioteer has already arrived."

Catlin felt adrenaline slide hotly into his veins, bringing his body to full alert. "When? Where?"

"That, too, is not for me to choose. I do not know the name of the person or persons in San Francisco who are working here with my enemies."

"Who do you suspect?"

"Everyone at Sam Wang's auction," Yi said bluntly.

Catlin grunted. That didn't tell him anything he hadn't already known. "What about Pao and Zhu—do your esteemed and treacherous comrades know about Wang?"

"They know that he has capitalistic ties to China. As for the activities of his partners—" Yi shrugged. "That may or may not be known by Comrades Zhu and Pao."

"Will Wang be the one who tells us where and when we can see the charioteer?"

For the first time, Yi hesitated. "An interesting possibility," he said finally, softly. In silence he lit another cigarette, exhaled a harsh plume and said, "I do not think so. He has lit-

tle to gain from my enemies, and much to gain from me. He is
a builder, as I am. My enemies are not. Ah!''

"That," Catlin said, looking at the very modern dragon
crouched on the table, "is very much a matter of opinion. And
as the owner of this dragon knows, reality itself is subject to
interpretation."

Yi laughed quietly, a sound that had little to do with amusement. "Remember that. Remember also that not all of Miss
Danner's enemies are Chinese. The honorable Mr. Stone has his
own plans and his own face to maintain. His own fish to cook
as you say. Be sure that Miss Danner isn't among them."

"If she were, it wouldn't be intentional."

"I am sure that fact would be a great comfort to the acci-
dentally cooked fish," Yi said dryly.

Catlin smiled. "I hear you, Yi. I've worked with men like
Stone before. I know what to expect. They'll take care of
Lindsay if they can, but she isn't one of theirs. They'll be more
worried about taking scalps than saving them." Catlin's smile
changed into something a good deal less pleasant. "It's the
same for you. That's why you came to me. If Lindsay dies at
your hands now, you won't suffer any loss of face. It will be my
responsibility, not yours. My loss, not yours. I understand that
Chen Yi. Just as you understand that you will die if I find you
anywhere near Lindsay."

Yi's cigarette glowed brightly, then vanished in a flat arc into
the ashtray as he turned and walked away.

"If we meet again, I will be surrounded by enemies. Ah!
Therefore I hope that we will not meet again, dragon, for that
would mean that I have lost and Qin's charioteer has been
found."

22

CATLIN LOADED the dirty dishes back onto the room service cart, pushed it into the hall and bolted the door shut again. As he turned he saw Lindsay sitting quietly on the couch, staring at the closed drapes. Her face was calm, but her eyes were very dark. She hadn't asked him any questions about where he had been or what he had been doing, though he had seen the questions in her eyes when she had unbolted the door to let him in. It had been the same while they ate a late lunch. No questions, simply indigo eyes watching him.

And now she was watching nothing at all.

"Half a penny for your thoughts," Catlin said, flipping the cut Han coin on his palm.

"Half? Let's see."

He tossed the bit of metal to her in a flat, hard arc. He wasn't surprised when she caught it with a quick movement of her hand. *Tai chi chuan* was good for much more than calming the mind. It also honed the reflexes.

Lindsay looked at the ruined coin lying on her palm. She could just make out the truncated outline of a flying bird. The line of the wing told her that it was a swallow. The shine of the metal in the cut told her that it was copper.

"Han?" she asked.

Catlin nodded.

With a sad smile, Lindsay looked at the coin. "The death of the ancient bronzes that we both love," she said. She looked up and saw Catlin's black eyebrow raised in silent query. "Copper money," she explained. "It came into general use in China with the Han dynasty. As money, copper was far more valuable ounce for ounce than it was when alloyed with tin to make bronze. Once that was realized, the great age of bronze art was over. And now, when gold and silver and nickel are used for coins, the last of the old bronze masters are long dead. We'll never see their like again.''

"Somebody made Wang's dragon," Catlin said, thinking of the extraordinary bronze he had seen just a few hours before.

Closing her eyes, remembering the dragon, Lindsay sighed. "Yes. Somebody did. What a shame all that intelligence and beauty is in the service of fraud." She opened her eyes and looked again at the half coin. "Where did you get this?"

"It was given to me."

A single look at Catlin's closed face told Lindsay that she had just heard all that he would say on the subject. She smiled sadly and flipped the coin back to him. He caught it without looking away from her eyes. They were haunted.

"Nightmares again?" Catlin asked softly.

"Just . . . thinking."

Catlin wanted to go to Lindsay, to pull her into his arms, to hold her until neither one of them could think of anything more than the wild, consuming fire that came when they touched one another. Yet he knew that it was more for him than for her that he sought the oblivion of their mutual sensuality; it was his need to forget rather than her own that made desire pulse thickly with every heavy beat of his heart.

"About what?" he asked, sliding the coin back into his pocket.

"I'm like that coin. So much cut away. Lost."

"I don't understand."

"China," Lindsay said simply. The word was both a curse and a sigh. "I was born there, Catlin. I grew up seeing myself as Chinese. My mother couldn't have loved the country more if she had been born there, too. She died an exile in every way that counts but one. She was among people she loved."

"Are you an exile?"

"Yes. No." Lindsay made a husky sound that could have been laughter or a sob. "I don't know. Sometimes I smell ginger frying in a hot steel wok and it's like I've been dropped into a time machine and I'm five again, washing vegetables for

Auntie Liu and laughing until I ache as I listen to her stories about wise peasants and foolish tax collectors. Sometimes I smell freshly turned earth under a wet spring sky and I'm six, following the women to the fields, pushing tiny onion plants into the ground while mud oozes over my sandals, and every time I look up I see figures rising out of the mist around me, surrounding me, planting as I am planting. The mist obscures all differences, mutes all voices into the sound of water falling to the earth. I'm in the center of people, always people, and they hug me and laugh with me and teach me."

"And the nightmare?" Catlin asked, his voice neutral.

"Oh, it's there, too. The sound of gunfire. My uncle's blood. My mother's tears. My screams. Yet now that I remember what really happened—" Lindsay closed her eyes. "It's sad—my God, it's sad, but—" Her voice broke. "But in the end it's just one death, just one child's horror. The Chinese people have suffered so much. Especially the peasants. All they wanted was to plant their crops, to marry and have children, to respect their ancestors, to live and die as Men of Han. All through the centuries, most of the rural Chinese didn't even care who was in control of the country, as long as there was some form of government that permitted peasants to live and die with a minimum of dignity."

Catlin sat down next to Lindsay. "That's all most people anywhere want," he said quietly.

"Most of them don't get it. Not in China. Not in this century. All they've had is war and famine and death." She looked at Catlin, searching his eyes as though she expected to find the truth reflected there. "It's going to happen all over again, isn't it? The People's Republic is going to use Qin's bronzes as an excuse to tear itself apart and then snarl over the scraps like starving dogs."

Lindsay closed her eyes and spoke before Catlin could. "For the second time in as many weeks, I'm glad that my mother is dead. She used to weep for her peasants until her eyes were the color of blood, and my father would hold her and talk of a time when it would all be changed, when the government that knew no God would be replaced by one that did. I used to lie in bed listening to them talk and wish that I could do something that would help. That's what I was thinking about, Catlin. My parents and China and tears.''

The pad of Catlin's thumb caught the drop trembling on the edge of Lindsay's eyelashes. He said her name softly as he pulled her into his arms.

''I'm glad she's dead,'' Lindsay said against Catlin's chest. ''She had been so hopeful in the years since Mao's death. She was so confident that the millennium had come at last. She was planning on reopening the old mission outside of Xi'an. She was going home again. It would have destroyed her to know that nothing had changed.''

''That isn't quite true,'' Catlin said as he smoothed away another tear. ''For better or worse, China's government is riding the tiger of change. No matter who wins this round—Mao purists or Deng progressives—the tiger has been summoned. The government can't go back. It can only hang on and hope to guide the tiger from time to time.''

''What about the people? What do they do while the tiger is loose?''

''They plant crops and raise children and endure whatever comes,'' Catlin said quietly. ''They've been doing it for five thousand years. They'll do it for five thousand more. They're one of the toughest people on earth.''

With a startled sound Lindsay looked up. ''That's what Uncle Mark used to say to Mother. And then he'd wish to God that the Chinese weren't so damned enduring. I guess he believed that if they would just fight back sooner they wouldn't have to suffer so much.''

Catlin thought of the men who had fought, and the ones who had died and how near he had come to being among the dead. He pulled Lindsay closer.

''Maybe,'' he said quietly. ''And maybe more of them would have died. You can't know. That's the hell of it. You just can't know. You can only hope that what you're doing helps more than it hurts.''

Lindsay turned in Catlin's arms until she was curled against him and could hold him as he was holding her. Though he said nothing more, she sensed that he was thinking about his own past. She wanted to ask about it, to know more about the man whose heart beat so strongly beneath her cheek. She wanted to comfort him as he was comforting her.

Eyes closed, cheek resting against the softness of Lindsay's hair, Catlin savored the moment of peace. When the phone rang, he tightened his arms instinctively, wanting nothing to interrupt. At the second ring Lindsay stirred reluctantly.

"I'll get it," he said.

"No. Just sit and relax. I'll take care of it. It's probably O'Donnel again, wanting to yell at you for losing the agents who were following you."

Catlin watched Lindsay walk into the bedroom and wished that she were back in his lap, warming him even as he warmed her.

Lindsay picked up the phone on the third ring. "Hello?"

An unfamiliar voice began speaking to her in Cantonese. She understood some, but not enough. "Wait, please," she said first in English and then in Mandarin. She covered the receiver with her palm. "Catlin? How are you with Cantonese?"

He came off the couch in a single motion. Soundlessly he strode into the bedroom and took the phone from her. He began speaking in rapid Cantonese.

"Miss Danner has difficulty with your dialect. Please permit me to translate for you."

"You are Rousseau?"

"I was. Now I am Catlin."

"The Chinese Christian Benevolent Society has a private chapel. Miss Danner knows its location. If you wish to look at some unusual bronzes, be there in ten minutes. If you wish to leave alive, be certain that you are not followed."

The line went dead.

Catlin looked at Lindsay. "Do you know where the Chinese Christian Benevolent Society's private chapel is?"

"Yes. It's one of those beautiful, unexpected buildings in the center of Chinatown's worst slum. Curved, tiered roof, high wall, inner garden. It's—"

"Can you get us there?" he asked, interrupting her.

"Yes."

"How long?"

"Ten minutes, maybe a little more."

Catlin punched in Stone's number and waited. He recognized the voice that answered. "O'Donnel, get Stone. Fast."

"What—?"

"Now." Catlin's voice was like a whip.

There was silence, then a harsh, "Stone here."

"We just got either a bite or an invitation to our funeral. Maybe both. They're going to be looking for tails. Make goddamn sure we don't have any. Clear?"

"But—"

"I'm turning the phone over to Lindsay," Catlin said. "She'll tell you where we're going. Don't come closer than two blocks."

"What if it's a trap?"

"Then we're in such deep shit that you couldn't help us if you followed us in with the U.S. Marines. Remember—Lindsay's your best hope of getting close to those bronzes. Don't do anything to burn her. Stay the hell clear. This is just a mutual show and tell. They didn't ask for money."

"Shit Marie," grumbled Stone. "At least let us wire you."

"No time. They're not stupid, Stone. We're on a deadline."

Without waiting for an answer, Catlin handed the phone to Lindsay. While she spoke he pulled out his gun, inspected the load and holstered the gun again. The whole process took only a few seconds. He opened the bedside drawer, pulled out two spare ammunition magazines and tucked them in the pocket of the corduroy sport coat he was wearing.

Lindsay hung up the phone and turned toward Catlin. "If you didn't want the FBI to follow us, why did you tell them where we were going?"

"We don't have enough time to flush FBI tails. Especially if one of them is O'Donnel. We'll have to pray that Stone is as smart as I think he is."

"Aren't you going to call Yi?"

"No," Catlin said. He looked up at her with hard yellow eyes. "Don't trust him, Lindsay," he said softly. "Don't trust anyone but me. I'm the only one in this whole goddamn game who will take a bullet for you."

She was too shocked to say anything.

"Ready?" he asked calmly.

Catlin took Lindsay's arm without waiting for an answer and led her out of the hotel. Less than ten minutes later they were outside the chapel. It was everything that Lindsay had said it was—beautiful, very Chinese and in the midst of a slum. The language of Canton swirled around them like atonal, staccato music. The street was alive with children and dark-haired women. Men stood in groups, smoking cigarettes and talking. The long white stucco wall surrounding the chapel grounds displayed a few spray-painted ideographs, New World graffiti telling of a feudal, territorial approach to life that had been old long before Christ was born.

As Lindsay and Catlin walked up to the high outer wall, a gate swung open. It was solid black with three ideographs carved in high relief. With a casual motion Catlin drew his gun and walked through the gate, laying his right hand along his leg to conceal the weapon. His left hand was on Lindsay's arm, ready to push or pull her away from danger.

The boy who had opened the gate was alone, but the cut of his hair and clothing marked him as a recent arrival to America. Catlin watched the gatekeeper very carefully; he had seen too many child soldiers in Asia to dismiss the boy simply because he was not yet sixteen.

"Lead us," Catlin commanded in Cantonese.

The boy's dark, slightly tilted eyes widened. He bowed, responding to the authority in Catlin's voice and body. If the boy noticed the discreetly drawn gun, he did nothing to show it. Without a word he turned and began leading them down the carefully raked gravel path. On either side of the path artistically trimmed evergreens rose into the late afternoon. An artificial stream wound like a silver ribbon through the garden, widening into a pool where lotus plants grew in circular profusion. Though barely a hundred feet long, the garden gave an illusion of space, serenity and peace.

Catlin absorbed the garden in a glance and dismissed it as a potential danger for the simple reason that there was no place in it to hide. Any ambush would have to come inside. He slipped the gun into the pocket of his sport coat, but kept his finger on the trigger. If he had to shoot he wouldn't bother pulling the gun out first.

The chapel itself was about as big as their hotel suite. Three doors opened off along the right side, and one along the left. All led to other rooms, and some of these led to still more rooms. The building was a warren that had grown over the years as money became available.

The boy led them through a small kitchen where the scents of fresh ginger, scallions, garlic and peanut oil had permeated the very walls. In addition to the usual gas stove and oven, there was a second stove. Instead of burners on top, there were three circular holes where big woks could be set and heated from below without any wasted energy. Next to the Chinese stove a small, erect woman chopped bamboo shoots with a cleaver. She looked up, bowed over her clasped hands and then resumed preparing the vegetable for its brief time in the fire.

"Know her?" Catlin asked Lindsay as they followed the boy into one of the rooms that opened off the chapel.

"No."

"She wasn't bowing to the kid," said Catlin. "Which means that the man we're going to see is not only feared, he is also respected. We're honored guests of the venerable warlord, as it were."

They saw few other people as the boy skirted the chapel by going through interconnected rooms. The rooms were small, redolent of pungent cigarettes and incense, and furnished with a melange of Oriental and European furniture. Traditional pictures of Jesus alternated with Chinese landscapes painstak-ingly done in silk embroidery using stitches so tiny that a sin-gle landscape represented a life's work for one woman, or decades of effort for several.

"What do they use all these little rooms for?" Catlin asked as they were led through yet another small space studded with chairs and small tables.

"Sunday school. Chinese language lessons. English lan-guage lessons. Civic meetings. Mah-jongg. Socializing. Most of the homes around here are tiny and overcrowded," added Lindsay. "If more than three people want to get together, they have to stand on street corners, yell over the chaos of one of the local restaurants or join one of the benevolent societies and use their meeting rooms. Places like this are the core of Chinese-American communities."

"Looks like a deserted core at the moment."

Lindsay frowned. The thought had occurred to her, too. In her memories the building had always been alive with voices. The silence inside, unlike the silence in the garden, made her uneasy. Reluctantly she realized that Catlin might be right to be walking with a drawn gun in his pocket. The thought didn't comfort her. The chapel was in many ways as much a home as her aunt's house had been.

"Here we go," muttered Catlin.

The boy had stopped in front of a carved, lacquered door. He opened the door, bowed to them and stepped aside. A single look told Catlin that the room was large, empty of people and had at least one other exit. An exquisite silk folding screen opened along the far wall, concealing any doors on that side. Two chairs were positioned with their backs to the folding screen. A third chair faced the others across a low table. A white teapot and three small cups were set on a tray. The cups had no handles. Their shape, like that of the teapot, raised simplicity to art.

Catlin released his hold on Lindsay's arm, allowing her to enter the room. He picked up one of the two chairs, placed it next to the single chair whose back was against a blank wall and gestured for Lindsay to sit down. He stood beside her, to the right. His gun was drawn again, muzzle held down along the side of his right leg.

"Do you—" Lindsay began, only to stop when Catlin's hand brushed over her lips in silent command.

After a few moments the utter, unnatural quiet of the building began to be almost tangible. The sudden sound of a woman walking in high heels into the chapel came like distant staccato thunder, swelling and then fading into silence again. A door opened and closed. The footsteps that came this time were much softer and yet somehow heavier, the measured tread of a confident man. But if Catlin and Lindsay hadn't been absolutely still, listening for just such sounds, the footsteps would have passed unnoticed, as would the slight whisper of a door opening behind the silk screen.

Lindsay reached out to silently warn Catlin that someone was coming. Her fingers touched only air. She turned quickly. He was gone. From the corner of her eye she caught a blur of movement as he vanished behind a fold in the long screen on the other side of the room. She sensed rather than saw him closing in on the concealed door.

Catlin waited to one side of the door, poised to strike if he didn't like what he saw coming into the room. Even as the flash of gunmetal and the large, blocky outline of Lee Tran registered on Catlin's mind, the edge of his hand slashed out. At the last instant he softened what easily could have been a killing blow. Pragmatism rather than sentiment made Catlin pull his punch—a dead man couldn't answer questions.

Air went out of Tran's lungs in a sudden whoosh. There was no sound of returning air, for Catlin's blow had paralyzed Tran's diaphragm, making it impossible for him to breathe. That was all that prevented him from screaming when Catlin's second blow landed an instant later, breaking Tran's wrist. Tran's foot lashed out in a belated attempt to return the attack. Catlin caught the foot and twisted hard as he heaved upward, all but wrenching Tran's leg out of its socket as he was thrown into the screen.

The screen exploded outward, crashing to the floor. Tran lay helplessly on his back, his eyes dazed, his right leg useless, his gun lying inches beyond his broken right wrist. Catlin's foot sent the gun sliding toward Lindsay even as he bent and dragged Tran to his feet.

"Pick it up," Catlin said curtly to Lindsay, never looking away from Tran's shocked, sweaty face. "It's the same model as mine. The safety is off and it's ready to go. Watch the other doors."

Without warning Catlin picked up Tran and slammed him full length against the wall. His right leg gave way as he fought for balance. Catlin held his old enemy upright by the simple expedient of a hand wrapped around Tran's throat and the cold muzzle of the gun jammed beneath his chin. After a moment, Tran's eyes focused and he began to take racking breaths again.

"You are the liquid stool of a diseased dog," Catlin said calmly in Cantonese. His hand began closing on Tran's throat. "You should have continued to buy your deaths, spawn of ex-crement eaters. You have the crotch of a snake and the face of an outhouse rat. What made you think you could kill a man?"

"Mei should have killed you!" Tran gasped in English.

"She was too hungry," said Catlin, switching to English, smiling, and his voice was as cold as his smile.

"What?"

"She was used to fucking you, but you don't have anything between your legs. So she waited to come before she tried to kill me. She died satisfied, Tran."

Impotent fury and lack of oxygen put color back in Tran's face. Catlin's smile didn't change as his fingers slowly closed on Tran's throat.

"You're—dead—" gasped Tran.

"Eventually. You won't have to wait, though. Your time is now."

"The bronzes—!" With a strangled cry, Tran tried to de-flect the death he saw in Catlin's eyes.

"You don't have them," Catlin said, but his fingers loos-ened just enough to allow Tran a sliver of breath. "You're a pimp and a pederast and a slaver. No one would trust you with a bucket of shit. The man running this show has the respect of the local people. All you have is their fear.''

"I know—who has them!" Air rasped and whistled through Tran's throat as he fought to breathe. "He asked me—to negotiate—with you!"

"That was his second mistake."

Catlin's finger began taking up slack on the trigger. Tran's eyes widened as he realized that he was going to die.

"Catlin, the door!" cried Lindsay.

"That is not necessary," Wu said from the doorway, his words overlapping her cry. Behind him stood three burly Chinese men.

"That's a matter of opinion," Catlin said without looking away from Tran. "Is Wu armed?"

It took Lindsay a moment to realize that Catlin was speaking to her. "N-no," she said, shaking her head as though stunned. "Neither are the men with him, that I can see."

She shook her head again, but it wasn't Catlin who had taken her off balance. She had known and accepted from the first that he was capable of violence. But she hadn't known that Wu was capable of betrayal. His presence was cutting the ground from beneath her feet, leaving her helpless as memories of her years in San Francisco whirled around her.

Lies. A world full of lies.

"Come over and stand to my left," Catlin said.

"I—" Lindsay said, trying to tell him of her discovery.

"Now."

Numbly Lindsay went and stood to Catlin's left side.

"Remember how I showed you to put the safety on my gun?"

"Yes."

"Do it."

With hands that trembled, Lindsay fumbled until she had the safety on Tran's gun.

"Put it in my holster."

As Lindsay holstered the gun, the contrast between its chill and the warmth of Catlin's body shocked her, forcing her to realize that it was not a nightmare she was caught in. It was real. There was no waking up.

"Sit down in the single chair, Wu," said Catlin. "Put your back to me and your hands on top of your head. Tell your bodyguards not to move."

"That, too, is unnecessary," Wu said.

"Do it, or I turn Tran into wallpaper."

Everything about Catlin from his calm voice to the controlled stance of his body underlined the fact that he meant exactly what he said. Wu spoke softly to the men with him, then sat in the lone chair and put his hands on top of his head.

"Catlin—"

"Not yet, Lindsay." Catlin's voice was the same as his body, utterly calm, as controlled as the lean finger resting lightly on the trigger. "Insulting me was a bad idea, Wu."

"I have not—"

"Bullshit," Catlin interrupted coldly, not looking away from Tran's terrified face. "Lindsay wouldn't kowtow to you, so you tapped Tran for the negotiations, knowing that he was my enemy. You thought he would hold a gun on me and watch me crawl. You thought that I would lose face with Lindsay and you would gain it. You were wrong. I don't crawl for sewer slime. I don't negotiate with it, either. Not for you. Not for anyone."

"Not even for Qin's charioteer?" asked Wu.

"Not even for that. That was your first mistake. Underestimating me. Say goodbye, Tran."

"Catlin!" cried Lindsay, unable to say more than his name.

Tran's eyes rolled back into his head. He slumped against Catlin in a dead faint. For long seconds Catlin looked at the slack face lolling against his hand. With a sound of disgust he stepped back, removing his hand. Tran fell facedown on the floor.

"That's the trouble with pimps and pederasts," Catlin said, nudging Tran's limp body with his foot. "No balls." He looked at the three bodyguards and spoke quickly in Mandarin. "Take

this miserable piece of shit out to the street and leave it for th
dogs to piss on. Don't come back.''

The men looked at Wu. He nodded. They picked up Tran'
slack body and hauled him unceremoniously from the room
politely closing the door behind. Catlin looked at Lindsay'
strained, pale face.

"Sit down, honey," he said gently. "The excitement is over
Wu won't make the same mistake twice."

Without a word Lindsay sat facing Wu and wondered why
she wasn't screaming. She hadn't been so frightened since she
was a child.

And then she understood that she wasn't screaming because
she wasn't really scared. Surprised, shocked, off balance—bu
not terrified for her life. Catlin had taken care of the danger
They were safe.

The realization took Lindsay's breath away. She put her fac
in her hands and let her whole body tremble in the aftermath
of the adrenaline storm that had begun when the silk screen ha
crashed violently to the floor.

"It's all right," Catlin said, coming to Lindsay's side
stroking her hair with his left hand and never taking his eye
from Wu.

"Dragon," she murmured, taking a long breath, turning to
ward him, brushing her mouth over his palm. "And thank Go
for it."

Catlin had been expecting Lindsay to shrink from him. He
acceptance of the unexpected violence surprised him in the in
stant before he remembered what her childhood must have bee
like. Whether she knew it or not, admitted it or not, her uncl
and father had been warriors of the Church Militant. She wa
no stranger to blood and death.

"Drink some of the tea, Wu," commanded Catlin.

He watched Wu pour and drink the tea without hesitation.

"Pour some for Lindsay. Slowly."

Wu poured very carefully, as though he were taking part i
a ceremony staged in a forbidden city hung with crimson sil

brocade. The first cup Lindsay drank from Catlin's hand. The second she managed for herself.

"Better?" Catlin asked softly.

She nodded. She had had a lifetime of practice coping with sudden fear of one kind or another, reality or nightmare. Already the old discipline was settling into place, the slow, measured breaths and soothing mental images of a blue-black pond gleaming beneath moonlight, silver rings of peace expanding outward from the center.

"I'm all right," Lindsay said, setting down the cup. Her fingers trembled very slightly, a motion so fine that only Catlin noticed it. She looked up at Wu with eyes that were as clear and dark as her imagined pond. "Uncle Wu, do you know who has Qin's bronze charioteer?"

Even as she said the words, Lindsay realized that Wu himself must have the charioteer. It was the only explanation that made sense. She looked quickly at Catlin. Without looking away from Wu, Catlin nodded his head.

"He's the one, honey."

23

"BUT HOW?" asked Lindsay. "You told me that whoever brought in the charioteer would need a smuggling operation that was already in place."

"Yes." Catlin said no more. He didn't have to.

Wu shifted. "Tea?" he asked calmly, his delicate hands poised over the elegant white teapot.

"Uncle Wu?" asked Lindsay, waiting to hear his denial.

Settling back into his chair with a cup cradled in his palm, Wu glanced again at Lindsay. "Do not look so shocked," he said tartly. "How do you think your honorable parents paid for smuggling their loyal flock out of China into Hong Kong, and from there to Canada and the United States? It was the same way your lover paid off his spies, whores and lackeys. Smuggled gold, smuggled opium, smuggled arms, smuggled bodies, smuggled bronzes. All become equal in the end. Smuggled. For that, one must have a smuggler of discretion and skill."

"You?"

"I," he agreed calmly. "I learned in Xi'an. Your esteemed uncle taught me," Wu said, sipping his tea. "He was a man of great honor, courage and, I am afraid, foolishness. He left rather too much in God's venerable hands, not realizing that God had many, many children who required His care. Sometimes even the most omnipotent and loving God must blink."

Lindsay closed her eyes. For an instant she saw again the time when God had blinked—shots and screams and her uncle's blood spurting between her fingers.

But beneath the image of violence Lindsay silently screamed a denial. Not of her uncle's death. She accepted that, finally. Yet she did not want to believe that her parents had been involved in anything illicit. The thought made her feel as though she were standing on the banks of a raging river and the earth were shifting subtly beneath her feet, warning of the disastrous crumbling to come.

How could she have been so wrong about so many things? How could she have been deceived so thoroughly?

"Arms? Opium?" she asked, her voice strained. "How many years did you smuggle for my parents?"

"Lindsay, you have to understand something," Catlin said quietly before Wu could speak. "In those years gold, opium, rice and tea were often the only currency Asians would trust. As for the arms—" Catlin's hand tightened for an instant as he remembered the file he had read on the early years of Lindsay Danner. As he spoke, he resumed stroking her hair slowly. "Your father and uncle chose to fight as well as to pray. Your uncle—" Again, Catlin hesitated.

"My uncle?" Lindsay asked, turning to fix Catlin with indigo eyes.

"Most Chinese missionaries reached some kind of accommodation with communism, or they left China. Your uncle did neither," Catlin said bluntly. "He spent more time teaching guerrilla warfare than saving souls. Your father was more circumspect. He had to be. He had you and your mother to think about."

"How do you know that?" Lindsay demanded. "How do you know things about my childhood that I don't?"

There was no answer except the measured glide of Catlin's palm over Lindsay's hair. She closed her eyes. She didn't want to believe, but she did. Catlin had never lied to her. He had no reason to begin now. And his words explained so much, including the reason her mother had so fiercely insisted that Lindsay forget everything about the night her uncle had died.

Forget it, Lindsay. Give it to God. Forget. It will be better that way, for everyone. Forget. Forget. Forget.

And Lindsay had, until this morning. Then she had remembered, and the same man who was even now stroking her hair had held her, let her cry, helped her to accept her dream of terror as a distorted reflection of reality. He had freed her from the nightmare...and now he was telling her about a reality that was in some ways worse. A childhood of deceit and lies.

It explained so much, so many fragments of memory and fear. Whispers and unnatural silences. Sudden gunfire and the sound of her mother ripping dresses into bandages. Men gliding through the night like black tigers, fighting for a cause that had been lost years before. Guerrillas. Outlaws. Her uncle had been one of them. So had her father.

No wonder Catlin had seemed so familiar to her, so right for her. She had been born among men like him, had laughed with them as they teased and hugged her, had felt their blood flowing between her fingers.

Lindsay let out a shaking breath and caught Catlin's hand. She held it against her cheek so hard that her nails left red crescents on his skin. His thumb stroked gently across her cheekbone. He urgently wished that it had been possible to shield her from knowledge of the gulf between her child's perception of her parents and their reality. This wasn't the time for Lindsay to have to adjust to a new view of reality, of herself. She had had to accept too many new insights in the past few weeks, none of them pleasant.

"Did Mother—" Lindsay's voice shattered to silence.

Wu understood. "This undeserving self was honored to serve your parents until your most venerable father died," Wu said quietly. "Your esteemed mother was a dutiful wife of unquestioned loyalty and obedience. She was a woman to bring honor to her ancestors and to her husband. Yet—" Wu shrugged. "No matter the weight and height of the evidence against her view, she steadfastly believed that the way to achieve God's ultimate victory in China was through the conversion of peasants rather than the honorable crucible of battle. She was a woman of infinite patience, with a generosity of spirit that must stand as an example to cynical mortals such as myself."

Wu sipped tea, sighed, and set aside the exquisite white cup. "From time to time she sent Christian peasants carrying ancient bronzes or other artifacts of value that would pay for the cost of introducing unexpected guests into a new homeland."

He bowed slightly toward Lindsay. "I regret to say that your honored mother lacked your fine eye in bronzes. Perhaps that was only to be expected. Her gaze was fixed always on a better future, not a glorious and honored past. I send my unworthy prayers to heaven in the hope that your beloved mother has found at last the gentle, bountiful God for whom she sacrificed so much."

"She used you to smuggle things after Dad died," Lindsay summarized flatly.

"Her calling was to the poor," Wu said obliquely. "The poor are forever in need of money. She kept nothing for herself from the sale of smuggled bronzes, no matter how great her own need. She insisted that God would provide for her. So she sent you to your American aunt and to me, knowing that I would train you to live in the world that your honorable mother had forsaken for her mission to the poor." Wu smiled slightly. "Apparently your mother did not have much faith that God would provide for others. That thankless task she took upon her own esteemed head."

Wu's smile faded as he measured Lindsay's reaction to the knowledge that her mother had been part of a smuggling operation. "Do not presume upon God's benevolence by judging your deeply honorable and most worthy mother," Wu said harshly.

"I was lied to."

"You were a beloved child." Black eyes narrowed. "Are you still a child? Do you expect the world to be as pure as your foolishness and as gentle as an idiot's smile? Are you as quick in your judgments of your own miserable self? Your esteemed mother never went whoring after a man who—"

"That's enough," Catlin said, cutting across Wu's tirade.

Wu's head turned with the speed of a striking snake. "Do you deny what the hotel maid has seen every morning? Two sleep in one bed. Each day one less pill remains in the little pink dispenser. Lindsay comes to you like a bitch in season. She—"

"No more," Catlin commanded. His voice was soft, vibrating with the promise of violence.

Rage glittered in Wu's eyes. He stared at Catlin while the silence stretched. Wu watched the yellow eyes staring back at him and understood that Catlin would be no more gentle with him than he had been with Lee Tran.

"Then let us discuss you, Jacques-Pierre Rousseau," Wu said finally.

Catlin became aware of the painful pressure of Lindsay's nails digging into his hand. He looked down at her face. It was pale, tight, and he could sense the tension that had her humming like an overstretched wire. Gently he eased her nails free of his skin and resumed stroking her hair, giving her the only comfort he could.

"We will discuss Qin's charioteer," Catlin said flatly, "or Lindsay and I will leave."

Wu weighed Catlin again, letting the silence stretch. At last Wu sighed. "I do not understand you. You corrupted a fine and honorable woman in pursuit of Qin's charioteer, yet you refuse to bow to a simple reality. I have the bronze. You do not."

"Enjoy it," Catlin said. He tugged on Lindsay's hand, pulling her to her feet. "Come on, honey. We're leaving."

"Wait!" said Wu.

Catlin turned from Lindsay to watch Wu with the unreadable eyes of a dragon.

"One question," Wu said, his voice clipped. "Rousseau was safely dead. Why did you resurrect him?"

"Would you have sold Qin's charioteer to Jacob Catlin?" he asked sardonically.

Wu hesitated, then bowed very slightly in acknowledgment of a point made. "You have sacrificed your safety to pursue your passion for bronzes, yet you will turn and walk out of here because I speak the truth about a woman."

It wasn't a question. Not quite. Catlin answered it, anyway.

"The truth is that you were accustomed to using Lindsay's gift for your own profit, and seeing that slip away makes you very angry," Catlin retorted. "People knew that Lindsay was your daughter in all but name. They knew her reputation. They assumed that everything in your shop had been vetted by her.

But not everything has. Some of it is, shall we say, of problematical origins?"

Only the tightening of the skin across Wu's cheekbones revealed the extent of his anger. "That is not true," he said, biting off each word.

"Neither is what you said about Lindsay. I will protect her from your cruel tongue even if it means walking away from the charioteer."

Wu watched Catlin through another long silence. The lines of anger on Wu's face slowly loosened, giving him again his normal, kindly expression.

"Rousseau would not have acted so," Wu observed.

"Rousseau is dead."

Wu nodded slowly. "What of the man called Catlin?"

"I will protect Lindsay no matter what it costs or who it hurts."

Wu's eyes closed for a moment. He bent his head over his folded hands like a man deep in thought or prayer. When he looked up, it was Lindsay's eyes he sought. "Forgive my unhappy words, daughter. You are like your honorable mother, after all. You have in your soul that which can summon gentleness from even the most savage heart."

Lindsay looked away from Wu because she could not bear to meet his eyes. She wanted to tell him the truth—that her relationship with Catlin was all an act, an elaborate lie to get to Qin's charioteer. That was what Catlin was protecting. Not Lindsay, but the ancient charioteer whose presence in San Francisco would tear apart the fragile relationship between America and the People's Republic of China. Catlin had sized up Wu's outrage and seen that it stemmed from a father's anger at a wayward daughter's foolishness. So Catlin had chosen the one sure way to disarm Wu—convince him that his daughter had tamed a dragon rather than been ravished by one.

Lindsay looked at Catlin and realized that Stone had been right. Catlin's genius was in analyzing people's weaknesses and then using them to his own ends. He was very good at it. Frighteningly good. Even now she was clinging to him, because he was the only truth in a world of lies. And she needed his truth. She needed it the way she needed air to breathe.

"You are too kind to me, Uncle Wu," whispered Lindsay.

Wu came to his feet and took Lindsay's hand, patting it. "It has been my privilege through the years to serve your parents and God. If it will reassure your gentle sensibilities, you should know that in the past few years my smuggling has been confined to Chinese Christians fleeing from the terrible curse of communism. The bronzes that have come to me have come because I have some minor esteem within the community."

"I understand," Lindsay said, her voice husky, almost shattered. "Forgive me for even thinking that you might have had less than honorable reasons for your actions."

The irony of Lindsay's apology went through Catlin in a razor stroke of pain. Lindsay, too, had honorable reasons for actions that appeared less than honorable—but Wu still did not suspect that.

"Yes," Catlin said dryly. "Tell us about your honorable reasons for dealing in stolen goods."

Wu's head came around sharply. What he saw in Catlin's face wasn't reassuring. "You will please explain," Wu demanded.

"Stolen. As in taken without permission. Or are you saying that Qin's charioteer was a parting gift from the People's Republic to a group of religious refugees?"

Wu laughed dryly, humorlessly. "Ah, that would be a fabulous day to see, would it not? That will be the same day that a ravenous tiger's tongue innocently washes the face of a newly born lamb." The papery sound of Wu's laughter faded. He looked intently from Catlin to Lindsay. "I will take no money from the sale of the charioteer."

"What will you take, then?" Catlin asked before Lindsay could speak.

"The satisfaction of a humble servant of God."

Catlin waited, and his silence was a pressure forcing Lindsay to be silent and Wu to speak.

"My shortsighted people turned to communism because they were hopeless, hungry and oppressed," Wu said. "Communism gave them much hope, a pittance of food and an oppression that is boundless. Now my people are becoming restless again," he said with satisfaction. "The hope of communism is a waning moon. The naive economic theories of the miserable dog Mao accomplished what the honorable armies of the venerable General Chiang could not—they nearly brought down the Communist Party in China."

Wu looked at Catlin, measuring his response. Absently Wu patted Lindsay's hand again and released it, concentrating only on Catlin.

"But nearly isn't good enough," Catlin suggested neutrally, forestalling whatever Lindsay might have said by squeezing her hand in silent warning. "You want it all."

Wu bowed slightly. "We will have what we want, eventually. We are patient and dedicated."

"You'll have to be, as long as Deng or a progressive like him is in power," Catlin pointed out. "He'll bring in new ideas, Western modifications of failed Maoist economic doctrines. Hope, in a word. People who have hope don't rebel. If you want to stir up another revolution, you'll have to make sure that things stay hopeless for the Chinese. You'll have to separate China from the hope of the West until your people choke and die on the drawbacks of pure communism."

Catlin felt the strength of Lindsay's grip on his hand and prayed that she could be quiet for just a few moments longer. Wu had disregarded her as any kind of threat to his political plans. In the Chinese community, women were not expected to have a vital interest in matters of state. Nothing in Lindsay's life up to then had suggested that she was an exception to that cultural expectation. Even if she were, Wu had no reason to believe that she would feel differently about the atheistic rulers of China than her father and uncle had.

Catlin wanted it to stay that way.

"You have an admirable grasp of politics at its most pragmatic," Wu murmured.

"I learned in Asia."

Wu smiled. "Then you understand the importance of Qin's charioteer."

"You're going to use it as a wedge to drive East and West apart."

"Just so."

Catlin showed his indifference with a shrug, but the pressure of his hand on Lindsay's was unrelenting. "Politics is your problem, Wu. Mine is getting my hands on Qin's charioteer."

"Charioteer, chariot and two horses," Wu amended.

Lindsay's breath came in sharply. "My God," she breathed, stunned. "All of it? Together?"

With a small smile Wu turned to her . "A spectacular coup, is it not?" He turned to Catlin again. "It is also a very expensive coup, I am afraid. The price is one million dollars. If you cannot manage that sum, there will be an auction. The bronzes will go to the highest bidder."

"I can manage it," Catlin said succinctly. "When and where do I pick up the bronzes?"

"As soon as the money is transferred to—"

"No," Catlin said. His voice was flat, ungiving. "Nothing gets transferred anywhere until Lindsay and I have inspected each and every piece of bronze."

"The pieces are genuine," Wu said reassuringly. His fragile hands hovered above the teapot like pale birds, but he poured no more tea. His attention was all on Catlin.

"Then there should be no problem with having Lindsay look at the bronzes. Take it or leave it, Wu. And remember," Catlin added in a smooth, hard tone, "a lot of people know that I'm looking for this charioteer and that I don't care about the price. If we walk away from this sale, there won't be another one. Everyone will assume that I turned my back because the pieces didn't pass Lindsay's inspection."

Wu's face became expressionless and his hands very still. What Catlin said was the truth, and no one knew it better than Wu. He looked at Lindsay. "You are in agreement with this, daughter?"

It took all Catlin's self-control not to turn to Lindsay and require that she ignore Wu's naked bid for her to switch her loyalty from lover to beloved uncle.

"I'm not the buyer, Uncle Wu," she said carefully. "Catlin is. It is for him to agree or disagree with the actual details of the sale."

Wu grunted and turned back to Catlin, who smiled slightly. It was a smile that Wu had seen once before, on the screen of his television surveillance apparatus after Catlin had kissed Lindsay, drowning her objections to his past in a hot torrent of desire.

"I assume you have some kind of bank account in Hong Kong," Catlin said.

Wu nodded.

"That will make it easier. When Lindsay approves the bronzes, I'll simply call and arrange for a transfer of funds between the two Hong Kong banks. You can call your bank and verify that the money has been transferred. Then we'll take the bronzes."

There was a slight hesitation before Wu nodded. "It is agreeable." He nodded again. "Yes."

"Good. When and where?"

"You will go back to your hotel. A call will come when the bronzes are ready. You will leave immediately. You will not be followed. At a designated location, a car will arrive and take you to the bronzes. Is that understood?"

Catlin shook his head. "Not good enough, Wu. I've got to have some way to move the bronzes. I'll drive a van to—"

"That will not be necessary," Wu said, cutting across Catlin's words. "For the sum you are paying, we will be honored to provide a truck and driver. You will of course have an opportunity to approve of vehicle and chauffeur before the sale is consummated."

It was less than Catlin had hoped for and more than he had expected. He nodded. "There's one potential problem," he said carelessly.

Wu's eyes narrowed.

"You know the FBI is keeping tabs on me," said Catlin.

Wu sighed. "Yes, that is a difficulty. With a man of Rousseau's background, it was not an unanticipated difficulty, however. We have succeeded in working around it thus far."

"I was lucky flushing tails on short notice today," Catlin said bluntly. "Next time they'll be a lot harder to lose."

"It would be very unfortunate if you were followed," Wu said. "It would be perceived as a definite sign of your unwillingness to purchase the bronzes. Under those circumstances it would not be difficult to arrange a second sale—without you."

Catlin ignored the threat and concentrated on what he needed from Wu. Time. "There's no real problem. All I need is enough time after the call to get rid of my admirers before Lindsay and I show up at the rendezvous."

"How much time would you require?"

"At least forty-five minutes."

"I will allow you ten."

"But—"

"Ten," Wu said sharply. "No more. My collaborators in this operation are very suspicious people. They would become much too uneasy if you were given more than ten minutes."

"I'll do my best. No guarantees, Wu. I'm not a miracle worker."

"You are Rousseau. That should be enough." Wu smiled rather grimly. "There is one last, insignificant detail."

Every nerve in Catlin's body came to full alert. "Yes?" he asked blandly.

"You will not be armed. This is not a matter of negotiation," Wu said, accurately reading Catlin's instant objection.

"I have too many enemies to go unarmed," Catlin said flatly.

"Lee Tran?" murmured Wu.

"He's at the top of the list."

"Lee Tran will not step upon your shadow again, ever." Wu bowed slightly toward Lindsay. "It is my humble apology for misunderstanding you, daughter."

"That's not—" Lindsay began, wondering if she had understood Wu correctly. And afraid that she had.

"Thank you," Catlin interrupted, bowing slightly in return. In Mandarin he added, "We are most appreciative that a man of your dignity would soil his hands removing such garbage rather than leaving it to stink in the presence of humble guests. If, however, you find that the stench so offends your honorable nostrils as to make Tran's removal impossible, you have only to call upon my miserable self. The removal will be accomplished with the speed of lightning walking over the land."

The papery sound of Wu's laughter rustled in the room. He took Lindsay's hand again, patting it fondly. "You have chosen well, daughter. Not wisely, perhaps, but well. Your honorable uncle and father would have approved."

Wu bowed to Lindsay, then to Catlin before turning and walking from the room.

Lindsay watched Wu go with a feeling of unreality. "Is he really going to—"

"I profoundly hope so," interrupted Catlin, pulling Lindsay close, kissing her almost roughly. "Move," he said savagely in her ear. Simultaneously his fingers dug into her arms, turning her toward the door. *"Now."*

Without a word Lindsay walked toward the door that led to the chapel. The room was empty but for a handful of candles and the pungence of incense swirling from a magnificent Han censer set by the altar. Nothing moved in the garden except the crystal dance of water over rock. The black gate opened at a touch.

Catlin went through first. There was no sign of Lee Tran or of anyone else who was interested in the two Anglos mixed among the Asian throngs. Lindsay neither looked at Catlin nor spoke to him all the way to the hotel.

"You can relax now. All we have to do is wait for Wu's call, but that won't be for a while. The banks in Hong Kong are still closed." Catlin glanced sideways at Lindsay as they climbed the service stair. "If it helps, you did a good job."

She said nothing. Instinctively she knew that she shouldn't relax, shouldn't let go of her tightly held emotions. If she did, she would fly apart.

"I'm sorry I was rough on you at the end. I was afraid that Wu or his partners would get smart and decide to keep us as 'guests' until the bronzes arrive," Catlin continued. "Besides, if Stone isn't already raising hell about our disappearance, he will be soon."

Neither by word nor action did Lindsay show that she had heard Catlin.

"Are you all right?" Catlin asked softly.

No answer.

"Lindsay?" he asked, reaching out to stroke her shining bronze hair.

"I'm just peachy," she said in a brittle voice.

"I know it was hard for you," he said gently, touching her hair.

"I don't want to talk about it," Lindsay said. "I can't. If I do I'll cry or scream or throw up or all three at once." She took a ragged breath and let it out slowly. "I'm pretty close to the edge, Catlin," she said, her voice flat.

Before the sentence was finished he had pulled her into his arms.

"Hold on to me, Lindsay," he said, kissing her eyelids, her temples, the corners of her mouth. "Hold on hard. It's almost over."

"Is it?" she asked hoarsely, wrapping her arms around his neck because he was the only stability in a swiftly spinning world. "Is it really? I feel like it will go on forever, worse and worse—lies, everything lies. And there's nothing I can do. I'm trapped. Nothing is real. Nothing but lies. My uncle, my father, my mother, Wu." Lindsay made an odd, broken sound. "I'm too tired to fight it anymore."

Catlin held her against his body as though he could take her into himself, give her some of his strength, some of his experience at surviving in a world of lies. "I haven't lied to you," he said.

Lindsay looked up at him with wild, dark eyes. "That's all that has kept me from coming apart. You knew it would be like this for me, didn't you?"

"Yes." *But I didn't know how much it would hurt you, me, us.* "Kiss me," he whispered even as he fitted his mouth to hers.

Lindsay didn't ask whether the kiss were act or reality, male passion or a response to her own need. She simply gave herself to Catlin's embrace, drinking his strength and warmth, letting it seep through her body to her soul. After a long, long time she felt herself eased down his length until her feet touched the ground again. His head tilted down once more. He gave her a tiny, biting kiss, and then another, as though he couldn't bring himself to release her mouth.

"Let's go to the room," he said.

Catlin took Lindsay's right hand, lacing their fingers together with a slow, sensual appreciation that made her breath catch. He heard the small, betraying sound and smiled.

"That's what I love about you," he said, his voice low. He brought her hand to his lips and inserted the tip of his tongue between her fingers, caressing the sensitive skin. "You're sexy everywhere. I want you so much I ache."

"Do you?" Lindsay whispered. "Do you really?"

His only answer was to take her hand and slide it down his body until she felt the hard reality of his hunger beneath her fingers.

"I've never lied to you," Catlin said, his voice taut with the hot flow of blood pooling between his thighs. "I—" His breath came out in a deep groan as Lindsay caressed him, then flexed her fingers so that his hungry, rigid flesh could feel the gentle bite of her nails through the layers of clothing.

"Come take a shower with me, honey cat," he said huskily. His fingers tightened on her right hand as he slowly drew her arm behind her back, arching her into his body. His hips moved against her, silently promising her the release that she needed as much as he did. "I'm going to love you until you scream with pleasure."

Lindsay's answer was a shiver of anticipation that went through Catlin like an electric current. He wanted to kiss her again but knew that if he did he might not stop until he finished what he had started, and to hell with anyone who might wander up the stairway. He wanted her now. She was wildfire spreading through his veins, burning him. The thought of sliding his aching, violently sensitive flesh into her took him right to the edge of control. He arched her into his thighs once more, trying to ease the fierce clamor of his body, wondering if he would ever get enough of her.

Finally, reluctantly, Catlin released Lindsay so that they could walk to the room. He was bringing the key to the lock when he remembered to check the tiny sliver of transparent tape he always put across the upper edge of the door.

The tape was gone.

Catlin spun and swept Lindsay down the hall before she could protest. He stopped in front of the stairwell, opened the door and pushed her through.

"Someone has been in the room while we were gone," he explained quietly.

"The maid—"

"I had the Do Not Disturb sign out." He watched the knowledge settle into Lindsay. "Stay here," he said. "If you hear any shots, go down to the lobby, call Stone and camp at the front desk until the troops arrive. Understand?"

"What are you—"

"Do you understand?" Catlin demanded, overriding Lindsay's question.

She searched his eyes and saw only the bleakness of the dragon staring back at her. "I understand," she whispered.

"Don't go near the room until I personally come down the hall and get you. If I call to you from the doorway and tell you to come to me, it means that someone has a gun at my back and I want you to turn and run like hell and not stop running until you're surrounded by the FBI. Clear?"

Lindsay nodded her head, unable to speak for the fear closing her throat. As he turned to leave she remembered what he had said before they went to meet Wu.

"Catlin!"

Lindsay's raw whisper was a wound in the silence. He spun back toward her, saw her unnatural stillness and her pale skin.

"I don't want—" Her whisper shattered. "Oh, God," she said fiercely, "I don't want you to take a bullet for me!"

Catlin brushed the back of his fingers over Lindsay's trembling lips and turned away without answering.

24

CATLIN STOOD WELL ASIDE from the door it
self as he turned the key with his left hand.
He pushed the door inward and pulled back flat along the
hallway wall at the same time. No sounds came from inside. He
waited.

Silence. No one spoke or shifted position or cocked a pistol.
He risked a quick look into the room. Empty. He entered the
room in a low crouch, because anyone waiting in ambush
would expect the quarry to be standing. From a crouched po
sition Catlin swept the room with a single turn of his body, left
hand locked around right wrist, arms straight before him, gun
ready.

There was no target, no one waiting in ambush, nothing but
the furniture and the closed bedroom door. Everything nor
mal—except that Catlin had not closed the bedroom door on
the way out that morning. He always left all interior doors wide
open, flat along the wall. Otherwise it was too easy for some
one to hide behind a door and wait for the target to open it and
walk blindly into gunfire.

Soundlessly Catlin crossed the room to the door that should
have been open. It wasn't latched. He heard nothing in the
bedroom beyond, neither movement nor word.

The door burst wide open as Catlin went through in a low
diving roll that ended as he came to his feet in a crouched
shooting stance. He found a target instantly, two men who
should not have been there. Even as Catlin's finger took slack
from the trigger, his mind registered the identity of the intrud
ers—Stone and O'Donnel. They were standing very still, their
arms held away from their bodies, empty hands clearly dis
played.

"That's a hell of an easy way to get yourself killed," Catlin said, uncocking and holstering the gun in a single motion.

O'Donnel let out his breath in a long sigh that was also a curse. "Mother of God," he said, shaking his head. He looked over at Stone. "You were right. I never even heard the son of a bitch."

Stone smiled slightly and wished he could light a cigarette. He couldn't, though. Neither Catlin nor Lindsay smoked. The smell would linger as a signpost to the maid or anyone else who might be interested in Lindsay's visitors.

"Lindsay?" asked Stone.

"Down the hall," Catlin said curtly, turning away even as he spoke.

He went quickly to Lindsay, saw the relief on her face as she ran to him, relief and something more, something that sliced through him until he wanted to cry out in a paradox of triumph and despair. She shouldn't look at him that way. The game was almost over, the lies nearly all spoken, the act all but complete. Her real life waited for her, and it waited without him.

"It's all right," Catlin whispered, lifting Lindsay off her feet as he returned her hard hug. "Just Stone and O'Donnel."

Lindsay nodded to tell Catlin that she understood, but her arms didn't loosen. She held him with all her strength, reassuring herself that he wasn't hurt. Finally she breathed deeply, filling her senses with Catlin's masculine scent. Her hands relaxed, stroking the soft corduroy of his jacket and the familiar textures of his hair and cheek and lips.

"I was afraid for you," Lindsay whispered, her voice catching.

Catlin closed his eyes for an instant as his emotions and his mind pulled him in opposite directions with racking force. Very gently he lowered Lindsay until her feet were on the ground again.

"Stone will have a lot of questions," Catlin said. "I'll try to keep Wu's name out of it."

"Would the FBI arrest him for smuggling?"

"No. Spying."

Catlin felt Lindsay stiffen.

"What?" she whispered, searching Catlin's eyes. There was compassion in the golden depths, but no confusion. He had said exactly what he meant.

"Think," murmured Catlin, holding Lindsay's chin in his palm. "Who stands to gain the most if relations between the U.S. and the People's Republic go to hell?"

She opened her mouth but no words came to her.

"Taiwan," Catlin said softly. "Every step we take closer to the People's Republic is one step farther away from the Chinese Nationalists on Taiwan. Without our support, the genteel fiction of two Chinas is dead, and with it, Taiwan. The Nationalists aren't stupid. They know that their only hope of survival is to keep the People's Republic and America at each other's throat."

"But Taiwan is our ally," Lindsay protested.

"And a spy is an unregistered agent of a foreign government," Catlin continued relentlessly, wanting Lindsay to understand even though the knowledge would not be comforting. "The Nationalists are rich in American dollars, so Taiwan can afford to contribute heavily to various American organizations, societies, politicians, churches and student groups whose interests are congenial with those of the Nationalists. Anti-Communist, in a word. I suspect that the Chinese Christian Benevolent Society enjoys the generosity of Taiwan."

"Is that illegal?"

"No. Every foreign government that can afford it buys favorable opinions in the U.S. It's called freedom of speech."

Catlin hesitated, searching the darkness of Lindsay's eyes, wondering if she understood yet. She said nothing, simply watched him in turn.

"I'm afraid Wu's involvement is much deeper than just accepting foreign contributions in the name of an American Chinese benevolent society," Catlin said after a moment. "I think Wu is a foreign agent paid directly by the Nationalist government. I think he has been for a long time. Since Hong

Kong, certainly, and probably before he met your uncle in Xi'an.''

"How do you know? Can you prove it?" demanded Lindsay.

"Why bother? Taiwan is a drop in a very large ocean of world power. The Nationalists in America are just one in a spectrum of refugee groups, and not even a particularly important one. The Nationalists are history," Catlin said bluntly. "They're like Albanians or Spanish Loyalists plotting political millennia in sidewalk cafes. Taiwan wasn't even enough of a threat to think of using the Qin charioteer as an international political football. It was Deng's enemies in the People's Republic who thought of it. Like the Nationalists on Taiwan, the mainland isolationists want to keep America and the PRC apart.''

"But aren't the Nationalists and the Communists enemies?"

Catlin shook his head and laughed harshly. "Yes, and politics makes strange bedfellows. But it's hard to imagine anything as strange as Wu, Pao and the tightly laced Madame Zhu in bed together. Yet there they are, flailing around in the dark, trying to screw each other without being screwed in turn. And then there's Chen Yi on the sidelines, trying to use me without losing his nuts in the process. And me, trying to pay off an old debt to the family of Chen.''

Impatiently, Catlin shrugged, dismissing plots and counterplots, old debts and recent payments. He wasn't there to help Yi or the isolationists, Wu or the FBI. He was there to earn back one half of a coin by protecting Lindsay Danner from the consequences of her own idealism.

"Once this mess is cleared up," Catlin continued, "the Nationalists in Chinatown can go back to hatching futile plots over tea and mah-jongg and watching their kids grow up to be neither Nationalists nor Communists, but Americans. Wu is a dinosaur. Burning down his political house of cards won't help the U.S. particularly, and it would hurt you a great deal. I don't see the point in that, but I'm not Bradford Stone. My job isn't to catch spies.''

"Is that Stone's job? Catching spies?"

"It's called the Foreign Counterintelligence Division of the FBI. Stone heads it." Catlin smiled sardonically. "You should be flattered, honey cat. You're being watched over by America's number one counter spy."

"What is your job?"

"Protecting you. Period," Catlin said bluntly. "I tried to do that by yanking you out of the game before it had really begun. You refused that option. Have you finally changed your mind? Have you learned that lies are contagious and the truth is a chimera? Will you let me take you out of the game now?"

"I was warned. I gave my word," Lindsay said simply.

Then she smiled at him, a sad, off-center smile that made Catlin want to cry out in protest. But there would be no point in protesting. He had given his word, too. He knew what had to be done. So did she.

The game would be played. Only the details remained to be decided.

"It's up to you," Catlin said. "Keep Wu's name to ourselves or give it to Stone."

"Is Wu really...harmless?"

Catlin thought of Wu calmly promising the permanent removal of one Lee Tran. Any man who could do that wasn't harmless, but that was different from being a continuing threat to the security of the U.S. "You mean harmless as a spy?"

"Yes."

"Wu will be safe enough once the bronzes are out of the way. I guarantee it," Catlin said.

What he didn't say was that he would make a special point of extracting a promise of good behavior from Wu as soon as the furor over Qin's bronzes died down.

"Thank God," Lindsay said raggedly. "I couldn't bear knowing I'd betrayed two uncles in one lifetime."

Catlin had known she would feel that way. It was the reason he had decided to protect Wu, if possible. Not for Wu's sake, but for Lindsay's. Catlin took her hand again. Her fingers were almost stiff with the tension radiating through her.

"Ready to face Stone?" Catlin asked softly.

"Do I have any choice?"

"Yes. Say hello, say goodbye and take a shower. I'll handle the rest."

Some of the tension left Lindsay's body. "Maybe that would be best. I still don't lie very well, do I?"

Catlin tilted her face up and kissed her tenderly. "Don't worry. I can lie well enough for both of us. But not to you, Lindsay. Never to you."

She smiled again, the sad, crooked smile that tore at Catlin's control. Neither of them said anything as they walked down the hall and into the hotel room. As soon as they were inside, he locked and bolted the door.

"Roll call," Catlin said loudly.

Stone and O'Donnel walked into the living room.

Catlin pushed Lindsay gently toward the bedroom. "Shower and then nap, if you can. The call will probably come late tonight."

"Wait a minute," said Stone.

"Hello," said Lindsay.

"I have some questions—"

"Goodbye," she said, walking past Stone.

Automatically O'Donnel put out his hand to restrain Lindsay. Catlin moved so swiftly that O'Donnel had no chance to react beyond a sudden gasp of surprise and pain.

"Back off," Catlin snarled, releasing O'Donnel's wrist as suddenly as he had taken it. "Can't you see that she's done? Waiting for the call will be bad enough. She doesn't need to be grilled by the two of you on top of it."

"What call?" demanded Stone.

The bedroom door closed firmly behind Lindsay.

"The one telling us where to rendezvous with Qin's charioteer."

There was a stunned silence, then Stone began laughing softly.

"I'll be damned," he said. "There goes my money." Stone looked at Catlin. "I bet the director a hundred that there weren't any stolen bronzes. But he said it didn't matter—we still had to kowtow to our great and good friend Chen Yi."

"Besides," Catlin said sardonically, "while you're helping Yi, you can learn a hell of a lot about Chinese spies, whether they happen to be Communist or Nationalist, overseas or right in your own backyard."

"How do you figure that?" Stone asked blandly.

Catlin's smile was almost cruel. "Pull the other one, Stone. If the bronzes really do exist, you know that they'll be handled by spies or dupes or both, because this was a political game from the word go. So all you have to do is sweep down on the rendezvous, gather up the bodies, twist them until they talk and then you roll up the spy pipeline all the way back to Taiwan and Beijing."

The FBI agent's smile was a perfect match for Catlin's. "Want a job?" asked Stone.

"There's just one problem with your little scenario," Catlin continued.

"Only one? That'll be the day," grunted Stone.

"Only one that matters," Catlin amended. "If you come cowboying in when Lindsay and I are looking at the bronzes, someone's going to get shot. Wait until we're clear."

"Can't do it," said Stone, shaking his head. "We need to have everybody there with the evidence. Airtight. No room for cute lawyers and bleeding heart judges to maneuver. Besides, what makes you think you'll be allowed to leave with the bronzes? It could be a ripoff. They get information on our foreign counterintelligence apparatus, they get money, and then they take off with the merchandise and bust a gut laughing at us."

Catlin had expected as much. In Stone's position, he would have done the same thing. "Then we've got a real problem. I'm not taking Lindsay into a trap. Without Lindsay, there's no deal, nothing to wrap up. School is out."

"Is that the way Lindsay wants it?" O'Donnel asked suddenly.

"That's the way it will be."

O'Donnel started to argue, remembered Catlin's speed and lethal skill and shut up.

"I know," Catlin said sardonically. "Safety is high on the FBI's most wanted list. But it's not first. Getting the job done is first."

O'Donnel didn't disagree. It was the truth, and everyone in the room knew it.

"Keeping Lindsay safe is the only thing on my list," Catlin said. "I'll do it any way I have to, including fight you. And I learned to fight in some dirty places."

Futilely, Stone wished for a cigarette. "Tell us what you want. We'll deliver if we can. We don't want anyone hurt, but we're going to get the bronzes and the spies."

Catlin nodded tightly. He had expected no less. "We're going to get a call. If the contact is in Cantonese, I'll call you and give you a translation immediately. We'll be given a certain amount of time to get to a rendezvous point. An extra ten minutes is built into that so that I can flush any tails I have."

O'Donnel laughed. "Ten minutes? You're good, Catlin, but nobody's that good. Not when we can cover you like a bad reputation."

"I know," Catlin said calmly. "Put four men on us. I'll do seven minutes' worth of flushing. At the end of that time, I don't want to see any tails. If I do, I'll take them out the quickest way I can."

There was a taut silence while Stone tried not to show how angry he was at Catlin's calm promise of violence.

"All right." Stone's voice was clipped, harsh. "But you won't have to waste time calling the FBI. Someone will be right here with you. A safety precaution."

Catlin weighed whether or not to argue the point, then decided not to. Allowing Stone to assign an FBI agent to cover them was the least confining way to let him feel in control.

"You can use the ten minutes, plus whatever our travel time is, to throw a surveillance net around the rendezvous point," Catlin said. "After that, it should be simple enough to keep track of us with the kind of rolling surveillance that the FBI invented. If it comes to a foot job, give it to O'Donnel. He's as good as anyone I've seen."

O'Donnel smiled. "Put it in writing, huh? It looks so nice in the file."

Stone smiled faintly. "That's okay as far as it goes. We'll put a beeper in Lindsay's purse to—"

"No." The word was flat, hard. "No wires, no beepers, no guns. We're going to be searched."

"Christ," muttered O'Donnel.

"Amen," Stone said. He smoothed his palm thoughtfully over his silver hair. "You're sure?"

"I'm sure."

"We've got some really small stuff that no one would notice."

"I'm not betting Lindsay's life on it. Besides," Catlin added, "unless they've upgraded those electronic 'burrs' a lot in the past few years, they're nothing to depend on."

Reflexively Stone reached for his cigarettes. He pulled out the pack, realized where he was and swore.

"I don't like it," he said, jamming the pack back into his shirt pocket. "We don't even know what you're going up against. Do you?"

Catlin thought of all the combinations of players that might occur. Wu might be foolish—or suspicious—enough to show up at the transfer. If so, he would have bodyguards. Comrades Zhu and Pao would doubtless want to be in at the kill, to witness the purchase of the politically damning bronzes. Yi would probably be there, too, whether willingly or not. His dear comrades wouldn't trust him out of their sight.

"How many people came to LA with the official Chinese delegation?" Catlin asked finally.

"Twelve," said Stone. He hesitated, then added, "Our intelligence is that at least six of them are soldiers. You'll have to assume that they'll be armed."

"Shit," Catlin muttered. "What does intelligence say about the bronzes?"

Again Stone hesitated.

"If anyone in this mess has a 'need to know,'" snapped Catlin, "I do."

"Word is that they came in under diplomatic seal along with a shipment of household goods for a member of the Taiwanese consulate staff," Stone said. "That's rumor, not hard intelligence."

Catlin shrugged. "I'll take it. It's the only foolproof way to get something the size of the four bronzes into the country."

"Four?" O'Donnel asked.

"Chariot, charioteer and two horses. Half to two-thirds lifesize, according to Chen Yi."

O'Donnel whistled. "No wonder they brought all the soldiers. That's quite a treasure they're guarding. How much do they want?"

"A million."

"You going to give it to them?"

"Yes," Catlin said.

"In cash?" O'Donnel asked dubiously.

"Bank transfer. Hong Kong."

O'Donnel thought about it, then shook his head. "Even so, you're running a hell of a risk. Just you and Lindsay against all those soldiers. Unless you figure Chen Yi to throw in on our side?"

"Not a chance," Catlin said succinctly. "He has his own ass to cover. That's why I agreed to be Lindsay's bodyguard."

Stone grunted, reached for a cigarette, remembered and swore. "I don't like it. If we lose you on the way to the bronzes, you're way up a very shitty creek with no way to paddle home."

Catlin shrugged. "I've spent most of my life like that."

Stone's smile was as thin as a razor. "Yeah, I guess you have, haven't you? If anyone could do it and come out smelling like a rose, you could."

"The bronzes are probably coming in by van," Catlin said. "They're giving me the van to drive away in."

O'Donnel whistled again. "When they do it, they do it right."

"Lindsay will inspect the bronzes," continued Catlin.

"How long will that take?" Stone asked.

"Given the fact that it might be the only chance in her lifetime to look at Qin's bronze army," Catlin said, smiling, "it will probably take as much time as I give her. Fifteen minutes, say. Then ten minutes to transfer funds from one Hong Kong bank to another."

"Which ones?" demanded O'Donnel.

"My bank's name won't help you, and I won't know the name of the receiving bank until Lindsay approves the bronzes."

"Any chance the bronzes are fakes?" O'Donnel asked.

"That would make Chen Yi a very happy man, and put our asses right on the firing line with the rest of the PRC," Catlin said dryly. "The people doing the selling are very confident of the goods, or they wouldn't let Lindsay within fifty miles." He hesitated, then shrugged. "But there's always a chance of fakes, I suppose, just like a snowball in hell has a chance of staying frozen."

Stone grunted. "Okay. Five minutes to get down to business. Fifteen minutes with the bronzes. Ten minutes with the banks. Half an hour total. That's not much time for us to get everything in place, especially if the bronzes are in a low traffic area where we'll stick out like daisies on shit. If that's the way it is, we'll have to come in on titty-fingers."

"If the deal goes down in someone's shop," Catlin said, "you should have a clear view of the bronzes being loaded. You can close in as soon as Lindsay and I get in the van. If it's a warehouse job, add fifteen minutes to load the bronzes. If a van doesn't come out by then, come in and get us."

Assuming, of course, that the FBI hadn't lost them somewhere on San Francisco's narrow, steep streets. No one mentioned that possibility, however. It was just one of the many risks that would be taken because there was no other choice.

For several minutes there was silence while Stone turned the plan over in his mind, probing for weaknesses. There were many, but given the restrictions of time and information, there was little to be done.

"All right," Stone said finally. He looked at Catlin and asked, "You recognize anyone you saw today?"

"Lee Tran, a.k.a. Tom Lee."

Stone paused. "You sure?"

"Very."

"Be damned. Spying isn't his style. Recognize anyone else?" Stone asked.

"No."

"Too bad. Well, I've got some calls to make," Stone said. "I don't want to tie up your phone. Stay here, Terry. I'll send over some more mug shots. Maybe Catlin and Lindsay can ID somebody for us."

Catlin went to the hall door, opened it and glanced casually up and down the hall. No one was in sight. Catlin turned away from the door and silently signaled. Stone walked out. O'Donnel locked and bolted the door behind him and turned back just in time to see Catlin closing the bedroom door behind himself.

"Going to help Lindsay shower?" O'Donnel asked innocently.

"I'm going to take my own advice," Catlin retorted.

"Which is?"

"A nap. Hong Kong banks open real early, California time."

The door shut firmly behind Catlin. He went to his suitcase and took out a small, narrow wedge. Using the heel of his hand, he silently tapped the wedge into the thin line between bedroom door and frame. Any attempt to open the door from the living room would only result in jamming the wedge in even tighter. It wasn't that Catlin thought someone was going to come sneaking into the bedroom. It was simply that he knew Lindsay would sleep better in the certainty that only she or Catlin could open the bedroom door.

The bathroom door was closed. The sound of the shower was very clear for a moment, then stopped. Catlin hesitated before he turned away from the bathroom door, went to the closet and looked at the clothes Lindsay had brought to San Francisco. When they went to see the bronzes, he wanted her to wear something easy to move in and not of a color that would make her an obvious target. As the call would probably come in the middle of the night, everything should be ready in advance.

The hum of a hair dryer came from the bathroom as Catlin went expertly through Lindsay's clothes. Finally he selected jeans and a soft blue-gray cashmere sweater. Her running shoes were next, followed by a supple suede jacket in a shade of blue that was as dark as her eyes. He draped the clothes over a chair and put the shoes nearby.

The sound of the hair dryer still came from the bathroom. Catlin hesitated, then went to the door and knocked lightly.

''Lindsay?''

''Come on in. I'm decent.''

Only the knowledge that the bathroom was bugged kept Catlin from expressing his disappointment. He opened the door and went in—and then stood very still, looking at Lindsay.

She was in front of the sink, drying her hair. The bathroom was steamy and scented with her perfume. Catlin hardly noticed the tantalizing aroma, for he was too caught up in the picture Lindsay made to have attention left over for anything else. She was wearing a pale rose teddy with lace flowers placed in such a way as to make the dark pink tips of her breasts into the center of the flowers. The sight of Lindsay's graceful twisting movements as she brushed and blow dried her hair drove everything from Catlin's mind but memories of how she had softened and run like honey in his hands, of her nails pricking him to full awareness and of her shivering cries of completion when he came deep inside her.

Quietly Catlin cursed the electronic eavesdroppers that would prevent him from hearing those elemental sounds again. And then there was O'Donnel in the living room with nothing to do but listen to the silence. There was no real privacy in the hotel suite, no chance to make love to Lindsay until she screamed with pleasure. They wouldn't be alone again until Chen Yi's game was over.

Which was the same as saying that Catlin wouldn't be alone with Lindsay again. Ever.

He went to stand behind her, not stopping until he was so close to her that he could feel the scented warmth rising from her body. Slowly he bent and kissed her bare shoulder.

"How are you feeling?" he asked, looking at her eyes in the mirror.

"Better every second," she said, tilting her head to one side to give him free access to the curve of her neck, smiling as his mustache stroked her like a silk brush.

"I put out some clothes for you," he said against her neck.

As Catlin spoke, his hands slid beneath Lindsay's raised arms. He smoothed down the curving, feminine lines of her body to her thighs before allowing his hands to move up her torso. He cupped her breasts in his palms and watched her in the mirror as she shivered. He bent his head again, found the sensitive network of nerves at the shoulder joint and caressed them with his teeth.

"Th-thank you. For the clothes."

The passionate catch in Lindsay's voice went through Catlin like heat lightning. He felt her breasts change beneath his hands, her nipples rising and hardening at his touch. Blood pulsed hotly, settling between his legs, making him rise and harden even as she had until he could count each heartbeat in the erect flesh straining against his jeans.

"When we go to see the bronzes," Catlin said, tugging at Lindsay's nipples, smiling at the ripple of response he could see in the mirror, feel beneath his hands, "I want you to be wearing clothes that won't hobble you."

"I—" Her voice broke as she watched his hands shift until her nipples stood out between his fingers and he squeezed gently, rhythmically. "Y-yes," she said. "That's—fine."

Hands trembling, Lindsay shut off the hair dryer and put it aside. The hairbrush followed. But when she would have turned toward Catlin, he held her in a sensual vise, keeping her back to him. With exquisite care he scraped his fingernails over her erect nipples. He bit the nape of her neck gently as he teased and tugged at her breasts, feeling her helpless response in the movement of her hips against his thighs.

"I knew you'd see it my way," Catlin said, looking up, watching Lindsay in the mirror. She didn't notice. She was watching his hands on her body, and the expression on her face made him want to groan with anticipation. He throttled the sound, knowing how close the bug was. "You see, I want you to be able to move freely," he added in a gritty voice.

Catlin's hard male hand slid down Lindsay's body, stopping only when his fingers were cupped between the warmth of her legs. He felt the hot silk of the teddy and the two snaps that held the lingerie in place, preventing him from caressing the soft, humid flesh that was so close and yet so far away from his touch. Slowly he eased his finger between the snaps.

Lindsay's breath came in sharply as she felt the tiny, probing caress. "Are you sure?" she asked, her voice husky, taut. "Are—"

And then she could talk no longer, for Catlin's other hand had closed over her mouth, stifling her moan of pleasure as he teased the hungry, hardening nub of nerves hidden within the soft, feminine folds.

"Very sure," Catlin said. He tugged in slow motion, feeling the teddy's snaps give way one by one. "And quiet," he said, his voice almost hoarse. "That's why I put your running shoes out. No one will be able to hear a thing. So just relax, honey cat. Don't worry. I'll take care of everything. Every...little...thing."

Lindsay met Catlin's eyes in the mirror. He smiled at her even as he caressed her. Almost helplessly she glanced down, and the sight of him touching her so intimately sent a wild, liquid pleasure coursing through her. He felt her sudden heat and wanted to groan in sheer male triumph. His hand slid up beneath the unsnapped teddy until he could feel her naked breasts. She arched her back, her eyes closed, and her tongue flicked rhythmically over the hard palm holding back her passionate cries.

Catlin's hand moved away from Lindsay's breasts, back down her body until he could tease the dark bronze hair concealing her velvet femininity. Fingers widespread, he pulled her suddenly against his aroused body, unable to bear the ache of his own hunger any longer. His palm rubbed rhythmically over her and his fingertips once more knew her liquid warmth.

Lindsay twisted slowly against Catlin, increasing the sensual contact even as one of her hands moved down to cover his, pressing him closer to her satin heat. Her other hand reached behind her back, hungry to pleasure him as intimately as he was pleasuring her.

After a small struggle that only increased Catlin's anticipation, Lindsay managed to undo his stubborn jeans zipper. The small sound of metal teeth parting was like a ragged breath. Her fingers sought the opening in his briefs, found it and released his hot male flesh from confinement.

Catlin clenched his teeth at the sweet torment of Lindsay's hand loving him. Slowly his fingers slid into her, stroking her until her hips moved in the rhythms of hunger and desire. He watched the languid movements in the mirror, felt her heat and sensual abandon and saw her hand warm and hungry around him.

And then he could bear watching no more. He closed his eyes and moved his hips as she was moving. For long, aching moments they caressed each other, wanting more but unable to do anything about it because what they had right then felt too good to stop. Finally he forced his fingers to withdraw from the wild honey of her body, only to return again and then again for the sheer pleasure of feeling her melt in his hand.

"You look like you'd be better off lying down," Catlin said, slowly releasing her hot, soft center.

Lindsay took a deep, ragged breath. "I think—" Her voice broke. "I know. You too."

Catlin ran his palms over the firm swell of Lindsay's bare buttocks, flexed his fingers sensually into the resilient flesh, and watched her tremble in response. Knowing he shouldn't, unable to stop himself, he smoothed each hand around her waist and then up beneath the teddy once more, caressing her erect nipples until she bit her lip in an effort not to moan aloud.

"Catlin—"

With a reluctance that said more than any words could have, Catlin squeezed Lindsay's breasts once more, then slowly pulled her teddy into place between her legs and fastened it, knowing that if he saw her uncovered just once more he would lose control and take her wherever they were, whoever might be listening.

As Lindsay brushed past Catlin on her way into the bedroom, she gave his exposed, aroused flesh a possessive look that made him bare his teeth in something more than a smile. He stepped out of the bathroom and closed the door, watching while she lay on her side and turned toward him. Her breasts were taut, full, and her nipples were the tempting centers of lacy flowers.

Catlin pulled off his clothes with impatient motions, wanting only to be naked. She watched while he came to her with a soundless, powerful stride that made her weak with anticipation. When he bent over her and his hand moved from her ankle to her thigh, she shifted, opening her legs in answer to the silent, hot pressure of his fingers.

"I thought—" Lindsay whispered, then bit back a cry as Catlin's nails raked lightly over the teddy's snaps, making her feel as though she had brushed against a live electrical wire. "I thought you didn't want to," she whispered, the words as ragged as the breath tearing through her body.

"Do I look like a man who doesn't want to?" he retorted very softly, smiling as her glance swept down his body and lingered with open hunger.

"Then why did you—" Lindsay's breath hissed in suddenly as Catlin's fingers toyed with the teddy's snaps.

"This?" he asked, running his fingertip maddeningly over the fastenings.

She nodded, unable to speak for fear that her words would come out as a passionate cry that would carry all too clearly.

"Because," Catlin whispered, sliding his finger into the opening between the snaps, "I like undressing you."

Lindsay's body arched in a sensual reflex that opened her completely to Catlin. He moved swiftly, kneeling between her legs, teasing her until she moaned very softly and he smiled.

"I fastened this," he murmured, watching her, feeling her heat come to meet him again, "because I knew if I saw you again, I would take you right there in the bathroom until we both screamed with pleasure. Then I remembered that damn bug."

"Does that mean we can't—"

Catlin's probing, teasing touch took away Lindsay's words, took away her breath, took everything from her but the hot race of pleasure as he found and caressed the tight feminine nub hidden within her folded softness. She twisted, trying to increase the pressure of his caress, and he evaded even as he teased her until she shivered and melted in his hand.

"Ahh, dragon, you're killing me by inches," she moaned.

"No, I'm not. Not yet." The teddy's snaps gave way with two soft sounds. Catlin slid his hands beneath Lindsay's knees and pressed until her legs flexed deeply, giving her to him without reservation. "But I'm going to."

As she looked from his hot golden eyes to the hard male body slowly, slowly taking her, she felt the tiny shuddering ecstasy well from deep within her. He felt it, too. She saw the pleasure that was almost pain tighten his face while he withdrew from her as slowly as he had entered. Then he was pressing against her again, filling her even as she melted around him, withdrawing, coming to her once more, slowly, slowly.

The incremental withdrawal and even more gradual return made Lindsay moan helplessly. Catlin caught the sound with his mouth as he slid by slow inches into her again. Her eyelids fluttered down and she moved with abandoned grace, matching his movements as though the two of them lived in slow motion, a lifetime in each joining, each retreat, and she moaned with each tiny movement, wanting him fully, all of him buried in her softness.

Catlin lifted his head, wanting to watch Lindsay, wanting to memorize each moment, to make it last forever because he had never felt so alive, so much a man, so many currents of wild pleasure making him tighten until he wanted to scream the release he felt gathering inside him.

Catlin withdrew again, drawing a husky groan of pleasure and protest from Lindsay. Her eyes opened slowly, dazed with the sensations consuming her. As he took her softness again, he felt it happen for her, tiny convulsions of ecstasy rippling through her, caressing the rigid male flesh held within her body. Gently he covered her mouth with his hand, muffling her husky, helpless cries. He watched ecstasy transform her as he continued the tender penetration until he was so deeply a part of her that he could feel her climax as though it were his own. And then he realized that it was his, a shuddering wildness sweeping through him that was both gentle and more overwhelming than anything he had ever known, coming in slow motion, exploding softly.

He saw her watching him, smiling in the knowledge of his release even as ecstasy swept through her again. He started to say her name but could not, for the intimate ripples of her body were his, too. He thought he would die from the endless, gentle explosions that were hotter and sweeter with each shuddering pulse. He had no breath, no thought, no sight, nothing but the ecstasy consuming him, and he wondered if this was what it felt like to die.

25

"COME ON, COME ON," O'Donnel muttered urgently, looking at the luminous face of his watch. "I told you to let Catlin lose you after six minutes and it's been—"

The sound of the radio cut off O'Donnel's words.

"This is Five. Is One on?"

"One here," Stone said, thumbing down the transmit button on the radio that had a built-in scrambler to discourage the thousands of citizens and crooks who enjoyed eavesdropping on police communications frequencies.

"I let them get away on Market. Am heading for the rendezvous on Stockton. Out."

O'Donnel sighed as Stone replaced the mike on its bracket beneath the dash. Stone gave the younger man an amused look.

"Relax, Terry. This is the easy part."

"No way," O'Donnel retorted. "Waiting is the hardest part of all. What if the whole thing was a ruse to draw Catlin and Lindsay off alone and then scrag them?"

"Easier said than done, with Catlin."

"He isn't armed."

"He still had his hands when I last checked," Stone said dryly.

"Not much range in them."

"Catlin didn't argue the toss," pointed out Stone. "It's his ass. He's used to covering it."

O'Donnel leaned back and settled in to wait. Just down the street was Wo Fong's All-Night Grocery—at least, O'Donnel assumed that was what the ideographs translated into. Catlin had told them the address and the name. The address on Stockton Street had been easy to decipher. The name they had to take on faith.

On either side of the street there were bars bearing flashing scarlet ideographs, two movie houses showing old spaghetti Westerns and Bruce Lee kung fu epics, several hotels that looked as though they asked no questions and told no tales and an "adult" bookstore for the unimaginative reader.

"Wonder if the pornography is in Chinese?" O'Donnel asked idly.

"What makes you think it needs translation?"

The younger man thought about it for an instant and laughed. "You're right. Grainy black-and-white close-ups transcend linguistic boundaries. Sort of an international hands across the water, as it were. Well, not *hands*, exactly."

Laughter faded into silence as both men watched Fong's All-Night Grocery in the truck's side mirrors. There was little chance of the agents being noticed, for they were more than a full block from the store and were driving a grimy Ford pickup with a camper shell. They could have been working men looking for somewhere to relax the night before beginning the weekly grind. Several collapsed beer cans decorated the dash, wordlessly explaining why the occupants were inside the car rather than prowling the streets along with the mixed Anglo and Chinese crowd outside.

Both agents wore work clothes that matched the grubby truck, although the effect would have been somewhat diminished if anyone had gotten close enough to see Stone's neatly clipped silver hair beneath the crumpled Giants baseball cap. Both men sipped coffee that had been substituted for Budweiser in their beer cans. Regulation FBI pistols and holsters were hidden beneath dark windbreakers. Sawed-off shotguns were clipped in a holder beneath the dash. A battered tool case under Stone's feet held extra rounds and binoculars that had been developed for night fighting in Vietnam.

"Uh-oh," said O'Donnel, setting aside his coffee. "Here come two more whores."

Stone watched the tightly dressed women stroll down the sidewalk toward them, rolling their hips and eyes at passing men. He let out a sound of relief when two eager customers snagged the women from a passing car. Short of flashing a badge, it was almost impossible to discourage streetwalkers looking for a fast fifty bucks and a few minutes out of San Francisco's raw night wind.

"How much more time?" Stone asked.

"Three minutes."

Stone bent down until he could use the radio without being noticed from the sidewalk. He punched in the transmit button.

"This is One. Anyone in place besides Three, Four and Nine?"

"Twelve." "Five." "Ten." "Two."

The calls came in. Stone waited for five seconds but no more units answered. "All right. Three and Four will follow the subjects. Ten will take the left parallel. Twelve will take the right. Five, stay in reserve behind Twelve. Two, back up Ten. Six, Seven, Eight and Eleven, call in when you get close enough to do us any good."

The units checked in one by one, acknowledging their orders. Stone glanced around casually, but could spot only unit Three, a man and a woman sitting close together in the front seat of a Plymouth parked just outside one of the bars.

"You know," O'Donnel said conversationally, looking at the stream of Toyotas, Nissans, Hondas, BMWs, Saabs, Volvos and Volkswagens surging down the city streets, "some day old Uncle Sam is going to get smart and realize that on the West Coast, damn near the only inexpensive American cars sold are bought by the federal government. Or state and local police." He made a disgusted sound. "We might as well wear a neon sign when we're on surveillance as drive a cheap American car."

"Don't hold your breath waiting for the light to dawn on Congress," Stone said. "Can you imagine the stink in D.C. if politicians were asked to appropriate funds for buying a fleet of unAmerican surveillance cars? Shit Marie. You'd hear the screams of outrage all the way to Alaska."

"Do the politicians want us to catch crooks or prop up Detroit?" retorted O'Donnel.

Stone gave the young agent a sideways look. "Guess," he said succinctly.

What O'Donnel said in return was lost in the sudden crackle of the radio.

"*This is Twelve. A cab just turned onto Stockton two blocks south of rendezvous. Male and female Caucasians in backseat. Could be them.*"

"Twelve, this is One. Are you north or south of the store?" asked Stone.

"*North.*"

As one, O'Donnel and Stone checked the mirrors. There were several taxis in view. One turned right at the stoplight behind them, one drove on past and one turned into the glass-sprinkled parking lot of Wo Fong's All-Night Grocery. A man and a woman got out. They were too far away for the agents to distinguish faces, but the man moved like Catlin.

"*This is Two. Subjects just entered the store.*"

"Ten, this is One," Stone said tersely. "Can you see the back door?"

"*This is Ten. The alley is covered. No one—Shit!*"

Stone didn't bother reprimanding Ten for breaking federal law by swearing over the airwaves. "Were you burned?" he demanded urgently.

"*Close. I saw the lights coming on in time to duck. I'm parked right on top of the damn thing. Black late-model Mercedes, tinted windows, four doors. Gee, can you imagine that,*" Ten added sarcastically. "*The license plate light is out so I can't give you the numbers. Car is pulling into the back of the parking lot. I can't see any more.*"

There were a few seconds of silence, then a different voice came on. "*This is Two. Subjects are being frisked. Professional job of it, too. Looking under collars for bugs and up sleeves for knives. They're getting into the Mercedes now. Can't read the license plate on the front, either. Confirm black and four doors. It's turning south on Stockton.*"

"I don't envy Ten," said O'Donnel, starting up the truck without turning on the headlights. "I'd hate to follow a snail through the center of Chinatown on Saturday night, much less attempt a parallel surveillance down Grant Street.''

Stone grunted. "Ten is Jackson. He's worked here for years. He should be used to the crowds, the narrow streets and the god-awful hills. Lord, to think people come from all over the world to this place. No accounting for tastes, I guess.''

The Mercedes moved south. Around it, surrounding it, unseen watchers fell into position.

Stone reached for the mike. "Two, this is One. Take the next street over so that if Ten gets bottled up on Grant you'll be in place."

"Roger."

Using a small, carefully shielded flashlight, Stone looked at a street map and tried to anticipate the Mercedes. He picked up the mike again.

"Five, this is One. Pull ahead and take Powell to Market. Turn south on Third. I've got a feeling they're headed for the docks."

As soon as Five had acknowledged, another unit came on.

"One, this is Seven. We're on Powell right now, heading north, between Post and Sutter."

"One this is Eight. We're on Taylor heading north, between O'Farrell and Geary."

"Roger, Seven and Eight. Five, try to stay at least a block ahead of the subjects. Seven and Eight will take Third. Do you copy?''

The units acknowledged. A half mile away, two inexpensive American cars simultaneously made illegal U-turns in the center of different blocks and headed south to converge on Third Street. Back in Chinatown, Four and Three switched places, changing the profile of the car that was working in close to the Mercedes.

"One, this is Four. Subject is pulling over to the side of the road just past Maude."

"Probably checking for tails. Go on by," Stone ordered. "Ten, switch with Four where Stockton crosses O'Farrel. Wait until the Mercedes moves before you take up position. Five, take the backup on the right parallel. Two, you're the lead on the right parallel now. Units on left parallel be ready to take over primary surveillance if subject U-turns.''

Units acknowledged one after another. O'Donnel waited with no outward impatience, watching traffic in the driving mirrors, ready to pull out onto Stockton at a moment's notice. The Mercedes stayed parked.

''Okay,'' Stone said to O'Donnel. ''Nice and slow. Make up about six blocks on them.''

O'Donnel switched on the lights and pulled into traffic. Thirty seconds later the radio crackled to life again.

''One this is Three. Subject U-turned. Going away fast!''

''Five and Twelve, do you copy!'' said Stone.

Both units acknowledged.

Stone sat tightly, swearing beneath his breath. Half his units were arrayed along the waterfront that the Mercedes was now heading away from. But the waterfront was the logical place for an overseas shipment to arrive. Stone was betting heavily on that. He was also betting that anything as old, cumbersome and valuable as the bronzes wouldn't be moved around any more than absolutely necessary.

''What if they shipped them into Marin County?'' O'Donnel asked suddenly.

Stone didn't answer. The same thought was haunting him.

''Subject turning left onto Bush.''

Stone waited, prayed.

''Subject turning left onto Powell.''

Stone held the microphone as though if he just squeezed it hard enough, the right words would come out.

''Subject turning left onto Sutter.''

''Come on,'' muttered O'Donnel, visualizing the Mercedes making a complete circuit of a city block. ''Come on, baby. One more time.''

''Subject turning right onto Stockton.''

O'Donnel let out a subdued whoop and then held his breath in case the Mercedes decided to do another lap just for the hell of it.

The Mercedes did just that, then pulled into a parking place along Stockton and watched the traffic go by for five minutes. The headlights of the cars had a subtle nimbus now, telling of moisture rapidly condensing in the air, forerunner of the city's famous fog. Stone watched the hands of his watch and tersely ordered the units to find a spot and stay there until further notice. Then he sat tight and thought of all the ways a surveillance could go sour. He had gotten up to fifteen separate disasters when the radio came to life again.

"U-turn. Repeat. U-turn. Subject now heading south on Stockton."

Stone's fingers loosened on the mike. He settled the map across his thighs and went back to positioning his units. Reports came in steadily. When the Mercedes turned south on Third Street, heading for the waterfront north of Hunters Point, Stone allowed himself a small feeling of triumph. He pushed down the transmit button.

"Unit Thirteen, this is One. Have you spotted the subject on Third?"

The distinctive *whap-whap-whap* of a helicopter's rotors accompanied Thirteen's response.

"That's a roger. We've got them dead center on the night scope. Southbound on Third. Patchy fog. Hardly any traffic. Better tell the guys down there to hang way back or they'll take a burn if he goes to ground again."

"Roger, Thirteen. All ground units, this is One. Rendezvous with me as per Plan Alpha. Thirteen, call me the instant that Mercedes chooses a warehouse."

Stone listened to the acknowledgments, then settled in and began to worry in earnest about the streamers of fog that were condensing across the face of the night.

INSIDE THE MERCEDES, Lindsay tried not to show her dismay when the driver shut off his headlights, made a sudden U-turn on the wet, gray waterfront street and pulled off onto a cross street that led between unlighted buildings. Though the engine remained on, the driver settled back in the seat, obviously not planning on going anywhere right away.

As before, Catlin had braced Lindsay during the sudden maneuver and then held her, letting her feel his relaxation, silently reassuring her that everything was all right. Privately he wasn't all that certain that everything was proceeding according to Stone's schedule. The Mercedes hadn't gone blasting the wrong way up a one-way street, but it had done most of the other things that were guaranteed to flush tails.

On the other hand, the FBI had a lot of highly trained manpower. That was what was required to combat evasive maneuvers on the part of a surveillance subject. The Bureau could afford to put a moving net of units around the Mercedes without giving away the game. Only once, back at Wo Fong's Grocery, had Catlin seen any sign of the Bureau's presence, and that had been a block away from the store, where Wu's men weren't likely to be anticipating surveillance.

But the waterfront road where they were now parked was deserted. The sheer numbers of the FBI would work against them here. Headlights would stand out like beacons against the drifts of fog. Catlin stared out the window and wondered if one of the aircraft he saw dancing above the city lights belonged to the FBI.

"It's all right," Catlin said softly against Lindsay's hair. "Look at all those lights across the bay. You don't get many nights as clear as this in San Francisco."

Lindsay took a deep breath and forced her fingers to relax on the fabric of Catlin's black denim jacket. "It's very pretty," she said mechanically.

Then she realized that Catlin was right. All around the bay, dots of incandescent silver and gold burned against the black velvet night. Patches of nebulous, translucent fog drifted over water and city alike, muting the brilliant lights without concealing them. The result was a view that was gauzy and crystalline at once, as though she were watching through a window where etched glass alternated with clear in a random pattern.

No traffic passed them. No other people were walking round. The driver of the Mercedes was a soundless, motionless silhouette against the windshield, and the mechanical purr of the idling car was barely audible. Only Lindsay and Catlin seemed alive within the black crystal and radiant fog of night.

"It doesn't look real," Lindsay said quietly.

"It isn't," murmured Catlin against her ear. "None of this is, remember?"

She turned and saw the harsh illumination of a distant streetlight reflected in his golden eyes. "It feels real," she whispered.

"It won't tomorrow."

Catlin's voice was a blend of certainty and regret. He knew what happened when the undercover game was over, how the mind adjusted very quickly to changed circumstances. Lindsay didn't understand that. Not yet. She would soon, though. She would be dropped back into her old life, her old reality reaching out to enfold her; and that reality didn't include him.

Lindsay rested her cheek against Catlin's chest and tried to imagine tomorrow. She couldn't. She could imagine nothing beyond the moment when she would see one of Qin's magnificent charioteers. She felt as though she had worked her entire life for the coming instant, the culmination of so many dreams, so many fears. That was all that was real. That was all that mattered. Nor would that change tomorrow.

"It will always be—" she began.

Lindsay's words ended in a startled sound as the Mercedes darted out and made another unexpected U-turn before resuming its slow prowling of Third Street. Buildings bulked blackly along the waterfront, warehouses where cargo was stored before being shipped across the face of America by truck or rail.

"I hope that's the last of it," Lindsay said tartly, suspecting that the Chinese driver spoke more English than he had acknowledged up to now. "Being dragged out of bed at midnight is bad enough. Being jerked around by San Francisco's answer to Mario Andretti is adding injury to insult.''

Catlin's laughter, like the silent pressure of his embrace, approved of Lindsay's resilience. He knew that the game of sudden starts and stops and wild turns were eating away at her nerves, reminding her of just how helpless the two of them had become once they had entered the black Mercedes.

"Oh, I think our silent friend up front has about accepted the fact that I lost any tails long before we showed up at Wo Fong's Grocery,'' Catlin said, shifting his arm until he could read the luminous face of his watch. "He's just shadow boxing to kill time before the banks in Hong Kong begin answering their phones. It shouldn't be long now.''

The driver's hands tightened on the steering wheel. Other than that, there was no response to Catlin's baiting. A few minutes later, the driver killed the headlights again. The darkened Mercedes prowled through the misty night, visible only in the pools of illumination thrown by occasional streetlights.

In a manner characteristic of the Bay Area, the streamers of mist that had been so fragile a few minutes before had swelled and thickened into true fog. The driver switched on the windshield wipers in answer to the wet, clinging fog, but not the headlights. He kept on driving as though confident that the street was deserted. Catlin hoped the driver was right—without headlights, the visibility was down to twenty feet.

With the usual lack of warning, the driver made a hard left into an opening between buildings that was too narrow to be called a street and too wide to be a driveway. No lights showed in any of the buildings, nor was there any gleam of reflected illumination from windows. The driver slowed, then blinked the parking lights on and off several times.

Ahead and to the right a slender glimmer of light appeared. Slowly it widened into a tall rectangular doorway leading into a warehouse. The driver accelerated smoothly up the road and into the warehouse. Three Chinese men appeared and wrestled the sagging door shut.

Catlin looked at his watch, marking down the instant that the Mercedes had vanished inside the warehouse. If the FBI hadn't lost them in the U-turns and fog, the clock was running. Stone would wait forty-five minutes before he blew the lid off the night. Catlin planned to be out of the way by then. He had seen too many hostages killed by desperate, foolish men to risk Lindsay's life that way.

A quick look around told him that the warehouse was small and probably had been abandoned years ago. Junk slumped amorphously in the corners, rotting and rusting in slow dissolution. Several cars and a truck had left tire tracks in the glaze of time and dust that covered the stained concrete floor. High up along the walls, openings that had once been windows were boarded over. The only interior illumination came from the headlights of two cars that had been angled so as to illuminate the far side of the small delivery truck parked sideways between them.

There were eight people visible. Three were Mrs. Zhu, Mr. Pao and Chen Yi. With them were four men whose body language fairly screamed *soldier*. Although no weapons were visible, the men hovered particularly close to Yi. All the mainland Chinese wore dark blue slacks and the military-cut jacket that Mao had made popular.

Hsiang Wu, wearing a pearl gray silk suit, stood apart from the representatives of the PRC. The three men who had dragged shut the old-fashioned door reappeared to stand impassively behind Wu.

"Aren't they—" began Lindsay, looking at the men standing near Wu.

"Yes," Catlin said softly, recognizing the bodyguards who had dragged Lee Tran away.

Wu's right hand gripped the handle of a rectangular leather briefcase that could have held anything from a bag lunch to an Uzi. Knowing Wu, Catlin would have taken bets on either possibility.

There was a distinct sound as the driver released the door locks on the Mercedes.

One of Wu's men came forward, opened the back door of the car and politely handed Lindsay out. Catlin followed, keeping track of the whereabouts of Wu's bodyguards and the Chinese soldiers at all times. It was more habit than necessity; at that point, Catlin didn't expect any trouble. If any problem arose it would be after the money had been transferred between banks in Hong Kong.

"I'll do the talking," Catlin said to Lindsay as they approached Wu. Before Wu could begin any lengthy Mandarin formalities, Catlin said crisply in English, "It's Monday in Hong Kong, the banks are answering their phones and there's no reason to screw around anymore. Where are the bronzes?"

"They are here," Wu said calmly, gesturing toward the truck. "The phone is here," he continued, opening the briefcase to reveal a cellular phone. "The truck is here, as is the man who will drive you." Wu signaled to the Chinese who had driven the Mercedes. "Start the truck for the very cautious Mr. Rousseau. Let him see that all is in proper order."

The driver opened the door, stepped into the truck and started the engine. It ran smoothly. The man looked at Catlin, who nodded.

"Fine. Shut it off, get out and leave the keys in the ignition," Catlin said. "I'm driving it out of here myself."

The man looked to Wu, who shrugged. "As I said, a cautious man. Wait in the Mercedes, Sen. I will not be needing you any further tonight."

Lindsay looked from Catlin to Wu. The harsh sidelighting from the cars made both men's facial bones stand out in high relief, set off by shadows that were angular, unexpected, almost satanic in their impact.

"The bronzes are uncrated on the far side of the truck," continued Wu. "Take as much time as you require, daughter. They are pieces of greatness that are infinitely worthy of your discriminating eye."

Catlin's hand closed around Lindsay's arm when she would have stepped forward eagerly. Startled, she turned toward him so quickly that her hair fanned out.

"We're doing this together, honey cat," he said, smiling, but it was a smile that made her remember how hard he could be at times. "Remember? I'm with you every step of the way. You're never out of my reach."

Lindsay looked into Catlin's amber eyes and felt cold. "I remember," she whispered.

Together they walked around the front of the truck. Then they stopped as suddenly and completely as though their feet had been bolted to the floor.

Glowing within the harsh radiance of the headlights, a Qin charioteer sat in ancient splendor, arms slightly extended to hold the tarnished silver reins of the two horses that stood at attention in front of the war chariot. The charioteer's hair was bound in a complex knot at the top of his head. His face was both serene and very martial. The thick sleeves of his uniform hung so gracefully from his arms that it was impossible to believe that the uniform was made of bronze rather than cloth. The hands were utterly lifelike, so much so that Lindsay felt that if she looked closely enough she would surely see calluses on the driver's fingers from a lifetime of handling heavy leather reins.

Slowly Lindsay approached the chariot. The horses stood alertly, eternally poised, ears pricked forward. The animals' eyes were carnelian and the plume rising gracefully between their ears was made of pure, braided gold. Muscles rippled beneath the horses' smooth bronze hides, giving them an aura of strength that was almost intimidating. Lindsay half expected one of them to toss its head and snort a warning of her presence.

The chariot itself was closed rather than open as the Roman war chariots had been. A rectangular box large enough to carry several men was balanced on the single axle directly behind the driver. An oval, umbrellalike roof extended beyond the edges of the box far enough to protect the driver from the elements or a rain of arrows.

Lindsay walked slowly, unaware of moving, totally absorbed in the bronzes. Their patina was a fine blue-green, with a jadelike texture that was both rare and exquisite. Gradually the bronzes' fine details began to penetrate the initial, almost overwhelming impact of the group as a whole.

With every step Lindsay took as she circled the chariot, inlays of gold and age-darkened silver, copper and malachite, turquoise and carnelian shimmered in a silent cry for her attention. The inlaid patterns were dense, intricate, magnificent, of an artistry that exceeded any she had ever seen. When newly made, Qin's charioteer must have resembled the colorful, complexly patterned lacquer boxes that had ultimately supplanted bronzes in Han times. Certainly the designs were very similar, a stunning, sensuous wealth of color, design and texture.

Lindsay's glance went from the horses' carnelian hooves to the gracefully braided silver harness. The bronze shaft of the chariot was suspended between the two animals. Her eyes followed the line back to the chariot itself. The vehicle was inlaid with a sinuous gold and silver pattern that could have been flowering vines or currents of wind and rain. The charioteer's uniform was almost a brocade of inlay, designs too dense to separate at a glance. His eyes were of beaten sliver and had been lightly polished to give them a lifelike gleam.

The man, horses and chariot were so perfectly proportioned that Lindsay felt as though she were too large, rather than that they were less than life-size. They were alive in a way that defied explanation or understanding. The hair stirred on her neck in primal response as she stood in the crumbling warehouse and watched Qin's charioteer driving toward her across a bridge of time, making a mockery of the millennia between the First Emperor's life and her own.

The charioteer's face seemed to come closer, a face both individual and a composite of every Chinese who had ever lived. She saw into his eyes and then beyond, suddenly feeling the presence of the countless peasants who had given their lives to the many-faced goddess of the land, sowing and reaping, birthing and living and dying, crying and laughing and enduring, always enduring, a river of humanity running down into the fathomless sea of time, their ghosts returning as a luminous rain of art that enriched the future's unborn generations.

So much time, so much endurance, so many lives, so little chance to laugh and live. Lindsay could hear a million million voices calling soundlessly from the richness of bronze and see her mother's tears in the beaten silver of the charioteer's eyes.

"Lindsay?"

She turned toward Catlin's voice, hearing him despite the endless wave of time and humanity breaking over her. The look on his face told her that he had called her name more than once, one name among many, one call among millions. Beyond time stood Zhu and Pao, Yi and Wu, the future watching her out of enigmatic black eyes. She felt their silent insistence on her answer, the future waiting for the word to be spoken so that the river could go on flowing down to the sea. Behind her came the aching, enduring cries of the past, lives beyond counting or numbering, people who had endured beyond reason or comprehension—

"Lindsay."

—and Catlin in front of her, the present beckoning. She half turned, her hand held out to the charioteer, her lips forming a silent plea that she not have to go on to the next instant, that she not have to speak the next words. The charioteer watched her with eyes the color of tears before he blurred and ran in hot silver torrents down her cheeks.

"Lindsay."

"Oh, Catlin," she said, turning toward him. "I'm sorry—so sorry. They're—they're fakes!"

26

THERE WAS an explosion of Mandarin and English shouts, indignation and disbelief, charges and countercharges. Catlin didn't bother to sort them out. At that instant questions and expostulations were irrelevant. Lindsay's life was not, and it was a very ancient tradition to shoot the messenger who brought bad news.

With cold yellow eyes Catlin measured the distance to the delivery truck, the obstacles to be neutralized on the way there and the various methods of doing so without getting Lindsay killed. Four soldiers of the PRC and two of Wu's chunky bodyguards were in a position to prevent the truck's escape.

Catlin never considered waiting for the FBI. Even if Stone hadn't lost them in the sudden fog, it had been less than fifteen minutes since the Mercedes had entered the abandoned warehouse. The FBI, assuming they were around, wouldn't act for another half hour. That would be far too late for Lindsay.

"Silence!"

Chen Yi's authoritative command sliced through the raised voices with the ease of a knife through water. He looked around disdainfully.

"Esteemed Comrade Zhu," he said in sardonic, staccato Mandarin, "and my equally esteemed Comrade Pao, you have the answer for which you have searched half a world with such great dedication. The face of China has not been blackened by contamination of Mao's pure policies. The honorable Comrade Deng has not permitted capitalist-induced greed to corrupt us. China's honor remains a model for the less civilized countries of the world. The truth of these statements is cast in bronze," he said, gesturing carelessly toward the charioteer and horses. "By the word of Miss Danner, your own carefully chosen and tested expert, those bronzes did not come from Xi'an. They are frauds."

Zhu, Pao and Wu burst into fresh protestations, their voices shrill, overlapping, chaotic.

Catlin kept his hand on Lindsay's arm, discreetly easing her around the charioteer that stood between them and the truck. She neither protested nor aided him. Tears ran silently down her cheeks. As Catlin moved closer to the truck, he chose and re-chose his targets with each shift in the group between him and the truck's door. He fervently hoped that everyone would be too caught up in the argument to notice the slow escape of the woman who had caused it.

It was Wu who first realized the futility of yelling at the impassive, subtly triumphant Chen Yi. Wu turned and saw Lindsay moving away from a bronze horse's eternally raised head.

"What have you done to me, miserable daughter?" he cried in Mandarin. "Why have you so foully lied? These bronzes are as true as you are craven! With their own eyes Madame Zhu and Mr. Pao saw the charioteer emerge from Mount Li's sacred earth! What has your lick-spittle paramour done to change your truths to lies?"

Lindsay looked at the charioteer's beaten silver eyes and shook her head, saying nothing.

"Control yourself, foolish one," Yi said coldly, snapping shut his lighter and exhaling a stream of smoke toward Wu. "The honorable Miss Danner has nothing to gain by calling the charioteer false, and much to lose in addition to her commission on the sale. It is known across the land that she has promised Mr. Catlin a Qin charioteer. It is also known that she is most humble and eager to please her chosen master. She has no reason to call the bronzes false except the obvious one: they are false!"

Using a theatrical gesture that was at odds with his normally controlled manner, Yi abruptly extended his arm to full length and pointed toward the chariot itself.

"Look at that miserable excuse for craftsmanship," he commanded, his voice vibrating with contempt. "Count the spokes in the wheel. Count them!"

The authority in Yi's voice was such that everyone except Catlin turned toward the wheel, silently counting spokes. With barely controlled urgency, Catlin took advantage of the shift in attention to move Lindsay closer to the truck.

"Stop her!" screamed Madame Zhu suddenly, catching the flash of Lindsay's bright hair from the corner of her eye. "The charioteer is from Xi'an! She is the paid lackey of the revisionist dog Chen Yi! Stop her!"

Several of the soldiers began reaching beneath their civilian tunics. Catlin shoved Lindsay behind himself even as he took two steps and leaped into the air in a high karate kick that ended at a soldier's head. The man went down as though shot and stayed there.

As Catlin landed he spun on the ball of one foot while the other lashed out in a series of controlled side kicks so rapid that they were a blur. Two more soldiers went down. The fourth one managed to pull his gun free of its holster. The callused edge of Catlin's palm broke the man's wrist. An instant later Catlin's elbow shot into the soldier's diaphragm. Before the man hit the floor, Catlin had taken the weapon and trained it on Wu.

"If your men move, you die," Catlin said, his voice flat.

Wu looked at Catlin for a long moment and found no reason to doubt him. Wu spoke sharply. The three bodyguards froze, weapons drawn but not yet aimed.

"Come here," Catlin said to Wu.

Slowly Wu walked toward Catlin.

"Closer."

Wu kept walking until the gun's muzzle was only inches from his chest. Catlin's left hand snaked out, spun Wu around and yanked him against Catlin's body.

"Tell your men to put their guns on the floor and then kick them as far as they can to the back of the warehouse. One at a time."

In the silence, the sound of a metal skidding over concrete was very loud as the bodyguards sent their guns spinning into the darkness one at a time.

"Now tell them to lie facedown and hold their ankles with their hands. If they let go, I'll assume they're reaching for a second gun. Make sure they understand that, Wu. Your life depends on it."

Within seconds the three Chinese had performed the awkward maneuver.

"Call your driver over here," said Catlin, watching everyone with rapid flicks of his eyes, waiting for the first covert motion toward a hidden weapon. "Tell him to walk backward. If I see his face or a gun, you both die."

Wu called out instructions in rapid Mandarin.

One of the Chinese soldiers on the floor groaned and vomited weakly. Catlin glanced at him for an instant, dismissed him and resumed watching Pao's hand creep toward his tunic.

"That's the problem with shoulder holsters and button-front Mao shirts," Catlin said conversationally. "By the time the second button is undone, you're dead. Take out the weapon, put it on the floor and kick it under the truck."

Pao's hand twitched, then resumed unbuttoning his military jacket. Very carefully he followed Catlin's orders, proving that Catlin had been correct in his earlier estimate of Pao: the man spoke excellent, colloquial English. Yi looked from Catlin to Pao and smiled. Catlin didn't notice. Wu's driver was backing around the front of the truck, taking great care to keep his hands visible and his face hidden.

"The keys to the Mercedes," Catlin said in a clipped voice.

The driver didn't bother to protest that he didn't know English. "They're in the ignition," he said quickly.

"Check on it, Lindsay," Catlin ordered. "Go around and to my right. If you see anything you don't like, scream."

At first Lindsay thought her muscles weren't going to respond to her commands. Then the urgent requirements of the moment overrode the adrenaline flooding violently through her body in the aftermath of violence. She walked around the truck. A few instants later her voice echoed back through the warehouse.

"The keys are here."

"Get in and start the engine," Catlin ordered.

Wu shifted as the Mercedes snarled to life. Catlin's arm tightened warningly across Wu's neck at the same instant that the gun muzzle pressed coldly into his ear. Wu froze.

Catlin turned toward Yi. "I overflow with desolation and abject apologies," Catlin said in Mandarin, "but I have to insist that you and your esteemed comrades open the warehouse door for me. Such manual labor is of course beneath your honorable station in life, but necessity must sometimes overrule custom. If the humble life of Mr. Hsiang Wu is not enough inducement for your labor, then I will add the miserable Comrade Pao's existence to the measure."

"We Chinese are great connoisseurs of necessity," Yi said in English.

The three representatives of the PRC turned to go to the door. Catlin dragged Wu to a point where he could watch the downed soldiers, Wu's bodyguards and the three people struggling with the warped door. Finally they managed to force an opening large enough for the Mercedes to pass through.

Catlin's face didn't show the relief that burst quietly in him. He had been ready to ram the truck through the closed doors if he had to, but had been afraid of triggering a barrage of gunfire if the FBI had managed to surround the warehouse. He glanced quickly at his watch. Nineteen minutes, seventeen seconds. He looked at the soldiers. Only the one who had gagged was moving, and he was no longer a threat.

With no warning Catlin turned and half carried, half dragged Wu toward the waiting Mercedes.

"Move over," commanded Catlin.

Lindsay scrambled over the gearshift into the passenger seat. In a single motion Catlin shoved Wu away, slid into the Mercedes, slammed the door and aimed the car toward the narrow opening.

"Get down," Catlin said curtly, not looking away from the slit leading into the safety of the night. "All the way to the floor."

Lightless, a black shadow knifing through the swirling fog, the Mercedes shot through the opening and accelerated south, going away from the FBI cars that were slowly converging on the area, combing the darkened warehouses for signs of life. The cars were still nearly a mile north of the abandoned warehouse, for that was where the helicopter had lost the Mercedes in the first condensations of heavy fog.

Driving quickly, yet skillfully Catlin threaded his way back to the city. After the first two miles he flipped on the headlights and pulled Lindsay back onto the front seat. He glanced at her pale, tight face and smoothed his hand once over her tangled hair.

"You don't have to be brave anymore," he said softly. "Go ahead and let it out. It's all over now but the cheering."

Lindsay looked at Catlin and wished that she could cry or cheer. But she could not. She was drained of emotion.

"I'm not brave," she said, remembering her raw fear when Catlin had shoved her away and exploded into the midst of the four Chinese soldiers, four men down before she could even scream. "I'm the kind who just—goes numb."

"You stayed in control of yourself," Catlin said, stroking Lindsay's cheek with the back of his fingers. "You could still think, still act. That's all that bravery is. The rest is posturing."

Lindsay let out a long breath and leaned against the seat. She said nothing. Neither did Catlin. No one followed them. No one noticed them. He parked the Mercedes a few blocks from their hotel and they walked through clinging fog. Catlin checked the rooms automatically. They were empty. With quick motions he removed the bugs and flushed them down the toilet. Then he pulled Lindsay into the hotel room and shot the bolt behind her.

"Why don't you lie down?" he suggested, guiding her toward the bed. "Stone will find the warehouse sooner or later, and then he'll be here in hell's own rush, looking for blood."

Lindsay sank onto the bed. "Shouldn't we call him?"

Catlin shrugged. "He'll find us soon enough. Close your eyes, honey cat. Sleep if you can. You'll need it. Stone will have a thousand questions, and then he'll have a thousand more. He'll keep asking them until you feel like screaming."

"Aren't you going to sleep?" Lindsay asked, wanting to have Catlin beside her, to curl up in his arms and let the world slide away, leaving only peace behind.

He looked at her for a long moment, wanting her, feeling as though someone were sawing on him with a dull knife. "Not yet," he said quietly.

Catlin turned away and pulled his suitcase out of the closet. Lindsay watched while he began folding and packing his clothes with the efficient motions of a man who has spent most of his life traveling.

"Catlin?"

His hands paused.

"Can't you do that in the morning?" she asked.

"It is the morning," he pointed out, then kept talking before Lindsay could object further. "When Stone goes at you like a cat after a baby bird, remember that you don't have to tell him one damn thing you don't want to. You don't owe him a handful of spit. If Wu is smart or lucky, he'll be gone before Stone finds the warehouse. If not," Catlin added, shrugging, "there's damn all Stone can do to prosecute Wu for being suckered by a batch of bad bronzes."

Lindsay looked away. Catlin watched her, remembering the emotion that had transfigured her face as she reached toward Qin's magnificent charioteer in the instant before she had denounced the bronze's worth.

"Is that why you said they were fake?" Catlin asked softly. "Did you figure out that was the only way to save Wu from his own reckless hatred of the People's Republic?"

Slowly Lindsay met Catlin's amber eyes. "That was part of . And Yi, watched over by Pao and Zhu. In their own ways, oth Wu and Yi are good and honorable men." She straight- ned and met Catlin's eyes squarely. "But most of all it was for e. I couldn't bear to have my honesty used to pull apart a untry and a people I love. So I—" her voice broke and then e went on. "I lied."

"Yi was right," Catlin said slowly, watching the golden fall f Lindsay's hair over her cheeks, hearing the shades of silver her husky voice, "You are your mother's daughter."

"I don't understand."

"He told me once that your mother loved the people of hina even more than she loved her God. And you love them ore than you love your god—truth."

Lindsay closed her eyes.

"It will be harder for you than it was for your mother," ntinued Catlin. "She never had to confront the results of her hoice, because she never admitted that she had made one. You ave. Every day of your life, every headline you read, you'll ask ourself if you did the right thing."

"Yes," Lindsay whispered, her eyes wide and dark. "I'm lready asking. I suppose it would be the same if I had told the uth about Qin's charioteer."

"No. It would be worse. Every time you read about crop ailure and famine in China for lack of Western fertilizer, or hinese children dying for lack of Western immunization, or hole villages wiped out by storms that could have been tracked y Western weather satellites, you would have asked yourself you could have prevented it. You would have felt individu- lly responsible for every death, every maimed life."

"How did you know?" Lindsay asked, her voice tight. "I idn't even know it myself until I saw the charioteer's eyes."

"In some ways we're a lot like each other," Catlin said, arning away again, folding clothes, packing them.

"I wanted to warn you, but I didn't know what I was going do until I did it." Lindsay laughed oddly. "And I haven't ven thanked you."

"For what?"

"Saving my life."

"I don't think—"

"I do," she said rapidly, cutting off his words. "Mrs. Zh
would have killed me and never looked back. I think Yi woul
have, too. And even—Wu. You were right again, Catlin. Yo
were the only one who would take a bullet for me."

"It's over now," he said. "You don't have to worry about *i
anymore."

Catlin pulled a suit coat from the closet. Methodically h
transferred the coat to a special hanger, folded the cloth and
wedged it into the luggage.

"Are you angry?" Lindsay asked hoarsely. "Did you wan
me to say that the charioteer was real?"

Catlin looked up quickly, pinning Lindsay with his glance
wanting her to be very sure of the truth of his answer. "I
wasn't my decision to make, but no, I'm not angry. You di
what you thought was right despite the cost to you. If it mat
ters," he added bluntly, "I think you're one hell of a woman."

"If it matters?" Lindsay shook her head as though sh
couldn't believe what she was hearing. "Catlin, don't you know
that I love you?"

There was an instant of silence, of stillness, and then he re
sumed packing.

"No, I don't," Catlin said matter-of-factly. "And neither d
you."

Suddenly he wadded up the shirt he was packing and fired i
into the suitcase. In two tightly leashed strides he was beside th
bed.

"That's what I've been trying to tell you all along, but yo
didn't want to hear me," he said. His voice was deep, gritty
"So listen to me now, honey cat. Listen hard. None of this i
real. You've been living on an adrenaline roller coaster, an
what you have right now is a bad case of emotional whip
lash."

"No!"

"Yes," Catlin countered softly, taking Lindsay's chin in his hand. "I've never lied to you. I'm not going to start now. But I'm going to tell you a lot of things you'd rather not know. Listen to them. Listen to the truth."

Catlin looked into Lindsay's shocked, dark eyes and cursed silently. He didn't want to do this, but it came with the assignment he had accepted. He was here to protect her. He wasn't here to pay off Chen Yi at the cost of Lindsay's future.

Gently Catlin released her, savoring the warmth and softness of her skin even as he turned away from her.

"When I was in high school in a small town in Montana," he said, picking up the wadded shirt, "I was as wild as a northern wind. I was ready to stand the world on its ear and shake it until everything I ever wanted fell out into my hands." Beneath the black mustache, Catlin's mouth shifted into a hard smile. "I didn't want to be a cowhand like my uncle or a rule-bound ex-soldier like my dad, and I sure as hell didn't want to make cheese in France with my mother's people. I wanted freedom and adventure. Adrenaline."

Lindsay watched Catlin's face, his hands, the smooth coordination of his body. She listened, too, hearing answers to questions she had wanted to ask since the first time Catlin had appeared in her office: *Who is he? Where did he come from?*

"I graduated from high school, signed up for smoke jumper's school and married the girl next door all in one summer." Catlin looked at Lindsay, saw the intensity and the surprise on her face. "You know what smoke jumpers are?" he asked, ignoring the more obvious questions brought up by the fact of his marriage.

Lindsay shook her head, afraid to speak, to break the flow of words ending Catlin's long silence about his past.

"They're the crazy bastards who parachute out of airplanes to fight forest fires in places so rough and remote that there are no roads, no trails, nothing to mark the way but black columns of smoke boiling into the summer sky," explained Catlin. "You jump out with your ax, shovel, sleeping bag and emergency rations. When the fire is dead, you hack your way out to the nearest road over country that even the Indians never used. Usually you spend more time getting home than you did fighting fires."

"That sounds—dangerous."

Catlin smiled slightly. "That was its appeal for me. That and leaving the world a better place than I found it." He laughed once, softly, shaking his head. It had been a long time since he had thought about his life as a wild kid. "But I didn't fight fires after I graduated. It turned out that the skills I learned in smoke-jumping school were just what Air America needed."

"Air America?"

"The CIA's civilian airline in Asia," Catlin explained. "They needed kickers and loadmasters for all the supplies they were dropping back in the highlands of Vietnam. So one year Air America came to the smoke-jumping school in Montana and recruited damn near the whole graduating class. My class." He went to the closet, grabbed a handful of clothes and returned to the suitcase, talking as he packed. "I was barely eighteen. In two weeks I was kicking loads out the open door of a DC-3 flying the nap of some of the wildest country I'd ever seen."

For a moment Catlin stood without moving, his arms overflowing with clothes, his eyes looking back into the past.

"I'd been a kicker for about three months," he continued, "when I heard my boss trying to understand what some very excited French planter was saying about guerrilla movements over what became known as the Ho Chi Minh Trail. My mother was French, so understanding the planter was no problem for me. In five minutes I picked the planter clean of information. My boss was surprised, but not stupid. He had me jerked out of the air and into a liaison job the next day."

Catlin looked at the clothes in his hands as though he didn't recognize them.

"Did you like it?" Lindsay asked softly when the silence stretched.

"Liaison?" asked Catlin.

She nodded.

"You mean, did I miss the thrill of nearly getting bucked off a DC-3 without benefit of parachute?" Catlin asked wryly. "Yeah. I missed it. Like I said, I was young. But I was learning other things, some of them as dangerous in their own way as jumping without a chute. One of them was the Vietnamese language. The other was Chinese. I soaked them up the same way I had French. I couldn't believe it when the Caucasians around me simply didn't hear the differences in the two languages." He shrugged and resumed folding clothes. "To Americans, the ethnic Chinese businessman was the same as the Vietnamese peasant. To this day most Americans don't realize how much of the economic power in Vietnam was in the hands of the ethnic Chinese."

Methodically, Catlin added another shirt to his suitcase. "I had a different boss by then, but he was no slower than the first. He recognized the fact that I had a gift for languages. I was jerked out of liaison and dropped into a CIA language school. I didn't fight it. I had discovered that I loved languages almost as much as I loved adrenaline. Besides," he added with a sardonic twist to his mouth, "the school wasn't limited to intellectual pursuits. They taught me some things that were a hell of a lot more lethal than words. I had a gift for them, too."

Lindsay remembered the explosive moments of violence, Catlin moving with a speed and skill that were unexpected, stunning. Yet that same lethal body could move with exquisite grace to the requirements of *tai chi chuan* and touch her with consuming sensuality as a lover, teaching her things about herself that she had never known.

"I stayed in Asia," said Catlin, "and I learned. Somewhere along the way to my twenty-first birthday I lost my wife. We were too young, separated by too much distance and different experiences, and I was too fascinated by Asia to go back home and patch it all together. So one day I opened up a 'Dear John' letter and found that Susie was having another man's baby. I felt betrayed, furious. I blamed her for everything." He smiled crookedly. "Like I said. I was young. Really young."

"Why don't you be generous?" Lindsay suggested ironically. "Share a little of the blame with Susie. Other girls sent their husbands off to war and managed to be faithful through all the years of waiting."

Catlin gave Lindsay an amused glance. "They must have had more going for them than habit. That was all Susie and I had. Asia broke the habit." He shrugged. "It was a long time ago. Last I heard, Susie was happily married and had enough kids to start her own baseball team. I don't blame her any longer. She taught me something very valuable."

Lindsay waited motionlessly, sensing that she wasn't going to like what she heard next.

"I said I felt betrayed and furious, and I did—for maybe a day." Catlin's clear amber glance held Lindsay as surely as though his hand were still beneath her chin. "You see, I was already hooked on the shadow life. The other life, the real one, just didn't seem *real* anymore. The highs and lows and the sheer excitement of what I was doing in Asia were all-consuming. There was no perspective. Undercover life does that to you."

"As you said—you were young," Lindsay said evenly. "Lack of perspective isn't unusual when you're under twenty-one."

He smiled sadly, understanding what she was trying to say. She wasn't twenty-one; undercover life hadn't caused her to lose her emotional perspective.

"It's not that easy, Lindsay-love," Catlin said softly. "It's not that easy at all."

For the space of several breaths he looked at her, memorizing her as she sat on the bed, her face intent, her eyes the haunted color of deepest twilight. He didn't permit himself to think about how much he wanted her, because he didn't trust himself not to take what she would have given him. But the double game was over. The last lie had been spoken. If he went to her now, she would hate both of them in a few weeks or a few months, when the adrenaline wore off and the other world was real again. He knew that. She didn't. Not yet. That was what he had to teach her before he left.

"Susie taught me something," Catlin said gently, relentlessly, "but it was Mei who taught me the most. Mei was extraordinary—delicate, exotic, skilled, and by far the most sensual woman I'd ever known. She was also an adrenaline junkie, a whore for Lee Tran, a double agent, my lover, and an assassin who had killed nine men. I was to be her tenth. I was the best man she'd ever had in bed, so she put off killing me on the excuse that the information she could get from me was worth more to Lee Tran than my death."

Lindsay went pale, remembering the vicious outpouring of Cantonese and English in Wu's office when Catlin had come very close to killing Lee Tran. She understood why now. It didn't comfort her in the least.

"By the time Mei came to me," Catlin said, "I was so far into the double life that I believed all people were liars, killers, whores, cheats and thieves. It was a necessary belief. It reminded me never to turn my back, never to pull my punch, never to care about anyone but myself.

"There were two ways to survive the parts of Asia I lived and worked in," he continued. "Vast money or sheer ruthlessness. The CIA didn't use its appropriations to make its officers vastly rich, but we survived just the same. Physically, that is. Mentally—" He shrugged. "Some burned out. Some burned up."

"You didn't do either." Lindsay's voice was taut, certain.

"No. I just believed I'd finally found love. I ignored all the little signs that Mei was both more and less than she seemed, and I kept ignoring them until the instant I was staring down the barrel of her gun and seeing my own death coming at me."

Lindsay wanted to look away from Catlin's eyes because it hurt too much to know the kind of hell he had lived in. Yet she met his eyes without flinching, knowing that in the end he had come out of hell holding the seeds of a better life in his hands. He was like the scarred bronze bowl he had given her—the quality of the original creation had transcended the battering of existence.

"In the end, Mei couldn't kill you, could she?" asked Lindsay, her smile both sad and bitter.

For a moment Catlin looked surprised, then he smiled gently and shook his head. "True emotions are nourished by the mind, not the body. Mei wasn't like you. She didn't have the ability to love or to hate. Her only responses were in her flesh. She would have killed me if it hadn't been for a man called Chen Tiang Shi. He took the bullets meant for me. He died killing her."

Lindsay shuddered. "And now you don't believe in love, because you loved the wrong woman."

Catlin hesitated, tempted to take the out Lindsay was offering him. Then he put away the temptation, knowing that he couldn't take the easy way with her. He had promised her the truth, and she had more than earned it. Only the truth would protect her—and him—from the adrenaline-generated response she believed was love.

"Not quite," Catlin said, his voice both sad and gentle. "I learned that while you're living undercover, you not only can't afford emotions, you can't trust them, either. Adrenaline pervades everything, heightens everything, makes each instant seem unique, extraordinary. Each drink you take is the best. Each meal you eat is the finest. Each time you make love is the hottest."

"But—"

"But nothing, honey cat. I'm the tour guide, remember?" Catlin continued ruthlessly, not giving her a chance to speak. "After a while the adrenaline high wears off and you lose the ability to feel anything at all. Then you know what adrenaline is and is not. It isn't love, Lindsay. Learning that takes time, though. Years, in my case. And more years coming out of it at the other end. You haven't had that kind of time. You still think that what adrenaline makes you feel is heightened reality. It isn't. It's the most subtle and dangerous lie of all."

"Catlin—" Lindsay said urgently, realizing finally where he was going, what he was trying to say.

"No," said Catlin, slicing across Lindsay's cry. "You don't believe me now, but you will. The truth is that you only think you love me. In a few days or weeks you'll come down off the adrenaline high. You'll remember what we said, how we made love to each other, and you'll blush to the soles of your feet. That's when I want you to remember that I understand. I've been there, I've felt all of it before, known it all to the last bittersweet drop."

"It's not true!"

"Lindsay, I know that you think—"

"No!" she said, overriding his words with her husky, urgent voice. "I know what is real and what isn't. I know what is true and what isn't. I love you!"

Catlin closed his eyes and silently condemned the manipulative Chen Yi to the deepest level of hell.

"In a few months," Catlin said, closing his suitcase, punctuating his words with the cold metal sound of locks taking hold, "you'll get past the aftershocks of adrenaline and emotion. You'll understand that you did the best you could with what you had at the time. And you did one hell of a good job, better than Stone and Yi had any right to expect. I want you to know that, Lindsay. It's the simple truth."

Catlin picked up the suitcase and went to the bedroom door. With his hand on the knob, he turned toward Lindsay. The look in his yellow eyes made pain twist through her until she clenched her hands against it, forcing her nails into her own flesh because that hurt less than the bleakness in her lover's eyes.

"Lindsay." His voice was soft, gentle, as desolate as his eyes. "Don't turn away from me if we stumble across each other in Washington. When you remember me, if you remember me, don't ever be ashamed. You're the most woman I've ever known."

He shut the door behind him, trying to close out the broken cry of her love. But the words were already in his mind, like her voice, haunting him in shades of silver:

"You're wrong, Catlin. My love for you is as real as Qin's charioteer!"

27

LINDSAY SAT AT HER DESK in the Museum of the Asias, staring at her hands as though if she just looked hard enough she would see through the present to the future and the end of her longing for something she could not have. She knew that the end of pain had to be in the future, somewhere, waiting for her; Catlin had promised she would stop hurting and he had never lied to her.

Maybe it would end today. Maybe today she would run into him on Washington's streets. Maybe he was out there right now, somewhere. Did he feel as she did—one half of a mutilated coin, a bird with one wing beating frantically, futilely?

The pungent smell of a Chinese cigarette sliced through Lindsay's thoughts. Her head snapped up and she saw Chen Yi standing in her office doorway.

"I apologize for the intrusion, Miss Danner," said Yi, bowing, "but I will be leaving soon and wanted to see you alone. If you would rather not speak to me, I will understand. I have caused you much grief."

Lindsay smiled sadly. "I was warned. I volunteered anyway. I don't hold grudges, Mr. Chen."

"You are very generous, daughter," said Yi. "If I may call you that?"

"You honor me," Lindsay said, but her expression tightened as she thought of the other man who had called her daughter. Hsiang Wu, the man she had betrayed. She stood up. "Please come in. Have you time for tea? With lemon," she added, remembering.

"Tea would be very welcome."

"Excuse me," Lindsay said. "I'll only be a moment."

The first thing Yi saw as he looked around Lindsay's office was a display case holding an ancient bronze rice bowl with a long diagonal scar. He stood before the bronze, absorbed in it, not looking away until Lindsay returned with a pot of fragrant tea and set it on a low table in front of a couch.

"You are a woman of subtlety as well as generosity," Yi said as he turned around.

Startled, Lindsay glanced up from the tea she was pouring.

"The scarred bowl," explained Yi. "It is China. Ah!"

He sat, accepting both the tea and the ashtray she offered him. She settled back into cushions that were covered with an Oriental design of golden bamboo against a black sky.

"I'm glad that you came to see me," Lindsay said. "I wanted to thank you, but I had no way of getting in touch."

"You wished to thank me?" asked Yi, his thin, graying eyebrows raised in surprise.

"For Hsiang Wu," she said simply. "I was his daughter, yet I betrayed him. You could have named him as a conspirator. He is your enemy, yet you protected him."

"You are wondering why."

Lindsay sighed. "I'm wondering about a lot of things, but I don't expect any answers."

"The answer to Mr. Hsiang is both as complex and as simple as that bowl," Yi said, leaving a signature of smoke as he gestured toward the scarred bronze. "If you have the time, I will be honored to explain."

"Oh, I have the time." Lindsay's mouth turned down slightly. "Nothing but time and time and time."

Yi saw the new lines on Lindsay's face, the subtle changes. She was more slender. Her skin was pale, almost translucent against the burnished wheat color of her blouse. Her cheekbones were more pronounced, as were her eyes. Their indigo clarity seemed different, darker than before.

"China has not used you well, daughter." Yi sighed and tossed his cigarette into the ashtray to smolder. "China uses few of her children well, but they endure, anyway. Perhaps that is her gift to them."

"And her curse."

"Ah! I hear your father speaking, but the voice is your mother's."

"You knew my parents?" Lindsay asked, startled.

"Your mother saved my life and the life of my eldest son. You would have been about three at the time."

Lindsay's eyes widened. She wanted to ask questions, but Yi was still talking. His words were unusually quick, as though he had much to say and only moments in which to speak.

"Neither my son nor I was Christian. This mattered not at all to your mother. We were human, and in pain. That was all she saw, all that mattered to her."

Yi's head bent as his lighter snapped open. He drew hard on the cigarette, making flame leap.

"You learned your generosity from her," Yi said, exhaling a veil of smoke and watching Lindsay through it. "Your courage is your father's. A formidable combination."

Lindsay shook her head helplessly, feeling about as formidable as a one-winged bird. The past was a turmoil of intrigue and lies and memories as vivid as wind-driven fire. Each new realization changed the shape of the flames, of the past, changed her memories, changed the way she saw the present. She had always thought of the past as static. She knew now that it was not. The past was a fire burning, changing with each breath of new knowledge, each shifting wind of understanding.

There was silence while Yi watched smoke and his own memories writhe, changing. The moment and the memories passed, and Yi's soft, staccato voice picked apart the silence.

"Throughout China's history, one thing has sustained both the people and the country: family. No matter who governed or whether no one governed at all, the generations of Chinese lives were interwoven like silk brocade," Yi said. "Daughters left their families to become part of the continuation of other families. Each son brought home a wife to bear his own family's next generation. The wisdom of the elders instructed the children and grandchildren. The strength of the parents fed and sheltered the generation that bore them and the generation that came after them, and so it was through the thousands of years. The cloth of Chinese history thus created had the strength, resilience and beauty of silk itself. That cloth is no more. Ah!''

Yi exhaled, watching Lindsay. She was motionless, listening, waiting. He nodded curtly, acknowledging her attention.

''Where there were once five children, or ten, there is now only one or sometimes two,'' Yi continued. ''Where sons once lived with parents, now a wife and a husband live alone. A single grandchild is shared among four family-hungry grandparents. A single child grows alone, never sharing, never learning the needs of others.

''The government tries to fill rooms emptied of the extended family. We care for the sick. We feed the poor. We punish the evil. We reward the earnest.'' Yi sighed a stream of smoke into the air. ''It is not enough. When the child's parents die, so does the child's history. There is no fabric of interlocking generations. There is no continuity.''

Lindsay remembered how she had felt at her mother's death—all those years lost, no one to ask or answer questions, no one who had survived her own childhood years to share them with her.

''You have filled your emptiness with art,'' Yi said. ''It is your history. It is your continuity. You can weave yourself into art's elaborate, elegant brocade and know yourself to be part of humanity and history. Ah!'' Yi's cigarette glowed twice, quickly. ''Most people are not like you. They cannot fill their own empty rooms.''

He looked at the burning end of tobacco and thought of his own diminished grandchildren, his own history ending. He grunted and continued speaking quickly, almost curtly.

''Yet China has no alternative except to weave a new fabric. If we don't shrink our population, we will spend our greatness scrambling to feed more and more mouths with less and less food. If we are to survive, we Chinese must take from the West the same thing that we have taken from all our conquerors throughout history—that which made the conquerors strong.

In the West, it is technology. Technology requires nuclear families. Thus the West has become what it is today, what China must become tomorrow."

Yi looked at Lindsay's dark blue eyes watching him and remembered other eyes, a woman's hair like a golden river, her voice dreaming in shades of silver.

"Mao tried to compensate for industrialization by making government what the family had been—the central fact of Chinese life," Yi continued softly. "He failed. Rigid ideology made us weaker rather than stronger. Yet the Chinese people must have something in which to believe, something which has preceded their births and which will continue after their deaths. The West already had it."

He looked at Lindsay and smiled, seeing her curiosity. "Religion, daughter. China has invented many things, but a religion was not among them. We had our extended family to explain our origin and place in life, to sustain our bodies and to care for our souls in the afterlife. We did not need God, so we did not invent him. Ah!"

Yi tossed his cigarette into the ashtray. Smoke rose in a thin, straight column until Lindsay stirred, creating currents in the air.

"After I realized that religion was necessary in the absence of the extended Chinese family," continued Yi, "I tried to discover which religion would be best suited to China's culture, history and future. I rejected the Eastern religions for the simple reason that they had neither encouraged nor permitted the habits of intellect that led to the development of modern technology. Islam was discarded for the same reason. Atheism has a personal appeal, but it is a luxury China cannot yet afford. Technology permits atheism, rather than vice versa."

Yi drank tea, sighed and set aside his cup. "In the end, there was only Christianity. It has been flexible enough to survive the drastic social dislocations of the modern age without demanding fanaticism in its followers. It can and does coexist with many forms of government and culture. It is capable of rapid change without losing its central reality. It is, in essence, the religion of industrialization."

Yi's lighter clicked open, flame hissed and the lighter snapped shut again. He inhaled sharply. "I saved Hsiang Wu because he is Chinese and Christian and we will need his kind if we are to survive the loss of the extended family and the gain of technology and still retain our identity as Men of Han."

Through veils of smoke, Yi smiled. "Does it offend you, daughter, that I support Christianity for reasons of state rather than reasons of spirit?"

"I think Christianity is protean enough to accommodate even you," Lindsay said dryly.

"Protean? Please explain."

"Flexible, resilient, able to shape itself to almost any situation without losing identity."

"Ah! Protean. Exactly. That I will remember."

Yi sipped his tea with enough noise to tell Lindsay that the brew was appreciated, but not enough to offend her Western sensibilities. When he looked up, Lindsay tensed subtly, sensing that the true purpose of his visit was about to be revealed.

"I also saved Hsiang Wu because I owed a debt to the family of Danner, a debt that grew greater when I could not save your other uncle, Mark Danner."

Lindsay froze.

Yi's black eyes narrowed. He nodded curtly. "An unhappy story," he said. "Do you still have nightmares?"

"If I do, I don't awaken." Then Lindsay realized that Yi could only have found out about her nightmares from Catlin. "He told you."

"The dragon and I talked of many things—Christianity and Hsiang Wu, half of a coin and a faithless woman, Qin's charioteer and truth, golden rivers and shades of silver, birds with one wing." Yi sighed. He puffed on his cigarette, coughed dryly, sipped tea and continued. "He protected you well, daughter. He earned back his half of the coin. His debt to the Chen family is fully repaid."

"Yeah. All day. Give me a minute, then put Wang through."

Lindsay sat back in her chair and tried to call calmness to herself through the discipline of *tai chi*. She was only partially successful. All the days had been Mondays since Catlin had walked out of her life. He had been right about the emotional seesaw she would go through as she went back to her normal life. He had been right about the difficulty of regaining her reputation despite the best efforts of Bradford Stone and the People's Republic of China to publicly and profusely thank her for her part in uncovering the "fraudulent" bronzes. Catlin had also been right about how quickly her real life would reclaim her. In fact, he had been right in everything he had said, save one.

And it was the only one that mattered.

Lindsay continued breathing deeply, slowly, until the phone rang once more. She punched in the second button and lifted the receiver.

"Hi, Sam," she said, her voice clear, her expression taut. Hearing Wang's voice brought back the auction where she had seemed to betray Wu—and the warehouse, where she had indeed betrayed him. "Did you get a line on that Shang bronze that Mr. White wanted?"

"Not yet. I heard something interesting when I was out in San Francisco last week, though. Thought you should be the first to know."

Lindsay's fingers tightened on the telephone. "Oh?"

"First Lee Tran disappears without a trace and now the honorable Hsiang Wu has decided to give up international politics and confine his efforts to the buying and selling of Asian objets d'art. Funny, huh?"

Eyes closed, Lindsay prayed that her voice wouldn't give her away. She hadn't mentioned Wu no matter how hard Stone had pressed for names. "I wasn't aware that Wu was actively interested in politics," she said politely.

Sam Wang's laughter came clearly over the line. "Come on, Lindsay. We're friends, aren't we? We both know that the only reason Hsiang quit spying for Taiwan is that Catlin came down on him like a falling mountain.''

"This is the first I've heard about it," Lindsay said flatly. "Why would Catlin do that?"

"I was going to ask you the same thing. The usual procedure in cases like Hsiang's is to turn the guy into a double agent."

"What?"

"Simple," said Wang, laughter curling through his voice. "You catch one of the other side's spies dirty and tell him that he can spy for your side or suffer some terminal inconveniences. Catlin knows how the game is played—hell, sometimes I think he must have invented it—yet he let Hsiang Wu off the hook. Now Hsiang Wu's an upstanding citizen instead of a newly recruited double agent. I don't mind telling you that Stone would be pissed off about it if he knew. He's dying to get his hands on a reliable Taiwanese double."

"Sam," Lindsay said, trying to keep her voice light, "I'm having a hard time following this conversation. Despite the affair of the Qin charioteer, I'm not the Mata Hari type. And how do you know Stone, anyway?"

"Who said I knew Stone?"

Lindsay felt like banging the telephone receiver on the desk in hope of improving the connection. She knew that it wouldn't work. Sam Wang lived in a different world than she did. They might speak the same language, but the meaning of the words was very slippery.

The sound of laughter floated up from the receiver. "I wish I could see your face, Lindsay. Catlin was crazy not to take advantage of you while he could. They don't make them like you anymore."

"Fools?" she retorted. "I disagree. I have it on the highest authority that there's one born every minute, which should give you a lifetime guarantee of full employment."

"Speaking of Catlin—"

"I wasn't," Lindsay said quickly.

"Ever see him any more?" finished Wang, ignoring her interruption.

"What does that have to do with Mr. White's early Shang bronze?"

"Nothing," Wang admitted. "But it has a lot to do with asking you out to dinner. If you're Catlin's, I don't want the kind of trouble he can deliver."

"Last time I checked, my rabies certificate didn't list an owner," she said evenly. "Does yours? Or wasn't there room for a triple entry?"

"Triple?"

"Stone, Chen Yi and adrenaline."

There was a long silence followed by laughter that was more rueful than humorous. "You're one of a kind, Lindsay. You really didn't like the game, did you?"

"No, I really didn't."

"Too bad. There's a whole world to play it in. We could have done it all."

"You go ahead. It's not my world."

"The world is whatever you think it is, remember?" Wang asked ironically.

Lindsay recalled the extraordinary bronze dragon and smiled in spite of herself. "Like I said, we live in different worlds."

"Anyone who could look at my dragon and see that reality is a construct, not a fact, can live in any world."

"I've been meaning to ask you," Lindsay said, determined to change the subject, "What did the lab tests say on your dragon's age?"

"It never went to a lab, and it's not my dragon anymore."

"There's one born every minute, right?" Lindsay retorted, unable to keep disapproval out of her tone.

"Not this one. The man who bought it knew exactly what he was getting."

Lindsay's relief showed in her voice. Despite their differences, she didn't like to think of Wang as an out-and-out crook. "Good. He must have had a very fine eye for art to buy your dragon for what it was, rather than what it was not."

"He had a rare understanding of reality," Wang agreed. "Like you. Thanks for seeing through my dragon's deception to the true art beneath. It cost me a bundle, but it was worth it. Every artist has a raging need to be appreciated—especially the artist who can't sign his own name. Ciao, Lindsay. I won't lean on you again."

Before Lindsay could speak, the line was dead. She sat motionless, phone in hand, realizing that it was Sam Wang who had created the extraordinary dragon. Slowly, she replaced the receiver, wondering what made an artist of Wang's caliber spend so much of his creative efforts in a shadow world of lies. Then she wondered if Wang had been trying to recruit her for one of his bosses, or if he had been on a personal fishing expedition for fun and profit.

Lindsay shook her head impatiently. It didn't matter whether Wang had been angling after her in the name of Yi, Stone, himself or a bizarre combination of the three. The answer was still no.

Automatically she glanced at her watch, then at the calendar. She realized that it still showed last Friday's date. Not that it mattered. Weekend or weekday, she worked. It was better than remembering. She had been alone before she met Catlin, but she hadn't been lonely. It was different now. She understood loneliness the way the ancient Chinese had understood bronze. Intimately.

With an abrupt movement Lindsay tore three pages off her calendar, adding them to the minutes and hours since she had sat in a hotel room in San Francisco and felt as though her skin were being pulled from her in thin strips, wanting to cry but unable to because it hurt too much even to breathe. Catlin had been right about so many things—why hadn't he been right about the pain? Why did she remember every moment they had spent together with such cruel clarity?

You're the most woman I've ever known.

Catlin's words returned to her, haunting her, hurting her. She hadn't been enough to hold him. He hadn't believed that real love could have been born from a world ruled by adrenaline and lies. He had given her no chance to prove him wrong.

Lindsay went to the window and stood without moving, watching office buildings bleed their population into the late afternoon streets. She tried not to think, not to remember, and most of all she tried not to feel. Yet her eyes searched the streets ceaselessly, looking for a man who moved like a tiger gliding through twilight. She didn't know what she would do if she saw Catlin again. She only knew that she wanted to see him with an intensity that left her weak.

Finally Lindsay forced herself to step away from the window and go home. She continued to search the faces of the city as she left the Museum of the Asias. Catlin wasn't among the people streaming down the sidewalk. He wasn't among the people milling around the bus and taxi stands. He wasn't standing in the foyer of the apartment building. He wasn't outside her apartment door. He wasn't inside—

Lindsay froze in the doorway, staring into her apartment with disbelief. Sam Wang's bronze dragon was crouched on her coffee table, radiating vitality. Slowly she walked closer. The slanting after-noon sunshine picked out every swell and flow of the dragon's muscles, every sinuous line of power, every metallic gleam of gold and silver. Her fingertips traced the timeless designs that spoke silently of intelligence, creation and endurance, and of the truth that reality is a work of art that changes even as it is viewed, containing all possibilities.

Magnificent, luminous with light and life, the dragon watched Lindsay out of hammered gold eyes as old as time and as modern as the future.

Behind Lindsay the front door shut with a distinct click. She spun toward the sound. Catlin stood motionlessly, watching her as the dragon had, golden eyes intent, fierce with life. She tried to say Catlin's name, but could not. She wanted to run to him but was afraid to believe that he was real rather than the creation of her own need.

"I wanted you to have the dragon," Catlin said matter-of-factly, as though it had been three minutes rather than three weeks since their last conversation. "I had business in D.C., so I brought it to you. How are you, Lindsay? Have you settled into your old life again? Is the nightmare gone?"

The questions didn't even register on her consciousness. She was too intent on looking at Catlin, memorizing him, noting all the changes from her memories. He was even bigger than she had remembered, harder, darker, with an almost overpowering aura of leashed danger. Dragon.

But the taut lines of his face reminded her that he was not immune to pain.

"Lindsay?" Catlin asked, his voice deep, as searching as his eyes.

She trembled as memories washed over her. He had always touched her so carefully, as though he were afraid that she was a dream that would awaken. She understood that fear now. She was frozen, afraid to move, afraid to breathe, afraid to awaken.

"It's too soon, isn't it?" Catlin said sadly. "You haven't forgiven me. You look at me and you see the man who led you into hell." He let out his breath with a harsh sound. "Sorry, honey cat. I didn't mean to upset you all over again. I waited as long as I could. It wasn't long enough."

He turned to leave, shocking her into speech.

"What were you waiting for?" Lindsay asked, her throat aching. "Me to stop loving you? That will take more than three weeks. That will take—" Her voice broke. "How long will it take, Catlin? You're the man with all the answers. Tell me how long!"

Lindsay watched the change sweeping over Catlin as he spun back toward her. It was as though he had been standing in shade and had stepped out into the sunlight. The lines of his face eased and his eyes no longer were like hammered metal. No more did he seem predatory, tightly leashed, dangerous. He crossed the room in two strides and lifted her off her feet in a hug that was both powerful and gentle. The familiar warmth and strength of him burst through her in a single shattering instant. Her arms closed around him and she shook with the force of her emotions.

"Don't cry, love, don't cry," Catlin said. He felt the shuddering of Lindsay's body, heard the ragged breaths. "Oh, God, stop, you're tearing me apart." He turned his head, searching for the softness of her lips, finding the taste of her tears. "I'm sorry, love," he said softly, repeatedly. "I didn't want you to be hurt. That's all. I didn't want you to be hurt."

"Then you shouldn't have left me!" Lindsay said, holding on to Catlin tightly, afraid that he would leave her again. "I said I loved you and you talked about adrenaline and lies and you walked away as though my name were Mei and I knew nothing about love. That hurt me more than all the rest, Catlin. That hurt until I—"

Catlin knew he had to stop the words that were too painful for Lindsay to speak or for him to hear. He took the softness and hunger of her mouth, filling her with his presence, being filled by her in return.

"It wasn't you I didn't trust," he said finally, giving her tiny, biting kisses between words. "It was me. I wanted you too much to trust my own judgment. I still do. I shouldn't be here. When I walked out of that hotel room I told myself I'd wait six months before I tried to see you again."

Lindsay made an involuntary sound of denial and her arms closed even more tightly around him. Catlin laughed roughly and kissed her again, felt her soften against his body, cling to him, and everywhere she touched him he knew again the sweet, consuming fire he had found with her.

"By the time I got to the hotel lobby," he said, kissing her eyelids, the hot trails of her tears, the corners of her mouth, "I'd decided that four months would be enough. By the time I was at the airport, I'd convinced myself that two months was plenty. Somewhere over Kansas I opted for two weeks, ten days, a week—three days—three hours—*turn around and fly back now, you fool. Don't give her time to come to her senses. Don't let her get away.*"

Catlin buried his hand in the fragrant softness of Lindsay's hair, tilting her head back until she was forced to meet his eyes. The pain revealed on his face made her cry out in protest.

"Do you understand?" he asked harshly. "I had given my word to protect you, and I was thinking about breaking that word. I knew that if I turned around and went back to that hotel I could have you. If the emotions you felt for me were really love—great, no problem. If not, you were too good, too generous, too kind to throw me out when the adrenaline wore off for you, because by then you would know how much I needed you. Either way, passion or compassion, you would be mine." Catlin let out his breath in a hissing curse, then said simply, "I waited as long as I could. Three weeks."

Lindsay looked into his eyes and saw his truth as clearly as his self-contempt. "Catlin, don't," she said, her tone dark, husky. "You could have waited three years and the answer would still have been the same. I love you."

His smile was bittersweet, painful. "I hope so, honey cat, because I sure as hell love you." Abruptly he let go of her and stepped back, shoving his hands deep into his pockets to keep from touching her. "Last chance. Tell me to go away and come back in three months. Two months. One—"

Lindsay smiled despite the tears aching in her throat. "None," she said. "Not a month, not a week, not a day. Not even an hour. A second, maybe. No more."

Catlin searched Lindsay's eyes intently, seeing through tears to the truth beneath. Slowly his hands came out of his pockets. In the palm of his right hand was the familiar blue-green of ancient bronze set in a circle of beaten gold. He caught Lindsay's hand and slid the ring onto her finger.

"It's not a traditional kind of ring," he said, brushing his lips over first the bronze and then Lindsay's lips, "but we've hardly had a traditional kind of courtship, have we?"

As Lindsay looked down at the small, ancient coin, her breath caught and she went very still. The halves had been welded together, revealing the complete outline of a flying bird. She tried to speak, to tell Catlin what his gift meant, but all she could say was his name and her love as his arms pulled her close, holding her as though he were afraid something would take her from him once more.

CROUCHED WITHIN an incandescent pool of light, alive with timeless designs, the dragon's eyes saw all truths, all lies, all fears, all dreams, all the billion possibilities of reality...and one of those possibilities was a bird with two wings, two lives soaring.

♥INTIMATE MOMENTS®
™ Silhouette

> *Dear Linda Howard,*
> *Won't you please write the story*
> *of Joe "Breed" Mackenzie?*

Ever since the appearance of Linda Howard's incredibly popular MACKENZIE'S MOUNTAIN in 1989, we've received literally hundreds of letters, all asking that same question. At last the book we've all been waiting for is here.

In September, look for MACKENZIE'S MISSION (Intimate Moments #445), Joe's story as only Linda Howard could tell it.

And Joe is only the first of an exciting breed here at Silhouette Intimate Moments. Starting in September, we'll be bringing you one title every month in our new **American Heroes** program. In addition to Linda Howard, the **American Heroes** lineup will be written by such stars as Kathleen Eagle, Kathleen Korbel, Patricia Gardner Evans, Marilyn Pappano, Heather Graham Pozzessere and more. Don't miss a single one!

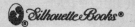